WINTER'S HEIR

WINTER'S HEIR

Book 2 of The Eisteddfod Chronicles

SARAH JOY ADAMS
EMILY LAVIN LEVERETT

FALSTAFF

WWW.FALSTAFFBOOKS.COM

Chapter One

At no point in Deor Smithfield's teaching career had she been this nervous. Not on her very first day, when she had been so nervous that she forgot to tell the students her name. Not even a few weeks ago, when she walked into this same classroom sure of her impending humiliation and termination (possibly literally). On that day, she'd put the Vampire Prince in his place, thrown the Goblin Prince out of her classroom, and exposed the Winter Court's Prince-to-be as a sneak. She'd also gotten her contract renewed.

Outside the lecture hall on the fourth floor, hand on the door handle, she rolled her shoulders and tilted her head side to side, stretching the tight muscles in her neck. In her back, her wings twinged and jumped. She thought briefly about putting them out through the slits in her clothes and academic robes, but instead clenched her muscles tighter. No need to make herself more conspicuous than she already was.

Slightly behind her, in the corner of her peripheral vision, a small glint. She ignored it and yanked open the door.

"I will be your..." Professor Ama Nefasta, chair of the English department and Bard in charge of the now-postponed Adoption stopped cold, her mouth slightly open. She and Deor hadn't spoken since the day Deor had interrupted the king's adoption of Rafe, Lord Farringdon by declaring that the king already had an heir—Deor.

"Good morning, Professor Nefasta," Deor said.

Everyone in the hall—a tiered affair whose other exit was on the fifth floor—shifted to face to her. From a quick scan, she noted that very few of her goblin students were in attendance, but if she had to guess, she'd say most of the other students were there.

A small breeze fluttered the hem of her robes, and the door clicked shut.

"Dr. Smithfield!" Ama recovered quickly and gave a soft smile—a strange sight on her sharp features, more often in a disapproving frown than not. Ama had a textbook case of "resting bitch face," and, to be honest, often a personality to match. Deor liked her very much. "I wasn't sure you'd be returning today."

Deor headed up to the lectern. "I came to teach my classes—you know, do my job?"

"Excellent!" Ama's smile shifted to a legitimate beam. "I'm very glad to hear it." She gathered her own materials and stepped out of Deor's way. "Why don't you stop by my office after class?"

"Perfect!" Deor said and put her book and notes on the lectern.

Ama patted her hand. "I am glad you're here." She turned her attention to the hall and scanned it, as if looking for someone. A small snort escaped her, and she threw another glance at Deor before showing herself out.

Deor opened her Shakespeare anthology to her bookmarked page. "Given the excitement of the past week, I'm not surprised that some students aren't here. So, I'll skip roll for today. When we left for the Adoption break, we were looking at *Richard III*. Let's review. Would anyone like to read the opening speech aloud?"

The students all stared at her, most of them with expressions of confusion plastered on their faces. Finally, from the second row, a young faerie with strawberry red skin and too-long black bangs hanging fashionably over one of his eyes raised his hand.

"Thank you, Aiden—Richard's speech. Go!"

"No." He pulled his hand out of the air. His book, in front of him, wasn't open. "I mean—*Richard III*? You're going to start class like nothing happened?" He shifted in his seat to look around not only at the cluster of his friends sitting near him, but at the rest of the class. Many nodded at him in agreement.

Deor sighed. "I had hoped to. But apparently not." She closed her book. "Okay," she said. "You've got two minutes to ask me what you want, and I'll answer what I can."

Hands shot up like the students had been zapped by electrical current.

Aiden did not wait to be acknowledged. "What happened? Was it you that interrupted the Adoption? Did it happen? Is it going to happen? Who are you? Where's the Goblin Prince?"

"Woah!" Deor held up her hands.

Several students nodded along again. "Is the king okay?" another shouted. "Is the Sword well?" Someone else—a lovely faerie girl—added her voice to the crowd.

"Alright!" Deor raised her voice, and it echoed through the room. A few students drew back. She cleared her throat. "Long story short. I found out that there was a conspiracy against the king and the Sword." So far, true enough. "I didn't discover it until after the final ceremony had started. I got away from the conspirators and interrupted the ceremony. Everyone is fine." That last bit was true, so long as she didn't count herself.

"Who was involved?" Jaromir, a vampire student, called from the back, perhaps the first time the kid had ever participated in class.

"I cannot say," she said. When the boy frowned nervously, Deor added, "Donovan had nothing to do with the conspiracy, and, in fact, helped expose it." Jaromir slumped back in his seat and sighed with relief, as did Danica, the woman next to him.

"Why are all the goblin students gone?" Zephyr, a lovely faerie woman, one in the circle of students around Aiden, asked. She had skin so black that it seemed to draw light in, leaving a halo around her. She had sapphire eyes that flashed with intelligence, though she, like the vampire students, rarely spoke. "I mean, I live in a dorm with a lot of goblin students—and they've left."

"I don't know," Deor said, though she could guess. "I am not—" she paused searching for the right words "—totally clear on the politics of the situation."

"What was the conspiracy?" Aiden asked. The students seemed to be deferring to him—like he was the elected representative from the class.

"I cannot say," she repeated. "I know that it will all be explained eventually."

"So you're a hero?" Aiden quirked an eyebrow.

"No," Deor insisted. "I found out information that was going to get me killed. Telling the monarch was as much for me as anything."

Aiden leaned forward in his seat, revving up for another question. He blew his bangs out of his face.

"And that's time!" Deor said. "Two minutes."

"Do you know—" Aiden started.

"I said time." Deor's voice was stern, and the kid cut off mid-word. Deor smiled at Aiden, trying to soften her tone. "Would you like to read the opening lines?"

Aiden frowned but opened his book and shuffled to the right page. "Now," he said, "is the winter of our discontent / Made glorious summer by this son of York..."

His immediate obedience troubled her. Members of the monarchy had voices of power. Eisteddfod University was no place for such magic, and in this place, she was a scholar and nothing else. How long that would last? She didn't know, but she would savor every minute of that she had left.

Outside the wind blew, stripping the trees of remaining leaves. A week ago, Fall had been in full swing, filling the world with oranges and reds and yellows. She sat on the throne, and it acknowledged her. She was the daughter of the house of Aethelwing, and with her came Winter.

An hour later, Deor knocked on Ama Nefasta's office door, tucked far back in the English department's main office.

Arthur, arms crossed in front of him, waited with her.

"Come in," the woman called.

"Behave," Deor muttered to Arthur before she opened the door. "And be polite!"

Lord Farringdon's secretary, and her temporary bodyguard, said nothing.

Deor walked in first, a move that she knew irritated Arthur, but if Ama wanted Deor dead, he wasn't going to be able to stop her. Not on Ama's own turf.

"Hello," Deor said. "I am sorry that you didn't realize I would be coming back. I should have thought to notify you. I'm sure you noticed my security." She gestured at Arthur. "I'm sorry that I wasn't able to get your permission first."

"I understand." Ama glared at Arthur, who remained impassive, his hundred-yard-stare perfect. "Will he be accompanying you all the time?"

"Unfortunately, yes." Deor shrugged. "Finn is immovable on this point."

Ama snorted. "Sit down." She waved at Arthur. "Both of you." She looked back and forth between the two for a few moments before finally addressing Deor. "His Majesty is—Creator, help me—right about you having security. And for now, I'll allow the captain here," she managed with barely a sneer, "to accompany you, and to use his magic to be unobtrusive." Ama turned to him. "You are here on my leave. If I, at any point, think you are violating any of our students' privacy or liberty, we will have words."

"I understand." Before Nefasta could ask, Arthur continued, in his best I'm-just-the-messenger neutral tone. "His Majesty is not satisfied with the current arrangement. And, frankly, neither am I. I have better things to do than sit in class. I am sure the literature is wonderful. I want nothing to do with it."

Ama snorted a laugh, as if the thought that Arthur could possibly appreciate culture was nonsense. Deor was rather sure that Arthur would like Shakespeare if he gave it the chance—especially the villains.

"Right now, no one knows who I am outside of the Palace except you and a few others," Deor said.

"I'm not sure I see a reason for you to continue teaching," Ama said. "While it is not my favorite, I am perfectly capable of teaching Shakespeare. Now that the Adoption is cancelled, I do actually have the time."

"No!" Deor snapped, and both Ama and Arthur started. "I mean, please, no," Deor said. She brushed a stray hair from her bun back behind her ear. The past few days had been insane, and magic and emotion roiled in her, barely controllable. A few small sparks spiraled away from her. Losing it here—crying in the boss's office—would not work. "I want to finish out my contract. I want to keep my work."

Ama sighed. "Your being here could cause absolute bedlam." Dark circles peeked out under her eyes despite the glamour hiding them. Deor couldn't tell if the circles were just that persistent, or if she was seeing through a glamour like she so often did. Probably both.

"I'll do whatever it takes to keep that from happening." When Ama didn't respond, she added, "Please, Ama. I've worked over a third of my life to be a professor—it's who I am. I can't give it up. And I promise," Deor leaned forward toward Ama's desk, "I will not disrupt the university or violate its independence. I'm even staying in my flat on campus. When I am here, I am a faculty member. No more. No less."

Ama stared at her for a long moment. Finally, with a shake of her head, she said, "Alright. Stay. Finish your contract." She turned to Arthur. "And you? Try to appreciate the material; it might broaden your horizons a bit."

"Whatever my king commands," Arthur said, voice razor sharp. He looked to Deor. "The king is foolish to let you do this—and I'm sure you'll prove that in time." He stood. "Until then, I'm your shadow."

Chapter Two

The sharp cold air stung Deor's face as she stepped out of the English Building. She trotted down the steps and chose the path that led further into campus, rather than toward the University Gates closest to the Palace.

"What do you think you're doing?" a disembodied voice whispered from behind her left ear.

"Going back to my flat," she said through nearly closed lips, struggling not to look like some crazy person walking along talking to herself. There were enough students milling about that someone might actually hear her. She pulled her scarf up around her mouth. At least it was cold enough to warrant that move. This was November. January would be a frozen nightmare.

"Your father wants you home for dinner," Arthur persisted.

"I know. I will be." Deor quickened her pace a touch, though she knew she couldn't outrun him. Still, the feeling of him at her back made the hairs on her neck stand up. His quiet, breathy voice in her ear sent chills down her spine. It reminded her too much of her first day in the Winter Court, detained in the Tower, him hovering behind her as Rafe—then known to her as the Sword of Peace and Justice—asked her questions. "But I need to stop by and let Penny know I'm back."

"Servants have already returned the clothes they gathered there."

"Good to know." She shoved her hands in the pockets of her new, heavy winter coat—a gift from her father, Finn, though she still thought of him as King Sweordmund. That, along with a bunch of newly ordered clothes—everything she'd need to look "presentable," even though she always wore academic robes. She'd have to remember to wear one of the pairs of gloves she'd gotten, along with new boots, socks, and long underwear.

The crowd on campus thinned out as she reached faculty housing, a lovely neighborhood of various flats and houses of different sizes. She lived on a street lined with three-story flats—and shared one of them with Penny—a medical student specializing in human/fae hybrids. Penny also worked on occasion with the Winter Court Civil Patrol and had done her best to help the victims of the Goblin's plot—young women Deor's age who had been attacked and interrogated as the perpetrators looked for Deor.

Deor shuddered, but it had nothing to do with the cold. She'd been attacked, too—the last victim—in an alley. A faerie woman and a goblin man lured her in there with will magic and tried to kidnap her. Only her own strength of will—helped by her unexpected left hook—had gotten her out of there. Swirls of black, fading slowly to grey, still spun across her neck and down her arms and chest, the physical evidence of the attack.

The woman's voice—the force of her will magic—haunted Deor's dreams, as did her eyes—a cold, washed-out blue like the bleak Winter sky. She'd seen the woman clearly, stared into her face, but the will magic was powerful, and every time she tried to piece together an image, nausea overwhelmed her. If she persisted, a raging headache would make her world spin, and she would vomit—the pain driving any coherent image from her mind.

At the gate to faculty housing, Deor laid her hand on the latch and it swung open, recognizing her as a permitted member of the faculty. Her flat was number 405. The apartments' front gardens were as different as their residents, some vine-covered and lush, others rocky. Hers was quaintly English—with a well-kept lawn and a small vegetable and herb garden in the back.

Today, a large woman waited at the edge of the walkway. Broad shoulders and a wide stance, vivid green eyes, with cat's pupils, and height at least a foot taller than Deor, "intimidating" didn't even begin to describe her.

"Good afternoon," she said and nodded at Deor as she approached.

"Hello," Deor smiled. "Can I help you?"

The woman returned the smile. "I am Kaya, a member of campus security." Her voice was a low purr.

"Oh. I'm Deor." She held out her hand. Kaya shook it, taking it gently in her own massive one. She reminded Deor of Bernie and Bob, the were-bears that guarded the western campus gate she used to go to the market or Palace. "Is there something I can help you with? Has there been some kind of trouble?"

Behind Deor, Arthur snorted.

"No." Kaya jerked her head at Arthur, even though he was still glamoured. "He has arranged for me to watch your home."

"Everything is in order here?" Arthur asked, remaining invisible.

"It is," she said. "Two people inside. Lady Penelope and her werewolf paramour." She wrinkled her nose.

"You don't like werewolves?" Deor asked, careful to keep her tone neutral.

Kaya shrugged. "I don't mind them—but they do have a very distinct smell." She looked to her left. "As do you, Captain. I do not have to see you to know you have moved. Your footfalls are not silent, and the breeze carries your scent."

Arthur, a few feet from Deor now, laughed. "That is why I requested you. A carriage will be at the western gate a six, Professor Smithfield." His voice had dropped all humor. "Kaya will see you safely into it. Do not be late."

"Okay..." Deor said.

The man did not bother to conceal his footfalls as he walked away, though Deor turned, squinting after him. When she focused, she could see him—small shimmers of magic in the air outlining his shape. Probably, if she really concentrated, she could break through the glamour altogether —but sometimes that dispelled the magic entirely, and besides, she had been told such behavior was rude.

"Thank you for watching out for me," Deor said to Kaya.

The woman gave a small nod. "Excuse me. I shall be right back." She disappeared behind the house and Deor walked to the front door, digging in her purse for the key.

A tiger—the size of Kaya—strolled around from the back of the house. "Kaya?"

The tiger bowed its head. She glided past Deor, barely brushing up against her, and took her position, sitting down to the side of the front door.

"I'll see you in a little bit," Deor said, and opened the door.

Penny and Rufus were in the living room. Penny's eyes were soft, and her smile made a person feel safe. The woman was born to be a healer. As usual, she wore a conservative dress, this one green, and her hair was back in a long braid. Rufus, also his normal self, had made a concession to Deor by wearing pants—and that was as much as he would do. Werewolves were generally more comfortable naked—with the exception of the red hair on his head and scattered over his body. Deor was happy to accept his gesture.

"Hello," Deor said, stopping in the doorway.

Penny smiled and stood. "It is good to see you. How are you doing?"

How much did she know? "I'm good," Deor said. "Glad to be back."

"Yes," Rufus said with a smirk. "I imagine the Palace has been quite trying."

"Hush!" Penny scolded him, but she smiled as she did it. "Would you like a cup of tea?" She gestured at the set on the coffee table in front of them. "There's plenty. Just grab another cup."

"Sure." When Deor returned and poured herself tea, adding ample sugar, they watched her carefully. When she sat down in a chair next to their couch, they smiled. "Okay," Deor said. "Go on and ask."

"Arthur contacted me and told me that you're—"

"Penny—" Rufus cut her off. "Let's not say things too loudly."

Penny glared at Rufus for a moment. "That you're who you are!"

"I am indeed." She smiled. "So you know that I'm...related to the Kingdom."

"Yes," Penny said. "Everything makes a lot more sense now. The wings suddenly appearing, your being attacked, you fainting during the Adoption ceremonies. Even Geoff's interest in you." When Deor quirked an eyebrow at her, Penny hastily added, "Not that he wouldn't have been interested in you anyway—you are quite interesting."

Deor snorted. "Right. Well, I was about done with that relationship anyway." Her smile vanished. "I am sorry that I might have put you in danger—there's a tiger out there now—"

"Kaya," Rufus said. "We know. She's a lovely girl—very good at her job."

"Oh, you know her." She relaxed. "Good." She took a sip of her tea and paused. "Look, I'd really like to keep who I am quiet—I just want to be a professor, do my job, live a normal life."

Rufus frowned at her like she were insane. "You can't do that forever. You probably can't even do it very long. I was there—I saw what happened. People will figure it out. And some people already know."

"Well, I'm letting the king decide when to tell people." Deor bit her lip. He was right. The secret wouldn't keep. But even when it came out—when Finn announced it—there was no reason for her to quit Eisteddfod. She was thirty, barely an adult by faerie standards. She should have a lot of time to be a professor. After all, if Geoff could be a student, why couldn't she have a job like a regular person? "Until then, I want to be a normal person."

"We'll do what we can to help," Penny said. "Are you going to be here for dinner? I was planning rabbit stew."

"No." Deor shook her head. "I have to go have dinner with my father."

"Dinner with the king?" Rufus grinned. "Yeah, you're a normal person, like the rest of us."

Chapter Three

R afe and the other officers stood at attention as Finn and Astarte entered the Tower War Room. Just a few days, ago he would have been thrilled to see his foster father and king taking charge of matters again. Now the sight of him made Rafe's stomach clench. Skulking off to the human world behind his wife's back to find an unwitting child bearer, then breaking the poor human's heart, not to mention losing the child, Deor, for thirty years it was unspeakable. Maybe unforgivable.

"Welcome back to the War Room, sir," he said. He gave Princess Consort Astarte a warm smile. She returned his look, but not the smile, moving to stand apart from Finn on the other side of the War Room table.

"It's good to be back," Finn said. He was the picture of health, nearly glowing with it. No, strutting. Here was a man who had everything he'd ever wanted.

"What is it you wanted to discuss today, sir?" Rafe said.

"Bring me up to date on this situation with the Summer Court, my boy," Finn said. "I gather you think trouble is brewing. Are you sure you aren't stirring it up yourself?"

It took all Rafe's discipline not to clench his hand at being called the king's boy. Never again. He would never again be the king's little boy.

"I'm quite sure, sir." He made a gesture over the wide oval table in the middle of the room and a three-dimensional map of the Winter Court's southern border appeared. "If you'll look at this pattern of 'training exercises' the Summer Court has been engaging in, you'll see that it's actually a subtle process of troop movement that's allowing them to amass a modest, but significant, number of units near vulnerable points on our border."

Finn contemplated the map, rubbing his chin. "As you said, it's a fairly modest number."

"But not nothing. And they're concentrated in key locations. I tell you, they're preparing for something."

"I see that you've also moved troops into parallel positions on our side of the border," Finn said.

"Yes."

"Pull them back and see if the Summer Court doesn't respond in kind."

"Sir, I think that would be extremely unwise."

Finn shook his head without taking his eyes off the map. "You're a general, Rafe. You think in terms of war all the time. Pull the troops back and let the ambassadors handle the matter."

"Sir, I cannot stress enough how much I disagree." He looked across the table to Astarte for help, but she stood with her head bowed, hands clasped in front of her. "This is an unwise move. You're leaving those border towns vulnerable. These are our people's lives we're talking about."

The king's eyes flashed silver. "Don't you argue with me, Rafe. I know very well how many lives will be lost if we provoke the Summer Court to war. Pull the troops back. Immediately."

"As you wish, sire."

Rafe dismissed the map. "Was there anything else you wished to discuss with me, sir?"

"The princess's security is my greatest concern at the moment. What steps are you taking to ensure that she's safe?"

Rafe swallowed hard, his jaw clenched. "As you know, sire, she would be much safer behind the Palace walls than living on Eisteddfod's campus."

Finn waved a dismissive hand. "Believe me, I know it. But I think we can afford to indulge her in this matter for a little while. After all, she still thinks of herself as having a job, a profession that she has to perform.

13

Soon enough she'll realize that being the heir subsumes all else. After all, I let you go on being Sword for quite a while during the Adoption process. As long as we can keep her safe, let her be a professor for a little while longer."

"Indeed, sir." Rafe felt a flash of sympathy for Deor. How betrayed he had felt when Finn and the members of Parliament had told him that he had to step down from his office in the interest of safety. She said she'd worked all her adult life toward being a professor. No doubt she loved what she did as much as he loved his own work.

Rafe licked his lips and went on. "I've assigned Arthur to escort her through campus. There's no one more covert than him. Eisteddfod won't hear of me stationing guards permanently on the campus, but they've agreed to put one of their own security personnel on permanent watch outside her door, so she'll be under secure watch day and night."

"Who is the guard?"

"A were-tiger. I understand she comes highly recommended."

Finn grunted. "I'd be more content if there were more people, but if you think that's enough…"

"I think that's the best we're going to manage. Our greatest safety lies in the fact that no one yet knows who she is. As long as we can keep that secret, I think she's more than safe enough with the arrangements we have."

Astarte spoke for the first time. "And what about *my* daughter's security? What steps are being taken for her well-being?"

"Astarte," Finn said. "This is really not the time or place. The two matters are not equal."

"They are to me." Her gossamer wings flared angrily behind her. "What surety do I have that Robbie will not be attacked again?"

Rafe cleared his throat. "We're fairly certain that the man who tried to kill her is dead, but you're right to be concerned. How is she doing, by the way? Has she woken up?"

"Not yet. They don't know when, or if, she'll wake again. I should be getting back to her soon."

"I'm sorry."

Finn cleared his throat. "If we could get back to business…"

"With all due respect, sir, I think this is business," Rafe said. "The Consort's child was attacked by the same people who attacked your heir, and Robbie may be vulnerable to further attacks. My office is deeply concerned that we find out who did it."

Finn frowned. "If you say so."

Astarte exploded. She struck the table hard enough to make the wood jump. "*I* say so! You'd like nothing better than for Robbie to quietly fade away and never be heard of again, but I am not going to let that happen."

Finn held out his hands, but Astarte waved them away. "My dear woman, you know…"

"I know you. I know you all too well to be soothed with a few easy words. If you won't take steps to ensure Robbie's well-being, then I will. I'm leaving."

"What? For where?"

"For the north. Roger of Northfalls has always been my friend and my daughter's. I'm taking Robbie somewhere she'll be safe." She turned and swept out of the room without another word.

Awkward silence hung over the War Room as the door slammed behind the Princess Consort. None of the men knew where to look. Certainly not at the king who stood alone by the table, his eyes and nails flashing silver.

Finally, Finn said, "Excuse me, gentlemen," and exited by the same door.

Rafe was the first to break the silence after the king and his Consort's abrupt departure. "Next order of business, gentlemen," he said. "Domestic matters. How many protests are we dealing with these days?"

Lieutenant Bolton, the member representing the king's household guard, picked up a file from a side table. "I have been going through household guard files—"

"Wait a minute," Arthur cut the blond soldier off. "What about the matter the king raised before he left?"

"Which matter?" Rafe asked.

"The Consort's child. He's right—her existence is a problem. If she wakes up, you may need to handle it."

The air around Rafe dropped several degrees. "Robbie is not a problem to be handled."

"If you say so."

"I do. Now let's tend to other matters that do need handling." Rafe returned his attention to Bolton. "How likely are these next sets of protests to turn into riots do you think?"

"That depends, I think—" the soldier started again.

"On the lovely Professor Smithfield," Arthur interrupted again. "That girl is going to cause no end of trouble. That girl's a walking, talking divining rod of chaos."

"She's not a girl." Rafe spun on Arthur. "She's a grown woman. And until we are otherwise informed, she is a professor at Eisteddfod University."

"She should behave like the heir she is," Arthur said with a casual shrug.

"She *is* behaving as the *person* she is. The king does not get to take people's lives away from them on a whim. Not Robbie's, not Deor's—"

"And not yours?" Arthur snorted. "The king hurt you, and you're right, as Rafe the foster son, to be angry. But you're the fucking Sword, and that woman is the living embodiment of a security breach. Sooner rather than later, she'll need to be handled."

"Handled." Rafe mimed the quotes in the air. "Yes, I'm sure the Winter Court would be much safer if I let you 'handle' all the 'security breaches.'"

Arthur shrugged. "Quick and painless, I promise."

Rafe jerked forward, his hands clenched into fists. Arthur did not flinch. The temperature dropped even further as the two men stared at each other.

"So, as I was saying," Bolton said, waving his file casually, "I've been going through the household guard files to see if there is anyone fit to temporarily replace Michael as Shield—it might be easier just to promote from within for now, and then once the heir settles in, the king can open up the position for applications."

Neither Rafe nor Arthur moved.

"Or we could burn all the files," Bolton said. "We could use the heat in here."

Rafe raised his eyebrows at Arthur.

"Fine." Arthur backed up a step. "I'm the spymaster, not the politician. The new Shield is up to the king."

"You're my secretary, Captain Maerhwer," Rafe corrected. He stepped away from Arthur toward Bolton. "Hold off on those files, Bolton. I don't know that's our best play. I'll speak to the king and see if he has any ideas.

For now, let's focus on the protests." He turned to Arthur. "While you're on campus guarding the princess, keep an eye out for anything to do with the protests—we know some of them involve students."

Arthur bowed and turned toward his office.

"Look into," Rafe repeated. "Look. Not touch, beat, or break, got it? They are *not* committing crimes. Hurt them and you risk martyrs."

Arthur did not turn back. "Right."

"They are not our enemies, Arthur."

"No," the man said softly. "Not yet." He closed the door behind him with a quiet click.

Rafe stared at the closed door for a moment. "Bolton," he said. "Look over those files, like you suggested. Give me an idea of who you think would be good to accompany the princess. I think Arthur's talents might be better served somewhere else."

"Yes, sir." He began to shuffle papers. "Sir?"

"Hmmm?" Rafe stopped at the door to his office and glanced back.

"I would like to volunteer, sir."

Rafe smiled. "Got a crush, Bolton?"

"Absolutely not," he said with a serious shake of the head and a wry smile.

"I will keep you in mind." Rafe nodded. He needed to review Bolton's file—how had a man so far out of Michael's social circle made it all the way to the Houseboys? He'd add that to the growing list of things he needed to do. "You're dismissed."

After Bolton left, Rafe glanced again at the War Table. "Show me the city." A wide map appeared. Most of the protests had been around the market, near the school, or in front of the Palace or parliament. Fairly typical, and none violent. He waved the map away and returned to his office.

"Hey boys," he said to the two piles of fur laying in front the couch at the far end of his office. Jake and Sam jumped to their feet, tails wagging. Rafe dropped to his knees and held open to his arms. He let them bowl him over, and he wrestled with them.

No question, the Winter Court had its traitors, and the princess would provide an excellent lightning rod. When the time came, he'd be the closest to the strike.

Chapter Four

After a relaxing bath, preparing for dinner with the king was surprisingly difficult. Deor had been provided clothes—including a pale pink dress embroidered with green crystal vines and yellow butterflies, with a pair of silk shoes to match. Some poor seamstress had probably been up all night so Deor could look like a rich five year old at a birthday party.

Deor opted instead for what she had brought with her: a simple black dress she had bought to teach in before the Adoption—something that would look formal enough when she wasn't in her academic robes. If it was good enough for Eisteddfod University, it was good enough for the king, she hoped.

A knock came at the door, and she glanced toward a clock on the wall. She still had time, or so she thought. "Come in?"

A young woman stepped in the room and curtsied. She wore a plain grey dress—not quite servant clothes. Her dark brown hair was up in a practical bun, and her pale pink face was free of makeup or magic, as far as Deor could tell. She carried a square case, worn around the handle and clasp.

"Hello," Deor said.

The girl bobbed. "I'm Melanie Griffith." She smiled. "I'm your lady's maid," she added when Deor stared at her blankly.

Images flashed through her mind: The young woman's face, sitting on the edge of her bed, giving her something to drink. A red-haired woman holding Deor's wrist, a look of concentration on her green-tinged face. Finn—the king—sitting in a chair next to the bed, watching her with silver-irised eyes. Melanie had been one of the people caring for her after the Adoption.

When she retired for the night, after all the commotion, something had happened—Deor hadn't remembered anything from that sixty hours, until now, and the bits of memory that resurfaced. The redhead, Asphodel, was a healer, and had explained, once Deor woke, that she suffered from magical exhaustion and fatigue from the whole ordeal.

"I remember you." Deor smiled. "You sat by my bed while I slept all that time. You brought me stuff to drink."

"I did." The young woman returned her smile. "I'm here to help you dress for dinner, though I see you've chosen something to wear already?" She glanced toward the pink, frilly monstrosity on the bed and back at Deor.

"I have. I prefer plain, simple clothes." She pointed at the case the girl carried. "You're here to help with hair and makeup, too?"

"Yes, Princess."

"It's Deor," she corrected automatically.

The girl curtsied. "I'm sorry, Princess Deor."

"No." She shook her head. "Just Deor. Just my name. No title. It's too —" Too what? Horrifying? She raised a hand to her mouth as her stomach rolled. She had sat on the throne. It showed her the whole of the kingdom, her kingdom, and later that night, she stood on the balcony and felt the kingdom and all its people all the way to the bedrock. She swayed slightly.

Melanie stepped forward and caught her arm. "Easy, miss," she said.

"Right." Deor shook her head to clear it and sat in the chair in front of the vanity. "What shall we do?"

Melanie set her case on the vanity and opened it. "What do you usually prefer? This evening is informal, so I didn't bring any of the family jewelry. Is that acceptable?"

"Sure!" Family jewels. It made sense that there must be some—every faerie she'd seen wore some kind of adornment, from the simplest of hair ornaments that her students wore to the elaborate jewelry sets. "Simple makeup—you know the kind that looks like I might not be wearing any at all? For my hair, pin it up in a bun so I don't have to deal with it."

The girl smiled. "No problem. That's easy."

It proved, however, not to be easy. Deor sighed and stared into the vanity mirror as her face melted and ran down her cheeks. Behind her, Melanie knitted her fingers together and bit her lip. This was their third attempt, but every cosmetic glamour, every attempt to pin up Deor's hair, had resulted in failure. The magic just wouldn't stick.

"I'm sorry, Your Majesty. I've never had this happen before," Melanie whispered.

"It's okay," Deor said. She shook her head, and the last shreds of glamour fell away. "Really, I don't need makeup to have dinner with my…with Finn."

She stood and turned to face Melanie. "This is not your fault. I've always been weird with magic—I see things I'm not supposed to be able to see. I think it's the human in me—the Winter Court feels so strange." She sighed. "Back home, my magic used to make mechanical things break. Here, my human makes magic break." She shrugged. "What can you do?"

Turning away from the mirror, Deor walked to a side table full of stationery. She selected a pen made of clear blue glass with silver filigree running through it to a silver nib. It was probably worth a fortune, but for the moment all she cared about was that it didn't glimmer with magic. She twisted her hair into a bun and jammed the pen through it. She wriggled her bare feet against the stone floor. It was cold, but the feel of stone grounded her, as if she were connected to the Palace all the way down to its roots.

"Thank you, Melanie," she said. "I'll see you later." Barefoot and skirt swishing over the floor, she headed for the bedroom door.

"Wait!"

Deor paused, one hand on the doorknob. "Yes?"

"I should call a footman to escort you to the king."

"No, thank you. I know the way." She left her maid staring after her in surprise.

The funny thing was, she did know the way. Besides giving her the ability to speak Faerie, the throne seemed to have given her a complete blueprint of the entire Palace. She just had to think about what she wanted, and the route opened up in her mind. Since dinner with Rafe on their shared balcony after the Adoption fiasco, she'd discovered a pantry full of snacks and an extra linen closet. She was also pretty certain that if she kept going left and went down two floors she'd find a library because every time she thought about books, her mind nudged her in that direction.

For the moment, however, she wanted something called the Amber Dining Room. Apparently, a common location for the morning briefing.

"Where are you, Amber Room?" she said.

The nudge in her mind took her down the long corridor past a pair of guards who saluted, down a short flight of stairs, around a corner. She paused at a three-way intersection of hallways. Something told her the left-hand passage would take her where she wanted to go, but something else told her she should just push straight ahead through the wall directly in front of her. The decorative panel in the woodwork looked like all the rest that lined this particular hallway, but she was sure it was a door. She pushed on the panel, and a lock clicked. The door swung in, leaving an opening just wide enough for her to enter.

Careful not to catch her skirt in the door, she ducked into the narrow passageway. It was lit from above with sunlight filtering down from two stories up. The panel clicked back into place behind her.

"Oh goody," she said. "I'm going to die in here and become a character in an Edgar Allen Poe story."

Nonsense, the Palace seemed to say. The stone floors under her feet pushed her forward. Twenty steps in, and she heard voices.

"Hello?" she called out. "Where's the door out?" As soon as she asked, a piece of the wall swung open for her, and she stepped from the dim passageway into a room filled with golden light.

Deor whistled. The Amber Room was quite literally that—every inch of the walls was paneled in slabs of amber. It was like being inside a jar of honey. In the center was a small dining table—fully set, it would hold probably eight—but it had been set for two. One at the head, one to the right of that. The golden cutlery and trim on the china complemented the amber of the walls.

Finn turned from where he was speaking with a servant and came at Deor with open arms.

She fended him off with a hand. "Don't hug me, please."

The king's face fell a little, but he took her hand and kissed it. "In time, my dear girl. I know this is all very new for you." He pulled Deor's chair out from the table and scooted her in once she was set. "I am pleased you are able to join me for dinner." He settled into his own seat. "And I see you found the passage from the middle hallway."

"Yeah," Deor said. "About that. It's like the throne imprinted a map on my brain when I sat on it. But it also feels like the Palace nudges me toward places I want to go. Is that normal?"

"Yes!" Finn answered, clearly excited. "It is a good sign—the Palace recognizes you, deep in its bones, and talks to you." He sighed, his eyes turning sad. "Legends say that it really did talk, centuries ago. Not impressions and glimpses, but words—and words that not only the king and his heir could hear. No one alive now ever saw it—back before the fae magic started to decline." He shook his head like he had snapped out of a dream. "Maybe it will happen again."

From the sad smile on his face, Deor doubted it. Though the idea that the Palace itself had spoken didn't surprise her at all. The feelings she got from it were as close to formed language as anything she had ever encountered.

"No Rafe?" she asked.

"No." He smiled. "He is with his fiancée Genevieve tonight. She is a lovely lady—quite good for him. I'm sure you two will be excellent friends."

"Oh," Deor said, and thought about the woman she'd seen in the papers with Rafe. Tall, blond, graceful—the kind of woman who belonged in a glorious Old Hollywood film. "I'm sure it will be interesting to meet her."

Finn nodded. "Perhaps Rafe shall bring her to dinner some evening. That would be nice, wouldn't it?"

"Sure." Deor laid her napkin in her lap. He seemed eager that she be happy, so she humored him.

A servant bustled in and filled their wine glasses while another served the soup course.

When Deor swirled her spoon through the clear broth, flakes of gold leaf danced around the bowl. She sipped it—salty, but not overly so. It didn't taste like fish, but there was a hint of the ocean. There was definitely meat in the soup. She'd had oxtail once. This soup reminded her slightly of that taste, if the ox used had been the original golden calf. She closed her eyes for a second savoring the warm, rich broth cut through with cooling herbs.

"What is this called?" she said. The white-gloved butler at the door stepped forward immediately.

"Green Turtle Soup with Rampion and Leeks, Your Majesty."

She put down her spoon. "Do faeries eat turtle often?"

Finn considered. "I couldn't really say. I've always been fond of it. We have it, oh, once a month or so."

"Green Turtles are a dying species. We really shouldn't eat them." Her grandmother had been a faithful donor to the World Wildlife Fund since before Deor was born.

He stopped, spoon halfway to his mouth. "Don't be ridiculous. If the kitchen staff had any trouble procuring them, I'm sure the steward would have notified Astarte."

Deor wasn't sure that household-running duties were foremost on Astarte's mind, but she let his comment pass—her stepmother was a topic for a different day, especially if she wanted dinner to remain pleasant.

"What I mean is that they may go extinct. We shouldn't be eating something that our children may only get to read about in books. It's like," she struggled for a suitable metaphor, "like eating unicorn."

Finn made a face. "You can't eat unicorn."

"That's my point. If we eat the turtles, they'll soon be nothing more than a story. Like unicorns."

"There's no good eating on a unicorn," Finn said. "They're carnivorous. The horns are highly valued though. Perhaps we'll have a chance to hunt them this Solstice."

If she hadn't already put down her spoon, Deor would have dropped it. Instead, she picked up her water glass, trying to process the new information. She was eating endangered animal soup. Finn hunted unicorns for fun. Unicorns ate meat?!

She opened her mouth, closed it again, drummed her fingers on the table, and decided to let it go. The unicorns and turtles could wait. She had bigger, hopefully not endangered, fish to fry. The servants cleared away the soup and set down plates of delicately roasted fowl. She didn't ask what species it was.

"So," he said suddenly. "Since you insist on teaching, tell me about it. You are teaching human literature, I understand. Shakespeare? Occasionally his plays are performed in the theatre here. Did you know him?"

Deor laughed. "Like did I meet him? No. He died almost four hundred years before I was born."

Finn rubbed his forehead. "Humans are so short lived. And what about Henry the Fifth?"

"The play or the person?"

"The person—you would not have known him either, correct?"

"Correct. He died more than a century before Shakespeare." Deor finished the last bite of meat on her plate and leaned back to let the waiter sweep it away. "Wait," she said. "Did you know him?"

"A bit." Finn let the waiter remove his plate. "We faeries went into the human world more then, and he was quite a mischief maker as a young man." He grinned at the memory. "Gregory, the Goblin King, and I helped him set up a fake robbery once..." He laughed. "Oh goodness, the look on that fat man's face." Finn's smile vanished. "But then Hal's father died, and like all princes in such positions, he turned serious. The English throne wasn't particularly stable, and foreign enemies were amassing against him. He died from battle wounds, you know?"

"Yes," Deor said. She wanted to ask him about a dozen other things, other people.

"I'm glad you understand," he said. "That is why I worry. A strong man. A good king. Cut down in battle. And his people? Lost."

"I'm not going out on any battlefields, Finn."

"Everywhere you walk, we walk, is a battlefield, daughter. I have come closer to losing my life off the battlefield than on it."

"Because you were way behind the front lines?" Deor snapped before she could think and immediately regretted it. She knew nothing of his own experience in war—she didn't even know if there had been wars.

"I fought for my Court. I led my troops into battle." His voice was ice cold, his eyes silver. The nails on his fingers had sharpened into inch-long silver blades. "And I don't like your tone."

Deor bit her lip. "I'm sorry," she said. "I had no right to question your track record in battle. You fought?"

He relaxed, any hint of anger suddenly gone. "Yes. Many times, before I was king and after. Though if Rafe has his way, I'll never see battle again, whether there are any or not." He laid his silverware across his plate and servants whisked it, along with hers, away.

"He does seem a touch protective." She let herself smile.

A servant placed a perfect small cake in front of her. Black like velvet, with silver piping and pearls, it looked like a miniature crown. "This is adorable."

Finn laughed. "I hoped you would like it." In front of him a servant settled a similar, though more masculine, version.

Deor wondered what cake Astarte would have had.

"Can I ask you about my mother?" she said as Finn took a bite.

He coughed, choking. He gulped down a bit of water. Once he had composed himself, he nodded.

"My mother was angry at you, and I was, too, for a long time—okay, I still am—but she was angry because you lied to her."

"I waited to tell her I was king—"

"Not that. She never knew that. You lied and told her you couldn't get her pregnant." Deor poked at the cake with her fork, finally breaking the surface and finding a beautiful white cake with jam filling inside. She took a bite.

"I didn't lie." He drove his fork through the cake and stabbed at a piece. "I was mistaken."

Deor rolled her eyes. "Mistaken. How could you be mistaken about something like that?"

"I don't know." He shook his head and set down his fork. "I'd never been wrong before. I wasn't anywhere near my time. I think maybe it was because your mother was human."

"What do you mean you weren't anywhere near your time?"

He squirmed, uncomfortable. "This isn't something I planned on talking about with you," he said. When she scowled at him, he continued. "You understand," he brushed a few hairs out of his face, "how fertility works? The human world didn't affect you that way, did it?"

"I know where babies come from, Finn." Deor sat back and crossed her arms. "Man and woman have sex. Man deposits sperm. Woman has an available egg. Bam! Baby. At least that's how it works in the human world."

"Yes," he said. "Provided the man is fertile."

Deor froze. No wonder he didn't want to talk about it. What man wanted to talk about impotence? "You thought you couldn't have children," she said. "Then it turned out you could."

"No," he said. "I had no reason to think I couldn't have children. I believed I wasn't fertile."

"What's the difference?"

Finn's eyebrows drew close together, and he regarded her for a moment. Finally, he seemed to come to a conclusion. "Male faeries and female faeries have different fertility cycles," he said. When she started to interject, he held up his hand. "Female faeries, starting at around the mid-twenties, are fertile for a two-month period, once every two years."

"Woah," Deor said. "That's interesting."

"Male faeries are fertile, starting around the same age, for a three-month period every three years. Babies can only happen when two are fertile at the same time. I was eighteen months from fertility when I met your mother. At least."

Deor's eyes widened. "You didn't lie."

"No," he insisted. "I would not have taken that choice from your mother—no matter how much I wanted a child. I am not a monster."

"Human men are fertile all the time. From the moment they're born until, in some cases, a couple days after they're dead."

Finn's eyes widened. "That's horrible," he said. He seemed to consider it. "That would explain the short life span and all the wars," he added, almost to himself. "But let's talk of other things." She continued to eat her cake and listen to Finn as he told stories about being young and fertile—about fist fights and amorous meetings. Deor laughed in all the right places, but she couldn't shake the memory of that night with Geoff, when he had promised her he couldn't get her pregnant. He'd sworn. What if he, like Finn, had been mistaken?

She wasn't late—well not yet. Who knew what being in the Winter Court was doing to her system anyway? Her hair was growing faster, and all the grey was gone. The typical eye-strain problems that avid readers suffered had vanished, too. Frankly, the thought of having a period once every two years, rather than every twenty-eight days, was alluring. There was no need to panic. Yet.

"Don't you agree?" Finn asked.

"What?" Deor said, snapping back to the moment. "Sorry, my mind was wandering."

"Are you well?" Concern pulled his face into a frown. "You look at bit ill. Was the cake too rich?"

Deor looked down at her plate—she'd eaten the whole little cake. "No. It was good. Maybe I'm a bit tired."

"I understand," he said. "It's been a rough few months for you."

"Yes." The world was a stress of its own. Magic filled the air around her; under her feet the stones were thick with it. Even the water she drank carried it along. Most of the time she didn't notice it at all. Right now, though, the stress made her hyperaware, and the magic danced along her skin. She drew in a deep breath and closed her eyes, focusing on drawing the faerie inward until it was just a tiny core, letting the rest of her be nothing but human for a while.

Think about oatmeal. Green peas. Tea with grandmother. She blew out a deep breath and felt more human than she had in days.

Where are you going? Don't go. Don't go. Don't go! All around her, the Palace was panicking. She could almost hear its voice, screaming like a frightened child. Hands seized her shoulders.

"Deor! What's wrong?"

She opened her eyes. Finn was shaking her by the shoulders, a look of panic in his eyes. Servants scrambled.

"Someone get a healer!" he shouted. "Call the Sword! Call Rafe! Now! Deor, sweetheart what's wrong?"

"I'm fine!" She struggled to push him away, but he was too strong, holding her by the shoulders, leaning into her space and trapping her against the chair. In her back, her wings jumped and twitched, trying to spring out. "Get off me."

"Stay awake. Just stay awake until the healers get here." He scooped her up from her chair and carried her, protesting, into the next room where he laid her down on a couch and gripped her hand.

"Finn, get grip on yourself. And let go of me." She pushed herself upright. "I'm telling you, I'm fine. What the hell are you screaming about?"

He kept ahold of her hand, his silver eyes peering into her own. "Your eyes are looking better. They were dead grey a second ago."

"They're supposed to be grey!"

"Shhh. It's okay. You'll be okay. The healers will be here in a minute. You're probably just exhausted from everything you've been through. It'll be okay, my little girl." He continued to pat her hand and talk in a soft voice as if she were a feverish five year old.

Deor rolled her eyes and flopped backward on the couch. There was no getting through to him, and trying to get up would only make him worse. "I'm perfectly fine," she said, more for herself than because she expected him to listen.

"I'll be the judge of that. Excuse me, Your Highness." Mac, the white-haired older healer who had worked on Rafe on Adoption Day sat down beside her on the couch, deftly shoving Finn aside and taking Deor's hand. The healer still had a napkin tucked into his collar.

Finn's voice shook. "We were at dinner. She closed her eyes as if she were fainting, and all her vitality just drained away. She looked like she was dying right in front of me."

Mac grunted and took her chin in his hand so he could look close into her eyes.

She frowned at him until he let go of her face and placed a finger on her throat.

"My...Finn's over reacting," she said. "I wanted to feel human for a bit. I'm sorry we interrupted your dinner."

Mac ignored her while he muttered about erratic magic balances and late puberty hormonal changes, one hand on the vein in her neck, the other still holding her hand. Finn hovered on her other side, close enough that she could feel his breath on her face.

"Alright, Princess," Mac said, "tell me if this hurts..."

Chapter Five

As Rafe stepped down from the carriage outside his club, the Junior Flaneur, the added guards who had ridden on the outside of the carriage held back the crowd of reporters who shouted and jostled. No doubt they had been waiting there for days on the off chance that he, or anyone else who knew what was happening inside the Palace, might show up. He ignored them and turned his face up to enjoy the cold rain even as he took the steps two at a time. He'd kept his fiancée Genevieve waiting long enough for some sort of word after Deor had crashed the Adoption. The least he could do was be on time for their dinner.

The porter coughed discreetly as he took Rafe's damp cloak.

"Shall I, sir?"

"No need, thanks." Rafe ran a hand over his hair. He gathered the droplets of rain into a globe and flicked the water into the waiting basin, relishing the easy return of his old water magic. One more reason to be glad that the princess had returned to her own in the nick of time.

"Is the Lady Genevieve here yet?" he asked the porter.

"Yes, sir. I believe she is waiting for you in the Arbor Room." The porter gestured down the club's hall to a door on the left.

"Thank you." Rafe tipped the porter and hurried down the hallway. Designed to look and feel like a gracious country home, the Junior

Flaneur offered its members a variety of spaces to eat, drink, exercise, gossip, hold private meetings, or simply fall asleep with one's feet stretched out in front of a good fire. The Arbor Room was one of the medium-sized parlors, just the right place to have a before-dinner drink with a few friends without the press and crowd of a bar, its walls ornamented with the interlaced branches of living trees. His earth faerie fiancée would be waiting for him there. He could hear her laughter as he opened the door.

Genevieve stood in the center of an admiring circle wearing a silver and white gown, droplets of diamond in her hair and around her wrists echoing the rain outside. The aquamarine ring he had given her at their betrothal winked, the only dot of color in her outfit. "Of course the little creature has gone missing," she was saying. "You don't suppose the Goblin Prince would leave behind his plaything, do you?"

"He's always left them before," someone else answered, and the group laughed again.

"Yes, he's terribly untidy that way," Genevieve said. "But can you imagine the incredible lies he must have told her to make her behave in that way at the Adoption? One almost feels sorry for the poor creature." She sipped her champagne before catching sight of Rafe.

"Darling, how are you?" she said, coming toward him with open arms. She kissed him on the corner of his mouth, smelling of jasmine and tart apples.

He kissed her back, circling her waist with his arms to pull her closer, but she held one graceful arm away so as not to spill her drink even while lightly hugging him back with her free arm.

Others in the room came forward as Rafe let Genevieve go. Delaney Overton, Rodney of Northfalls, and his paramour Clarissa Rangley— friends old enough to know they'd be welcome to press him, if only a little. Others who knew him less well hung further back, just within earshot.

"Yes, Rafe, how are you?" Delaney asked, a faint crease of worry on his forehead. At their last meeting, he had hardly been able to meet Rafe's eyes.

Rafe gave them all a wide smile. "Better and better every day," he said. "Like my old self again."

Audible sighs of relief went up from his friends.

"What else can you tell us?" Rodney said.

"Not a blessed thing. It's all classified."

"Was that really Geoff's little lady friend who went screaming up the aisle at the king?" Delaney said.

"If you mean Professor Deor Smithfield, yes, that was her." That much had been publicly broadcast. No need to be coy about it.

"And where is she now?" Clarissa said.

"In the Tower, I hope," Genevieve said. "That creature should be charged with treason."

"That's hardly fair," Clarissa said. "For all you know she's a hero. And it can't be treason because she's not a Winter Court citizen."

Genevieve sniffed skeptically.

Rafe sighed. "I can't comment on the lady's whereabouts, but I assure you we have the situation under control."

"And what about the child she claimed to know about? What on earth was that all about? Any truth to it?" Delaney asked.

Rafe held his tongue as Genevieve snapped, "It's absurd. There's no child."

"You never know," Clarissa said, lifting her chin.

"Just another goblin trick," Genevieve insisted.

Rodney put an arm around Clarissa's waist, saying, "The woman is clearly insane."

But Delaney frowned into his drink. "What if it's the Gemalsdottir girl? A long game between the Consort and the king to allow them to have a child after all?"

"Why do you think the Bards are being so closed mouthed all of a sudden?" Rodney said. "Normally they can't be made to shut up."

Rafe said nothing and sipped his drink.

"Oh, come on, Rafe," Rodney said, coming closer. "Don't put on your press conference face with us. Tell us what we really need to know. When will the Adoption be finished? Or is it finished already and that's why you're looking healthier?"

"I'm not at liberty to comment on any of that, Rodney."

In a quiet voice, too low to carry beyond their immediate circle, Delaney said, "I see that you're still wearing the Sword's uniform and insignia." He raised his eyebrows at Rafe.

Rafe simply smiled back. He offered Genevieve his arm and as she took it, said, "You'll all have to be patient a bit longer. The king will be making a statement soon."

He led Genevieve away to the private dining room he had reserved for the two of them. They made happy small talk as the supper was laid out and their glasses filled. After the last servant had whisked out of the room, Rafe threw up a quick privacy spell just for good measure.

"The Palace is going to make an official announcement soon," he said. "But I wanted to let you know first so you wouldn't be caught off guard. You absolutely must not mention this to anyone else."

"You can depend on me."

Rafe smiled and took her hand. Genevieve was trustworthy. She knew very well what to do with politically explosive information if she needed to, but she had never been one to gossip, and she was deeply loyal to her king and crown. It was one of the reasons he had proposed to her. A future Consort needed discretion. Not that she would be Consort now, but a Sword's spouse needed the ability to keep their mouth shut just as much. "I'm not going to be king."

"Oh, Rafe." The color drained from her face.

He reached across the table to take her hand. "Don't be worried. The kingdom is safe—safer than it would have been with me as king—and the king is finally healing. It's all going to be alright."

Tears glistened in the corners of her eyes, but her face held its delicate composure. "You always think of the king and the kingdom first, not yourself."

"I don't know about that." He still wanted to punch Finn square in the eye for what he had put him through, not to mention what Deor had suffered, and Astarte and Robbie were still suffering. At least Deor had gotten in one good slap.

"I'm happy for the kingdom," Rafe went on, "but I'm pretty well pleased with my own fate too. In fact, I feel like I escaped the hangman's noose at the last second." He reached for a roll and slathered it in butter.

"Oh, Rafe," Genevieve said again. She rose from her chair and came over to him, pulling him into her arms. "I'm sorry, my darling. It's alright. You don't have to put on a brave face with me." She kissed him and held him close.

He hugged her back, patting her awkwardly on the shoulder. "You're not crying, are you? Don't cry for me. Really, Gen, I'm happier than I can tell. I'm over the moon about this, in fact. I get to go on being Sword. I can't give you more details, but everything has worked out perfectly. Or as close to perfect as it can get."

Genevieve returned to her seat but left her food untouched as she watched Rafe eat. Finally she said, "I'm not stupid, Rafe. If you're not the heir, then the king must already have an heir of his body."

"I can't tell you that."

"Was the king afraid of his Consort's anger if he announced that he had taken a child bearer?"

Rafe snorted. "As if that ever stopped Finn before."

Genevieve frowned at the indecorous noise he'd made but pressed more. "So, what's wrong with the child that he needed to be forgotten and replaced? Is the child deformed or defective in some way? Or," her eyes grew wide in horror at the thought, "does he have his grandfather's madness?"

Rafe laughed. "Thank the Creator, no. But let's talk of other things. You'll just have to wait and learn with the rest of the country."

Genevieve frowned at her plate, then at him, before picking up a fork and spearing a piece of asparagus.

Rafe dug into the roast capon in front of him. Ah, it had been too long since food tasted like food. Now everything he ate had an extra savor to it. Freedom—that's what it was. He was free. He was a Farringdon and himself once more, and he'd never let anyone take that away again.

"Trust me, Gen," he said. "It's all worked out for the best."

"You know I don't like that nickname, Rafe."

"I'm sorry." He took her hand and kissed it. "I won't do it again."

Genevieve's mouth drew tight. "How can you be taking all this so lightly? It's...it's monstrous."

"You'll get no argument on that point from me."

This did nothing to slow Genevieve's building rage. "How can he do this to you? You've been adopted. You're the king's flesh and blood as much as anyone else. You've been a son to him your whole life, and now he's simply going to replace you on a whim? You have to fight this."

Rafe stopped mid-mouthful. "Why?"

"Why? For the sake of your honor. For the sake of the kingdom! This nation has suffered enough. Think about how vulnerable we'll be to the Summer Court, to the goblins' machinations if some hidden child is produced at the last minute with no preparation at Court. What if the king dies and leaves us with a child monarch? The Princess Consort would become the Regent. We cannot have that."

A faint chill stirred the air around Rafe as he unconsciously drew heat from around him. "Princess Consort Astarte would make a magnificent Regent, if that were necessary."

Genevieve waved her hand as if shooing off a gnat. "Don't give me that threatening look. This is politics, not personalities. I don't care how pleasant and self-effacing she's been over the years, Astarte is still a Summer Court faerie. It would be a political and magical debacle."

Rafe shook his head. "Gen...Genevieve, you're working yourself up over nothing. There isn't going to be a Regency. The king is in no hurry to die. You'll just have to trust me on this."

"And what about you?" Genevieve pleaded. "What about everything you've suffered for the sake of the crown? You deserve to sit on that throne."

Rafe put down his knife and fork. "I suffered for the love of a man who I called father, not to win a kingdom. Don't you understand? I never wanted it."

"I know, darling. I know you never had the treasonous ambitions of your parents, but to have the kingship within your hand and to have it snatched away from you at the last moment. Literally, the last moment. It's heartbreaking. It's too cruel. Too humiliating."

"To whom? Not to me. Don't you understand? I didn't want it. I forced myself to obey the king's wishes. They were never mine. And there is no humiliation in being what I am. I am a Farringdon and damn proud of it."

"How can you be? The Farringdon name is tainted, mired in treason. Your parents skulk in their fortress and plot against the king. Your brother stirs up rebellion in the streets. You could have been an Aethelwing, the noblest name in the kingdom, a name befitting you!"

Needles of frost spread out from Rafe's fingers across the tablecloth. "My name fits me very well, thank you. Perhaps it's you who can't stomach the thought of being linked to the Farringdon name."

Genevieve didn't blink or look away at the accusation, but her left hand toyed with the aquamarine ring on her finger. "Don't be ridiculous," she said.

The silence stretched between them, growing wider every second that it lasted. Rafe tried to bridge it, clearing his throat awkwardly. "I realize this is a shock to you. It's not what you expected when you agreed to marry me. Perhaps we ought to talk more about what we expect our lives to be like once we're married."

Genevieve opened her mouth and closed it again. She took a deep breath, straightening her already perfect posture and returning to the benevolent smile that had warmed the hearts of all the Harvest Queen judges. "We'll have to consider buying a house in the town."

"Yes, I agree."

"Now that you're no longer Sword, you'll have much more opportunity to speak freely in Parliament and to take on public works you couldn't have entangled yourself in before."

Rafe frowned slightly. "I'm still the Sword."

She blinked in shock, as if she'd never heard anything so stupid in her life. "Darling, you can't be."

"Why not?"

"After the way the king has treated you? And I doubt this new heir wants his rival breathing over his shoulder every moment, reminding him of what he isn't. Not to mention, you'd have to be continually deferring to him." Genevieve sighed, tracing plans on her napkin with her nails. "It's a good thing the Consort's daughter has returned to the north. One fewer fly in the ointment."

"What have you got against Robbie?" he almost shouted.

His tone startled Genevieve, and she jumped slightly. "Nothing. Robbie's a nice girl, if a bit silly, but politically, she's troublesome. We don't need that sort of trouble right now."

"Robbie's birth is hardly her fault." Crystals of ice spread across the surface of his wine glass.

Genevieve pursed her lips and shivered in a pointed way. "I'm simply saying that if the girl stays quietly in the north, something she has not been good at lately, she won't force the king into doing something harsher like forbidding her to enter Caer Eisteddfod, or banishing her to the human world."

Rafe nearly protested that Finn wouldn't do something so rash or so stupid, but he stopped himself. Yes, Finn might do exactly that, especially if Astarte refused to conciliate him or Robbie became more outspoken.

Genevieve went on talking, making plans, considering alliances and the purchase of land, even suggesting that a tentative, and temporary, reconciliation with his parents might be a judicious political move.

"Really? You expect me to side with them now? Just a minute ago you were denouncing them as traitors and claiming their name irrevocably tainted. Which is it, Gen?"

"You must learn to remember that this is politics, darling, not person- alities. That's why you need me, you see. You're a marvelous strategist in the field, but you've been far too aloof from the day to day working of the kingdom."

Rafe stared at his plate, drawing circles in the gravy. "Genevieve," he said. "Do you love me?"

"What? Naturally, I love you, darling. Now tell me what you think—if we purchase land in Scotland, we can strengthen our ties to the Lord of the Admiralty and perhaps even find some useful connections with the werewolves. Not that they matter much, but it never hurts to make friends. And then we'll have a northern home for those times when the heir is less pleased to have his predecessor around."

Rafe's pocket jolted as his mirror buzzed to alert him. He pulled it out, keeping it below the table, and flipped it open. "Shit." He snapped it closed, standing as he did so. "Forgive me, but I have to go. I will be back as soon as I can." He kissed her on the cheek and hurried out of the room.

He placed his hand on a part of the wall and slipped into a small, secret room. A guard saluted him from his place next to the doorframe. Rafe nodded at the young man and slapped the lintel, muttering the pass- word. Magic swelled through him, and he stepped through to the private quarters of the Palace.

Chapter Six

R afe hurtled through the door, face flushed purple from running and his fingers wreathed in magic as if he were preparing a spell to hurl. He was panting.

"What happened?" he said.

"Good grief. Enough of this." Deor yanked her hand out of Mac's and stood. Her wings flared out through the slits in her dress, fanning her hair around her face. She drew herself up to her full height, not that her five foot five meant much. "Everyone calm down. I'm not a hormonal teenager. I'm not a fragile flower. I'm not a hysterical girl. I'm not dying of some mysterious magic illness. I'm human, and I was taking a minute to be human." She didn't have to look down to know her nails had gone sharp as knives. "Now, everyone calm down and go back to your dinners."

She turned to Rafe, pausing to take in the unusually flamboyant deep blue suit with vines and flowers embroidered on the sleeves and the moonstones dotted through his hair. Lady Genevieve had had a hand in both.

"Rafe, you look..." She paused. He wondered what descriptives she worked through until she settled on one. "Very nice. I'm sorry we interrupted your date. Please apologize to Lady Genevieve for me."

"So I just force-portalled my way across the entire city and left my fiancée alone in private dining room across town because you were feeling a touch human?"

She glanced at Finn, who had not yet gotten the grace to be embarrassed. "Apparently so."

He gritted his teeth and growled something under his breath that her magically inserted Faerie dictionary translated as having to do with sodomy and wild animals.

"I'm sorry we ruined your date. Maybe you can get back there before the next course?"

"I hope so." He glanced in a mirror and reset a few of the jewels in his hair. "Can't I leave the two of you alone for one evening without trouble?" He didn't wait for a response, just portaled back to the club the way he had come, startling the guard.

"Sorry," Rafe said. "I know this is usually one way."

The young man nodded. "Yes, sir."

Rafe straightened his jacket and headed back to the private dining room. The table was there, as were the remains of the course he had abandoned along with the half-drunk glasses of wine. Genevieve, however, was not.

"Dammit," he said under his breath.

After a moment's thought, he went to the Arbor Room where Rodney and Clarissa were still chatting.

"Rafe!" Rodney said. "You came back." He looked around the room and waved at a waiter. "Drink?"

"No, thanks," he said. "Where's Gen?"

"Gone," Clarissa said. "I'm not sure where, perhaps home."

"Delaney escorted her out, hon, remem—oof." Rodney stopped as Clarissa kicked him in the shins.

Rafe laughed. "It's okay Clarissa, but thank you for sparing my feelings. She went out on the town?" He sighed. "Good for her. Goodness knows that there will be a lot more nights like this than I'd like. She needs to have friends."

"Stay and have dinner with us," Clarissa insisted. "We haven't gone in to dine yet."

"Oh, no," Rafe said, giving a small bow. "It's been one of those nights. I think I shall retire for the evening. If I don't see you before, I shall see you in Parliament."

Once he was away from the Arbor Room, it only took him a minute to head for the secret gate in the club's back garden. The rain and the dark ensured that the garden was empty except for a pair of merfolk lounging in one of the farther pools and utterly unaware of his presence.

Rafe slipped through the gate, shaking his hair free of the watery blue moonstones his valet had woven into it. The jewels securely dumped into his pocket, he turned his face upward to the rain and breathed deeply for a moment. He wished his dogs were there with him.

Well, no matter. He threw a faint glamour over himself, ensuring that anyone who noticed would see only a common soldier on some errand. He stretched his long legs and ran through the rainy streets, breathing freedom and loss with every stride.

Eventually, his run took him out of the St. George district into less prestigious streets where the buildings crowded closer together. Here shops and homes mingled, and gardens were more likely to be small patches of ground behind the building than expansive lawns. Rafe slowed in front of a pub with a simple sign showing a rounded green hill crowned by a circle of stones. Technically called The Faeries' Rest in the city registers, but to its patrons, the pub was simply the Mound. Warm light glowed from bow windows on either side of the door.

As Rafe entered, he dropped the glamour that had covered him. Nearly every one of the many patrons were in uniform, but few even looked up at his entrance, and none stood to salute. That was the unspoken, but long-standing rule of the Mound—officers and enlisted, noble and common—everyone's money was the same and everyone had equal right to a quiet pint or two. Come to that, everyone had an equal right to get punched in the head if he couldn't leave others to drink in peace, but it usually only took one or two lessons before hot-headed youngsters learned to value the peace and quiet. If you were after a brawl, you went In The Back.

Rafe passed by the bar where the twins, Evan and Eva, were busily pulling pints.

"Your usual?" Eva ask him.

"Thanks. And how's your mother?"

"Like a bear with a bad tooth over this year's barley harvest. She's had to buy from the pixies to make up the usual amount, and she's sure some of what they sold her came from the human side. She tossed a whole batch of malt into the trash just this morning. Said it smelled wrong."

"Did it?"

Eva thought about the question as she filled his glass. "It was off-ish. Not bad mind you, but she was right. It just wasn't up to standard. Still, I don't know what we'll do if there's a shortage again this year. Dwarf brews are alright, but Mother'll close the place before she serves a goblin ale."

She slid the glass across the bar to him, and Rafe took a long, appreciative drink.

Rafe strolled to the back of the room where a soundproof door waited. As he swung it open, the sound of men shouting spilled out briefly. He shut the door.

The room was bare of furniture except for the raised circle in the center. The faintest distortion in the air around the circle showed where a magical barrier kept the two combatants in and their audience out. Rafe leaned against the wall with his drink and admired their skill. One of the fighters was slow, but he punched with a scientific precision that never failed to strike his opponent. The faster, but less precise, of the two fighters swung three times as often as his opponent, but not every blow landed. Rafe recognized him as a major in a cavalry brigade. The younger, more careful fighter he didn't recognize at all, a sure sign the man was new to the military. Too new to have come under Rafe's notice.

"Evening, Your Majesty," a quiet Welsh voice said beside Rafe.

Rafe raised one eyebrow. Bolton stood beside him, an enquiring look in his eye.

"Last time I checked, rank didn't exist back here," he said. He gestured pointedly to the two fighters now circling each other, the faster, sloppier fighter clearly flagging as his opponent wove and dodged, looking for the perfect shot. An opening came, and he took it with lightning speed. The other man went down like a landed fish.

Cheers and groans went up, and ring's healer rushed in to check on the downed man.

"Rank may not count for much back here, but I doubt the king would look kindly on someone pummeling his boy bloody," Bolton said.

"The king knows nothing about this place," Rafe said. "Nor will he from me." He set down his empty glass. "Care to go a round or two? Show the other Houseboys what a real fighter looks like in action."

Bolton took a long drink from his own glass. "I do believe the honor of the *household guard*—not boys—is at stake," he said. "You know I can't let that stand."

As Rafe climbed into the ring, an old familiar fire burned in his belly. Stripping off the embroidered jacket, jewels still clinking in its pockets, he rolled up his sleeves as Bolton did the same.

"Come on then," Bolton said, a wide grin on his face. "Let's see how out of practice you are."

Rafe grinned back, the fire inside him spreading with joyful heat, and raised his fists.

Chapter Seven

Deor slapped her hand against the lintel of the portal on the first floor of Hrofstag Gwythferth Hall, the English Department building. "Fourth floor," she said. She lingered a moment, rather hoping that Arthur might get stuck. The movement of air around her as she made her way down the hall suggested otherwise.

"You know, you didn't have to be hidden when you came to get me at the flat this morning," she said as she slipped into the English Department office and checked her mailbox. Nothing. A good start to the day.

Arthur's voice whispered in her right ear. "I'm supposed to be stealthy."

"You thought I wouldn't see you," she mumbled to the mailboxes.

"Luck," Arthur insisted, but his voice was sulky.

She wondered, had it been luck, too, when she'd seen through his disguise in the Tower her first day in the Winter Court? She should let it go—not acknowledge him. It might make him feel better—and that might put him in a better mood.

She left the office, nodding politely to another professor walking down the hall—a man whose name she didn't know, though she recognized him, sly features and all, from a picture on Ama's desk.

The hallways were sparsely populated—empty really—given how early in the morning it was. The students with early classes wouldn't arrive at the building any sooner than absolutely necessary, and most of the faculty who didn't have to be in early weren't. She climbed the last flight of stairs to the fifth floor, heading for her office. It wasn't like she couldn't simply pick up the textbook and go, she could, but a quick reread beforehand was always nice.

Today, though, it appeared she wasn't going to have the time.

"Good morning, Aiden," she said as she approached her office. The red-skinned faerie student sat in the chair outside her door, exactly where Robbie should have been waiting for Deor—who had been running late—when she was attacked. The girl had almost died, might still die.

Aiden's head jerked up, and he stood. "Good morning, Professor Smithfield."

Deor unlocked her door and gestured for him to enter before her. She held the door for him and waited for the breeze marking Arthur's movement to pass before she followed and closed the door. "Have a seat," she said, pointing at the chairs in front of her desk.

She stripped off her heavy coat and scarf, hanging them on the coat rack just inside the door, and took her place at her desk. "What can I do for you?"

"I have questions," Aiden said.

Deor sighed. "I am quite certain of that," she said. "And they do not pertain to Shakespeare, correct?"

"No," he said. "They don't. But I deserve answers!" He slapped his hand down on the table and then winced at the pain. To his credit, it was a tiny flinch, and he recovered quickly. "The people have a right—"

"No, you don't," Deor cut him off. She knew—believed—that wasn't true, but for now, for a few brief days, she was still an ordinary person, no title but the one she had earned. Aiden remained standing. For the first time, she noticed his t-shirt, just visible under his open coat, a silkscreen of Che Guevara. She smiled, barely containing a laugh. "Did Robbie bring you that shirt from the human world?"

"What?" He looked down and back up. "Yes." He plowed on. "Something is going on in that Palace! The king is hiding something! If you know, you have to tell me!"

"Even if I were in a position to say what was going on at the Palace, why should I tell you?"

"The people have a right to know what's happening."

"You're not *The People*, Aiden," Deor said gently. "You're one man."

Aiden drew himself up and shoved his bangs out his eyes. They immediately fell into his face again. "I represent the Student Action Committee of the Loyal Sons of London. You can't silence all of us."

"I'm not trying to silence any of you." She folded her hands on the table and leaned forward. "Have a conversation with me instead of delivering a speech."

Aiden frowned, biting his lower lip.

"I thought London was a slur," Deor said, remembering the warning in her mother's letter. "Why would you name yourself that?"

Aiden flushed a bit. "It is controversial," he admitted. "But we wanted to show where our loyalties lie—with the place, not the person. It's not really a bad word, just a human one. Caer Eisteddfod is locked in autocracy, under the absolute sway of a single ruler. London, the other side, has a House of Commons and not just for show. They have a Constitution, guaranteed rights for all citizens, the rule of law over the rule of whim." He leaned forward, face lit up with sincerity of belief. "It's an idea whose time has come. Do you have any idea how many more people, not just students, came to our meeting after the interrupted Adoption?"

"No," Deor said, as her eyes flicked to Arthur lurking in the corner. "And I don't want to know, nor do I want names. Now do you have a question I can answer, or do you just want to lecture me about democracy?"

He deflated, his momentum quelled by her sharp tone. "You've been at the Palace—you stayed there, right? Is Robbie there? Is she okay?"

Deor drew in a deep breath, and a wave of fatigue washed over her. The kid—though he was her own age—seemed young. He radiated that passion, that absolute confidence in his beliefs that only inexperience could produce. Had she ever been that naïve? That unbroken? Her heart ached at the vast space between eighteen and thirty—in years, in experience, in broken hearts.

"I did not see Roberta when I was at the Palace. But, from what I have gleaned, she is safe and recovering, with her mother, out of town."

He squeezed his eyes shut and pressed his palms into the desk for a moment.

"We are on the same side, you and I," Deor went on. "I know you think we are not. I care very much for Robbie, and I am aware that she is where she is because of me."

"Why? Tell me why being in your office almost got her killed," he demanded.

"I can't explain that right now."

He crossed his arms over his chest. "Right."

"I can tell you that the man who hurt her is dead, and the Sword has not given up hunting down his accomplices." Tears stung the corners of her eyes. "For now, the best we can do—you and I together—is our jobs. Be the best student you could be." She smiled at him. "You know Robbie will be mad if you don't do the reading."

Aiden gave a small laugh. "Yes."

"And keep fighting your political fight." Deor sat back in her seat. "From what I've seen, I think you and your friends are right. Did you read de Tocqueville, like I suggested?"

He shook his head. "I've got it, but…"

"And that fellow on your shirt," Deor pointed. "Do you know who that is?" When he shook his head, she sighed. "His name is Che Guevara." She waved away any answer. "Go out into the human world. Go to a bookstore. Ask for a book or two on him. Ask for a book on the American Constitution too. Particularly the Bill of Rights."

"You're giving me more homework?" But at least he was grinning.

"Yes. Whatever political wrangle is coming, the best thing you can do is be prepared." She glanced back to where Arthur lurked. "Now," she smiled, "let me do some preparing for class, okay?"

He nodded and stood. "Thank you, Professor." He paused, as if wanting to say something else, but turned and walked to the door. "See you in class!" he said before he left.

"See you," she said as the door closed behind him. "Don't." She held a hand up to Arthur—now visible—before he could speak. "Just don't."

"The Bill of Rights?" he asked. "Fomenting rebellion, are you?"

"Maybe," she said. "You should read a copy, too—you and Rafe. And Finn, except the shock of it might kill him." She flipped her textbook open and took out a pencil. "That poor kid. I hope Robbie loves him back."

Arthur laughed. "Yes. Or he might die of a broken heart—or at least feel like he will." He took up his sentinel position at her door. "Young love," he sighed dramatically. "Thank the Creator I'm done with that."

45

Chapter Eight

"Alright," Deor said, closing her textbook and nodding at the class. "I think that about covers it. Have a good weekend, and be ready to talk about *Twelfth Night* next week—we're going back to a comedy, which should be a nice breather after all that political tragedy."

The students rose to leave, and several faeries flicked their wings in and back out again as they donned their coats, slipping their wings through the vents. Deor's own wings twitched in her back. Outside, even before the addition of a chilling wind, the temperature was barely above freezing. The thought of having her wings out made her shiver. The students seemed not to care—was it adaptation? Or more like her willingness to wear four-inch heel to class in grad school—worth the discomfort for the fashion?

Aiden smiled at her as he left with his friends, and several other students said or nodded their goodbyes. Maybe she was making some progress—progress that might vanish entirely once the world found out who she was. Hopefully the students would still recognize she was the same person—she'd been their professor, she'd stay their professor.

As the door clicked closed behind the last student, Arthur dropped his glamour, appearing right next to her.

Deor squeaked and a few sparkles spun off her. "Stop doing that!"

He chuckled. "I knew you hadn't seen me."

"Nope," Deor said through clenched teeth. "You got me there." Her silver nails punctured through several onion-paper pages of her textbook.

She forced her fingers to relax, one by one. The magic that tipped her nails had spread, turning her fingers silver almost to the second knuckle. She gathered up her belongings, tucking her hands below her books, and hoping Arthur didn't see. He seemed to enjoy getting a rise out of her, so no need to encourage him.

As this morning, someone waited at her office door—but not a student.

Victor Farringdon stood in front of her office door, speaking urgently with two students—one a part of Aiden's coterie. Victor's coat hung open over a dark blue day suit, and a scarf hung down his shoulders. His black hair was free and fell a few inches below his collar. His pale blue skin mirrored Rafe's, though his features were much finer. Both the brothers, though differently so, were as handsome as any men she had seen.

Victor frowned at the students and shook his head. He glanced her way and started. "No. You wanted my opinion, now you've got it. No. Now, go on." When one protested, he shook his head, silencing the younger man. "Later." The students—a young man and the beautiful young faerie woman from class—glanced Deor's way, nodded, and headed off down the hall away from her.

A look of tired exasperation flashed across Victor's face as he watched them go. By the time he had turned toward Deor, his face was calm, a pleasant smile replacing the scowl. "Professor Smithfield," he said.

"Lord Victor." She unlocked the door, feeling Arthur hovering behind her. "What can I do for you?" She pushed open the door and dropped her things on a side table.

"I hoped that you had time for a brief conversation." His eyes searched the space between them, alighting here and there. He had to know someone else was with them—but could he see Arthur? Or did he expect her to be guarded?

"Please," she gestured toward her open door, "come in and we will have a chat." Once Victor sat, Deor glared at Arthur, focusing all her attention on the wavy magic obscuring him. When she had first arrived, staring at him under one of his glamours made her head hurt. Now, whether she had grown accustomed to it, or her anger kept the pain at bay, she wasn't sure.

"Stop it," he hissed, clearly trying to keep his voice low.

"It's not like he doesn't know you're here."

"Is that the captain?" Victor called from his seat. "So nice to almost see you again, Captain Maerhwer."

At last, the lines of magic across Arthur's face came into focus, sharp and clear. Deor pushed just enough magic through her hands to tip her fingers in silver. She swiped her hand across his face, barely missing his nose, and dragged the magic away. With a flick of her hand, she sent the broken bits of magic—twined threads of gold and brown—spiraling to the floor.

She backed up a few paces. "There."

Arthur glared at her, or at least his seemingly-disembodied head did—she hadn't stripped away the whole glamour. "My being here is meaningless if everyone knows it."

"Get out," she said.

"No." Arthur crossed his arms. "He's dangerous."

Deor snorted. "You don't tell me who I can and cannot see."

Victor cleared his throat. "If it would help," he said, "I am happy to have the captain check me for weapons, magic, etc. I will swear that I am here with no ill intent."

"Perfect," Deor said. She looked to Arthur. "Well?"

Victor stood and stepped toward the two of them, stopping a few feet away. He held his arms out. "Captain?"

Arthur glared at her, the gold flecks in brown eyes glittering, before inspecting Victor. Waves of magic rolled over Victor, spilling from above his head and pooling at his feet. None seemed to cause physical pain, but he winced slightly with each new spell.

"He's fine," Arthur said. "Let's sit." He pointed to one chair for Victor and moved to stand behind him.

Victor sat.

"Thank you, Arthur," Deor said coming to stand next to him. "You can wait outside." She laid a hand on his chest and gently pushed backward. He hesitated but relented, walking backward toward the door.

"This is a bad idea," he said. Magic flowed over him until, once again, he was nearly invisible.

"I'm sure it is." Deor opened the door and waited until the glittering magic she could still see was in the hall. She closed the door, gently but firmly, in his face.

She took her place behind her desk. "I hope what you have to say is worthwhile. I'm going to get an earful when you leave."

Victor chuckled. He was and was not like his brother. His posture was more relaxed, but he had the same eyes, with their laser focus. Slighter in build and a touch shorter, he was less imposing, but that came as much from his manners—he gave off an air of indifference, as if, even if he could hurt someone, he simply couldn't be bothered.

"I think you'll find it so, Your Majesty." He gave a slight bow of his head.

"Ah. I see." Deor stared at him. "So you have come to confess that you and your family tried, with the help of the goblins, to have me, and my father, the king, killed?"

"No." He jolted back. "I had nothing to do with you being attacked, or the attempt on your life."

"But the king's?"

He settled back in his chair and drew a deep breath. "I had heard you were nothing if not to-the-point. My family knew the king had a bodily heir. They knew the king believed she was dead. They knew her approximate age."

"How?"

"Michael Monteblanc," he said. "He was Shield when the king had his most fortunate affair. He was sent to find the heir when her mother fled. He lied and told the king that both the mother and child had died."

"Why are you telling me this, and not, say, Rafe? Or Arthur? He is right outside." She crossed her arms. "Didn't you commit treason? I just yell for Arthur, and you'll never see the light of day again."

He frowned. "The knowledge itself was not treason. Neither was having nothing to do with the king. His choice to make my brother his heir was nothing to do with me or my family. Yes, the king's lie might have killed him. But it was his lie. His risk."

"It almost got me killed."

"If that is the case, I am deeply sorry. I know Geoffrey tried to kill you, but I do not believe that the king's lie would have—neither you nor my brother would have been permanently harmed because neither of you participated in the lie."

"I damn near killed Rafe!" Deor snapped.

"I did not know he was being hurt by you until the last ceremony." Victor grimaced. "I was not sure you were the heir, even after I met you with Geoff at the restaurant that night. He thought you were, and thought he was clever, taking you as a mistress. Keeping an eye on you—as he put it." Disgust rang in Victor's voice. "I had no way to get you away from him, and I foolishly thought you would be safe, whether the heir or no." He gave a small smile. "It seems that you handled everything perfectly."

"Perfectly? Oh, fuck you."

Victor's jaw dropped for a moment, and then he began to laugh. "No. I mean it. You disgraced Geoff, you strengthened the ties with the vampires, you provided the kingdom with an heir, you have, it seems, healed your father, and you did all of this with grace and style."

"No," she said. "You don't get to come in here with this fake flattery and think this is all okay. Do you want a cookie for coming clean? If you want to tell me who was in the alley, that might help."

"You know who was in the alley." Victor's voice was flat. "If you expect me not to be disingenuous, then at least extend me the same courtesy."

"I don't know. When I try to remember, I throw up!"

"You know," he repeated. "My brother knows. It couldn't have been anyone else. But you'll never put her behind bars. You'll never identify her. I have no evidence. My advice? You survived. Call that win and let it go."

"Your advice?" Deor stood. "I think you should leave."

Victor stood. "Your Majesty—"

"Professor Smithfield," Deor corrected.

"Professor Smithfield," Victor said with a sigh. "Please. I am sorry for what happened. Had I known you were...all you are, I would have run screaming to the king with you in tow. I am not a traitor—my parents may be—but I am not. I have left my family's home. I am here to help you."

"So far, it seems you've bragged about getting away with it."

Victor looked down at the table. "That was not my intention." His voice was barely a whisper. "I came to warn you." He glanced up at her. "My parents know who you are. Your father is a fool if he doesn't tell the world. They will do it for him, in the most inconvenient of ways. I don't know when or how, but every moment that you lie about who you are—"

"I'm not lying!" Deor shouted. When Victor merely raised his eyebrows, she went on. "I am not announcing it. I have never lied about it."

"Really?" the man smirked. "Not revealing important information is not a lie? Many people will think your stint here is ridiculous—insane. The captain clearly does. And I'm sure my brother does as well. This is a security nightmare. You must know that."

"I'm fine as long as no one knows—"

"People know!" It was Victor's turn to shout.

Deor glared at him.

He did not apologize. "People know," he repeated, softly. "You're pretending they don't."

"So, what shall I do? Will you protect me?"

"With my life," Victor said, as nonchalantly as though he had agreed to pass her the salt at dinner.

Deor opened her mouth, closed it, and opened it again. Nothing came out. They stared at each other for several moments.

"I...I would never ask that," she said, a deep frown creasing her forehead.

"I know," he said. "Which is a part of why I would make the offer. Your lack of pretension, your lack of experience here. You're a blank slate—no political alliances, no preconceived ideas. You can make this kingdom better. But," he shook his head, "these are also weaknesses. You have no idea what's coming at you. The captain, for all I dislike him and his ilk, and my brother, for all our strife, both have some idea. Both will protect you if you let them."

"I don't want protection. I don't want politics. I want the life I had," she snapped.

"Well, it's gone." Victor crossed his arms. "It's not coming back. Quit the charade before you get hurt."

"I don't—"

"Before you get someone *else* hurt then, whether you ask them to or not."

"I think you're being overly dramatic," Deor said. Except she knew he wasn't. He was smooth and politically savvy, and he was here—even knowing Arthur was too. "Look, maybe—"

Arthur slammed open her door, completely visible, sword drawn. "We have to leave. NOW!"

"What? Now?" Deor stammered. "Why?"

"A mob," Arthur said. He glared at Victor. "Somehow, word of who you are has gotten out."

"Shit," Victor said. He launched himself over her desk, and she jumped back. He took her arm. "Come on."

Mouth agape, she followed him as he led her toward Arthur.

"Here." He grabbed her coat off the rack.

"Cold isn't the first priority, Victor," Arthur snapped.

"It's one more layer of cover," he said, helping her on with her coat. He grabbed her scarf and threw it at her. "Cover your head, hair, face—as much as you can and still see."

Deor did as she was told.

"Victor," Arthur said. "Stay next to her."

"Right." He took her arm.

Arthur vanished into a glamour again but said, "Follow me. Down the far stairs, out the back door. I've mirrored for help, but I don't know if they can get here in time. Kaya—Eisteddfod Security—should be down there, hopefully, when we get there."

"Right," Victor said. "We head for the West gate?"

"Bob and Bernie are there," Deor said. "They'll help."

"It's the closest to the Palace," Arthur added. "Any help will come through there."

Victor paused and took Deor by the shoulders, turning her to face him. "No one out there is your friend—even if they are. They may even hurt you by trying to help. Do not stop. Do not look back—no matter what—and do not respond to anyone calling your name or title. People will be watching for that. Got it?"

"Yes." Deor nodded.

Victor flung her books and papers into her satchel and shoved it at her. "Here."

"Thank you." She flung it over her shoulder.

"Come on!" He tried to take her hand.

"No." She pulled her hand away. When he started to protest, she said, "Take my arm." She held it out. "I don't have my gloves." When he looked confused, she added, "I don't want to cut you." She waved her hand at him.

His eyes widened as the silver magic sharpened her nails to razors and spread down toward her hand. "Right. Maybe keep your hands in your pockets." He took her arm. "Let's go."

They hadn't gone ten feet down the corridor before office doors began banging open. Bards, mirrors in hand, stuck their heads into the hall, calling to one another.

Aiden, his wings out for extra speed, raced up to the open office door. "Is it true?" he shouted. "You're the heir?"

"Shhhh! Not so loud," Deor said. "Yes, it's true."

Aiden's eyes grew even wider. "No wonder you stopped the Adoption."

"I wasn't trying to become the heir…"

Arthur cut her off. "We don't have time for this. We have to go. Now." He grabbed Deor by the upper arm like a toddler who might run off and pulled her toward the door.

"I'm coming too. I can help," Aiden said.

Arthur rolled his eyes but didn't respond. Instead, he focused on Deor. "Keep your head down and keep moving," Arthur hissed, his hand on the middle of her back. Her wings twitched and clenched at the overly-familiar touch. She shrugged off his hand and stepped closer to Victor.

They bolted out the stairwell door at the end of the hall and down the stairs. Classes were still in session, though not for long.

They made it a hundred feet from the front of the building before someone shouted, "There she is!" A crowd surged toward them, more people converging from all different directions.

"Run!" Arthur had her by the sleeve of her coat, dragging her along toward the wooded path that led to the gates.

A crowd of reporters headed for Deor's group, though they hadn't yet figured out Deor was standing right in front of them.

"Not that way," Deor called to him. She veered to the right, headed for faculty housing. Victor and Aiden kept pace beside her, giving Arthur little choice but to follow.

The long skirts of her academic robes tangled around her legs, and Deor hiked them up, exposing her legs to the cold wind.

Her chest burned with the exertion even as Arthur growled, "Can't you run any faster?"

The best she could do was shake her head.

"Maybe. We should. Just stop. And talk to them," Aiden panted.

Deor threw a glance over her shoulder at the pursuing crowd. Nope. Voices, both hostile and friendly, called out after her, but she knew that, even if she turned to face them, they wouldn't stop a few feet away. They would get their hands on her and, friendly or not, it would not go well for anyone.

She grabbed Aiden's arm and pulled him along. They'd be safe once they got behind the magical gate barring the entrance to faculty housing. They had to be.

But they weren't. The gate hung open, one hinge melted.

"Goblins," Arthur and Victor said in unison. A knife appeared in Arthur's hand, and lines of pale blue magic wreathed Victor's.

"We still have to get to my place. We have to warn Penny." Deor fumbled in her pocket for her keys. "Come on."

The four of them charged down the street only to hear snarling and yelps of pain coming from Deor's front yard.

Rufus, in dog form, stood on the steps ringed by six goblins, their hands wreathed in fire. Penny crouched on the top step behind him, one sleeve of her dress charred and burned away. Kaya, in tiger form, crouched surrounded by a ring of three goblins. A nasty wound forced her right eye closed.

"Stay here," Victor said to Deor even as Arthur grabbed Deor and pulled her the opposite direction.

"Not our fight," Arthur said. "Quickly, before they notice you."

"Are you insane? We have to help them." Deor swung her satchel off her shoulder with both hands, prepared to bludgeon any goblin that came at Penny again. It might not be magic, but there was a good twenty pounds of books and papers in the bag.

His pale white wings out, Victor leaped over the garden gate in a gale of stinging snow that drove into his enemies' eyes. Deor charged after him, satchel swinging. She caught the nearest goblin square in the back and sent him sprawling.

Cursing, Arthur followed.

The next goblin wasn't quite as easily taken by surprise. He rounded on Deor and flung strands of green magic at her that tangled her arms and knees. She stumbled and fell, but shredded the sticky magic with silver fingernails.

"Don't you hurt her!" Aiden shouted and got a fiery punch to the face from another goblin. He reeled back, screaming.

Someone grabbed Deor by the back of her coat, hauled her to her feet, and half dragged, half flung her toward the house steps. "Get inside," Arthur shouted. "You're the target."

Penny reached out from the front steps to grab Deor's hands, pulling her inside.

"We have to go out and help them," Deor said.

"The devil you do," Penny said. "You stay right here, and we'll all be safer." She held the door open, and a second later, Aiden and Arthur rushed through it. Arthur seized the door and began muttering over it, even as Victor, Kaya, and Rufus squeezed past him.

The second they were inside, he slammed the door. His peculiar shade of golden brown magic spread along the door frame, sealing it shut.

"Back door?" he said. Deor pointed back along the corridor to the kitchen, and he charged off to perform the same magic there. Penny, despite her own injuries, had already given Aiden ice for his face and was tending to Kaya. Rufus growled and paced in front of the parlor window. Victor joined him, a knife of ice in his hand.

Standing on tiptoe to see out the front door, Deor looked over the goblins in the front yard. They weren't retreating, despite their injuries—more goblins were joining them, ringing the house.

"This is my fault," she said to no one in particular. The sheer arrogance of thinking she could go on being just another adjunct on campus while being the heir felt like a rock in the pit of her stomach.

She reached into her pocket for the mirror Finn had given her.

"Rafe," she said. "I need you to come get us. Bring reinforcements."

Chapter Nine

Deor returned to the front door and peeked out of the glass at the top again. Rafe had said he'd be there soon. She counted the gathering goblins, frowned, and counted again.

"Come on!" Penny grabbed her arm and jerked her toward the parlor. "We're all safer in the same room."

Deor let Penny lead her but shook her arm off as soon as she could. Arthur had drawn the curtains, but stood at the window, one curtain cocked aside and stared out.

"I think there are more of them," Deor said as she shed her coat and scarf, as well as her academic robes, and dumping them on the floor by the front hall. "I counted twice and—"

"Of course there are more of them," Arthur snapped, not turning from the window. "They're coming to get you."

Deor rubbed her hands up and down her arms, though she wasn't cold. Under her the sleeves of her sweater, magic crawled. Her own magic, she knew by the feel of it. The same feeling she got when sparkles exploded when she was frightened. But no sparkles—or at least they weren't dancing off her into the air. The magic coated her skin, like a tight, supple bodysuit of pure power.

She shoved up one of her sleeves a bit and choked back a gasp. From her wrists up, her arms were coated in silver—like the tips of her nails.

She looked like she'd been dipped in armor. She poked her wrist, and to her relief, her skin felt normal, but the silver curled around her touch, like cloth at first, and ripples of magic flowed away from her finger like water around a dropped stone.

"Are you alright?"

A voice hovered at the edge of her hearing.

"Princess?" the voice repeated. "Deor?" It was more urgent now.

"What?" Deor tugged her sweater back in place and looked up at Victor, who eyed her with concern. "Sorry," she said. "I'm fine."

"You're sure you're not hurt?" He gestured at Penny. "We've got one of the best healers—"

"I'm fine," she repeated. "Nothing hurt me. No magic or fire landed. The magic that one goblin threw at me I wiped off." She managed a smile. "Remember, Victor, I know what goblin magic feels like."

"True, but—"

Rufus leapt toward the fireplace, barking and growling.

"Dammit," Victor said. He lunged after the hound and leaned in to glance up the fireless chimney. "Oh no you don't!" A flash of blue magic filled the room as Victor shot a shower of ice shards up the chimney. A strangled cry followed the sound of ice entering flesh, and a small burst of flame rolled out. Victor repeated the spell, but there was no sound. "I think he's retreated." He looked at Arthur. "Can you enchant it to keep them out?"

"I'll do what I can." Arthur stalked over to the chimney and created a mesh web of magic over the fireplace, like a massive netting. "Can you help?" He glanced over his shoulder at Victor, his voice cold.

"Sure." He stepped up. "What do you need?"

"Ice spikes would be a nice touch. A welcome for someone dropping in. I can cloak them."

Victor nodded and went to work. After a few minutes, only close inspection revealed the protective magic covering the fireplace.

Deor retreated to the window, on the opposite side of Arthur, who had returned to his post. She glanced out but wasn't really looking. Around the room, people fidgeted. Kaya's face looked better, though the fur around her eye was burned away. At least it looked like she could still see. Penny stroked Aiden's cheek, her own magic dancing around the now darkening bruise around his swollen eye and nose.

"You'll be fine," she said softly, with a smile. "No scarring or anything."

"Thanks," Aiden muttered, his gaze on the ground.

Rufus sat in the entrance to the room, eyes flicking back and forth from the front door, down the hall toward the kitchen and back. Victor remained by the chimney, head cocked as if listening.

Deor wanted to blurt out that she was sorry—that this was all her fault. But she knew that at least one of them would try to say it was okay, not her responsibility—even though they didn't believe it. No, the best thing she could do was remain as quiet and unobtrusive as possible.

Arthur let out a small sigh of relief.

"Victor, Rufus? Rafe's here, let's go."

Rufus bolted for the front door, Victor following. He charged out, ice knife in one hand, magic swirling around the other, wings behind him like a banner, their edges glistening in the light. Despite her wounds, Kaya was hot on their heels.

"You three," Arthur said before darting outside. "Stay here. Don't leave until one of us gets back. If a goblin gets in, run."

Deor and Penny nodded. Aiden looked disappointed but did not argue.

From the window, the three watched. The fight, if it could be called that, was brief and brutal. The goblins went down in a hail of magic and swords that they clearly were not prepared to face. In moments, the goblins—many much worse for wear—were bound and being dragged away. Deor turned away from the window, dropping the curtains in place.

Rufus was first through the door and charged to Penny, returning to human form as he leapt. He caught her in his arms and clung to her, whispering words in a language Deor didn't know—Gaelic?—almost too soft to hear. She hugged him back. Deor turned away to give them some privacy.

Rafe followed. After a small frown in the werewolf's direction, he turned to Deor. "You're safe. Let's get you back to the Palace." He turned to the couple. "Lady Penelope, would you and your paramour like to return to the Palace with us? We will leave guards here, but retaliation is a very common goblin trait."

"No, thank ye," Rufus said. "I'll be takin' her to the Embassy—we'll be safe there."

Rafe nodded. "Wise move. We'll be out of here soon."

He looked at Aiden, who shoved his hand through his hair and clasped his hands behind his back. "Where can we take you, young man?" Rafe said. "Do you need a healer?"

"No, sir," he said. "Lady Penelope has helped me." He glanced from Rafe to Deor. "Your Maj—I mean Professor Smithfield, are you alright?"

Deor smiled. "Yes Aiden. Thank you for your help, and for using my preferred title. Do you have family in the city?"

"I do," he said. "I was born and raised in Caer. But I'd rather go back to my flat," he said. "My parents already don't like my involvement in politics."

Arthur snorted. "Wise people."

"Hush," Deor scolded. "I'm sure the Sword can have soldiers escort you back to your flat." When Aiden looked panicked, she added, "To make sure you get home safely."

"Thank you," he said, with a sideways glance at Victor.

"With the University's permission, we'll leave some guards for a few days, to make sure that it's safe." Rafe said. "Unobtrusively. And we'll keep your name out of the press, too. If you like."

"Please," Aiden said, a brief look of panic sweeping his features. "I don't want people to know I got beat up by a goblin."

"Nonsense," Victor said. "You fought a goblin." He smiled. "No one needs to know that you might not have exactly won your encounter—we won the day. I can walk back with you if you like."

"Yes," Aiden said, relieved. "Thank you."

Victor gave a small bow toward the princess. "Your Majesty, Professor." He smiled.

Deor laughed. "Thank you for trying to warn me, Victor. I appreciate your help." She glanced at Arthur and Rafe, neither of whom looked pleased. "Perhaps next time we meet it will be less...violent."

He bowed again and led Aiden from the room.

Kaya trotted out after them.

Arthur turned to follow.

"Don't even think about it," Deor said. "Leave him alone."

Arthur started to protest, but Rafe shook his head. "She's right. We've got other things to deal with right now. Victor isn't going anywhere. We know where he lives."

"He was behind this, you know," Arthur said conversationally, heading for the door.

"I don't think so," Deor said. She paused and turned to Penny. "I am sorry. Please, if there is anything I can do, let me know." Before Penny could speak, she added, "Don't worry—I won't be back. I obviously can't stay here. I shouldn't have put you in such danger." Deor flailed. "Again, if there is anything…" Oh God, she was caught in a loop, and if she didn't stop talking, she'd say the same thing five-hundred times.

"Thank you," Penny interrupted. "If I need anything, I'll let you know, Your Majesty." She gave a stiff, formal curtsey. Slightly behind her, arm about Penny's waist, Rufus eyed the princess, but said nothing. His gaze briefly met Rafe's, and he nodded. Whatever needed to be communicated had been.

Deor let Rafe lead her through the campus surrounded by a ring of soldiers. A young, blond soldier walked at Deor's side. Arthur took up the rear. As they walked, the circle around her kept the crowds at bay, though their heavy arms meant that no one actually got within ten feet of the circle. Some people shouted questions, others curses. Many had their mirrors out. Most seemed to be students and faculty, but Deor couldn't be sure, and most seemed content just to stare.

"So," Deor said, to do anything but walk in silence. "You look familiar to me. Did we meet?" She gave a dark laugh. "Maybe you were one of the men with pikes at the Adoption."

The man gave a wry smile. "No ma'am," he said. "We met on the first day you arrived. I was the officer at immigration."

"Oh my God, yes." The memory of the patient but weary man, and her absolute failure to follow directions, flooded back. "I am sorry if I inconvenienced you," she said.

He laughed loud enough that Rafe glance back. "Not at all. It's a great story now." He winked at her. "It'll great for pulling in bars."

Deor laughed at that, and with it, the knot in her chest loosened a bit. The tears waiting to spill out retreated. "Do you have a name?"

"Lieutenant Steven Bolton, Your Majesty. I am a member of the King's Guard—Palace Guard under the Shield."

"Well, Lieutenant Bolton, it is a pleasure to meet you again." She smiled. "So. Tell me about yourself," she shrugged, "to take my mind off the utter mess I've made."

"You're about what I expected," he said. "Given what I saw of you that day in the Tower, and that day in the Palace." He was smiling and didn't pause for her to respond. "I am from Yorkshire," he said. "My family are sheep farmers. I joined the military at thirty and worked my way from the sticks to the Palace."

"Sheep?" Deor nodded. "How charmingly pastoral."

Bolton's eyebrow shot up. "If you've never shoveled sheep shit," he said with a smile, "I can see why you might think so."

Deor grinned and took his arm. "Fair enough."

Chapter Ten

Deor paced back and forth in front of the fireplace in the same place she had been brought after she had halted the Adoption—the main parlor of the Household—the royal quarters. There were substantially fewer people—only Deor and the king. He sat on the sofa facing the couch, one hand resting on the arm, the other in his lap. He watched her movements, but said nothing.

She stopped, one hand covering her mouth, and stared into the fire. The glowing embers had warmed the area of the stone floor not covered in a rug, and she curled her toes against the rock, savoring the connection to the Palace. She had noticed that Finn also almost never wore shoes.

"I can't believe I'm so arrogant and selfish," she said to the fireplace. This was about the tenth time she had said it. Again, her father let her go. He seemed to be waiting for her to speak directly to him.

Finally, she faced him. "I can't go back," she said. After he merely looked at her, offering no response, she added, "To Eisteddfod, I mean. I can't be a professor anymore." As soon as the words were out, the tears followed, damn them.

Finn rose, came to her, and wrapped his arms around her, pulling her into a tight but gentle hug. She held still for a moment, trying to keep from sobbing, her head turned to the side, silent tears rolling down her cheeks. When he didn't let go, she wrapped her arms around his waist and, pressing her cheek against his chest, she closed her eyes and sobbed.

The oppressive guilt didn't lessen with her tears—she wasn't only weeping for the people who had gotten hurt. She wept for herself—for the life she wanted, worked for, and lost. The life she would never, ever get back. Clinging to it had been pure, selfish fantasy.

Now that they had started, the tears, the sobs, wouldn't stop.

Finn cradled her against him and scooped her up.

She wanted to protest. She should stand on her own, but she couldn't.

He eased himself to the floor, lowering her with him, and set her on the stone, between his legs. He continued to loosely hold her.

As her sobs subsided, weariness overtaking her, he stroked her hair. "It's okay," he said. "Cry as long as you need. I'm here."

That brought another round of tears. How many times in three decades had she wished for a father to say that? A furious anger rose in her, and she pressed her palms to his chest, ready to push him away. He had no right to comfort her. She shoved, and he immediately dropped his arms, letting her go.

She stared up into his face—tears wet his cheeks, too.

"I am sorry, daughter," he said. He wiped a tear from her face, oblivious or indifferent to his own. "I would do anything to give you what you want."

"You think I should quit, too, right?" she asked.

He gazed down at her. "I will do what you want to do," he said. "There are ways to keep you safe at Eisteddfod. If you want to be a professor, we can find a way."

She sniffed, frowning. "I expected a lecture on duty, on my job as heir."

Finn smiled sadly. "That lecture can wait. The duty will always be there. You're young—though I know you do not think so. Had you been raised here, you would be decades away from any real political responsibility. I think, once you are no longer as fascinating to the public as you are now, you could teach at Eisteddfod with little fuss. After all, many children from noble houses spend a part of their thirties or forties at Eisteddfod—albeit on the opposite side of the desk."

Wiping at the tears on her face, she asked, "Are you serious? Do you want me to go back?"

He sighed and leaned back, bracing himself on his hands. "Not really, no," he admitted. "I worry. I also think it would be wise for you to learn here—Eisteddfod is in the Winter Court, but it is not *of* the Winter Court. It is its own world." He searched her face and looked away. "I chose Rafe as Sword, and he was so young. Not yet ninety."

"Has he done a poor job?" Deor's tone came out sharper than she meant it to be, but if Finn noticed, he didn't show it.

"Not at all. He is a brilliant general and will continue to grow as a wise counsellor. He will be, I believe, one of the Winter Court's greatest Swords. But in making him Sword, I stole away some of his youth. And that of others, like Arthur, who came with him. Rafe should have had more time to be young and, frankly, silly." He took her by the shoulders. "I don't want to make that mistake with you—and you're even younger." He laughed. "When I was your age, I'm not sure I could have gotten all the buttons on my fancy clothes fixed right by myself. You have a coming of age there, right? Your mother talked about not quite an adult, not quite a child?"

Deor nodded. "Yes. Eighteen-year-olds are legal adults, but many go to college, which isn't quite adulthood, perhaps. They may stay living at home, that sort of thing. They can't drink alcohol legally until they're twenty-one."

"And when you were eighteen?" he asked.

Deor chuckled. "I was a happy mess. I'm amazed I didn't give my grandmother a heart attack."

"Well, at your age here, that's what you should be—whether it gives me a heart attack or no. And your brother had his fair share of incidents."

"Brother?" Deor asked. "Oh," she said realizing. "Rafe. Right. I'll bet he did."

Finn stood and helped her to her feet. "Come sit on the couch with me." He pulled a handkerchief from his pocket and handed it to her. His own tears had long since stopped, but their trails remained.

She sat with him. *He is handsome,* Deor thought. She could see why her mother had liked him so. Deor herself had been overly fond of mysterious, and Finn had mystery. There was a gentleness to him, too, that she hadn't seen before. No wonder a woman like Astarte, or like her own mother, would be drawn to him. He made her feel safe, too.

"So, are you sure you want to quit Eisteddfod? You could, perhaps, take a break?"

"No." Deor shook her head. "No. As long as I'm there, I'm a danger to the people around me. Plus, how would we keep me safe? The school doesn't want soldiers, and I don't want to be an exception. Plus, the thought of Arthur following me around makes me ill."

He laughed. "Arthur is very good at his job."

Deor did not ask what, exactly, Arthur's job was. "Still, no soldiers."

"I agree with that," Finn said. "But there are other options. Geoff had a bodyguard. Donovan's wife, the Lady Chloe, has performed such a task. I could see if she were willing?"

"No." Though the thought of someone who could dish on Geoff's former vampire was intriguing. "Geoff did that, and it made him look like more of an ass than he already was. No matter what I do, as long as people know who I am—and I'm certainly not going to try to disguise myself—I'm a distraction, and a danger."

Finn patted her leg. "I know that is a hard choice for you."

Deor blinked back tears. "I wanted to be a professor for years—I spent twelve years in school. That's almost half my life!"

"I know," he said. "You have every reason to grieve for this loss. Take some comfort knowing you will never stop being a professor. Your accomplishments will not go away." He frowned, gaze focused on a spot between them. "Being a part of the monarchy means making choices for others, not ourselves. They may be the right choices, but we are not required to like them."

"I know you're right," she said.

"But it doesn't make it better." He sighed.

"Right." She drew a deep breath and blew it out. "Now that we've decided, I need to let Ama know. I have to tell her myself."

"I think it is best that you do," Finn said, "though we can have the secretary notify her."

"No." Deor shook her head. "Can I do it now?"

"Here?" Finn pointed at the mirror. "Mirror: Eisteddfod, Ama Nefasta."

After a few long moments of darkness, Ama appeared.

"What can I do for you, Your Majesty?" She did not bother to hide the weariness or annoyance in her voice. Deor wondered how many times the woman blew off the king's calls. "Oh, professor...princess—"

"Either works," Deor cut her off. "Or you could just call me Deor." She smiled.

Ama's look suggested that she would use Deor's first name when hell froze over.

"I'm calling to resign," Deor said, getting straight to the point.

The woman jolted. "Resign?" Her eyebrows shot up.

"Effective immediately," Deor added. A sigh of relief escaped her chest. "I can't stay. I'm too much of a distraction. What happened today," Deor choked back the tears, "it was my fault for believing I could stop being a princess when I crossed into Eisteddfod. I was arrogant and stupid. I don't want to put people in danger—that's not what the students are there for."

Ama regarded her for a long time, her gaze flicking from Deor to Finn and back. "And this is your own choice?"

"Yes." Deor nodded emphatically. "Finn offered to find a way for me to stay. He even suggested a bodyguard, like Geoff, but I still think it is bad for the school."

"Unfortunately, I think you're correct," Ama said. "I am quite sure we will have a lot of trouble finding as…unique a professor to replace you." She smiled. "Take care, Professor Smithfield."

"Take care, Professor Nefasta."

The mirror went black.

"Very good," Finn said. He stood. "Now, if it isn't too soon, I would like to think about what you will do here."

"Well," Deor stood, too, "I've got a lot of free time on my hands."

"We will be announcing your existence formally at Parliament. There's nothing else to do. I had planned on waiting until the opening of Parliament next February—that would give you some time to settle in. But I can't wait that long. Parliament closes soon for the Solstice holiday."

"Do I need to go to Parliament?"

"Good heavens no!" Finn shook his head. "I go as rarely as possible. We will have Rafe announce it as the Sword. The monarchy has a very hands-off relationship to Parliament. While we do have a seat, we do not go often, and, frankly, they prefer it that way. Appearing there can feel like bullying. Even if it isn't. So, no. We will watch from here."

"Got it. So, I lay low for a bit?" That would be a relief. She hadn't had a moment's peace in months. The idea of sleeping for a month straight seemed like a good one. She could read the papers and learn all about society that way, while not risking making the papers—again—with some sort of faux pas.

"You need to get some suitable clothes," he said, glaring at her outfit. It had been perfectly suitable for teaching, especially since she wore robes over it. "Do you have a favorite designer? I know some women do."

Deor considered for a moment. Nope, she couldn't name more than one: Wham! and Thorsen, the pair who designed her Adoption outfit. "I liked the folks I worked with for the Adoption," she said.

"Excellent. The secretary can have them come here, if you wish to discuss things with them. Or, like Rafe and I do, you could simply tell them what you want, and they will make it and deliver it."

"Option 'B' I think." Deor said.

He nodded. Now, aside from clothing... Perhaps..." Finn turned his attention from her and walked to one of the many bookshelves lining the walls. He scanned for a moment. "Aha!" He snatched a book from the shelf. "I think you should start to step out into society. You need friends, and you won't make them by hiding in the Palace." He paused. "Unless you want me to have Solstice parties here? We could bring people to you."

"No." Deor shook her head. She wasn't sure how to be a guest at a faerie party, let alone host one. At least at someone else's party, she could claim fatigue and leave—it looked much worse to suddenly disappear from your own shindig. "I'll go out."

"Perfect," he said. "I want you to go somewhere that is fundamentally sympathetic to the monarchy. You don't need to be around hostile people."

"Amen to that!" The time for winning over skeptics would come. Deor liked a challenge, but not a firing squad. Especially when the ramifications could last centuries, rather than a few days in the twenty-four-hour news cycle.

"Here," he said. He handed her a beautiful, leather-bound book about the dimensions of phonebook. "This should help you with some of the finer points of faerie culture."

The tooled-leather cover showed a smiling faerie woman, her wings spread out behind her, holding the hands of two cutely chubby children, who gazed up at her adoringly. *The Nobble Babees Nobble Booke.*

"Oh," she said, opening to the cover page where the title was repeated, followed by the subtitle—*A Prymer in All Manere of Curtesie for the Instruction of the Lewed and Innocent Chyldren of the Nobble Classes.* "Is this a children's book?"

"Yes." Finn had the grace to look embarrassed. "It is usually given to children who are about to start behaving in public. Somewhere around age twenty, give or take." He pointed at it in her hands. "You hold in your hand the copy that my mother gave me. And I gave one to Rafe, too." He waved his hand, encouraging her to flip the pages. "Look at the Table of Contents."

She flipped to it and scanned down the page, turned it, and scanned down the next. Everything from how to sit still at a table, what cutlery to use, appropriate titles and manners of address, to hosting duties, and formal letter writing filled the pages. Literally any social situation possible seemed to be covered. She held in her hands the definitive *Miss Manners* for the Winter Court.

"I see," she said and looked up. "This will be very helpful. Thank you."

Finn sighed, relieved. "I'm sure you know how to behave—you certainly drew the undivided attention of the crowd at the Adoption," he grinned at her, "but this might help you with the finer, most subtle points that differ from the human world."

She laughed. "Indeed, it might help. And," she said with a grin, "it gives me something to do all day. Surely within a few weeks, I will be the epitome of a well-mannered faerie."

A person barked out a laugh behind her. Deor started and turned to see Arthur and Rafe standing in the doorway. Arthur smirked.

Rafe cleared his throat and bowed. "I am sorry to interrupt, Your Majesties."

Deor snapped the book shut and fought the urge to hide it behind her back like she was a naughty child.

Finn waved the apology off. "What do you need?" He frowned. "Is there some news?"

"Nothing of major importance." He came farther into the room and handed the king a folded-up newspaper. "That is the first public document we can find releasing the identity of the princess."

Deor moved to read over her father's shoulder. The headline was clear: *Goblin Mistress is Winter Court Heir.* The sub-headline as well:

Professor Deor Smithfield of Eisteddfod, the woman who stopped the Adoption, is the bastard daughter of King Fionnleigh. The byline was familiar as well.

"I know that woman." She pointed at her name. "She was one of the reporters Geoff gave information as an anonymous source."

"So, it was Geoffrey who leaked the news to the papers?" Finn asked.

"It seems likely," Rafe confirmed.

"Perhaps," Arthur said, stepping forward. "But it could have been Victor Farringdon. He was on Eisteddfod's campus when the news broke there. He might have been the one to spread the information on campus."

"He came to warn me that people knew and it might come out," Deor snapped. "Why would he warn me if he were responsible?"

"To gain your confidence. Perhaps he mistimed—or the people in the know didn't keep it quiet as long as they should have. He was chatting with a couple of students when we arrived at your office."

Deor rolled her eyes. "He admitted his parents are traitors, and he came to warn me about this. When we were attacked, he fought as well as the rest of us, and got hurt for his trouble."

Arthur shrugged. "I have no doubt that Victor was not working with the goblins—everything my intelligence says suggests they have long since fallen out. He had every reason to want to keep you out of goblin hands even if—perhaps especially if—he wants you for himself. Politics is complicated, Your Majesty." He glanced at the book in her hand. "Especially for one still learning the ropes."

Anger flared in her chest, and for a moment, the world shaded silver—her eyes were changing. She blinked hard, clearing her vision. He'd found one of her buttons and delighted in pushing it.

"Regardless," Rafe said, glaring at Arthur, "it seems clear that this came from the goblins. Geoffrey fled the country immediately after the Adoption, as did a majority of his entourage. There are some people in the Goblin Embassy, but we'd have to attack it to get them out—and even then, we might not."

"So we let it go for now," the king finished for him. "That seems best. It doesn't matter who spread the information. What matters is what we do now. Rafe, you've got your speech for Parliament?"

"Yes, sir. All set."

"Good. As for the princess—"

"Keeping her safe at Eisteddfod has gotten a lot more complex," Arthur interrupted. "I think we should consider—"

"I've quit," Deor said.

Arthur froze, mouth still open mid-word. He snapped his jaw shut. "Oh?"

"Yes. It is too dangerous for the students for me to be there. You don't need to worry about that anymore. I'll be safe and cozy here."

"Excellent," he nodded.

The king stepped up behind his daughter and put his hand loosely around her waist. She didn't rebuff him. "I am proud for her decision. If she wanted to go back to Eisteddfod, we would have made that work." He stared down Arthur. "But she worries for her people, as a monarch should. It was a hard choice for her. I support her, and you should as well."

Before Arthur could speak again, the king went on.

"Rafe, I want you to find something for Deor to do to enter society. Some party or event. It needs to be safe, friendly, and small enough for her to handle. Perhaps one of the parties to open the Solstice season? Somewhere she could accompany you, if possible?"

Rafe nodded. "I have a few ideas."

The king smiled and squeezed Deor. "It's time for my daughter to take her place as heir."

Deor glanced down at the book in her hands. It was. Whether she liked it or not. She stroked the cover. At least she knew how to study.

Chapter Eleven

Deor followed Finn through the portal from the Household to the first floor. Though the Palace could have guided her perfectly to the king's office, as it had with the Amber Room, she enjoyed the grand tour.

"When I was a young king," Finn said as he led her to the main foyer, the doors through which everyone had entered for the Adoption, "the Palace was open. There were dozens of people—friends, courtiers, ambassadors, foreign dignitaries—coming and going. Everything was lit up. It was beautiful."

He led her to the Throne Room. Undecorated and unoccupied, the room seemed much smaller. The black and white checkerboard marble of the floor was the same, as was the stone throne, roughly hewn out of a single slab of rock, like it had emerged from the ground in some tectonic upheaval. A flash of magic surged between her and the throne, tugging her toward it. She stayed in place, but though the magic couldn't physically move her, it irritated her, like an uncomfortably starched collar.

"Don't worry about the pull," Finn said.

She spun to face him, worried she would see silver eyes and nails. There were none. "You feel it too?"

"Eventually you won't notice it as much. When the throne is calm, I have to search to feel it, but of late, things have been quite exciting. It's still very uneasy." He placed a hand on her back and guided her out of the room.

Finn led her through the dining hall, fit to hold hundreds, and the grand ballroom where the sweeping double staircase to the second floor was yards from the far end of the room where grand glass doors led to the balcony. Curtains covered all but the center doors, and the chandeliers, including a gigantic centerpiece, were dark, leaving the room dim and melancholy. In her mind's eye, though, Deor could imagine Finn, younger, happier, sweeping in on the balcony with his new bride, Astarte's sheer wings glittering in the light.

"I think that is enough for today," Finn said, heading back the way he came. "We'll head to the other side now, where the more banal work gets done." He offered her his arm, and she took it.

If not for the map in her head, Deor certainly would have lost her way in the warren of hallways winding through the hub of the Winter Court Palace. "This way." Finn led her to a foyer off which five doors stemmed. A sword and a shield marked two of the doors, and a crown another. The five-pointed Winter Court star glittered from the fourth door. The final door—the simplest—had nothing.

"The offices of the Sword and Shield, and my office, as is likely quite obvious." He turned to the fourth door. "Come with me." The handle was dust covered and the star, up close, was clearly in need of dusting. "It's been far too many years since this was opened." He folded his hands and gazed at her.

"What?" Deor asked. "Me? Oh, okay." She laid her hand on the handle and felt the magical lock slide free. The handle turned easily at her touch, and the door, silent as though it had been oiled that day, swung inward.

"After you," Finn said with a bow.

Crossing the threshold bathed Deor in magic, like stepping through a waterfall. There was no resistance, but the magic told her as soon as she set foot in the room that this was her space. Indeed, more her space than the heir's suite—with its goblin-flattering decorations still in place. "My office," Deor said.

"Exactly." Finn's voice was quiet, nearly a reverent whisper, behind her.

"Lights on," Deor said, and the room was illuminated. As she scanned the room, lit by large fixtures on the ceiling, the coat of dust covering the furniture and shelves disappeared. A heavy desk sat opposite the door, in front of a window, curtains drawn. A small sofa, two chairs, and a coffee table huddled around a fireplace. Shelving, almost empty, lined the walls except where filing cabinets, built in like the shelves, took up space. A circular table with five chairs, sat to one side.

"Obviously not today," Finn said, "but over time you can decorate this how you like. We can change any or all of the furniture. In fact, that desk is a placeholder. I took my desk from this room when I moved next door." He gestured toward his room, and Deor noticed that one of the bookshelves had hinges. A passage connecting the monarch and heir.

"It's lovely." She could hardly wait to fill the shelves with books. There was so much to learn. She'd have to raid the library—the Palace nudged her toward the third floor.

"I'm glad you like it," he said. "Now, unfortunately, we must go. The fifth door out there is the conference room. There is a mirror there from which I usually watch Parliament. I can arrange it so that I can be seen and heard, but mostly I watch. If I want to pronounce things, I do it from the throne." He grinned.

As she followed him to the conference room, she wondered if his pleasure at his own displays of power might be some of the reason the people were so upset. He seemed perhaps more a stick leader than a carrot one. Inwardly, she shook her head at herself. She was filling in the gaps with her own imagination, tainted by years of hurt and anger. Some of her wrath he deserved, but it was unfair to assume that he was a poor ruler, arrogant and condescending, based on what little she'd seen of him. After all, he had been dying when she arrived—what person facing death, coupled with leaving a whole nation in turmoil, wouldn't turn a little snappish?

They settled in at the table, with Finn at the head and Deor on his right.

"Mirror, Parliament, private." As Finn spoke, the glass went dark, then cleared revealing a room of people milling about. A gallery was above the main floor, though Deor could barely see it. The whole scene reminded her of watching *C-Span*.

"Let's see what the nobility has to say about my little girl." He smiled at her and patted her hand, though she wasn't as reassured as he clearly wanted her to be.

Before she could ask how he thought it should go, a banging gavel brought the members to their places and quieted them.

Chapter Twelve

The Speaker of the House of Lords banged her gavel for silence as Rafe took the seat on the king's dais reserved for the Sword of Peace and Justice. The Sword's squire, Gordie, took his place just to the left of the seat and slid Rafe's slate into place on the attached table leaf. The slate displayed the order of planned speakers. His own speech would come first.

Interesting—Rufus, the son of the Werewolf Alpha from Ireland, had been given a chance to speak as well. Not an unheard of event, but uncommon—and hopefully nothing to do with the attack on his paramour. By tradition, the Alpha's representative addressed concerns directly to the Palace. His seat was considered more of a courtesy to the non-faerie enclave in Ireland than an invitation for them to meddle in Winter Court politics.

"Remember not to lock your knees," Rafe murmured to Gordie, even as his eyes scanned the gathered crowd. This was going to be a long, long day for all of them. Finn and Deor were watching from the Palace by mirror—at least they could pace or make comments to each other. The rest of them would be sitting on their best behavior in the stiflingly packed hall.

Even Roger, Lord of Northfalls, was actually in his chair for once. Rodney, his nephew and heir, had been speaking for his uncle for forty years. Now Rodney stood beside the chair holding the Admiralty Staff for his uncle. Both wore the family tartan. Delaney Overton and his brother George also both stood behind their father, Delaney Overton Senior, who wore his heavy chain of office as Master of the City of Caer Eisteddfod. Every family's heraldry and badges of office were on prominent display today.

Genevieve's were particularly well done. Along with the snow-scattered green of her dress, her family colors, she wore a crown of ivy, holly berries, and wheat, reminding everyone who saw her that as Harvest Queen she had done far more than merely symbolize the kingdom's prosperity. With her plant magic, she had worked tirelessly to keep the harvests full. If crops in the last few years had failed, it had not been her fault. Their eyes met, and she glared at him—no doubt unhappy that she found out about Deor like the rest of nation—in the papers.

Even the Farringdon seat was occupied. His mother and father were prominently absent, but his brother Victor sat in their mother's chair, signaling that he was present not merely as a witness, but was authorized to speak for the family. That ought to be interesting. If their positions had been reversed, Rafe would have planned to keep his big mouth shut. Everything a suspect said could and would be used against him, especially if Arthur were listening, which he was. Victor didn't operate that way though. There was no doubt he'd make some sort of speech.

Not only were all the nobles' seats filled, but the galleries above were packed elbow to elbow with commoners, gentry, and the lesser nobility. Only those holding a title of Earl or above were granted a seat, and thus a voice and a vote, in the Parliament. A contingent of Bards, Ama among them, sat in the honorary seats granted them on the House floor. Though technically the university stood apart from every nation's politics, even kings had the sense not to meddle with the Bards or prevent them from observing. Every one of them had their arms crossed.

The Speaker banged her gavel again. "Silence. I will have silence from the galleries or I will have them cleared of all spectators." A few lords and ladies clapped their approval of the threat.

"We have a right to be here! The people have a right to know!" a young man's voice shouted from the very top balcony. Aiden—Deor's hot headed, but brave, student.

Without a word, the Speaker signaled to the guards, and Aiden was grabbed and dragged out, still shouting. Another person took his place immediately. Poor kid. Rafe shook his head. He could object, but the Speaker had every right, and this early in the proceedings, there was no point getting sidetracked.

"Gordie, go out there and make sure they aren't rough with him," Rafe said under his breath. "You won't need to say anything. Just make sure the guards see that you're wearing my badge."

"Yes, sir."

Gordie disappeared through the curtain-shrouded door behind the platform.

"Rafael, Lord Farringdon, Sword of Peace and Justice," the Speaker said, "as the king's representative and heir presumptive," she gave a slight cough, "you have privilege of speaking first." The entire room rustled with whispers, from floor to galleries.

Rafe stood and bowed to the Speaker, then to the rest of the nobles. As he rose from his bow, he made sure to turn his eyes toward the galleries, including the commoners in his courtesy. Many of them leaned out over the railings, straining to hear. He flexed his sword hand at his side, recalling the speech he had written and rewritten a dozen times.

"My duty to you all," he said. "Today I speak on behalf of His Majesty." A pause—make sure he had their attention. He raised his eyes and his voice. "But I do not speak as the heir. Nor will I ever again speak in that role."

Chatter broke out in the chamber—mostly some form of "the papers were right?"

"As some of you heard at the Adoption, King Sweordmund does indeed have a child of his body, one naturally conceived and not created through magical means. It is my honor and duty to relinquish all claims to the throne and kingdom in her favor."

He held his tongue as voices shouted from every side and the Speaker banged her gavel furiously. At last the room was gaveled to silence, and he picked up his speech. "The king's daughter is the offspring of a liaison between the king and a human child bearer." He'd spent a good hour deciding how exactly to phrase that particular sentence. "She was raised under her mother's name among her human family and has only recently returned to the Winter Court."

"So Sweordmund lied to our faces?" Delaney Overton, Senior said, loudly enough for the question to echo. "And left us to find out from the goblins? In the newspapers?"

"No. The king was cruelly deceived. Michael Monteblanc, Shield to the king, conspired against the kingdom. He convinced the king that his daughter had died in infancy, along with her mother."

A lord from the Southern Coasts leaped to his feet. "But who is she? Where is she? If she exists, why is she not here in person?"

Because her first experience in Parliament shouldn't be facing a mob, Rafe thought to himself, *and she should be marking papers and preparing lessons.* How it would stick in all of their throats if he were to imply that the princess counted her time better spent talking about books with a bunch of students than addressing the peers of the realm. That part of her life was gone now, though. Lost to being the heir.

Instead, he said what Finn had told him to say because, in this case, it was also true. "The young lady who so bravely intervened at the Adoption is none other than the heir herself. Her name is Deor Smithfield, and for the time being, she is safely in the Palace. Given her recent ordeal— including an attack on her life on the Eisteddfod campus—the king prefers not to subject her to the questioning of the Parliament."

Let them all think the king and his long lost little girl were closeted at the Palace, enjoying a tearful family reunion. He risked a glance at Genevieve. She was flushed with rage, her bosom heaving. Oh dear. Perhaps he should have told her a bit more, especially after the papers.

All around the room, people were standing to demand proof that Deor, or "that changeling the Goblin Prince was shagging," could possibly be the heir.

Rafe cleared his throat for silence. "If you all recall, I was present when the Adoption was interrupted. After the ceremony was ended, the throne tested Deor. We have the witness of the Consort, the king, and a Bard that she is indeed the rightful heir." He nodded to Ama Nefasta who stood.

"It is exactly as the Shield says. I was present and acted as witness. The throne acknowledges Professor Deor Smithfield as the king's heir."

"And no one in the kingdom is more delighted at her arrival than I am," Rafe added. "I have never wanted the crown. I agreed to the Adoption solely out of duty to the king and to the Winter Court. My ambition is, and ever was, to bring safety to this kingdom and honor to the Farringdon name." He paused, looking over his audience until his eyes met those of his brother. How much good they could do together if only Victor could be free of their mother's treason. It would take decades, maybe even centuries, for him to escape that association—especially in the king's mind. Victor's cool look said nothing in return. Rafe took a deep breath. "Princess Deor has my complete support. I have no doubt of the good she will do the Winter Court."

Applause answered him—loud and enthusiastic from some quarters, hesitant in others. A few openly refused to applaud at all.

Delaney Overton Senior rose to speak next, deploring the king's secrecy and carelessness in the way Deor came into existence, but expressing sympathy for the lonely grief the king endured thinking his daughter dead. "I have seen my eldest ride off to battle and feared I would never see him again," Lord Overton said. "It is no wonder the king's grief sapped the powers of the entire kingdom. Now is not the time for recriminations! We ought to be rejoicing for him and for ourselves. Long live King Sweordmund! Long live the heir!"

Before he could sit down, five other members of Parliament had risen and were shouting questions at Rafe. How long had he known? Why hadn't she been identified before? Had the Palace leaked the story? Were the Bards in on the conspiracy? Why wasn't the kingdom informed sooner? Why weren't the Farringdons in jail? What was Victor Farringdon doing here with that smug look on his face?

"Waiting his turn to speak, unlike some of you," Rafe said.

That got a chuckle from some nobles and an outright laugh from the galleries. Victor smiled a half smile and nodded his head once. Rafe went on, "If there are grounds for a warrant to be issued against any member of my family, or indeed anyone else connected to this matter, I assure you I will sign it personally." Victor's half smile didn't waver.

The original questioner sat down muttering about blood being thicker than water, but another noble popped up before the Speaker could point to him and shouted, "Then why isn't the Goblin Prince chained to a wall somewhere? Half his staff left the country unscathed and the Goblin Embassy is still occupied."

Even angrier cheers met that question.

"That is a complex matter of foreign policy, and indeed many goblins have fled the country, including His Majesty Prince Geoffrey," Rafe said. "Right now, the goblins are not the king's priority."

"But the king's not bloody well here, is he?" a woman in the gallery called out. "He's sent his pretty little boy to pat us on the arse and tell us it's all being handled, hasn't he, but how do we even know she's a faerie? She looks more like a pixie on stilts if you ask me!"

Rafe turned on his heel toward the woman, rage flushing his face. "I am not the king's boy!" He took a deep breath, forced himself to unclench his fists. "I uphold the cause of peace and justice in this realm, even if it means saying no to the king. That is my office and my promise to you."

Even louder shouts broke out. Boos and hisses. Cries of "down with the king!" were met with "traitors!" Everyone shouted at once.

The Speaker banged her gavel so that the roof rang with the sound. "Order! I will have order! Officers, clear the galleries."

"No, please. Milady Speaker, allow them to stay." Victor had risen to speak, edging out Genevieve by half a second. The Speaker signaled that he had the floor first and Genevieve could follow.

His eyes fixed on Victor, Rafe lowered himself into his seat.

Victor raised his hands, turning both to the galleries and to the floor of Parliament before speaking. He let the silence settle around him before he opened his mouth. "Ladies and gentlemen, my esteemed peers. Loyal common folk. We are not here today to speak treason, but to seek redress. The king has wronged us, it is true." A few booed at that, but more cheered. "From the moment he ascended the throne, King Sweordmund's rule has been erratic, without foresight or thought for the common good. Look at the heedless way he chose a wife. Could there have been a more foolish choice in all of Fae? And then to endow her with Office of Consort, ceding power to a member of the Summer Court Royal family—how blind, how self-centered an act. Such behaviors belong in the pages of adolescent romance, not the annals of great kings."

Rafe gripped the arms of his chair. *Leave Astarte out of this, whelp.*

Victor went on, "And see how obdurate the king has been, how resistant to counsel. He chose himself a Sword who would never say him no." Laughter from the gallery.

Rafe's ear tips burned. Victor had a point, about Finn and himself. It would be different now—he would be saying no a hell of a lot more often, if Finn didn't start listening to him and confiding in him as well. Creator only knew what other secrets the king had kept from him in the ten years since he had taken office. He made a mental note to speak to

Bartholomew, the former Sword who now lived in virtual seclusion in the remote north-east of the Winter Court. Perhaps Deor had been part of the reason Bartholomew had retired from the Office of Sword. Officially the reason had been that he was old, having served two successive kings, the second longest serving Sword in the history of the Winter Court. But then again, Rafe remembered being a young knight standing his watch in the Household and overhearing the late-night argument between king and Sword, when Bartholomew had stormed out shouting, "You're a damned fool, Finn, and I won't be a part of it. I'm too old for this basilisk shit." If the first rule of the Household Guard was "hold your post," the second was "keep your ears open and your mouth shut." He hadn't even blinked as Bartholomew stormed past him.

Victor went on, enumerating Finn's manifest failings—the failing crops, the declining fertility that forced family after family to seek child bearers, the king's disastrous trust in the goblins, which they had repaid with humiliation and attempted murder. Rafe's face burned. He should have stood up to Finn about Geoff long ago.

Victor laid a hand on his chest, a smile on his face. "I hardly expect the king to listen to me personally. After all, he barely listens to my elder brother, and he has earned far more honors than I have." Laughter from nobles and commoners at that.

"But I myself have spoken with the princess, while she was still in her position at Eisteddfod. Unfortunately, because of the press and the attack on her life it caused, she has resigned her position." Another piece of information over which the king had lost control. "She is very unlike her father," Victor said.

Gordie had rejoined Rafe. He leaned in and whispered, "The young man was sent off on his own, unharmed."

"Thank you. Gordie. You've arrived just in time to see quite the show."

Victor scanned the room and continued. "She is thoughtful and reasonable. She is both well-educated and eager to learn about the Winter Court. She manifests concern for her people at every turn." Victor risked a sly smile. "She was raised in a democracy and brings many of those ideas with her."

Sometimes I really hate you, little brother. The rabble are going to latch onto this idea like a wildcat on a unicorn's leg.

When the murmuring from all sectors finally quelled, Victor inclined his head. "As I said, I do not expect the king to listen to me, or even, as a wise ruler would do, listen to you, his peers. Perhaps, though, he will listen to his heir. And I know, without a doubt, she will listen to us. She is our opportunity to have a voice, one that the monarchy, bound by honor and law, will heed."

Cheers and boos echoed through the chamber. Aiden's remaining friends shouted in unison "House of Commons! House of Commons!" with the commoners around them mostly cheering and shouting their support. Even members of the House of Lords came to their feet, applauding wildly.

But there were just as many who scowled from their seats, arms crossed or who stood, shouting "Traitor!" at Victor. For his own part, Victor nodded briefly to those who cheered him and took his seat with a smile as if he were deaf to the opposition.

The Speaker banged her gavel. "Lady Genevieve Lascaris?"

Out of the corner of his eye, Rafe saw Genevieve leaning back in her seat, signaling to the Speaker that she ceded her chance to speak next. No use would come of following that speech. He caught Genevieve's eye, and for a split second, the look she gave him made him quite grateful she wasn't a fire faerie. He had warned her! Not enough, apparently. Genevieve turned away to whisper something to another member. Meanwhile the Speaker banged her gavel vigorously on the podium and shouted for order until the din died down.

Four others slated to speak quietly passed notes to the Speaker's chair, and she nodded. Their names disappeared off the roster on Rafe's slate. Other people were hastily scratching out whole paragraphs of planned speeches. One simply tore his speech in half and slumped in his chair, glaring at Rafe.

Rufus, on the other hand, showed no interest in giving up his plan to speak. He stood in his place, arms crossed over his chest, glaring at the House Speaker until she was forced to notice him. He was weaponless, but he wore a wide-sleeved linen tunic and saffron short trews, leaving him bare-legged below the knee and barefoot as well. Rafe leaned his face on one hand and pinched the bridge of his nose, recognizing the clothing of a traditional Irish kern, or *ceithern*. At his feet sat a basket sealed with magic.

"Is he going to make a declaration of war, sir?" Gordie whispered.

"I hope not. Though I could imagine him thinking it is an appropriate response to recent events. No matter what he says, he'll certainly make the papers in that getup. He's like all the rest of them—too fond of dramatic gestures." Even as he said it, Rafe eyed the basket at Rufus's feet. Some gut instinct told him its contents were going to cause a commotion that put all Victor's fiery words in the shade.

"Enough of this gasping and fluttering," Rufus said, his Irish accent lengthening out the vowels. "The whole lot of you were present at the last Adoption. Were none of you awake? Did you not see the girl's silver nails and bloody wings? The Goblin Prince has played you all for fools and conspired against your own monarch, yet now you sit and squabble like schoolchildren over matters of precedent. When is the muster of armies to be? The goblins have sold out the Winter Court, and they hoped my people would do the same. But the wolves of Ireland have already taken steps against the foe, while the lords of the Winter Court sat on their fat bottoms."

With a sweeping gesture, Rufus kicked the basket, breaking the magic and spilling the contents at the Speaker's feet. Two goblin heads rolled across the polished oak floor to bump wetly against the podium. One of them Rafe recognized as a minor goblin noble. A battlefield smell, of blood and fear and festering meat, wafted from the heads. Three days old, experience told him. No more than that.

Around the room, faeries were gawking or turning away. Some held handkerchiefs over their noses while others leaned as far forward as they could for a better view of the gory mess. Victor had one hand over his mouth as if covering his disgust, the first sign of real shock Rafe had seen on Victor in half a century.

"Rufus," Rafe said, his own voice sound strangled. "What the hell have you done?"

"Not I, but my father," Rufus said proudly. "While you and the Winter King dithered, these two maggots approached the Alpha with offers of a secret bargain. They promised our people gold and more if we would wink at certain comings and goings on our mutual borders. A mere matter of smuggling, they claimed, but my father saw them for the spies that they were."

Rafe clenched his fist at his side, wishing he had a sword hanging there. "It is not the place of the Alpha to execute criminals without trial."

"Neither is it a crime to destroy spies and informers in a time of war," Rufus shot back. "Or would you have had us pat them on the bottom and send them home again, as you did with the Goblin Prince? Should we expose our loved ones to the same disregard the king shows for his heirs?"

Rafe had always rather enjoyed the young Irishman's blistering tongue and roughshod ways, but at that moment, he wanted nothing more than to punch Rufus square in the jaw. Rufus spat in the nearest goblin's eye and gave a short nod at a job well done.

The galleries erupted with shouts, boos, cheers, and chants of "House of Commons! House of Commons!"

The Speaker pounded her gavel, shouting for the galleries to be cleared of commoners, but the commoners resisted. Their massed bodies formed a wall against the guards who clustered in the galleries, trying to shove onlookers toward the doors. Fist fights broke out. A banner reading "Give the People a Voice" was unfurled and hung over a balcony.

"Let them stay!"

Rafe turned to see Victor standing on a chair toward the front of the gallery, his voice magically enhanced to project over the hubbub. But Victor was no air faerie. Rafe scanned the crowd. There—just behind Victor—a redheaded woman with an arrow in her elaborate hair lent him her abilities.

Others—a small, but loud cluster of minor nobles and lesser sons and daughters—took up Victor's chant.

"Let them stay! Let them stay! Let them stay!"

Victor raised his hands high over his head, waving them back and forth. "The people have a right to be here. History is being made. Let them witness it and have their say. Let them stay!"

"Get down, you young idiot," Rafe muttered under his breath, forgetting that Victor was barely six years younger than him.

"Guards, remove that man!" The Speaker pointed her gavel at Victor, and a wholly new sensation of pure brotherly anger filled Rafe's chest as Victor disappeared into a scrum of guards and nearby Parliamentarians where fists and wings swung in place of sharp words.

"Let him stay! Let them all stay!" Rafe shouted. Battlefield trained, he didn't need an air faerie to make his voice echo off the back of the room. He strode forward across the open floor and pulled aside the guards swarming Victor. "Take your hands off him. This is a lord of the realm you're handling, and he has a right to speak."

Several of the guards fell back, confused, their glances darting from Rafe to the Speaker. Rafe gripped Victor by the front of his jacket and hauled him to his feet. A shiny red spot over Victor's left eye promised to be quite the bruise later, but from the bloody nose of the man with whom Victor had been grappling, Victor had given as good as he'd gotten.

"Everyone, shut up, or I'll have you arrested!"

A shocked silence took momentary hold of the room. Even the Speaker blinked and held still for split second. It was all Rafe needed.

"Is this a Parliament or a riot?" he said. "Because last time I checked, only the Civil Guard had the authority to quell riots. You guards—you're authorized to escort people out, not haul them out by their hair. Settle down, or I'll charge you with assault. That goes for you, too." He glared at the nearest lords who had been "helping" the guards subdue Victor and his friends.

Victor cleared his throat. "Thank you...brother," he said. "You can let go of me now. Ahem."

Rafe let go without much gentleness. "Try not to incite anything you can't control, *brother*," he said in a low voice.

Turning to Rufus, he said, "Pick up that damned mess this minute and take them to the king the way you should have in the first place."

Perhaps Finn hearing him say that would help, though he doubted it would help much. Already the mirror in his pocket was buzzing. He didn't need to answer it to know Finn would be shouting his name, especially after seeing him defend Victor.

Finally, Rafe bowed toward the Speaker's podium. "Madam Speaker, I believe my younger brother had the floor last."

The woman puffed up like an outraged grouse at hunting season. "How dare you? Who do you think is in charge here?" She sputtered for another half minute before bringing her gavel crashing down. "This Parliament is adjourned!"

Without bothering to find Genevieve, Rafe grabbed Gordie by the shoulder and steered him toward the nearest portal.

In the conference room, Finn flung his personal mirror on the table where it skidded across and dropped to the other side. His eyes and nails were silver—usual for anger—but his hands had sprouted small spikes, too.

"This is, I take it, not usual for Parliament?" Deor asked.

Finn turned his silver gaze on her, and she shrank back a little in her chair.

"It is not." He pointed at the now blank mirror. "You see what your conversation with Victor has done? He has, before you have even been presented to the realm, planted the idea that we are at odds. That you will contradict me. It bordered on treasonous."

Deor shook his head. "I don't have any plans to try to unseat you." The whole thing seemed ridiculous. "He's right about where and how I was raised, though. We can't deny it."

"No," Finn said, drumming his nails on the table. "We can't."

"At least Rufus's scene—were those really people's heads in the basket? —distracted people. That might be the more talked about story."

Finn shoved himself back from the table and stood. "Come on," he said. "Rafe will meet us in the Household parlor. There's no need to meet in the Tower where others will hear our council."

"You don't trust your soldiers?" Deor rose and followed her father, having to hop every few steps to keep up.

"After Michael," Finn's voice was low and dark, "I'm not sure I trust anyone."

Chapter Thirteen

When Rafe and Gordie stepped through the portal to the Palace office, Arthur was waiting.

"Was it as bad as it looked?" Arthur asked, a wry smile on his face. "You and your brother seemed to have a nice family moment."

Rafe glared at him. "Not now." He waved at Gordie to follow them—he might have noticed things Rafe had not. "And it was worse than it looked —those heads were real and around three days old. That, and Victor's speech? The king will go through the roof."

"My mirror's been pinging non-stop," Arthur agreed. "He's in his parlor."

Rafe nodded. "Don't say anything at all unless the king asks you something point blank. No commentary on the people or the princess or my brother—don't say anything that will get him more riled up. Understand?"

Arthur flicked a salute. "Absolutely, sir."

Rafe let the mocking go—he'd deal with Arthur's newfound attitude later. Right now, he had to calm the king.

Deor gripped the arms of her chair in Finn's parlor and tried not to flinch as the king raged up and down in front of her. His nails and eyes were living silver, flashing like knives as he paced and swore. Beneath Deor's feet, the Palace quivered.

Finn shouted at the mirror, "Rafe! Where the devil are you?"

The parlor door dissolved, showing a brief glimpse of an unfamiliar hallway as Rafe and Arthur, followed by a very nervous Gordie, stepped through the portal.

"Here, sir," Rafe said.

"What took you so long? Never mind. Did you see what that fool has done?"

"Seen and smelt it, sir. I was feet away."

Deor patted the floor with her foot, thinking at the Palace, *It'll be okay. He'll calm down soon.* She hoped she was right. Gordie was doing his best to press his back into the doorpost without actually cowering, his eyes wide as he followed the king's movements.

"That was the Goblin Ambassador's chief aide in that basket, wasn't it?" Finn said.

"Yes, sir. I didn't recognize the second one."

Finn swore. A knife appeared in his hand, and he hurled it across the room. It buried itself up to the hilt in the wall. With a gesture, Finn pulled the magic back to himself, and the knife vanished. The hole in the stone did not.

"Alright, that's enough," Deor said as she rose from her chair without thinking about it. Finn spun around to face her, mouth hanging open. Arthur rolled his eyes.

Finn drew himself up to his full height. "I will not be spoken to like that by you, missy."

"Somebody has to speak to you." Deor fumbled for words to explain it. This was his home, his parlor. He certainly had every right to yell. Plus, he wasn't—well, he hadn't been—directing any hostility at her. The walls around them pulsed, vibrations spilling out around the newly-carved hole in the stone, and resonating through her body into her spine. Finally, she blurted out the only thing that made any sense. "You're scaring the Palace."

For a second, Finn looked contrite. He put a hand out, his fingertips brushing the mantelpiece, and took a deep breath. "I think you fail to understand the gravity of the situation, daughter."

"I doubt it. Killing an ambassador is pretty much an act of war where I come from. I assume it's the same here or you wouldn't be so angry. But the Goblins didn't declare war when you kicked Geoff out. They went sneaking around looking for a back door via Ireland, or at least that's how it sounded to me. They're likely not going to declare an all-out war on us now, right?" She looked to Rafe for confirmation.

Hands clasped behind his back, his feet spread as if on parade rest, Rafe nodded. "The Goblins have a substantial army, but not nearly large enough for a full-scale war against us."

"Besides," Deor went on, "aren't the concerns of the Winter Court Parliament and the people more pressing than a couple dead spies? Shouldn't we worry more about that? Are you going to take their desire for a House of Commons seriously?"

"I will when the Summer Court freezes over," the King snapped. "And now is not the time for you to argue with me about this."

Deor opened her mouth to protest, but snapped it shut. Perhaps referencing Victor's speech right now wasn't the best idea.

Finn turned his back to her, addressing Rafe. "The Goblins will demand restitution, with every right to do so. The Alpha will be lucky if I don't send them his head and the heads of all his sons packed in ice. Have Rufus detained immediately."

Rafe sighed. "On what charge, sire? Accessory to murder or treason? Because in either case, his father will argue the ancient right of the Irish Alpha to execute justice in his own territory up to and including capital punishment. And they'll claim diplomatic immunity as well. Those goblins were killed in Ireland."

"Isn't Ireland a part of the Winter Court?" Deor asked before she could stop herself. Even as she said it, she wished she hadn't. Still, murder was nothing to wink at, even if she had patted the murderer on the head and called him a good doggie once.

"Tricky question," Rafe said. "There are many were-folk in the Winter Court that are full citizens, either by immigration or marriage, but the Irish werewolves are technically citizens of Ireland, which is a protectorate of the Winter Court, which gives them the same rights to a trial and protection as our citizens. Being the Alpha's son makes it even more difficult since Rufus is hardly a private citizen. If I charge him with accessory to murder, it makes it seem he was acting *in propria persona*, in which case he'll argue that he was acting merely as an agent of a foreign state, and..."

"Charge him with being public nuisance for all I care," Finn snapped at Rafe, ignoring Deor. "But throw him into the Tower. He'll be lucky if I don't hang his body from Tower Bridge for the crows to eat."

"Are the Irish going to rebel if you do that?" Deor asked.

"They might," Rafe said.

"Not if they know what's good for them!" Finn said.

Deor thought about the aggressively protective nudist she'd first met at the flat she shared with Penny at Eisteddfod, about the way her werewolf students always wore something green around their person, and seemed more than eager to debate any point at all, either among themselves or with other students. She doubted their idea of what was good for them matched with Finn's.

"Why not take the Alpha's side?" Deor mused out loud as if she were sitting in a graduate seminar, debating the rhetorical possibilities of a situation instead of trying to manage an international disaster and the possible death of her ex-roommate's lover.

"Because he's wrong!" Finn snapped.

"She has an interesting point," Rafe said. "I can't defend his methods, but it might be better to chastise the Alpha in private and publicly praise him as a defender of the realm. After all, the goblins were engaged in espionage."

"Don't you think I know that? But we need the Goblin alliance far more than we need that upstart in the north thinking he can make international policy for himself and get thrown a biscuit for it afterward." Finn drummed his fingers on the mantel, silver nails striking sparks of magic off the stone surface.

They watched him in silence as he glowered and thought.

"That's the real crux of this, isn't it?" Deor said, her voice quiet. "You're afraid he's challenging your authority as king."

Finn's shoulders relaxed, and he smiled at her, like she was a pet that had performed a good trick. "Yes, exactly, daughter. I can manage the Goblins. Geoffrey will accept some form of wergild, and we'll pass it all off as a tragic misunderstanding over trade. But Angus has usurped my role, and I cannot tolerate that."

"With all respect, sir, I doubt Angus sees it in the same light," Rafe said. "Quite the opposite. I'd bet good money that Rufus and his father both believe their actions were a defense of the realm."

Finn didn't seem to hear him. He paced back and forth in front of the fire as Deor and Rafe exchanged glances. Gordie still stood by the doorpost, eyes wide, and Arthur had faded so far into the background, he nearly blended in.

"Finn..." Deor said, but the king held up a hand for silence and continued to pace. The seconds ticked by.

When he finally stopped, pacing his eyes had returned to their calmer grey and his fingers were no longer bladed. But beneath Deor's feet, the Palace still quivered with faint distress.

Finn spoke, his voice firm and clear but not raised, and the stones of the Palace echoed with his authority. "I, Sweordmund the VIII, hereby banish from my realm all were-folk, wolf and otherwise, citizen or not. They have forty-eight hours to leave my borders or be treated as foreign spies."

"Finn, you can't do this!" Deor shouted, her voice echoing against Rafe's angry, "This is outrageous!"

Slashing his hands through the air, Finn said, "It is done! Carry it out at once." Without another word, he strode from the room.

Rafe and Deor stared at each other in horror. "He can't..." Deor said, even as she knew he could and he had. "This is insane. Rafe, you have to go reason with him." To her fury, she could feel hot tears brimming in her eyes.

"Gordie," Rafe said. "There are two weres who serve in the page program, yes?"

"Yes, sir."

"Go see the Master of the Pages and then help the girls pack. Tell them to report directly to my office, and I'll see that they are portaled home safely." After Gordie left the room, Rafe turned to Deor. "I'm sorry. I know you must think I'm a coward, but once the king has spoken like that, there is no calling it back. The best we can do is make sure his orders are carried out in as humane a way as possible."

The sorrowful stone under her feet confirmed what he was saying.

She nodded, grimacing hard to keep the tears from spilling over. She sat down heavily in a chair, thinking about Bob and Bernie, her students, Penny. The werefox whose picture sat on Ama Nefasta's desk. Where would they all go? Who would care for their property while they were away? "This isn't right," she whispered.

"You don't get to make that decision," Arthur said, as he stood behind her.

"I know that," she snapped. "I wish there was something I could do to help."

"Behave," Arthur said.

Deor did not respond.

Rafe came over and put a hand on her shoulder. "I'm sorry, but Arthur and I must leave you. We have to make sure that our soldiers are safe."

Deor patted his hand. "Thank you."

Rafe dropped into his chair behind his desk in his Tower office. "This is such a mess," he said to no one in particular, though Arthur stood nearby.

"No question," Arthur said. He waved a hand over Rafe's desk, and a map of the city appeared. "While most of the protests are in the Marketplace, on the university campus, or at the Palace gates, the protesters don't live in one particular area." He waved his hand, and the map zoomed in closer to a very middle class, non-noble neighborhood not far from the river. Nice enough, people who owned shops or who maybe had a small farm in the country, but definitely nothing special. "There's a pub in this neighborhood where a lot of meetings take place."

Rafe looked at the map. The pub was called the Burning Heretic. He'd never been in it, though he had heard some local soldiers mention it as a place neighbors and friends gathered. The name was an obscure reference to the human world—apparently the pub lined up on maps of London with a spot known for burning people. Charming.

"What of it, Arthur?" He knew, but was too tired to play games about it.

"I thought some of my lads and I might nip over there for a drink. Maybe invite some folks back for a chat. I do know that when he's not on campus, that firebrand student of Deor's spends time there. He might have some interesting things to say, considering he was right near the princess when the news about her identity broke."

"He's a student in her class," Rafe said.

"Class had been over for hours," Arthur said. "Especially for him—he's in the first class, in the morning."

"He's a kid, Arthur," Rafe insisted.

"He's in his thirties."

"A kid," Rafe repeated. "And so what if he's involved in protests? There's nothing illegal about it."

"He's quite the supporter of the House of Commons, much like Victor. And Victor did see him home from Penny's after the attack."

"Fine," Rafe said. "Keep an eye on him. But no, do not go to the bar. Do not follow him. Do not do anything unless he reveals himself to be something other than a student radical."

"Yes sir," Arthur said and saluted. He headed for the door. "You know," he said conversationally, "being Robbie's friend doesn't make the kid a good guy." He didn't wait for a reply.

Rafe waved the map of the city and leaned his elbows on the desk, head in his hands. He rubbed his temples, fighting the niggling headache growing there. He hadn't been up to see Robbie since Astarte had taken her there. In the flurry after the Adoption, he hadn't looked into the case at all either. Not that there was much to do—the man who attacked her was dead—he would never explain the magic he used.

He couldn't fix Robbie. He couldn't fix the banishment of the werefolk. His relationship with Genevieve was on thin ice, and he didn't know how to fix that either. Arthur's desire to "invite folks for questioning" irritated Rafe in ways it never had before, which led him to Deor. She was disruptive, no doubt, and that was another thing he couldn't fix.

He wanted to punch something. Or someone.

Time to take another trip to the Mound.

Chapter Fourteen

A few days after Deor's identity was out, and Parliament had failed to be as receptive as Finn had hoped, Finn insisted that Deor make her social debut. He suggested that her appearing casually in public would settle the distress—everyone would see that things were under control at the Palace, and specific friends of the Palace would have access to the princess.

It had taken negotiations more delicate than those required to settle some wars, but between the four of them—Finn, Rafe, Arthur, and Deor—they had finally agreed that the princess would accept an invitation to the Overton brothers' Saturday card party. The yearly Overton card party was elite rather than massive. And as Rafe pointed out, if Delaney Overton were anymore upright, he could be used for a ship's mast. It was also the first major party of the Solstice season.

As Rafe entered the Overton's grand salon with Deor on his arm, he automatically pulled his elbow in against his side so that Deor wouldn't slip away from him before he could scan the room.

"Why are you squishing my hand? I'm not going anywhere," she said in a low voice, her lips barely moving. She was almost as good at it as Genevieve.

"Just being security conscious," he whispered back, nodding and smiling at people around the room. Curtsies and bows rippled through the room, but very few smiles. Genevieve's little circle of friends smiled at him, but in a way that reminded him of circling sharks. She had not been pleased when he informed her that instead of escorting her to the party, he would be playing chaperone to the new princess.

Deor smiled at the room, but the tips of her fingernails pricked through the fabric of his jacket. "What a delightful, cozy gathering this is. Everyone here looks like they want to eat me or watch me take a pratfall."

He would have said something reassuring, but they'd already spent too much time in the carriage reviewing the names, faces, and varying degrees of hostility to be expected from every guest in the room for reassurances to mean much.

Across the room, Delaney was pushing through his guests toward them, his younger brother George in tow. The two brothers both made low, elegant bows. At his side, Deor managed to bob and incline her head, but she rose from the gesture too quickly for good manners, dragging Rafe up with her. Good thing she was the highest ranked person in the room.

"Your Majesty, you are gracious to attend our little party," Delaney said.

"You're very gracious to have invited me," Deor said. "I hope I didn't upset your table arrangements. It was so inconsiderate of me to have arrived when all the winter season's party planning had been done months ago."

George gaped at her, not sure how to respond, but Delaney chuckled. "May I introduce you to a few people, ma'am?"

So, she had at least looked over part of the *Nobble Book* since this morning.

"I'd be delighted," Deor said, slipping her hand out of Rafe's elbow. For a split second, he had the urge to grab her hand in his, but he squelched the impulse. She didn't need him holding her like a toddler in the grip of its nursemaid. Still, his eyes followed her as she walked off between the two brothers. George was already inquiring as to whether she played cards, and she was nodding. Finn had warned her sternly not to gamble in public until he had time to teach her a few basic card games.

Deor had argued. She'd told him that she'd been playing cards with

SARAH JOY ADAMS & EMILY LAVIN LEVERETT

her grandmother since she was old enough to count. Rafe's stomach rolled over at the thought. During the ride over, he'd failed splendidly at convincing Deor that playing for buttons with one's granny was not the same thing as gaming in a faerie salon.

Still, she had made no move toward the card tables in the next room. Rafe breathed a sigh of relief just before George said, "Dashed bit of nonsense about a House of Commons, what? Terribly distracting from the real issues at hand."

Delaney frowned at his brother, but it was too late. Debate broke out immediately among those closest, with arguments ranging from those in favor of jailing all the protesters to those who argued just as passionately that a House of Commons was long overdue.

"But dash it! The Lords speak for their people," George pleaded.

"Do they?" Deor said, her voice neutral. She took a glass from a waiter's tray as it passed and sipped the fizzing liquid, her eyes following as the argument bounced from person to person, but her face carefully blank.

"What do you think, Your Majesty? It's your opinion that really matters, is it not?" a middle-aged woman said.

A tense hush fell over the crowd around Deor, spreading through the room as people leaned forward to hear. Deor sipped her drink.

A trickle of sweat ran down Rafe's back.

"I think," she said with a smile, "that I will play cards after all. What are we playing, George?" She set her glass on a tray and took George Overton's arm.

Rafe followed her into the card room. For a moment, he debated sitting down with her, but that would be too obvious a gesture and would automatically raise the table stakes. People knew he played to win. Besides, George was introducing Deor to two other players not too much older than her and neither of them known card sharps. The four of them were sitting down to Ombre, a game that bored him silly. Deor was nodding patiently as George explained the concept of trumps.

"This sounds a lot like Spades," Deor said, gathering her cards into her hand. "I played that with my grandmother. This should be fun." She tossed a modest number of tokens into the center of the table.

Rafe breathed a sigh of relief and sipped his drink. She wasn't betting too high too soon. Without losing sight of Deor, he shifted his position nearer the fire on the far wall so that he had a better view of the entire room. If only Finn hadn't forbidden him from taking Arthur along.

Deor was making her table laugh. Perhaps he ought to leave her here and go find Genevieve. But he'd promised Finn he wouldn't lose sight of her. As he watched, she played a low card and lost the trick with a look of cheerful innocence. The last time he'd seen her look that way, she had goaded Donovan into a public tantrum. Bother Genevieve. She'd have to wait.

"Enjoying the party, darling?" Genevieve appeared at his elbow. Her cluster of friends had moved closer, spreading out, but leaving a discreet distance between them. Delaney was elsewhere, presumably tending to his non-gambling guests while George played cards with the princess.

"Yes. Lovely party."

"I realize that you're on guard duty at the moment, but I do think you could have at least introduced me to the woman you came in with."

"What are you talking about? You know perfectly well who she is."

"Yes, I do. Now. I was delighted to read about it in the papers like everyone else. It made for so many interesting conversations with other people, especially the ones who called to assure me they didn't believe a word of it."

"I'm sorry if that made things awkward for you."

Genevieve gave a ladylike sniff. "Awkward doesn't begin to describe it, Rafe. I assume she is the reason you rushed off so quickly the other night as well?"

"Yes, I'm afraid so."

"Well…"

"Well what?"

"Do I merit an introduction to the new heir by my fiancé, or shall I simply wait to read about it in the social papers tomorrow morning?"

Rafe grimaced. "If you wanted an introduction, why didn't you just say so?"

"Because I am not some court hanger-on currying favor with the Sword. I'm your fiancée, Rafe. I shouldn't have to ask for your attention when we're standing in the very same room. Especially when you were supposed to be my companion for the evening in the first place."

Rafe laid a hand on her arm. "Please don't make a scene."

Her icy smile didn't waver, nor did her voice go up a single notch. "I am not making a scene. I am simply having a little chat with the man who seems to keep forgetting that we're engaged to be married."

"Are you telling me that you're jealous?"

"Of a thirty year old? Don't be ridiculous. If anything, I pity her for the mess she's been thrust into. It's you I'm annoyed with, Rafe, not that poor creature."

Rafe glanced across at the table where Deor was laughing and pulling a rather large pile of counters toward herself. Even her losing companions were laughing at the joke she had just made. Poor creature indeed.

"Brute. Genevieve deserves so much better," someone stage whispered nearby.

Rafe didn't bother to turn his head as he snapped, "Shut up, Phipps. This doesn't concern you."

Phipps's answering gasp was as dramatic as it was feigned, but Genevieve was unfazed. "I will not have you speaking to my friends that way. Apologize at once."

"If Phipps wants an apology, he can come ask for it himself." Rafe's sword hand flexed at his side as he spoke. To his left, Phipps squeaked and took a step back. Delaney Overton was hurrying toward the two of them, not even bothering to apologize to the guests he shoved aside.

Genevieve's knuckles were white around the glass she clutched. She drew herself up to her full height, seizing back control of the conversation. "I am tired of making excuses for you everywhere I go. You left me behind on your little vacation. You abandoned me at a moment's notice at the club. You deliberately misled me into thinking the king had an infant child, and then you left me behind in Parliament to answer questions about which I had no information. You made me look like a fool."

"You deceived yourself! I never said she was a baby."

"You never said she was an adult! Or a changeling! Or the Goblin Prince's floozy!"

"Do not speak of the heir that way."

"I will speak however I please, Rafael Farringdon. You lost the chance to tell me what to say on your behalf when you abandoned me on the floor of Parliament."

"How in hell was I supposed to know Rufus would drag a pair of lopped-off goblin heads onto the floor of Parliament?"

"You could have said *something* to me before you left!"

"I had more important things to do."

Genevieve recoiled as if slapped, and the crowd gasped. Her lower lip trembled ever so slightly. "I am never on your mind, am I? Not unless it suits your convenience."

An acid chill ran down his insides. She was right. She was his own betrothed, and he thought of her more as an asset to be used or an inconvenience to be managed. She deserved better.

"You're right," he said, his voice so low that everyone else in the room leaned forward to hear. "We should…we should talk about this later."

Delaney stepped out of the crowd, nodding. He put his hand out toward Genevieve, as if to move her away, but she jerked her elbow out of Delaney's grip.

"Genevieve…" Delaney pleaded.

"No!" She stamped her foot. Actually stamped it. Delaney pulled back, his eyes flashing from Genevieve to Rafe and back. Genevieve was far from done. "Half our engagement has been me making excuses for you. Explaining why you didn't come to the theatre after all. Explaining why you suddenly had to leave a dinner. Explaining why you'd taken a vacation away from me! Do know how that made me look—to be left behind by you—my own paramour—because he 'needed some rest'?"

Rafe blinked. He hadn't. It hadn't even crossed his mind—all he had wanted was to fall into his bed and be lulled to sleep by the rocking of the ocean, as far away from the throne as possible.

"I'm sorry."

Delaney bent toward Genevieve and murmured something, but she ignored him. "Sorry isn't enough."

"You're right. You deserve better." He lowered his voice, stepping closer to her. "But must we talk about it here and now?"

"If not now, then when, Rafe? You never answer your mirror. You only answer letters when it suits you. We're never alone anymore, and even when we are, you can be summoned back to the Palace at a moment's notice. You're married to your post, and I'm merely an afterthought."

"Don't say that…"

She drew a deep breath. "Very well. I will be at home tomorrow morning. You can visit me there and we can talk in private."

The back of his neck burned with the sense that dozens of eyes were on him. "I'll make it up to you."

She looked up into his eyes, her own eyes uncharacteristically wet with tears. "Will you? We shall see." She turned toward Delaney, all smiles. "Do forgive me, Delaney. I don't feel well, so I think I should be going. Please apologize to George for me."

Delaney took her hand and kissed it, bowing as he did so. "You mustn't stay if it distresses you, though I'm sorry to see you go. Let me escort you to the door." He offered her his arm and walked away with her, his head bent over hers. Rafe caught the faint hint of a laugh from Genevieve just before she passed through the parlor door.

There he was, alone at the party in an open circle of partygoers all staring in his direction. For once, he didn't know which direction to turn, so he stood there, more awkward with every passing second as he turned the gold, vine-shaped engagement ring around and around on his finger.

Already other guests, particularly friends of Genevieve, were beginning to cast reproachful glances at him. He gazed at the door through which she had gone.

Dammit I am not a bit player in some melodrama, no matter how skillfully Genevieve performs her part.

Through the other guests' whispers, Deor's voice rang out. "Rafe! Rafe, come and help me, would you? I've lost my partner to his hosting duties, but I'm determined not to let Quincy here beat me, even if he does seem to hold every trump card. Come and play with us."

She waved her hand of cards at him like it was fan. A few people laughed along with her, and young Quincy blushed delightedly to be considered a player worthy of the Sword.

He breathed out in gratitude and bowed low. "Just as you wish, Your Majesty."

"Now which card is Manillo again?" Deor asked as Rafe took his seat opposite her. "It's already down, isn't it? Yes, yes it is. Right, I think that makes it my turn. Isn't this fun?"

All around the room, people returned to their games and their conversations. Servants moved to circulate once more with trays full of bite-sized snacks.

Later, in the carriage home, Rafe slumped against the seat.

"I'm a cad," he said.

Deor cocked her head to one side. "No, I wouldn't say that. A bit of an asshole, but not a cad. You didn't cheat on her. But the two of you do need to have a serious talk."

"Oh, we will." Flowers and jewelry weren't going to solve this one. He watched Deor jingle her golden winnings from hand to hand and wondered if he even wanted to solve it.

Chapter Fifteen

Rafe saw Deor as far as the door to her suite and said goodnight. He considered heading down to the kennels or perhaps out to the wall for a late-night run—anything to blow away the lingering anticipation of dealing with Genevieve's anger whenever later came around.

Then he had a better idea. Without bothering to call for his valet, he stripped out of his party clothes and into plainer garb. A few portal hops across the city and he was, once again, less than a block from the Mound. He pushed open the heavy wooden door and stepped into the darkened room. The streets were only slightly brighter, so his eyes adjusted quickly. Though people rarely turned to see if someone walked in, even fewer eyes than normal glanced his way. The bar was mostly empty—soldiers stationed in London were on leave for Solstice and many would have headed home today at the latest. Those who lived here were also unlikely to spend the first of their holiday in their work bar.

He saw a few familiar faces, but no one he knew well. Lieutenant Bolton was a regular here and was on the duty roster for all of Solstice but nowhere in sight. He must still be working.

Rafe slid into the far corner of an empty booth in the corner. Peace, quiet, and calm—he needed that. He shuddered at the thought of spending Solstice in the Alps, hosted by Phipps, all of Genevieve's friends watching to see how he treated her. There was no way he could beg off the trip now, not with her already feeling—justifiably—that he had been ignoring her for weeks.

Before the princess showed up, it had been easy to say what he wanted from life. He wanted to please the king. If that meant being the heir, so be it. Marrying Genevieve had seemed like such an obvious choice. Who in the kingdom would make a better Consort for the future king?

He shuddered at the naiveté. He barely recognized the man he had been proud to be just a few months ago. He could barely stand to be in the same room with Finn for any length of time. Every time His Majesty gave an order, Rafe stiffened, wincing under the strain. No. The king may have raised him from the age of five, but he had no desire to be the king's man —and certainly not his boy.

Being the Sword though. He'd dreamed about that since he was a child. One of his earliest memories was peering over a table edge at a three-dimensional map of the world as the king and old Bartholomew, the former Sword, talked politics and troop movements. The two had even let him play with the intricately-carved troop markers as he imagined himself a great general at the head of a vast army, defending the kingdom from all comers. Leading death or glory charges against the enemy. Had it all just been a childish fantasy?

His grip tightened around his glass.

"Mind if I join you?" His brother slid into the booth across from him.

"Yes, I do mind. What do you want?"

Victor didn't leave. "Happy Solstice to you too, brother."

Rafe shot him a glare. "Shouldn't you be home by now, fawning on Madeline?"

"I won't be returning to Wellhall for the holiday." Victor's jaw tightened. Looking straight ahead, he said, "Did it ever occur to you that I didn't ask to be born the replacement child? It's not exactly a warm and comfortable role being constantly reminded that you're loved primarily for your ability to not be someone else."

Rafe grunted. No, he never had considered Victor's life to be anything other than that of a pampered lapdog.

"At least you were loved. Try growing up with the knowledge that you're a hostage and your foster father could have you killed at any moment if your parents, who want you dead, overstep themselves."

Victor offered his own grunt. "So that's what we've come to? The two Farringdon boys, whining at each other in a bar at Solstice. Aren't we precious?"

"Indeed." Turning to face his brother, Rafe said, "What do you want, Victor?"

"How about a fair fight for once?"

"When the hell have I ever been unfair to you?"

"When have you treated me like anything other than dirt? I was a born traitor in your eyes. When I turned thirty and came to Caer Eisteddfod on my own for the first time, you acted like I didn't exist. Never answered a mirror call or a letter. You and your glittering circle of friends were the toast of the town, and I was a pariah. Do you know how many doors were closed to me because you wanted them to be?"

"I never set out to harm you. You, on the other hand, couldn't seem to leave me alone." Rafe pointed to the scar on his cheek. "Remember this? You're lucky I wasn't fair to you or I could have had you arrested for cheating in a duel."

Victor blushed purple. "Madeline gave me that knife. I didn't know it was poisoned."

"I find that hard to believe."

"It's the truth."

"Prove it."

"How?"

Rafe stood, pushing the table away from him and toward Victor. "You want a fair fight out of me? Well, here's your chance." He gestured toward the back of the room. "No weapons this time. Just us and whatever magic we can summon. And no repercussions if you win. On my honor as the Sword."

Victor regarded him for a long moment. "Alright then, Sword of Peace and Justice. I take you at your word."

Without another word between them, they left the bar and walked, shoulder to shoulder, to the Back. For once, the room was empty, no audience, neither gamblers nor seconds to see a fight that half the town would have given their eyeteeth to witness.

In silence, they stripped off their coats and shirts. Rafe slid his heavy ring of office off and tucked it into a coat pocket as Victor tied back his hair, stripping out the garnets that dotted his long, dark locks. Still silent, they entered the ring from opposite sides, circling each other.

Victor's fingertips twitched faintly. Before Victor could throw whatever magic he was gathering, Rafe punched him in the eye. Rattled, Victor stumbled backward, shaking his head. Rafe followed him, stepping in for a closer blow.

The floor under his feet slicked with ice, and he slid, knee twisting as he fought to regain his balance. Victor's left foot caught him just above the knee as he fell, but Rafe locked his hand around Victor's ankle, and they both went down hard. Knees and elbows, fists and teeth. This was no gentlemanly boxing match.

Rafe bashed his forehead into Victor's nose and was rewarded with a gush of blood. Arms locked around each other, they rolled, one on top of the other, across the ring, each scrambling to keep the other down.

Victor hissed a word, and stinging particles of ice like sand flew into Rafe's eyes. Blinded for an instant, Rafe lost his view of his brother, but not his grip. Victor chopped him in the throat with the edge of his hand. Rafe let go, gagging.

Victor half rose to his feet, but Rafe kicked at Victor's knee. As Victor fell, Rafe locked a hand onto his brother's wrist, driving magic into the flesh. Blistering frostbite spread out from his hand.

But Victor pushed back, his free hand flat against Rafe's chest. Pain bubbled up inside Rafe, flowing along every major vein and artery. He grabbed Victor's arm with both hands and wrenched. Victor's shoulder separated with a sickening pop. Victor shrieked.

But the bubbling pain went on, spreading to every joint. Rafe fell forward to his hands and knees, gasping for breath. Victor fell backward on his ass, cradling his arm and groaning.

"Truce." Impossible to tell which of them said it first.

"Make it stop," Rafe said.

"I have to touch you."

A beat as Rafe weighed the pain against the risk.

"I promise. I'm not tricking you," Victor said. He held out his hand.

Rafe took it. The pain receded, the bubbling pressure like iron needles in his blood fading. It left behind a whole-body ache and exhaustion he hadn't felt since the Adoption.

They half sat, half lay on the ring floor, panting.

"What was that trick?" Rafe said at last.

"Humans call it the bends. It happens when they dive too deep and come up again too fast."

Slowly, painfully, Rafe hauled himself to his feet and held out his hand. "Let's find a healer for that arm of yours."

Victor winced and nodded.

An hour or so and a trip to a discrete healer formerly attached to Victor's regiment, and the two brothers found themselves back in the Mound enjoying the near emptiness of the place.

Victor took a long drink of his beer. "When we were younger, I was so jealous of you."

"And now?"

He smiled. "Less so. At the time, all I saw were the perks."

"Perks?" Rafe said, arching an eyebrow.

"The rings of lovely women around you and your friends? That was a young soldier's dream." Victor raised a hand before Rafe could object. "I get the bad now—the scrutiny. Ever since I got to London a couple months ago, I've gotten a lot of attention. Very little of it good."

"The Farringdon name," Rafe said. "Blessing? Curse? I sometimes wish I had a stately, boring name. Like Overton."

Victor laughed. "And be that boring? You? No." He glanced around the nearly empty bar. "Where's your spymaster?"

"Don't call him that," Rafe snapped. He winced. "Sorry."

"It's true," he said. "Everyone knows it."

"Arthur, my secretary, is at the Palace, working late so that everything will be done when he eventually goes home for Solstice with his family."

"No doubt," Victor said and smiled. "I was surprised to see you come in here tonight," he changed the subject.

"Were you following me?" Rafe looked around the bar again, but he recognized most of the people in there, at least by sight, even if he didn't know them well. No thug-looking folks.

"No." Victor shook his head. "I saw you walking and was interested since you didn't seem to be heading to the Palace. I know you've got a place in town, but it looks pretty shut up to me. And before you worry about that, it is only two streets over from my own."

Rafe nodded. "I remember that you bought a home in the city."

"You remember?" Victor smirked. "Surely your 'secretary' must have told me I was there and living in town."

Rafe stared at him for a moment and relented. What Victor said was true—that Arthur was far more than a secretary was an open secret among much of the military nobility. He was too good at being invisible to not be more. "Actually," he smiled at his brother, "the princess let me know that you had moved here."

"Ah," he nodded. "She told you about that?"

"Arthur mentioned it to me and to the king."

Victor wrinkled his nose. "You'd think Arthur might be more discrete. How much did the old man beat her?"

"Victor," Rafe warned, but the shock sounded feigned even to his own ears. He'd been on the wrong end of Finn's temper more than once—and far too long into his adulthood—to pretend that the king wouldn't strike his heir.

"You know it is possible," Victor prompted.

"He hasn't laid a hand on her, except the occasional hug."

Victor snorted. "Wiser man than I thought. He tries that, he might lose the hand."

"She is not a traitor!" Rafe snapped.

Victor jolted back like he had been slapped. "No..." He stumbled. "I didn't mean that." He took another drink. "I meant that she doesn't seem particularly tolerant of people in her space."

Rafe rocked his head back and stared at the ceiling. "No. She's not." He looked back at his brother. A small flare of irritation blossomed every time he really looked at his brother. He was so much like their mother— sharper angles and long lashes. Elements that made him both more handsome and less intimidating than Rafe. He had to have known about Geoff, about the attack on the changelings, and on her. Might as well poke the bear. "Geoff found that out the hard way, as did *some woman* in an alley."

"So I have heard. I would have liked to have seen the prince after it happened." He sat stone still, meeting Rafe's gaze. "I knew she was attacked—you could see the marks on her at the Adoption."

"Yes," Rafe nodded. He had been so distracted that day that he hadn't paid too much attention, but she had stood out, even then. Her size—so short compared to most of the other women, and unabashedly displaying the marks from the will spell attack. She was daring someone to say something. "I wish I could see what happened to the one who made it out of the alley."

"A goblin died there, correct?" Victor cupped his mug in both hands, and frost ferns spread up the glass from beneath his fingers.

"Yes," Rafe said. His anger rose and the temperature around him dropped. "The same one who damn near killed Robbie."

Victor shuddered, upset. "That poor girl."

Rafe grabbed the edge of the table and almost slammed it forward, pinning Victor to the wall, but he paused. Regret seemed palpable on his brother. He sat still—his gaze locked on the swirling liquid in his stein, as if focusing there would block out other things.

"Why did you follow me in here?" Rafe asked, trying to keep his voice steady. He let go of the table and took another drink. "Did you have something specific?"

Victor waited a long moment, not raising his eyes from the mug in front of him. Finally, his voice a rasp, he said, "Yes." His gaze darted back up to meet Rafe's. "You know as well as anyone who was responsible for that attack on the changelings, on the princess."

"You mean Geoff?" Rafe sneered.

"Yes." Victor held his gaze. "And others." He laid his hands flat on the table—a gesture of goodwill—flat hands mean no gathered magic, especially for a water faerie touching wood. "You'll never get evidence, nor a confession."

"A witness could come forward."

Victor barked out a laugh. "No. No witnesses will come forward. You won't pin this on mother, no matter how much you want to. And you need to stop trying."

Rafe glowered at him.

"I mean it, Rafe." Victor did not wait for a response. "You have to let the attack on Robbie go—you have more pressing things to worry about."

"Victor, so help me if you know anything about anything, I will see you beheaded. Hell, I'll do it myself."

"I don't," Victor snapped. "But I don't need to, do I? You think after centuries of this vendetta against the king, mother is just going to stop because there's a princess now? Somehow she's going to think that everything will be okay, and she can settle back and live in quiet, loyal obscurity in Wellhall? I don't have to have heard anything to know something is coming. And—"

"And what?" Rafe sat back and crossed his arms. "Or should I ask Arthur to help you find your voice?"

"Don't threaten me, brother." Victor's voice was flat—the same toneless sound their father would make when he had lost all patience.

Rafe settled back against the booth. "You're right. Why are you telling me this?"

"I don't know," Victor said. "I wasn't planning on speaking to you at all, but…"

"It's her, isn't it?" Rafe gave a small laugh. "I shouldn't be surprised. When did you first fall for her? At the Adoption? Or before?"

Victor shrugged and dropped his gaze. "I didn't *fall for her*. But the moment she told the whole world to stop at that ceremony, I sat up and paid attention. How anyone didn't know she was the legitimate heir is beyond me. The whole Palace resonated. I think if they had tried to continue the Adoption, the stones themselves would have shattered beneath the king's throne."

"I should have figured it out before then," Rafe said.

"No," Victor shook his head. "You couldn't have—you were too close."

"You can say that again." Rafe took another long pull of his beer. "She's the one who made those marks on me, you know. She didn't mean to," he added hurriedly, "but even in her dreams, if she feels threatened…"

Victor chuckled. "Creator help the next man who sleeps with her. Geoff's probably only alive because her magic hadn't fully come out yet."

"Yes," Rafe said. "If she'd known how to use it when he attacked her, he might have survived, but he'd have been in ribbons more than he already was."

Victor leaned forward. "Want to hear some Goblin gossip?"

"I have people—"

"Not who will have told you this." Victor grinned like the cat that ate the canary. "He's still got the marks. The ones her wings made down either side of his face? Those. They've healed, but he's still got fine lines."

"How do you know? How did you know about Geoff's injury?"

"Goblin connections," Victor said. "There is a lot of trade and smuggling around Wellhall, you know that. The Summer Court and Goblin Court both push those boundaries. I've got friends."

Rafe finished his beer. "Deor will likely be delighted to hear it. She wanted Finn to call him out—she understands why he couldn't, but—"

Victor finished his own beer. "Listen—whatever you and I were, however we felt about each other, and still feel, I have thrown in, one hundred percent with her. When I talked to her in her office, there was a raw honesty there. She's naïve in some ways, sure, but she cares for the Winter Court. And she charged right into the goblins attacking Penelope and Rufus. Too little care for herself, but impressive." Victor stood. "Be careful."

"Because of her?"

"For her. The king's enemies, most of them, are hers now too. They are coming for her."

"Any more sage advice?" Rafe stood, too, happy to look down slightly at Victor.

"About that? No. If I knew anything, I would tell you. My best guess is that whatever they decide to do, it will be public and permanent."

"I'll keep that in mind." There was no sarcasm in his voice. He wanted to reject what his brother said, ignore him as stirring up trouble, but he saw the look in Victor's eyes.

"Together, you and I could protect her," Victor said.

They would certainly be more powerful that way, Rafe knew. "If you ever know anything, come to me directly. It might be a good idea to keep our newfound civility to ourselves."

"True," Victor said. "But the most dangerous place for her, you know, is the Palace." Before Rafe could object, he plowed on. "The king chose for an heir someone he believed he could utterly control. What do you think he is going to make of her?"

"The king—"

Victor held up a hand. "Don't finish that sentence." He dropped a few bills on the table. "For the perfect lack of service," he said. The bartender was studiously cleaning the counter on the far side of the bar, his back to them. The few other patrons didn't seem to notice at all. "You know the king better than just about anyone else," Victor said. "Think about what kind of man he is, about how he is going to respond to an heir like her."

He turned for the door, grabbing his cloak and twirling it around his shoulders as he stepped out into the cold.

Victor had been wrong. Rafe didn't have to think about what kind of man Finn was at all. He already knew. She was permanently in the Palace —her own choice—so she had done what he wanted. That would never last. The princess was going to need all the help she could get.

Chapter Sixteen

In the days following the Overton's party, Deor was happy to snuggle in front of a crackling fire, warming her winter chill, but she was in danger of getting bored. She wore flannel pants, a tank top, and a sweatshirt over that. Her feet were still bare, though. Finn had been right about that—she couldn't stand to have shoes on in the Palace if she didn't need them, no matter how cold it was. She flopped back on her bed. Though the bed had a canopy, it was pulled back, as were all the curtains. She stared at the ceiling with its pattern of snowflakes gently spinning as though they were falling.

In the corner, something glimmered—in fact, the same glimmer of magic was in all the corners of the room. It hadn't been there the first nights, or if it had, she hadn't noticed. Last night she knew there was something there but didn't think much of it. Tonight, though, she got out of bed and stood underneath the clump of magic. The glimmer coalesced into a clear spell—multi-colored threads of magic twisting and turning into a complicated cat's cradle.

The vaulted ceilings meant that there was no way she could reach the spell standing on a chair. But there was her vanity, though it wasn't directly under any of the spells. She leaned against the table, bent her knees, and pushed. For a few seconds, the thing refused to budge, then lurched forward, and she almost slipped off. She drove it along the wall and into the corner.

She hopped up on it and stretched her hands toward the spell. If she had a stick, she might reach it, but knocking it down like a wasp's nest might break it—she wanted to get her hands on it in tact, touch it and feel the magic.

She crouched and eased off the table. The vanity's chair wasn't particularly stable. The designer had beauty on the list before utility and didn't put "ability to be stacked and climbed" on the list at all. She hoisted the chair onto the table—the surface was barely wide enough to accommodate it—and slid its back against the wall.

Again, Deor climbed onto the table. She put one foot in the center of the chair, one hand on the back, and eased herself up. The tower teetered a bit, and she froze. She reached for the spell. It was still too far—but only by an inch or two. She turned around and scanned the room. Her textbook! God knows the tome of all of Shakespeare's works should be good for something other than breaking the backs of those who had to carry it. She set the cinder-block-sized text on the ground to test it. Her toes and the back of her heel hung off the edges, but it felt sturdy.

She centered the book on the chair and made the climb again. Once again, she swayed slightly. She evened her weight across her feet as much as she could.

She reached for the ceiling.

Flat footed, her fingers almost brushed the spell.

She stood on her toes.

"Gotcha!" she called as she shoved her fingers through the magic and tugged. It stuck to the wall. She yanked at it, stretching the strands. She dropped back off her toes, flailing slightly as the chair and book teetered, tearing a bit of the spell free.

The spell looked like a bird's nest—and a poorly made one at that. Far away, it had seemed that the winding strands had a pattern. Now, not so much. The remainder of the spell hung from the corner, the broken strands black, like they had been burnt.

She pinched one of the threads of magic and pulled, careful not to tighten the knots her destruction had made. The threads faded, gold and green washing out to grey and black. After a few moments, the magic disintegrated and fell away.

"Dammit." Deor reached, on tiptoe again, for the rest of the spell. The broken strands were curling and blackening, crumbling away to ashes. The rest of the spell, though, was pulsing brighter, frantic, like an adrenaline-driven heart. She reached up again.

The door to her bedroom slammed open, crashing into the wall behind it. Deor started and nearly fell, grabbing the back of the chair for balance, and hoping that the tower wouldn't topple her.

Arthur bolted into the room. Naked to the waist and in lounging pants, he brandished a sword. His free hand was slightly cupped, and around it, threads of gold and brown magic swirled.

Behind him, by only a fraction, was Rafe. He was in a suit, but no tie, and three buttons on his shirt undone. He, too, was armed with a sword in one hand and some kind of magic, strands of white and blue, in the other.

"Princess?" Arthur demanded.

"Over here." She steadied herself on her perch.

Arthur stepped toward her, and Rafe headed for her dressing room and bath.

"Are you okay?" Arthur asked.

"Yes."

He reached the desk on which she stood. "Is anyone else here?" Arthur demanded.

"Not that I know of." She kept still—he looked like the might stab her if she moved.

Rafe emerged from the bathroom. "Nothing in here."

Arthur lowered his sword. "What the hell are you doing?"

She pointed at the ceiling. "There were spells up there. I wanted to know what they were."

"So you built and scaled a tower of furniture and books to find out." Arthur chucked his sword on her bed. "You didn't think to, I don't know, *ask* someone?"

"No," Deor said. "It's my room."

Rafe set his sword on the bed, too. He rubbed the bridge of his nose. "Those are security spells," he said. "They go off if anyone not allowed comes in here. Or, apparently, if someone tries to take them apart. "

"Sir?" Lieutenant Bolton stuck his head in the door and paused when he saw her. "I've got a small contingent of Houseboys in the hall..."

"Stand down, Bolton," Rafe said. "Go back to your posts. False alarm."

"Out of my way!" Finn shouldered his way into the room, black silk robe fanning behind him. "Are you alright?" he said before he took in the sight of Deor on the table, chair, and book. "What are you doing?"

"She's fine," Rafe said. "You can go back to bed." He walked over to Deor and reached his hand up. "Come on down."

She waved off his hand, eased off the chair and dropped to the floor.

"You deliberately destroyed security spells?" Finn demanded, his nails and eyes flaring silver.

"Well, I—"

"It is a yes or no question." He cut her off.

"Then, no. I did not *deliberately* destroy anything. I didn't know what they were."

"You..." he trailed off. "You broke the spells to find out how they worked?"

Deor crossed her arms. "When you put it that way, it sounds bad."

"Don't you ever do that again! Do not touch spells if you do not know what they do. You could have hurt yourself."

"They were spells in my room. In my private space!" Deor protested.

Finn snorted. "If you can't be trusted not to endanger yourself, I'll have guards up here at night too." Before she could argue, he added, "Do you still think you shouldn't be treated as a child?" He didn't let her answer but turned and left the room, slamming the door shut behind him.

"I wanted to know—"

"How it worked," Arthur finished for her. "Did you figure it out?"

"No. Every time I would try, it disintegrated. Is it supposed to do that?"

"When someone who isn't supposed to touch it does? Yes." He flicked out his wings—deep brown, as dark as his skin, and shot through with gold threads. With a small jump, he was in the air. He chucked her textbook to the floor and lowered her chair only slightly more gently. He waved his hands over the remnants of the spell, muttering.

"Next time, ask someone before dismantling something," Rafe said. A chill blew around him matching the coldness in his eyes.

"Yes." Deor nodded. "I will." Groping for anything to change the subject, she added, "That's a lovely suit. Did you go out tonight?"

"Out in public?" he said. "No."

"That's too bad," she babbled. "You're all dressed up. Did you do something else fun?"

As the last words escaped her mouth, she noticed on the collar of his shirt a small smear of pink. The kind that happens when a woman is wearing lipstick and kisses the neck of a man with a collar.

"I can't fix this here!" Arthur snapped, dropping to the ground. "I don't suppose you would like to have a try at fixing it?" He waved at her vanity.

All that remained in the corner were a few sad silver threads of magic. "I don't think I can help."

"No!" His raised voice bounced off the walls. "You can't. These took hours of work. I have to build a new one."

"Surely that can wait until tomorrow?" Deor asked.

"It will have to!" He dusted off his hands and flicked in his wings. "Unless you plan on letting someone who shouldn't be here in?"

"No." Deor's voice was almost a whisper. "I think I'll go to bed."

"Excellent!" He snatched his sword from the bed and stormed out, flinging the door open and not bothering to close it behind him.

Rafe tugged his jacket back in place. "I think I will be off, too."

"I'm sorry for interrupting your..." Deor fumbled for the right word, "...date?"

"Really?" Rafe arched an eyebrow at her. "Shall I pass your apologies on to my fiancée?" Rafe bowed slightly, gathered his sword. "Goodnight, Princess." He left, gently shutting the door behind him.

Deor sat down on the bed and covered her face with her hands. Number of days without an embarrassing incident? Zero.

Chapter Seventeen

The next afternoon, Deor rolled her shoulders and stretched. Memorizing the degrees of nobility and the attendant titles that went with them was as arcane as wading through literary theory had been in graduate school. But it had to be done. She yawned and stuck her pencil into her bun. Time for a break.

Big as they were, without her job to go to, her suites started to feel all too confining. With the winter weather closing in outside, Deor took to wandering aimlessly around the Palace, trusting her newfound instinct to keep her from getting lost. She discovered parlors and bedrooms and curio rooms. Portrait galleries and dining halls with musicians' galleries. Linen closets and secret passageways. Entire rooms with no apparent purpose at all. And most of what she discovered was empty. It was all scrupulously clean, but clearly unused.

She got used to nodding hello to Lieutenant Bolton as she came and went. Occasionally, she let him accompany her, but for the most part, she preferred to wander alone. She rarely saw Rafe except at mealtimes and those seemed to be further and further apart as he spent more dinners with the Lady Genevieve.

Which he had every right to do, she reminded herself, even as she had to admit that having him around made dinners more interesting and less awkward than when it was just her and Finn.

Every once in a while on her rambling, she got the impression she wasn't alone. She started to anticipate coming around a corner and finding Arthur traveling the opposite direction. He always had a very good reason for being there—most often that her father wanted to speak to her about something or that she was entering a restricted area and should return to her own quarters. But still it unnerved her that it was always Arthur.

One day she found an entire hall full of taxidermied animals. From floor to ceiling, the walls were covered in skulls and horns and mounted heads. Birds poised in motionless flight hung from the ceiling. Full sized beasts—snarling wild cats, elk with six-foot racks of horns, a creature like a blue water buffalo filled the floor. Cabinets of tinier animals, some of them posed in charming tableaus, lined the walls.

She was just staring in fascinated horror at a tavern scene made up entirely of pygmy shrews in tiny jackets and hats when a glimmer of fuzzy magic caught the edge of her eye.

"Hello?" She turned toward the glimmer.

Hands seized her. Arthur materialized out of thin air, right in front of her, his hands gripping her upper arms.

She screamed. Sparkles shot off her in every direction, hissing like fire. Her wings shot out of her back, banging painfully into the display case behind her.

Arthur yelped and leaped back wringing his hands.

"What the hell are you doing?" Deor shouted.

Arthur's palms were bloody, as he held them up in a gesture of truce. "A test," he gasped. "Just a test."

"Of what? My patience? Because you've been testing that for weeks now."

Through gritted teeth Arthur, said, "I apologize, Your Majesty. The king has charged me with ensuring your safety. I wanted to test how you might react under an attack."

Deor narrowed her eyes at him. "Somehow I doubt this is what he had in mind. Now get out of my sight, you creep." She shuddered as she said it, but kept her eyes fixed on him until he had exited the hall and she could hear his footsteps retreating.

When she was sure he was gone, she breathed out, a long shuddering breath and ran her hands up and down her arms, shivering. That's when she discovered the cause of the blood on Arthur's hands. Where he had seized her, her skin had erupted in needle-sharp points that stuck out even through the thick sleeves of her sweater.

When she pressed a tentative finger to the largest point, it went straight through her with no pain, only the faintest ripple of silver-like water meeting water. And the points wouldn't go away. As she stood there shaking in the aftermath of the adrenaline rush, surrounded by long dead animals, the skin over her hands rippled and spiked with silver.

"Okay," she said. "That's enough. He's gone." Nothing changed except the longer the effect went on, the weaker she felt.

Her knees buckled under her, and she lowered herself to the floor, waves of nausea and dizziness flooding over her. She tried to breathe normally. In with the good air, out with the stress. It only helped a little.

She sat on the floor for a long time, smoothing her hands over her arms again and again, trying to ease the spiking lines of magic back into place. Eventually only the tips of her nails were silver, and the dizziness was gone.

But she felt like she'd run ten miles. Muscles jumped and twitched all over her body, and she wobbled when she stood up. Finally, she pulled out her mirror. "Lieutenant Bolton?" she called. "Could you come get me? I think I need an escort back to my rooms."

But it was Arthur that showed up. "Princess?" he called from the open door. "Your father wishes to see you."

"Now?" Deor said.

Arthur stepped into the room. "Your Majesty," he said, voice dripping with something—not quite disdain, nor sarcasm. He sounded bored, like anything to do with her was tedious. "The king is not accustomed to waiting."

"Right." She pushed off the case she had used to steady herself and stepped toward him. One of his hands was bandaged, she noted, but said nothing. "Let's go."

Arthur gave a slight nod and led the way from the room. He stalked down the hall and up the staircase leading to the top floor and the king's suites. Like most of the faeries, he was taller than she was, and he moved just fast enough that it took effort for her to keep up—either she stretched her stride so much it almost hurt or concede and take up a light jog.

"You don't like me, do you?" Deor said, conversationally, trying to keep a breathless gasp from escaping as she kept pace.

Arthur stopped so abruptly that she almost ran into him. He turned his head and spoke at her over his shoulder. "I don't care either way." He remained still for a moment. "I dislike chaos. It is not good for the kingdom, for the king, for Rafe, for any of us. And you," he jerked his head slightly in her direction, "are chaos incarnate." He looked forward again but didn't move. "And you don't do anything to fix that."

"I'm not—" Deor started, but Arthur resumed walking, his pace even faster. Deor gave up staying with him and instead took her own time down the hall. He could wait.

The tall, wide windows cast squares of pale light on the dark red rugs that ran the length of the hall. Beautiful paintings of Winter Court landscapes lined the other wall, moving through the seasons as she walked. Spring vistas of blooming trees and gentle rains, the lush green grass of summer, trees topped with vivid autumn leaves, and blankets of pure white. Every painting featured the castle from a distant perspective, the final one at night, the Palace lit with torches of magical light, and the ice crystals on the roofs and spires glittering like diamonds under the full moon.

When she caught up with Arthur, he opened the door without knocking and bowed her in. She turned to the parlor, but it was empty. There were no footmen, nothing. All the doors leading from the parlor were closed. She had made him wait too long, it seemed, and now he returned the favor. Fair enough.

If this suite followed her own, then the bedroom would be to the left, but the parlor was so much larger, and she was sure there was more than a small dining room. Astarte must have had her own suite of rooms, as the parlor looked as bachelor as she had ever seen.

Everything was dark wood and leather, with heavy rugs on the floor, though there was a lot more exposed stone than in her own suite. There were a few bookshelves, a beautiful fireplace, and several framed maps on the walls. There were various ornaments, including both shields and swords of different styles on the walls, too. She moved to look more closely at some of them, and a flicker caught her eye.

A long tapestry hung on the wall at a corner. A plain wooden door on the left and a bookcase on the right had shielded it from view. It was on the same wall as the door into the parlor. The elaborate tapestry had four scenes, from the top to the bottom. A man and woman, standing tall, arms outspread, a halo of gold and silver light above their heads. A hunting scene with a man and a woman riding full speed, both laughing. The pair sitting in a shared throne, each holding a child, smiling. The last panel, though, was different. A jagged line severed the thrones, beneath it two figures, a man and a woman, with crowns, their backs to each other, gazing out at the world beyond the tapestry.

Deor ran her hand down the front of the tapestry and it split—two panels, not one, but so well disguised that she would have never known without touching them. She pushed them apart revealing a stone door. The rock was iron grey, a single slab. The seam between the wood of the wall and the stone of the door nearly invisible, as though the material morphed from one to the other. She ran her fingers down the stone, smooth under her fingers. She laid both her palms on the door and closed her eyes. Cool to the touch, the stone was several degrees cooler than the room.

With her eyes closed, Deor could see that the stone was solid and porous. Sparks fluttered in her vision as she pressed her palms harder into the rock. Her eyes flew open when the stone gave way and her hands slipped forward into it. The air filled with silver sparks, but not her own, and they burned her everywhere they landed. She yelped but didn't pull back her hands. Her own skin rippled, shifting from flesh to silver—but not spikes, smooth silver armor, sending the sparks bouncing back. She leaned forward, lifted a foot to step forward.

Whatever was on the other side of the door, she could feel it, hear it, calling her toward it. Power. Never in her life had she felt anything like it. Not even when her wings exploded out to protect her from Geoff. Lines of knowledge fell into place next to instinct, and the world of magic opened. This was magic she understood, magic she could touch, she could shape. The spells in her room were nothing compared to what she would make.

"Deor!" The voice was a scream, tearing through her ears and her flesh.

She shuddered, and the world blurred.

"Stop!" The command struck her to the spine, and she froze.

Her skin's protection faded, and the sparks seared her skin. The stone began to close around her hands, her arms. Solid rock crushing her bones. She hurled herself backward, landing on her back with enough force that it drove the air from her lungs. The panels of the tapestry fell back into place, seeming whole and hiding the door from her view.

Above her, Finn loomed. His eyes were pure silver, and his hands, nails sharp, rested on his hips. Anger rolled off him, and sparks—like her own—spat from him at wild angles. Those that hit her burning enough to singe through her clothing.

"How dare you?" he boomed again.

Deor raised a hand to cover her face from the onslaught of magic. "I—I—"

"What?" he demanded. "What is your excuse for this?"

"Please," she said, her voice small. "Please stop."

The anger lines on his face softened. He knelt next to her, took tender of hold the hand he held out against him. "Deor? Look at me."

She focused on him—his iris were still silver, but the anger had faded.

"What were you doing?" He shifted his weight and sat on the floor next to her. As she tried to sit up, he put his hand on her shoulder. "Lie back," he said. "I'm not going to hurt you." He guided her hand down to his lap and laid his other hand on top of hers.

"I got here, and you weren't here. I was looking around, and I saw the tapestry." She glanced at the wall, but there was nothing—no tapestry, no door, just the wood paneling that lined the rest of the room. "It was there! I swear!" Panic rose in her chest. Had she hallucinated?

"Shhh," he said. He stroked her forehead. "It's still there. You just can't see it. You didn't see the magic shielding it?"

Deor blinked. The tapestry *had* seemed strange. That's why it had fascinated her. Perhaps she had seen the magic on it. "I didn't realize—then the door. There's something behind it. There's so much power..." She shuddered at the thought of the power she'd touched. Here, free from it, on the ground, it terrified her. So much power—she would have drowned in it.

"That's my private workroom. The king's workroom. No one can go in it without my leave. Or so I thought. Why did you try? Even after it rejected you?"

Deor stared at the ceiling. The vaulted ceiling was painted to look like the sky, and as she stared at it, she realized that it was like glass, not any sky, but the one that passed overhead at the moment. Deep twilight had come—it came so early these days—and a few small stars had begun to peek out.

"I don't know," she admitted. "I wanted to know what it was."

Finn laughed, loud and full.

Deor jerked her attention to him. "What?"

He let out a few more chuckles and smiled at her. "Oh, my daughter. You take apart spells to see what they are. You talk to people who intrigue you, no matter the politics. You defend the weak even at your own peril." He shook his head. "You need to look before you leap, as they say. Or at least learn to fly before you jump out a window."

He stood and held out a hand to her.

She took it, and he hauled her to her feet and pulled her into a hug. "I wanted to speak to you about your misplaced confidence in Victor Farringdon," he said, a whisper in her ear. "And then I come in and think I'm finding you breaking into my workroom." He let go and stepped back, resting his hands on her shoulders. "Come, let's talk."

He moved to a chair near the fire and sat, gesturing for her to sit across from him.

"I've tried to keep you out of politics, at least for a short time. I've failed. But as you go out into society, you must promise me you will not speak against me," he said. "At all. Period."

"Forever or for the next few months?"

He rolled his eyes. "Must you negotiate everything? For the next few months, since I would like to go to dinner, and saying 'no' would mean a longer conversation."

"I will not speak against you personally. I promise."

His eyebrow shot up. "That's quite a thing—to promise. Take care not to break it." He clapped his hands on his knees and stood up. "And when that is all done, I shall help you set up your own workroom. I have been remiss in not teaching you magic yet. Until today, I think I did not fully understand your power."

Deor nodded as she stood. "Rafe has said that you should be teaching me. He says he can't do much because our magics are different."

"He's right." Finn offered her his arm. She took it. "Why were you here? In my suites?"

"You wanted to see me, Arthur said. He brought me here."

"Huh." Finn shrugged. "He must have misunderstood. I was wanting to see you in my office downstairs, where we could look at the reactions to your event on campus."

"Yes," Deor said. She glanced up at Finn, but it seemed the matter was closed. "I'm sure it was just a mistake."

From the man who didn't make mistakes? The sneak. Deor shook her head slightly. Not bloody likely. Whatever this was about, Arthur surely had a plan. "Chaos incarnate," he had called her. How exactly, she wondered, did he intend to quell the chaos?

Chapter Eighteen

A couple days later, Rafe enjoyed the quiet of the mostly empty Palace. Arthur had left for his family's home, and the majority of the servants were also with their families. It was the quietest time of the year. Whistling, Rafe shrugged on a coat and headed out through the parlor he shared with Deor. Genevieve was well on her way to the Alps with her friends, and most of the Caer Eisteddfod garrison was on Solstice leave. In the week that had passed since Rafe had conversed with his brother, the bruises had faded—mostly. Aches and pains still followed him a bit, but nothing that a quiet Solstice holiday of good food and drink wouldn't cure. Sam and Jake danced about at his feet.

"Going somewhere fun with Genevieve?" Deor called from her spot on the couch.

His cheeks burned for a second, but he put on a light-hearted tone. "Fun, yes. Not with Genevieve, I'm afraid. We've decided to…to take a hiatus in our relationship."

"Oh, I'm sorry." Deor sat up, a look of concern on her face.

He paused, one hand on the door. "I'm going down to the royal kennels to check on Sam's puppies. Want to come?"

"I love puppies!" She stood. "And I deserve some fun after wading my way through the names and political positions of every member of Parliament. I'll get my coat."

Ten minutes later, Rafe held the kennel door open for her, and Deor darted inside, her scarf clutched around her nose and ears to keep them from freezing off. Rafe hadn't so much as turned up his collar.

"You're sure you're not feeling sick?" he asked.

"I'm fine!" She laughed. "I'd like to see how well you do when it's a hundred and six degrees in the shade with the Santa Ana winds blowing." She shook snow off her hair and looked around.

The royal kennels abutted the royal stables but built on a slightly less grand scale since the doors didn't need to accommodate temperamental war horses and equally large carriage animals. The building was a long rectangle, its stone walls divided on either side into wooden loose boxes strewn with deep straw. Most boxes had swinging doors set into the outer walls that let the dogs take themselves for a walk in the open yard beyond. Deor could just manage to get her chin over the wall of the boxes to see the dogs inside.

As Rafe led her down the hall, he pointed out the different types of dog. Long, lean dogs called Coursers for chasing swift game and racing. Small, fluffy dogs with big egos for hunting rats and other vermin. Alaunts that looked to Deor like thick-haired bulldogs all sleeping in a snorting, farting heap in one box.

"How do you hunt with a dog that short?" Deor said.

"*A goode, long haired Alaunt shall be uglie, stupid, and slowe, with a bite like a trap. He arriveth last to the hunt and bears down the prey by sheer force of stubborn wille,*" Rafe quoted. "Gervaise's *On the Matter of Dogges.* One of my favorite books as a boy. And here," he gestured grandly, "are my Molossians. *The noblest of the Royal Hounds, excelling in all points. The Molossian is the very parfait picture of a dogge.*"

She had to agree with Gervaise—the Molossians were the very doggiest of dogs. Sharp pricked ears, thick fur, giant fanged mouths that smiled with delight as Rafe passed and tails that wagged non-stop. On either side of the hall, dogs stood on their hind legs, front paws draped over the box doors, tongues lolling and tails wagging. Rafe stopped to pet each and every one of them, laughing as they slobbered on his face and shed fur over his clothes. A few leaped out of their boxes, wiggling and play bowing for extra attention.

"Not today, lads and lasses," he said. "You'll scare the mothers. Off you go. Jake, lead." He snapped his fingers, and Jake took off with a bark, shooting for the far end of the building. Molossians disappeared through their swinging doors into the exercise yard, and Rafe led Deor to a closed off portion of the kennel, where a loose box was tented over and heated.

"Let me go in first," Rafe said as he opened the box door. "The bitches are extra protective when they have pups. This one is my favorite. She blue ribboned four times before I stopped showing her."

Deor nodded and watched as he let himself in, going down on his knees next to a dog with a face like a razor blade and unfriendly eyes. She let Rafe scratch her under the chin and around the ears, but she kept her eyes fixed on Deor the entire time.

"Come on, Madeline, there's a good girl. You know I wouldn't let anyone hurt your babies," Rafe said.

Deor choked. "You named your prize bitch after your mother?"

Rafe grinned back at her. "She knows it, too. Come in. It's safe now. Just don't make any sudden moves."

"Hi Maddy," Deor said, keeping her voice low and friendly. "I'm just here to admire your puppies. No need to eat my face." She settled into the straw, hands folded in her lap where the dog could see them.

Madeline's head bobbed, sniffing Deor from across the box while Rafe petted her back. At last she gave in and relaxed, laying her head across Rafe's lap with a sigh. Four fuzzy puppies nursed at her side, ignoring everything else.

"Aw! They are so cute!" Deor said. "How old are they?" At the sound of her voice, one of the puppies stopped head butting his mother long enough to look around at Deor.

"Just eight weeks." Rafe sounded like he was the proud father himself.

The puppy that had responded to Deor's voice broke away from the pack and struggled through the deep straw, yipping and sniffing the whole way. His top fur was dark all over, but the reddish undercoat showed through. Madeline leaned forward and grabbed him by the scruff of the neck with her teeth, setting him down by her side. But after a few seconds, the puppy set off again, charging away from his siblings in search of something.

"Here, puppy, puppy," Deor said. The puppy misstepped, tripped, and tumbled end over end, bounding up in her direction with a happy yelp. This time, Rafe picked him up and petted him.

"You're a brave little fellow, aren't you?" he cooed to the puppy. "Yes, you are. Such a bold little mariner." The puppy wriggled happily, licking Rafe's hands and face, but the second Rafe set him down, the puppy bounded toward Deor again. A few of the other puppies broke away from Madeline, yipping and sniffing to see what all the excitement was about.

"Well hello," she said, gathering the bundle of warm fur and wet tongue into her arms. "Aren't you just so cute?"

She spent the next ten minutes cuddling and tickling the puppy, getting her hands and face thoroughly licked in the process. Every time she put the puppy down, he would bound back to her within half a minute. The other puppies tumbled over each other and explored the loose box.

"Have you named them yet?" Deor said.

"Not yet. Do you have names in mind?" Rafe asked.

She picked up her puppy friend and looked into his eyes. "I think this one is named Brand," she said. He licked her nose.

She looked up at Rafe. A strange, almost wistful smile, crossed his face as if he were laughing at some old, double-edged joke.

"Did I say something wrong?" Deor asked. "Please don't tell me I picked the name of a dead friend of yours or something ham handed like that."

"No, no. Nothing like that. It's just you've picked out the best of the litter without even thinking about it."

Deor's face flushed hot all the way to her ear tips. "Just like my...like Finn." She held the puppy up for a moment and stared into his eyes. "As if I had a right to waltz in here and take over your dogs. I'm sorry. I didn't mean it that way. He's your dog. You've probably got a stud book name all picked out for him already." She cradled the puppy against her, holding it in the crook of her arm.

Rafe leaned back against the loose box, stretching his legs out in front of him until his boots almost rested in her lap, one hand patting Madeline's head as he stared at Deor for a long minute.

"What?" she finally demanded. "Tell me what you're thinking."

"I'm thinking you haven't put Brand down yet," he said.

Deor's cheeks burned even harder, and she set the puppy down on the other side of Rafe's booted legs. Brand immediately tried to scramble up and over them, yelping pitifully as he did so.

"Go on. Go back to your mother," Deor said. She made little shooing motions at the puppy, shoving him gently away from her, but every time she did so, he struggled back. Even a playful sibling grabbing him by the tail couldn't distract him from his quest for long.

"Go on," Rafe said. "You'd better pick him up, or he'll think you don't like him."

Without a second's hesitation, she scooped Brand up in her arms.

"I don't ever sell my dogs," Rafe said. "But every once in a while, I give one away as a present."

Deor's heart beat faster. "I shouldn't ask for something like this," she said. "But I'm not going to say no. I can't." She bent her head over Brand's, burying her face in his soft, puppy fur.

"Just promise me you won't get bored with him. Molossians aren't ornaments. They're smart, fierce, and loyal to a fault. You'll break his heart if you turn him away."

"Never," Deor said.

Chapter Nineteen

D eor flopped back on her bed and stared up at the ceiling—the canopy of the bed had been rolled back. No matter what she had on the ceiling—a scene of her own devising, the weather outside, or the plain ceiling itself, the filigree and wainscoting at the edges never changed. The same was true with the rest of the room. It wasn't so much that Deor disliked peacock blue—it was that it was the color of Geoff's house. Every speck of decor reminded her that this was—and still is—the prince's room. In her house.

She thought better of climbing the furniture again to scrape the accents off the walls. Even if she didn't disturb any of Arthur's security spells on purpose, who knows what trigger she might trip? She glared at the small pulses of magic in every corner and didn't like what she saw. Security was important, but if anyone unacceptable got this far into the Household, the Houseboys and Arthur would have much bigger problems than her security spells sounding an alarm. She would talk to Finn about it—again—later. Surely he didn't have spells in his room? Or maybe he did, and years of living like that meant he didn't notice—sort of like contestants on reality TV shows claimed to forget the presence of the cameras.

"Excuse me, Miss Deor?" Melanie peeked in through the open door.

Deor sat up. "What can I do for you?" She had, for the time being, given up on getting the woman to call her by her simple first name. The honorific "Miss" seemed as far as the lady was willing to drift into informality. Melanie was right, too. Erasing differences in status felt nice, from Deor's point of view, but familiarity probably would cause her lady's maid more trouble than the faux intimacy of first names was worth.

The lady stepped in the room and gave a quick curtsey. She was dressed differently than normal, with a heavy coat open over a dark wool dress. She wore boots and carried a scarf and gloves. "I wanted to see if you need anything before I go."

"Go?" Deor asked.

Melanie frowned, a crease of worry across her brow. "For Solstice? I was planning on accompanying my father home. But if you need me...?"

"Oh!" Deor stood. "I didn't know you were leaving. No, no. I don't need anything. Have a lovely holiday!" She smiled, and a wave of guilt rose in her. Was she supposed to give her maid a present? Probably. That seemed like something royalty would do for their staff. She'd talk to Finn.

"Thank you."

"Can I ask you one question before you go?"

"Yes, Your Majesty." Melanie stepped farther into the room. "What do you need?"

"I was thinking about my rooms. They're lovely, but I would like to make them a bit more my own. Can I redecorate?"

"Certainly." Melanie ran her fingers along the wainscoting. "I've never liked peacock blue." She smiled shyly at Deor.

Deor laughed. "Me either!"

At Deor's laugh, the girl relaxed. Hopefully she would relax more over time. Deor could do with some comfortable companionship. "So, after the holiday, we'll look into changing the room?"

"I will have the Palace decorators come in for a meeting. You let me know that date and time." Melanie looked around the room. "We'll get rid of the elaborate style—you want something a bit more thoughtful? Cozy?"

"Exactly." Deor sat back down on the bed and leaned back on her hands. "The linens, too, I think. And the bathroom."

"Everything," Melanie agreed. "So I will be off then?" She curtsied. "You have a..." She paused. "Happy Christmas? That's what one of the stable hands said he heard in London."

Deor laughed. Close enough. "Happy Christmas to you, too."

Melanie curtsied once more and left through the servants' door, a narrow wood panel hidden between two bookshelves.

Deor took a shower and puttered around some more, finally settling in to read more about the Winter Court's history. The history read a bit more like a novelization than a statement of fact, but she at least got the general idea of Summer/Winter Court relations at the time. They seemed as cool then as now. Lots of skirmishes, the occasional full-blown war, and almost no change in borders—with a small area of semi-disputed land that functioned as a demilitarized zone.

After a particularly vitriolic passage on the tensions between Parliament and the king, Deor closed the book and picked up her tablet-sized mirror. "Playback last Parliament."

The mirror came to life, showing the scene from days before. It began with the Speaker banging her gavel. Deor watched as soldiers dragged Aiden from the room. When the mirror finally stopped—some minutes after the Speaker had adjourned the session—the room was mostly empty, with a few members milling about looking baffled.

She drummed her fingers on her knee and stared at the tablet. It was worth a try. "Call Aiden Kirby."

The mirror's surface rippled like a pool disturbed by a falling stone for a few moments, and then cleared, the young man's face in view.

"Ya? Who's this then?" he said before the picture had cleared.

"Hello Aiden, it's Professor Smithfield." Deor smiled, trying not to look as nervous as she felt.

The picture swung wildly, careening around the room, flashing the ceiling and the floor before going dark. A muffled voice said something incoherent in the background.

"Aiden? Are you okay? Are you still there?" Deor was leaning to call in a soldier from outside to send to see if the boy had been hurt when the picture swung again, and Aiden reappeared.

"I'm sorry, Your Majesty," he said. He shoved a hand through his hair, an attempt to comb the spiky mess. It did little to help. "I dropped the mirror."

"I'm sorry to disturb you. If you are busy, I'm happy to talk some other time."

"No!" he shouted. He cleared his throat. "I mean, no, now is fine. I was..." He glanced around the room searching for an answer. Finally, after moments of silence dragged on, he said, "Asleep." He hung his head.

Deor laughed. "Good for you. I always slept for a week at the end of the semester, too." She glanced at the clock on the wall. Noon was a bit early to be calling a student on break.

He blushed, turning his already vivid skin a deeper red. "I'm sorry for snapping—I didn't recognize the call."

"No worries." Deor smiled. "I was calling about Parliament the other day. I was watching."

"Ah," he said, non-committal.

"I saw you dragged away," she said, and plowed on before he could offer excuses or explanations. "After your aid on the last day I was on campus, I wanted to make sure you were okay. Those soldiers didn't hurt you, did they?"

"What?" He gaped, eyebrows raised. "I mean, no. No, they didn't. Lord Farringdon's squire followed them out and was watching them. When the soldiers saw him, they gave me a shove and told me to go home. I went back to the Burning Heretic."

"The what?" Some sort of rally or something? Like Guy Fawkes day?

"A pub by my house. My mates and I meet there sometimes. There were some friends who didn't go to the session there watching. I had a couple pints, watched the show, and went home."

"Good. And you're healed from the fight on campus? Thank you for defending me, by the way. You were brave to take on goblins."

He blushed deeper. "I'm fine. Lord Farringdon—the younger—took me to a healer he knew. I was fit as a fiddle before I went home. He said he didn't want my mum to worry."

"How nice of him," Deor said. It was also a kind way of gaining the trust of a young firebrand in the movement—an opening to a group very distrustful of nobility. Smart.

The young man stared at her in silence for a few moments, like he was screwing up his courage.

"Go ahead and ask what you want, Aiden. If I can answer it, I will." She paused. "There's zero chance this is about Shakespeare, right?"

"Less than zero," he said, face serious. Though he had the same coloration as a ripe strawberry in summer and the haircut of goth from the eighties, there was nothing silly about him. He looked young to her

—had they been in the human world, she'd have guessed he wasn't quite old enough drink—but she saw the adult there, too. He was ready to be taken seriously by the world, whether the world was ready or not.

"Go for it."

"Do you agree with what your father did to the were-folk?"

Points for directness. She sighed. "I don't know. I haven't been here long enough to understand the history." She hated herself more than a little as she said it. What he was doing was wrong. Punishing an entire group for the crimes of one person, depriving citizens of their rights—or whatever they were called here—it was as bad as what had been done to the Japanese during WWII. And here she was, pretending she could be neutral on the question.

"The history isn't that complicated." He frowned, holding her gaze. "They're people. This isn't fair."

"No," Deor said, shaking her head. "It's not fair. Let's put it that way. I don't know what I would have done to respond, and let's be real here, dumping goblin heads on the floor of Parliament does deserve a response, but blaming all the were-folk isn't doing any good."

As she had spoken, a look of shock and, increasingly, horror formed on Aiden's face. She hadn't sounded that ridiculous, had she?

"What do you think?" she asked him.

His eyes widened even more, if that was possible. He opened and closed his mouth, but no sound came out. Finally, he flailed and pointed frantically at her.

"What?" she said. Then she noticed his gaze—it wasn't on her. It was on a spot behind and above her. She turned.

Finn's arms were crossed, his frown was deep, and his eyes weren't silver. They were iron grey. His anger was palpable.

"Please," he said, voice quiet, "don't let me stop you. Do go on. What, exactly, would you have done in my place?"

Deor froze. If she started babbling at the king, flailing and apologizing, she'd look like an idiot child. If she didn't defer, she'd be defying the king in front of a known protester, which could bring all sorts of hell down on Aiden. Stall. "Like I said, I don't know what I would have done." She turned from the king to Aiden. "I am glad to hear that you are safe," she said with a smile. "I won't take up any more of your time. Have a good day." Before the kid could speak, she disconnected the call with a tap of the mirror.

She turned her attention back to her father. "So...? Do you want to sit down and talk about it?"

The anger washed off his face, replaced with shock. She hadn't apologized, she hadn't flailed, she hadn't cowed.

"No," he said. "Do not forget your promise. You will not, ever again, speak against me to anyone—in private or in public. I understand that this is all very new to you, but the Palace must present a united front at all times. Not to do so is to foment disruption and even treason. There will be consequences. Do you understand?"

"Yes." A tight knot of fear pulsed in her chest.

He did not yell or storm about. He wasn't emotional, as he had been with her when she broke the spell in her room or accidentally broke into his workroom. That was Finn playing the upset, but loving, father. An emotional display for her benefit. This was the real Finn, the real king, demanding absolute loyalty. She had no doubt that, whatever threat he was implying, he would follow through.

"Yes, what?"

Deor's mind raced. "Yes, I understand?"

His frown deepened. He eyed her, gauging her reaction. "Try again." His tone said there wouldn't be another chance.

She blinked at him. Tall, imposing, arms crossed, he glowered over her. She got it—what he wanted. "Yes," she paused, "Your Majesty."

He nodded once. "Good." He looked about to say something else, but the door opened again.

"Good afternoon." Rafe came in smiling. He was covered in dust and fur. "I've been down to see the puppies. They are doing well! All of them look like they could be blue ribboners." He took off his coat and draped it over his arm. By the time he reached the two of them, his cheery mood had dissipated. "Is everything okay?" he asked, his eyes locked on Deor's.

Deor gave a tiny inclination of her head, and then looked to the king.

"Everything is fine," he said with genuine cheer.

The tension evaporated, though Deor's heart pounded and the knot of anxiety in her chest wasn't easing up anytime soon. As she exhaled, trying to release some of the tightness in her body, she knew anxiety wasn't the right word. It was fear. She was afraid. Not quite terrified, not yet. Even in the alley, fighting for her life, she had not been this kind of afraid. The lump in her chest, the tremble in her hands, the slight silvering of her nails, they all were born of the certainty that he would hurt her. There was no doubt in him at all—only the cool assurance that, if he wanted to, he would hurt her. To get what he thought was right. To, in his mind, keep her safe. Or, Deor knew, to satisfy himself.

Even worse, she knew "if" was wishful thinking. It wasn't a matter of *if* he would deliberately hurt her, but *when*. A flash of anger flared in her chest, momentarily overwhelming the fear. She'd have to stay here—in this anger—if she were going to stand up to the king. She drew in a deep breath and let it out. Someday, she would defy him—she would have to—but not today.

"Come sit down, Rafe," Finn said rounding the couch and taking a place in the chair nearest the fire.

Rafe followed him and took a seat in the other chair. A small line of concern creased his forehead as he stole a glance at her, but he said nothing.

"Solstice is a time for family," Finn announced. "It is also a time for making amends. I need to do so."

Deor and Rafe exchanged glances.

"I have been remiss with my Consort." For an instant, he looked contrite. "I need to set things right between us. So, for Solstice, I have decided that we shall all go up to Roger's. Roger and Pookie are so full of cheer that I know all our spirits will be lifted. After all our suffering, a bit of a holiday will help."

Rafe relaxed, allowing Deor to do so too. "That is an excellent idea. When do we leave?"

"I am going up there tonight," Finn said. "But you two can come when you wish. Rafe, Genevieve is welcome to come, and I understand if you two have plans—perhaps you could spend a few days with us?"

"No plans," he said. "Genevieve is in the Alps. I wanted a quieter Solstice here. Roger's would be delightful."

Finn quirked an eyebrow at his response but didn't press.

Deor tried to repress her own sense of relief that Genevieve would not be joining them. She didn't know what about that woman got her hackles up—Genevieve had never been anything but charming to her.

"Alright. You can help Deor to portal there, can't you?"

Rafe nodded.

"Good. Be there by the twentieth." Finn rose, beamed at both of them, and left.

"Well," Rafe said, "that was…interesting. Are you okay? This isn't ruining any plans you had, is it?"

"I'm fine," she lied. "What plans could I possibly have?" She forced a smile. "Will Roger's really be fun?"

"Actually, yes." Rafe eased back into his chair. "I've known them both since I was a child. They're more like family. There won't be any more formality than there would here—maybe even less. Hot toddies, sweets, good food, walking in the snow—really it will be the epitome of Solstice. Roger will love you, I'm sure, too. As will Pookie."

Deor relaxed some. "That sounds nice." A thought shot across her mind. "Will Robbie be there?"

"Yes," Rafe said, his voice turning sad. "Though I don't know if she will celebrate with us. She has only recently woken up, and I'm not sure how well she will be."

"Especially after finding out who I am." Deor stood. She needed to move, do something. She'd pack. Something to focus on, to take her mind off of Finn. "No matter what, Robbie won't have any problems from me. I'll support her—I don't care what Finn says."

"Thank you." Rafe stood, too. "That means a lot to me. It will to Robbie and Astarte, too. I imagine she's quite afraid for her daughter, with you here. If you and Robbie were to be on good terms—not even friends, but friendly—it would relieve Astarte."

"I'll do my best," Deor said. "I'm off to pack before dinner." She turned and headed for the door, letting Rafe say goodbye to her back.

Chapter Twenty

Two days later, Deor and Rafe stood in front of the Tower portal. They'd taken the portal from the Household here, and Deor already felt slightly woozy—like she was trying to stand on an uneven floor.

"You okay?" Rafe said.

"I guess." Deor shook her head to try to clear it. At least the cold chill of the air helped some.

"Good. I know this is tough—the first few times you portal any distance is always awful." He leaned in. "Truth is, it's still awful for me. I hate it. So, we're going to portal from here to the garrison at Yorkshire, and from there, we can portal into Northfalls. We could go straight from our household to theirs, but it takes a lot more effort and magic—we only bother with it on formal visits where we need a pomp and circumstance arrival."

"Let's get this over with, then."

Rafe held out his hand to her. Around them, Jake and Sam snuffled the ground and pawed anxiously. They looked like she felt. She took his hand and followed him through the portal.

The Yorkshire garrison was a blur—one step and they were in a large, mostly empty courtyard under a bleak grey sky. One or two soldiers saluted, and Rafe returned the salute. Holding tight to her hand, he said, "Ready?"

"Yep." Deor swayed slightly.

He laid his hand on the lintel of the brick arch, and they stepped through again. Deor's brain tried to tell her she was falling left and floating to the right and spinning in place at the same time. Slowly her eyes came back into focus, revealing a wide foyer flanked by a double staircase. The walls were painted pale green with gold rococo accents echoing the living greenery that wreathed the balustrades. Overhead a chandelier of mistletoe supported hundreds of white candles.

"Hello, Pookie," Rafe managed before pausing to catch his breath. "May I present Her Majesty, Princess Deor." He gently pulled her toward the man and let go of her hand.

"Hello," she said to the grey man in front of her. Still too dizzy to curtsey, she nodded her head at him. She remembered him from the Adoption —the severely plain husband of Duke Roger.

"It's lovely to meet you, Princess," the man said and held out his hand.

"Please," Deor said, her voice soft, "it's just Deor." She swayed, and the hand in front of her blurred slightly. She reached for it and tumbled forward, the room spinning, into Pookie's arms.

"Sorry," she croaked as he caught her and eased her back up to her feet.

"Not to worry, my dear." He kept a firm arm around her waist—the strength of his arm not matching the short, thin body. He waved over a servant with a tray and took one of the tiny crystal cups for Deor.

She took it and drank the golden cordial. It lit up her insides like sunlight. A thrill of magic power returning after the portal hopping. Crossing an entire Kingdom had taken so much more than a simple step from the first floor to the fourth, as she had done at Eisteddfod. She straightened and stepped slightly away. "Thank you..."

"Pookie," he said. "Everyone calls me that."

"Thank you, Pookie."

Rafe took a cordial as well and swallowed the drink in one gulp. "Miraculous," Rafe said. "One of your brews, Pookie?"

The man smiled modestly. "It's mostly dandelion with a bit of goosefoot grass. The trick is to use both the flower and the root in the right season."

"Well, it's done me good. Thank you. Where is everybody?"

"Roger and the king are out for a ride. Astarte is upstairs with Robbie, and both will be thrilled to see you."

Rafe looked to Deor. "Do you mind if I leave you in Pookie's capable hands?"

"Go," Deor said, waving him away. "See your little sister. I'm sure Pookie and I will be fine."

"Thank you." He turned to Pookie. "Is there anything I should know before I go up to see Robbie?"

"She hasn't been told anything yet," Pookie said. "She doesn't know about the princess. And she doesn't understand why she's here instead of in London. She keeps asking when she can go back to Eisteddfod." He shook his head sadly. "Also, don't bring up goblins—the healers feel she's still in a fragile state and shouldn't be agitated." Tears brimmed in his eyes. "And her voice is weak. The spells that monster put on her throat to silence her... Our poor little girl."

"I'll keep all that in mind. Don't worry. Thank you both for standing by her."

"How could we do any less?" Pookie said. "She's in Astarte's suite—you know where that is."

"I do." Rafe bowed slightly to Deor and headed up the stairs.

"I am sorry for what happened to Robbie," Deor said, not quite looking at Pookie. "It's my fault that poor girl—"

"No," he cut her off. "You didn't do anything wrong." He frowned. "There are people at fault, but you are not one of them." As suddenly as it had appeared, the darkness in his face vanished. He offered her his arm. "Come on. I'll show you your rooms."

"Am I rooming with Finn?" Deor asked, trying to keep her voice neutral.

"If you like," Pookie said. "But I thought you might prefer a suite of your own."

"Yes!" Deor said. "I would. Thank you." She took his arm. Perhaps this would be a nice Solstice after all.

The suite where Robbie and Astarte were staying looked north over Loch Ness. Swathed in blankets and wearing the black and white bantam knit cap of her favorite human football team, Robbie sat in one of the deep bow windows. Her forehead rested against the glass, the pallor in her cheeks making her freckles stand out even more than usual. On the other side of the room, Astarte slept on a couch, her embroidery hoop slipping from her fingers toward the floor.

"Rafe!" Robbie's exclamation came out as a rasp, but she held out her arms to him.

After a long hug, he pulled back. "They told me you were sick. You look as healthy as a horse."

Robbie giggled, sounding like pebbles grinding together. "It's all the greens and oatmeal and other horse food Pookie keeps feeding me. I think he's trying to turn me into a Pooka like him."

Rafe squeezed her hand, smiling at the old joke. He settled himself on the window seat. "So, how do you feel?"

"Like a kitten someone tried to drown. And I sound like an old crow."

"You'll get better. Give it time."

She sighed. "Time. How much time, though? No one is telling me the truth, Rafe. They won't tell me when I'll be better or how long I was out or anything. They just tell me not to worry and bring me more blankets. But I do worry. Something awful happened to me, but I can't remember it, and that's worse than knowing for sure what it was. I have this awful feeling—like it might happen again or that it might happen to someone else and it would be my fault because I didn't warn anyone."

Rafe studied her face for a minute, his mouth closed. No, she wasn't a little girl any more than Deor was, although she'd lived a far more sheltered life. In a sense. In another sense, she'd had less shelter—Deor at least hadn't grown up with the papers saying nasty things about her to fill column space.

"You were attacked a second time by the goblin who attacked you before. He snuck into Deor...er, Professor Smithfield's office and ambushed you, probably so you wouldn't get your memory back and testify against him. You don't have to worry about him coming after you ever again, or anyone else. He's dead."

Robbie slumped in relief. "Did you kill him?"

"No, but I saw his body. How are you doing? I'm not supposed to be telling you things that might agitate you."

"Is Professor Smithfield safe?"

"Safer than the House of Lords. I saw to it personally."

Robbie's smile widened. "So you like her now?"

"I do," he said.

"Do you think she'll be my friend after I graduate? When she's not my teacher anymore? It would be nice to have someone who understands being a changeling and everything."

Internally, Rafe winced, but he said, "She will always be on your side. I've heard her say so, and she's the kind of person to take her word seriously."

Tears sprang up in Robbie's eyes, and she turned to look out the window. Seagulls flew through the snowfall over the loch. "Weather like this always makes me feel like flying," she said.

A familiar pain lodged in Rafe's throat as she said it, and he struggled to smile at her. How many times had he seen her reach out her arms to the sky over the years, stretching for flight with a body that would never fly? She had inherited her mother's way with plants, her wit, and, thank the Creator, her depth of power. But her stature, and her lack of wings, were the legacy of her human father. Robbie would never fly.

"We could go riding tomorrow," Rafe suggested.

Robbie snuggled back down into the blankets the swaddled her. "Maybe. I don't think I'm strong enough to go galloping yet." She smiled up at Rafe and nudged him with her foot. "Don't look so sad. I'm not feeling sorry for myself, I'm feeling better. That's all I meant. Besides I get enough sad looks from my dad. He's frantic that I won't come back to London and see a human doctor."

"What good would that do? Lady Penny knows more about bimorphs like you and the...I mean, Deor than anyone in the world."

"It would make him feel better. That's all. I'll go see him when going through a portal doesn't make me feel nauseous."

She turned to face him. "So, what are you all hiding from me? It must be huge and terrible if even you're in on it. I know it has to do with Professor Smithfield, since you stumble every time you say her name. Spill it. All of it this time." She glared at him. Like the bantam on her cap, she seemed more than fierce enough to kick the truth out of him.

Rafe sighed and smiled down at her. "I suppose it's pointless to say we're all trying to spare you any distress while you recover."

"Totally."

"First, let me say that we're going to be up here for Solstice, which you know, right?"

"I've seen the king." She rolled her eyes. "I know I must be poorly when he's nice to me. Or he actually thinks he might lose Mom. But you're stalling. I can tell."

Rafe drew in a deep breath. There wasn't a gentle way to say it. "Deor, Professor Smithfield, is Finn's daughter. He took a human child bearer the way your mother did, only he didn't handle it quite so well as your mother did and he lost track of both of them for about thirty years, with Michael's connivance. Deor's the heir now, not me. Finn's moved her into the Palace. Astarte was worried for you and nearly tore him to pieces over it, so she packed you up here and came with you. I don't know if she'll ever be willing to share a home with him again."

"Ugh." Robbie blinked in surprise. "That is a lot to swallow. So, I suppose we won't be friends after all." She dug her hands under her blankets. "I should probably transfer to a human university, then." She shoulders slumped even further. "Do you think the king will officially exile me, or will he let me come and go if I keep quiet and out of the way?"

Rafe put his hands on her shoulders, bracing her up. "You listen to me, Roberta Ellington Gemalsdottir. Finn is not going to exile you. We won't let him."

Robbie shook her head. "Don't be stupid. You're going to live too long —*he's* going to live too long—to make me the hill you die on. I can live in the human world. If you and the king fall out, you don't have anywhere else to go, and the Winter Court will suffer. Do you think I haven't been paying attention all these years? I don't go to rallies and student government meetings just to meet boys and make trouble. You and Mother and Roger and Pookie are all wonderful. I know you love me and would keep me safe. But you can't pick a fight with the king over me. It's not worth the trouble it would cause, especially if it makes the Kingdom vulnerable to the Summer Court."

"You're worth it."

"Not politically, I'm not. This is politics, Rafe. It's not personal."

"Everything is personal to Finn. That's why he's so damn touchy."

Robbie sighed. "I know. He may not know me, but I've studied him."

"I told you, Deor is still your friend. She said so to Finn's face, and I heard the power in her words. She won't go back on that promise. As for

Eisteddfod, Deor has stopped teaching there—it's too dangerous. And she would have a fit if you didn't go back. So, put off your self-imposed exile a while longer, alright?"

"If you say so." She chuckled, sounding like she had gravel stuck in her throat. "Are you sad about not being heir?"

"Absolutely not!" He smiled at her. "You knew my heart wasn't in it. She's only been here a few months, and I can already tell she'll be much better than I ever would have been. So, tell me," he steered the conversation in a new direction, "what good gossip have you heard from Roger? There's always something."

They sat in the window seat chatting for another hour until Robbie's head started to bob and her eyelids fall. He scooped her up and put her back in the bed, pulling the covers up. Astarte still slept on the couch, her embroidery fallen to the floor. Rafe took one of Robbie's extra blankets and draped it over Astarte. Then he settled himself in an armchair by the fire and let his own eyes close for a well-deserved nap.

The dinner bell was ringing when he woke up. Astarte stood by his shoulder, shaking him.

"I thought you'd want to eat," she said.

He ran a hand over his face, wiping away the mental cobwebs. "How is she?"

"She's up and ready to eat with the rest of us. The healers said it was alright as long as she didn't over exert herself. It will keep her from being alone up here. Roger sent two footmen up to carry her, but she insisted on walking between them."

"I'm not going to dress for dinner." He stood and stretched.

Astarte laughed. "I haven't dressed for dinner since I got here. You know Roger and Pookie are just old homebodies when they aren't throwing one of their gala parties. Roger comes to breakfast every morning in the most disgraceful slippers you can imagine."

Together they left Robbie's room, turning down the plushly-carpeted hall for the portal. "How are you holding up, Mother? You seem tired."

"Exhausted. I feel like I've aged a hundred years just sitting and watching her, waiting for her to wake up." She turned to face him as they came to the portal, a trompe l'oeil painting of a door standing half open, ready to be walked through into the main hall. "How is the princess doing? Is Finn making life miserable for her?"

"They seem to be getting along. I think he sees himself as being indulgent and giving into her whims. The days is coming, though, when she will cross him and not back off. I'd like to say that's decades away, but I'd say a couple months. At most."

"That's a hard lesson." Astarte took laid a hand on Rafe's arm. "Do you think Robbie is safe from her? Am I?"

"I think Robbie would be safe from Deor even if you walked up and tried to stab her with a knife. The two of you don't have to be enemies, you know. You could become allies—Finn has wronged you both."

She arched her eyebrows at him and took half a step back, considering. "I can't leave Robbie. Not yet. But I'll think about what you say. I never wanted the role of wicked stepmother."

"Good," Rafe said. "She's got a few months' experience in the Winter Court, and politics are about as rocky as they could be without open rebellion. She's going to need all the friends she can get."

Deor trotted down the corridor from her suite in what she hoped was the direction of the dining room. She rounded the corner and saw Rafe, facing Astarte, in front of a large painting. Deor backed up and stepped around the corner, peeking out. They were definitely talking about something serious, though she couldn't hear them. Astarte's hand rested on Rafe's arm, and her brow was creased in a way that projected worry, not anger.

Whatever their conversation, they did not need to be interrupted, and certainly not by her. She waited until they disappeared through the painting and headed down the hall herself. Along the wall, there were elaborate paintings of what she assumed was the area's landscape interspersed with mirrors. Though she'd spent plenty of time in front a mirror already, she couldn't help but pause in front of the last one to check one more time.

Pookie had insisted that this was informal—that any old thing would do for dinner. He'd probably adopt the trend of athleisure wear as formal wear in a heartbeat. But what the master of the house could get away with in his own home was not the same as a new guest, trying to impress. Deor opted for a plain but appropriate dress. She would have loved pants but knew Finn would prefer this, and why rock the boat on the first night?

She stepped through the portal into the parlor where everyone was to meet before dinner. Pookie chatted with Astarte and Rafe in one area, near a bow window, while Finn and Roger stood closer to the fire. Each of them had a drink in their hand, and, sure enough, a servant appeared with a tray and a single glass of red wine. She took it and thanked him.

All alone, sitting in the bow window with a glass of her own, was Robbie. She wore a plain floral dress that, like Deor's grey one, seemed to fall into the category of "suitable but comfortable." She was staring out the window—looking a touch like a forlorn Jane Austen heroine.

Deor walked up. "Hello, Robbie."

The girl spun, snapped out of whatever world she had been daydreaming. When she saw Deor, she opened her mouth to speak, thought better of it, and snapped her mouth closed again. She hauled herself to her feet—slower than someone healthy would—and glanced around for a place to set her half-full glass. She settled on the windowsill.

"Your Majesty," Robbie said, dropping her eyes and clutching her skirt to make a curtsey.

"No," Deor said. It was her turn to flail around for a place to put her drink. Finally, she leaned past Robbie and set her own glass down on the sill. The girl still held the curtsey. Deor caught the girl's arms gently—she felt skinnier than Deor had remembered—and lifted her up. "None of that title nonsense now," Deor said. "Look at me." The girl raised her eyes. "My name is Deor—that's what you call me. Understand?"

"Y-yes." She stared at Deor.

"Good." Deor let go of her arms. "It is so good to see you. I was thrilled to hear that you had woken up and were recovering." She didn't need to turn around to know everyone else was watching. "Robbie," she said. "I am so sorry about what happened to you. I'm sorry I was late to my office, and I'm sorry that you were attacked by people looking for me. If there is anything I can do to help you, please, tell me."

Robbie's gaze darted around the room, and she bit her lip. "Can you help me with my Shakespeare paper so I can catch up with my studies?"

Deor burst out laughing. "I would love to." She flung her arms around Robbie in a hug, then immediately let go and jerked back. "Sorry. I shouldn't have touched you without asking."

Robbie hugged her. "I was afraid you'd been hurt," she said as she let go and stepped away.

"Not much," Deor said. "But whatever hurt I had, I'm fine now."

"Dinner is served." A voice from across the room spoke.

Deor glanced over her shoulder and saw a valet—dressed in Northfalls finery—bowing deeply and holding open the door. Finn beckoned her. Astarte stepped forward and took Finn's arm, drawing him in. Rafe, Roger, and Pookie turned to follow.

"Come on," Robbie said. "We must follow the leaders." She offered Deor her arm.

"In every good thing," Deor said. She linked her arm through Robbie's, subtly positioning her arm so that Robbie could lean on it if she needed the help.

The dining room revealed that this was not a simple family gathering after all—or at least not of only her family. Everyone stood behind his or her seat, waiting for Deor and Robbie, before taking their seats. The table was quite full. Roger sat at one end, with Pookie on his left. To Roger's right was Rodney and then Clarissa—she recognized them from the peerage she had been studying. Rodney was Roger's nephew and heir, and Clarissa his paramour. Finn sat at the far head of the table, Astarte on his left.

Rafe deftly pulled out the empty chair to Finn's right. "Princess?"

Deor nodded, leaving Robbie in the hands of a footman who held a chair for her next to Clarissa. "Thank you," Deor said.

Rafe smiled and took his seat next to her.

Roger cleared his throat. "Since Solstice is traditionally a time of family, and of restoration—for after the Winter Solstice, the land begins its journey back to spring—I thought that this would be a perfect situation to mend fences. Please, be seated and let us enjoy the feast!" He bowed.

Finn looked a bit annoyed—that dig at reconciliation seemed to have stung, as he seemed to keep his gaze off his wife. Everyone took their seats as the first course was served.

Rafe engaged in conversation with Finn over things she had no idea about—descriptions of troop movements or hunting locations. Across the table, Astarte talked quietly with Robbie.

She took the tiniest possible sip of the wine. No telling how many different glasses there would be with each course. A small pang hit Deor's heart—Solstice was a couple days before Christmas, but there was no way she could go home. Certainly Finn would freak out at the thought, and it would be on Rafe and other soldiers to get her there and back safely—effectively ruining their holidays, too.

"Rafe," she said quietly, once Finn and Astarte had fallen into vaguely polite conversation, "could I mirror the human world?"

"What?" He set down his knife and fork. "If a person there has a functioning mirror."

"Can I send my family a functioning mirror?"

"Probably." He dabbed his face with his napkin. "We have portable secure mirrors at the Tower. We have a few soldiers who regularly go into the human world. One of them could send it. Once we get back to the Palace, we'll check. Is there a specific time you'd like it by?"

"The twenty-fifth, if possible."

Rafe drew a breath between his teeth. "That's cutting it close. I'll mirror the Tower tonight and it get started."

With any luck she'd get to talk to her grandmother on Christmas. The only problem was, what would she say?

Chapter Twenty-One

❦

Well and truly bundled in a heavy coat, boots, scarf, and gloves, Deor trotted down the stairs to find Rafe waiting for her in the foyer.

"Good morning," he smiled. "You look ready for a winter storm. You might be a bit over-protected in all of that."

"Nope," Deor said, shaking her head. "And good morning to you, too. Where is everyone else? Am I late?" She frowned. She hated the thought of being rude to her hosts.

"No," Rafe said. "Everyone else has already gone down to the boat, but it isn't set to sail for another half an hour or more." He offered her his arm. "Shall we?"

They followed a winding path down from the main doors. The bushes lining the trail were bare and the grass beneath their feet brown. The sky above, though, was bright blue and full of light—not a cloud to be seen. Stretching out in front of them, Loch Ness sparkled in the sun, small ripples flashing in the near-still waters.

"Lovely day to be out," Rafe said. "He'd be taking the boat out no matter what—this is a Solstice tradition, you know. He also takes it out at his annual Season's Closing party in late January."

He led her up a wide, railed plank onto the deck.

"Excellent timing!" Roger came out of the cabin with a jolly smile.

"We're about to be off." He was dressed in something that looked a bit like a naval uniform, but far more elaborate. He wore a captain's hat, too. "Shall we?" He led them to the prow of the boat where the others were already set. Even Robbie was out on deck, though she stood between her mother and Pookie, more than arm's reach from Finn.

Deor joined Robbie. "Ready for this?"

Robbie nodded. "I've been going out with Roger for years. I love this part of Solstice. Sometimes, if the weather was bad, it would just be Roger and me. He hasn't ever missed a trip."

The ship lurched slightly as pulled away from the dock.

"Are you keeping the *Admiralty* in ship shape, Roger?" Finn asked.

Roger laughed as though it were a joke.

"I'm not kidding," Finn said, face stern. "We might have need of your fleet if certain allies prove disloyal."

"I am prepared, sire," Roger said, his bow stiff.

Rafe offered Deor his arm. "My lady, shall we return to the prow and watch the loch from there?" Astarte, Pookie, and Robbie had already wandered away from the conversation together.

Deor nodded and took Rafe's arm. "Excuse us," she said with a nod to Finn. "Thank you," she whispered when they had moved out of earshot.

"Finn is referring to Geoff, right? I know he was a part of the plot," Deor said. "Why isn't he being arrested right now?"

"Politics." Rafe let her to a place at the bow that allowed them to enjoy the view while keeping far enough from Finn that the sounds of the waves would hide their conversation. "Finn and Gregory have been friends since they were youths."

"I remember the portrait in the gallery—the young goblin looked up to something." Deor wrapped her hand around the top of the rail and leaned into the wind. The sting of it on her face made her smile. The crisp air was filled with the light scent of the water and the sharp snap of recent snowfalls. The sun on her face gave a small hint of warmth, too.

Rafe snorted. "They were thick as thieves back then, no doubt about it. Gregory's father gave Finn advice when he was a young king—so far as I know it was good advice, except for the part that led to the formal treaty between the two nations. Finn swore to support the goblin nation and come to their aid if necessary, in any capacity. Gregory promised the same."

"Will he keep his promise?" Deor already knew the answer, regardless of what kind of spin Rafe put on it. The mere fact that Geoff had been involved in a plot that could have—would have—killed the king suggested that goblin promises meant little. "He had to know that Geoff was involved in the plot."

"I'm certain he knew. He's got Geoff on a short leash, though you wouldn't know it to look at his behavior. Geoff doesn't do anything without his daddy's permission."

"That sounds like fun."

Deor leaned on the railing and stared out at the water. Six months ago, she hadn't even made the decision to come to the Winter Court. Now here she was on a duke's yacht for a winter pleasure cruise on Loch Ness. Six months ago, she'd barely been a for-real, signed-and-sealed PhD. Now she was a princess. She missed home—she'd be in Bakersfield for the holiday now, if she had followed her plans to be a professor. he would also probably be dead.

"Poor little rich girl me," she whispered to herself.

"What?" Rafe asked, leaning in to hear her.

She shook her head. "Nothing. Just thinking about home, that's all."

"The Palace home or human world home?" He shifted position, turning his back to the sea and leaning on the railing.

"The Palace isn't home to me," she said, a touch more petulance in her voice than she liked. "I mean, it's lovely and all, but it's not..."

"Where family is? Childhood memories? That sort of thing." He nodded. "I feel that way about Wellhall. Someday it will be all mine. I literally could not find my way around the place without a map."

"Why are your parents giving you Wellhall if they hate you?" Deor scowled. "Sorry, that was rude."

"It's fine," he said. "Good question. Most of the time families pass on the major title to oldest child, though that's not always the case. Younger children, if they exist, get the lower-titled parent's lands and seat, and so on. Again, it depends. Some families do things differently for whatever reason. If there is no will, it works this way. But not for the Farringdons. A million years ago, back when we were actually part of the Aethelwing family, the oldest child wasn't made heir. She took what she thought of as her consolation prize, the Duchy of Wellhall, and disowned her family. She also magically bound Wellhall to the first child—it will always fall to the first living child, no matter what. I'm sure my mother loathes the irony of it now."

"That's...kind of petty."

"What is the luxury of nobility if not the means to be petty?" He shrugged. "But yes. I don't know what I'm going to do with it. There's a part of me that loves it—even as foreign as I am—I can feel it in my bones. But I'm here. I'm Sword. Is that best for Wellhall? It's not some small plot of land. It's strategically important—another of a few likely places for an invasion—and holds almost as many people as Caer Eisteddfod."

"What about your brother? What will happen to him?"

"Victor? Oh, don't worry too much about him." Rafe grinned. "My father was no slouch. He came into the marriage with a much smaller, but still impressive, county. That, and all the land and wealth that goes with it, will go to Victor. It's not Wellhall, but it's not a country house either."

Deor nodded. She hadn't even considered property. The Aethelwings must have property all over the nation—and it would be her responsibility. Ugh. She'd been proud of herself when she managed her own little finances—an apartment, utilities, a Netflix account. "There's someone who runs all this stuff for Finn, right?"

"The exchequer. Yes."

"Oh, thank God." Deor scanned the horizon as something caught her eye. A burst of wind, or maybe a fish surfacing. "Are there fish in the loch?"

"Sure." Rafe turned to face the ocean too.

"What the hell is that?" Deor pointed. Out of the lake rose a grey-green hill, about ten feet across. Water poured off it. Slowly, another mound appeared, much smaller, a few feet away. The smaller one climbed toward the sky, supported by a grey-green column as thick as a young tree trunk.

"Oh good. I was get tired of waiting for her to show."

"Her?" Deor squinted. It wasn't some sunken island emerging. No, this was a creature—a leviathan, if she were to be dramatic about it. As it shook its massive head, spraying water like a wet dog, Deor pushed off the railing and stepped back. "Is that the Loch Ness Monster?"

"Oh," Roger trilled behind her. "That's a horrid title the humans gave Nessie centuries ago." He joined Deor at the railing, shooing Rafe over a bit. "She's not a monster—she's a sweet little pet." Roger let out a call, something between a whistle and a holler, that rolled out across the water, loud enough to make Deor wince. Air faeries.

Nessie returned the call and glided toward the boat, faster than any duck on the water could manage. Smooth and gentle, she barely rippled the waves. She came right up to the railing and lowered her head for Roger.

Up close, Nessie was the size of a whale with the long-necked body of a dragon. Her color came from rows upon rows of tight, fist-sized scales that shifted color in the light from green to blue to grey and back again. She had the diamond shaped head of a dragon, too, with a scraggly grey beard to match. She didn't have any wings, only massive flippers. Her eyes didn't show the same cunning that dragons were supposed to have. They were large and a dull green, and slightly watery, making her seem more like a friendly-but-dumb dog than scourge of man.

Nessie knocked her enormous head into Roger's shoulder like a cat wanting cuddles.

Roger complied, rubbing her neck. "That's my beautiful girl," he cooed. "Fish!" he called out over his shoulder. A servant brought a tray laden with stinky fish and Roger took one. "Does my sweetie want a fish?" He held it up.

She sniffed it a bit, and then opened her mouth. Roger threw the fish into the air, and Nessie snatched it, tossing her head back and swallowing it with minimal chewing.

"Very nice, Roger," Finn said. He stood a fair distance back from the railing, Astarte and Robbie even farther behind. Rodney and Clarissa were nowhere to be seen—they'd probably been to this show so many times they could quote it from memory. Pookie, too, kept his distance. Only Rafe remained with Deor and Roger.

"Is she dangerous?" Deor asked as Roger tossed her another fish.

"Do you mean will she hurt you? No. In her younger days she might toss a boat or two, but never killed anyone. She was just playful. Her pups, now, are the ones that cause mischief. This old girl is pretty much retired in that department." Roger was rubbing Nessie's neck again, and the dragon's eyes were half closed. If she could have, Deor was sure, she would have purred.

"Can I give her a fish?" she asked.

Roger stepped back, delighted surprise on his face. "Would you really like to?" He took one and handed it over. "Make sure you throw it far enough out for her—she'll lunge at the boat and knock it around if she can't catch it."

"Right." Deor took the fish and waved it. Nessie caught the scent and turned her eyes toward Deor. "Here you go, girl." Deor tossed the fish, with more force than she needed, into the air. Nessie lunged, driving her body out of the water to reach the sailing snack. When she dropped again, waves rocked the boat. "Oops, sorry," Deor said.

"No, that's good for her—she needs to stretch a little. Go on."

Deor threw more fish until the tray was empty. "That's all, girl."

Nessie leaned to Roger again, a rumbling noise in her belly. Turns out she could purr.

"That's my happy girl." He scratched under her chin. "Would you like to pet her?"

"Yes!" Deor clapped her hands like a little girl.

Behind her, Finn laughed. "Careful," he called.

"She's got some thick scales, so you've got to really give it some pressure," Roger said.

Deor pulled off her gloves and shoved them in her coat pocket. She concentrated and sharpened the tips of her nails before reaching up and scratching the beast under the chin.

Nessie leaned in more and gave a snort of pleasure.

"Good girl!" Deor stepped closer.

"Princess..." Roger cautioned. He took hold of her arm to pull her away, but it was too late.

Nessie drew a deep breath and chuffed, sending a glob of clear mucus right into Deor's chest, splattering some of it across her face and into her hair.

"Ah," a small squeak was all Deor could manage as she stared down at the mess.

"Princess!" Roger flailed toward her, a handkerchief waving. "She does that when's she happy." He dabbed frantically at her. "She was being friendly. She—"

Deor held up a hand and Roger jerked back. "That hankie is not going to do the job." She looked at Roger and laughed. After a moment, he joined in, waving his hankie and dabbing at his eyes.

"The look on your face," he said, between gasps of laughed.

Behind them, the rest of the folks laughed too. She caught Finn's eye, and he grinned at her.

"That's happened to me before," Robbie said, covering her mouth as she giggled.

"Go on, Nessie." Roger gave her a friendly shove and waved her away. She slipped away from the boat, sending rocking waves in her wake, before diving. A small splash of water as she disappeared, and she was gone. Moments later, she emerged several yards from the boat and gave a long hoot. Roger made some call in return, and she vanished once again under the lake.

"I think this coat is done for." Deor tugged her scarf free. "And the scarf." She held it out at arm's length and dropped it. A servant swooped in and caught it before it could land. "Sorry," she muttered to him. She'd planned on dropping the stuff in a pile and then gathering it to take back to the Palace herself once they'd docked, forgetting there would be servants for that. She unbuttoned her coat, slipped it off her shoulders, and handed it off.

"You look lovely," Finn said.

She glanced down. Wham! and Thorsen had done a good job. She wore black leather pants lined with something—silk maybe—that kept her warm, a black turtleneck under a black sweater and warm, but stylish, winter boots. Conservative, except for the fact that she wore pants, and the Aethelwing house color—black—a lucky coincidence. "Thank you."

Though she had on multiple layers, they were nothing in the face of the wind coming off the Loch as they sailed. She rubbed her hands up and down her arms.

"Here, Princess." Rafe stepped toward her and in one smooth movement, he had taken off his cloak and wrapped it around Deor's shoulders. On Rafe, the cloak—a deep blue—had fallen below his knee. On Deor, it pooled around her feet like she was a child playing dress-up.

"This certainly will keep me covered," Deor smiled at Rafe, catching his eye.

His gesture was a friendly one—brotherly care, even. Why then did Deor feel like the school quarterback had given her his letterman's jacket? She blushed. And why did she suddenly wish the head cheerleader would fall off the top of the pyramid?

She bit her lip, and with great effort, broke their gaze.

Chapter Twenty-Two

The pounding sounds started in her dream. Deor was working on a syllabus for a class that started later that day—that she had no idea she was teaching—and now someone was pounding on the door. When she turned to open it, there was no one there, but the pounding kept right on going. Finally, she blinked open her eyes.

The room was dark, and she sat up in bed, peering around.

"Come on!" a voice called from the hall.

She didn't recognize where she was—college dorm? Nope. Wait, grad school apartment, maybe? Nope—too big. Northfalls! She was at Northfalls, for Solstice. Today was Solstice.

"Light," she muttered, and the lamp on the side table blazed. The clock on the mantle above a dwindling fire in the fireplace said seven o'clock. No light peeked in from around the heavy curtains on the windows—designed to keep out the cold more than the light.

Why was someone pounding?

She flung her covers aside, stood, and grabbed her robe.

She yanked open the door. "What?"

"Happy Solstice!" Finn and Rafe both said in unison. "It's getting late! Why aren't you downstairs yet?" Rafe asked.

"Are you feeling ill?" Finn asked, his face exchanging mirth for concern.

"No, no." Deor shook her head. "I'm fine. I was sleeping." Like a normal adult.

Rafe laughed. "You can't sleep on Solstice morning!"

"Clearly." She yawned. "I'll put on clothes and come...where?"

"We're in the parlor downstairs," Finn said. He grabbed her hand. "Don't worry about clothes. We're all in our pajamas." He tugged her hand.

Deor relented and smiled. How could she not in the face of such joy? "Okay." She stepped out of the room and closed the door. "Lead on!"

In the parlor, Roger sat in a chair next to a decorated living tree. Magic lights like lit candles flickered on each bow. Crystal spheres of different colors sparked in the light. Ribbon in Roger's tartan had been strung around the tree.

"It's beautiful," Deor said.

"Thank you," Roger said. "It's all Pookie."

The grey man smiled from his position crouched in the center of the room. The coffee table that had been there before was gone, and the couches and chairs had been pushed back. In the center was a huge basin filled with logs crackling with a warm fire.

"What's this?" Deor approached.

On one couch, Robbie sat, legs tucked up under her, leaning against her mother. Astarte's long hair was free down her back. She had one arm secured around her daughter and a happy, if cautious, smile on her lips.

"Good morning, Lady Astarte, Robbie." Deor smiled at them.

"Good morning, Princess." Astarte smiled back, a sense of relief crossing her face.

Finn took a seat in a chair next to Astarte's couch.

"Come on." Rafe took her hand and led her toward another couch. "It's bad luck to eat Solstice breakfast before everyone has gotten their first present," Rafe said. "We already opened ours."

Pookie handed Deor a box wrapped in an elaborately painted and folded leaf. "From your father."

She tore off the paper to find a leather-bound book inside—but this time it was no book of manners. The cover read *Sir Gawayne's Marriage and Other Tales of Arthour's Court.*

Deor gasped. "Oh, my goodness! How did you think of this?"

"I spoke to Ama about what you might like, and she said this was what you study," Finn said. "You do like it? It's a very old-fashioned book. Are you sure you wouldn't prefer something a bit more contemporary?"

"It's perfect!" She threw one arm around his shoulder for a quick hug and just as quickly pulled away. "Thank you."

Deor stared at the book as tears welled in her eyes. "I'm sorry," she said to the room. "I don't have any presents—I didn't even think about Solstice gifts, I should have, but—"

"No," Finn said, standing up and taking her in his arms for a hug. He let go and put his hands lightly on her shoulders. "Your being here is present enough."

A few tears escaped, and Deor wiped at them with her sleeve. "I'm still sorry," she said. "But thank you. I promise I'll do better next year."

"Let's eat!" Rafe said, taking her hand and pulling her away from Finn. "It's the best part of Solstice. Today we make our own breakfast. Come on."

Laid out on trays around the fire were three types of sausage, slices of bread and cheese, a bowl of raw eggs, and piles of fruit from the greenhouses. Even the tea was unmade—just a stone jug of water waiting beside a tin of loose tea leaves. Rafe was already threading sausages onto a three-pronged skewer while Jake and Sam watched closely, drooling.

Soon they were working on the meal, Deor cutting fruit while Rafe crouched in front of the fire and toasted things. A swing arm held the jug of water over the coals until it boiled, and Deor tossed in a generous handful of tea.

"You really like doing this, don't you?" Deor said, laughing a little.

"My favorite part of the day," Rafe said, carefully laying cheese onto a slice of bread and holding it over the fire. "It's like a hunting trip in your own house. No formality, no servants bustling in and out, no schedule to keep. We just cook and eat at our own pace as much as we like."

Roger and Pookie joined them, and they sat on the floor cooking.

"Robbie?" Deor called to the girl. Neither she nor her mother had gotten up from the couch. "Why don't you come and help?" She patted the empty space between her and Rafe.

Robbie glanced at her mother, who nodded. "Are you sure?" she asked.

"Absolutely." She glanced at Rafe. "He says this is the best part—surely you can't miss out on that?" She waved a piece of fruit stuck to the tip of her knife at her. "Doesn't this look like fun?"

After a moment, Robbie laughed and hopped off the couch. She went the long way around the room—taking care not to come within arm's reach of Finn, who did not look at her. She settled in next to Deor. "What can I do?"

"Here." Deor handed her another tray with more fruit and a knife. "Help me with this." She bumped Robbie with her shoulder and smiled at her as she went back to her cutting. Once done with the fruit, Deor judged the tea to be about right and poured each of them cups. "Cream? Sugar?"

Rafe shook his head at both. "None, thanks."

Finn took his with lemon.

Robbie poured a cup for her mother and took it to her, and Pookie prepared tea for Roger and himself.

Once all the food was ready, each took a wooden plate—another quaint detail of the event—and sat. Deor, Rafe, and Robbie remained around the fire, while the grown-ups, as Deor thought of them, retreated to couches.

"This reminds me of Saturday mornings with my grandmother. No need to get dressed until we felt like leaving the house. Sometimes Grammy would fall asleep in her recliner with the crossword on her lap while I lay on the couch and watched cartoons."

"Exactly." Rafe slid a couple perfectly browned sausages onto a plate and handed it to her to share with Robbie, gave himself another, and split the last one between his slavering dogs. "What's a cartoon?"

"It's a moving picture story. Usually they're funny."

"Oh, movies. Donovan told me about those once. I thought you had to go to a special theater to see those."

"No," Deor said. "You can watch them at home, too." A lecture on various human entertainment technology could wait. Rafe would probably embrace binge-watching. He threw himself wholeheartedly into everything else she'd seen him do. That trait was much more appealing now that it wasn't directed at proving she was some kind of criminal.

They ate sausage and toasted cheese at a leisurely pace, comparing notes on childhood traditions.

Finn sat next to Astarte on the couch, as close as he could get without touching her, glancing at her every few seconds, as he twisted his tea cup back and forth in his hands between sips. He nodded at whatever Pookie was saying, but his gaze was off—far away. Deor almost felt sorry for him, not being able to touch his beloved. Almost.

"I'm sorry," Finn blurted out, loud enough to startle himself.

"What?" Pookie said, wide eyed.

Finn caught Astarte's hand in his. She froze in place, a blank look on her face. She did not pull her hand back, but did not lean toward him, either. She risked a glance at her daughter.

"I'm so sorry, Astarte," Finn continued. "For the affair, for the way I treated you and your daughter, for everything. And I'm sorry it took me so long to see how badly I was behaving." He kissed her hand. "Please tell me that there's still a chance for me. For us."

Astarte remained still and silent for several moments. "Thank you, Finn." She laid her free hand on his cheek and glanced at the rest of the room. "Of course there is a chance for us." She smiled softly at him.

"Thank you." He turned his face and kissed the palm of her hand. "I wanted to do this in front of everyone so you know I'm serious—"

"I know," Astarte said and dropped her hand to her lap. She leaned forward and kissed him on his lips—a small peck. "I understand."

"Good," he said. He beamed at her and shifted his gaze, and his smile, to the whole of the room, catching the eyes of each one of them in turn, even pausing on Robbie. "See! Solstice is a time for reconciliation." His eyes fell on Rafe who shifted his body back from the fire, but said nothing.

More moments of silence passed.

"Happy Solstice!" Roger said, breaking the silence. He waved his empty plate toward Rafe. "I could use another sausage, dear boy."

Rafe's shoulders dropped in relief. "Right away, Roger." He busied himself preparing more sausages, and the conversations in the room began again.

"That was quite the performance," Robbie said softly—Deor almost didn't catch it.

"Indeed, it was," Deor said. "Has he done this before?"

"What?" Rafe said, twirling the sausages over the fire. "Publicly apologize so that you'll look like you're the bad guy if you don't accept it? Never."

Deor looked up from the fire and caught Finn staring at them. She forced a happy smile and raised her cup of tea at him. He smiled back. He turned back to his conversation, sliding his arm around Astarte and pulling her back toward him. She did not turn to look at him, but she didn't resist his touch either.

Next to Deor, Robbie cursed under her breath.

Chapter Twenty-Three

The days since Solstice had passed with silly games and an increasing tension as everyone pretended that everything was fine. Deor chafed under the faux cheer. Roger and Pookie were charming and friendly as ever, and Finn walked around like all was right with the world—and it might have been, for him. Everyone behaving that way, at least. Robbie was never more than a few feet from her mother or Rafe, and always as far as possible from Finn. Rafe avoided the king whenever possible, which wasn't often, since Solstice was about family togetherness. At least that was what the king said.

Christmas morning came and went without comment from anyone—not even Robbie. Though it was possible that no one knew that human holiday or how important it was to American culture.

Deor had kept to herself, in her room, reading her new book and staring at the snowy landscape. By late afternoon, though, messages from the king had arrived—she would have to make an appearance at dinner or risk offending the hosts. Neither Roger nor Pookie would be offended at her absence, but Finn would be on their behalf.

A knock came at her door and she sighed.

"Come in?"

Rafe stepped in and closed the door. He carried a tablet-sized mirror with him. She had left hers behind at the Palace. "I got a message," he smiled at her. "The mirror made it safely to your grandmother. It was hand delivered minutes ago."

"You had it hand delivered? By faeries?"

"Yes, and no. Not by faeries. Once we got it to the human world, I have connections there and people who move freely."

Deor frowned. "What kind of connections?" Had he put her family in danger? She certainly did not need a bunch of faeries knowing where her human family lived.

"Mostly vampires," he said. "Donovan's aunt, who is also his mother-in-law, lives in northern California. They were going to be with her for Christmas—that's the holiday, right? Christmas?"

"Yes," Deor said, filing the "aunt and mother-in-law" thing away for later.

"So they had a minion drop it off."

"Oh, good." Not good. A faerie knowing where her family lived had struck her as terrible, but a vampire? Even worse. At least faeries were allergic to iron, something that her grandmother, with her fondness for wrought iron furniture and cast-iron skillets, had for days. "That's not dangerous, is it? For my family?"

"No," Rafe said. "We've been allies with the vampires for centuries. Chloe—Donovan's wife—is an American, so it made sense to contact them. You'll meet her at some point, I'm sure."

"Right." The tall woman that Donovan had pointed out at the Adoption. "I'm looking forward to it."

"Good." Rafe sat on the couch and patted the seat for her to join him. She did. "Here," he handed her the mirror. "The mirror we sent is secure and will only react to calls from other secure Winter Court mirrors, like the ones you have, and this one. Otherwise, it is an ordinary mirror. It can also call secure mirrors, but for now, you can do the calling. Say 'California' and it should connect, if they answer."

"Okay." She looked at the mirror in her hands and up at Rafe.

"Do you need anything else? Aren't you going to call? I thought you wanted it by today."

"I did—I do. It is just that, I haven't told my family anything. I haven't contacted them at all. I think their first sight of me should not be with some strange, but handsome, blue man on a couch." She stood. "I think I'll sit in front of the fireplace. We had one at the flat, and it could be anywhere."

"Right." Rafe stood. "Sorry. Is there anything I can do to help?"

"No," Deor said. "I'm not going to tell them the truth—not yet."

"Is it wise to lie?" Rafe's tone suggested that the answer was no.

"Probably not," Deor said. "But that's what I'm going to do. The less they know, the safer they are. I don't want them to worry. I'll give them a broad sequence of events that is as close to true as possible, but edit it."

"So, no king for a father; no almost killed? That sort of thing."

Yep." Deor settled in front of the fire. "I'll see you at dinner? Will you tell Finn that I'll be there, and not to come storming in while I'm talking to my family?"

Rafe nodded. He left, closing the door quietly behind him.

Deor adjust the mirror on its stand on the coffee table so that she would be easily seen and framed. She drummed her fingers on her knee and her silver-tipped nails pricked through her pjs. She shook out her fingers to release the tension. Her wings, carefully held back under one of her few sweaters without vents, quivered and twitched.

Either Bill and her grandmother answered the mirror or they didn't. She stared at her own reflection and tried not to think of all the things that could go wrong—both with the mirror and the conversation. Outside, the sky was already dark, but in the human world, assuming time even worked the same way between Fae and the human world, it was only ten a.m. in Bakersfield.

The mirror went black. Her heart raced, and she clutched her hands together.

Her grandmother's face appeared, squinting suspiciously at the mirror with Bill's equally worried face over her shoulder.

"Bill, I told you to step back," Deor's grandmother snapped. "No telling what this thing will do."

"The delivery guy said this was sent directly from her."

Deor waved frantically at the mirror. "Can you see me?"

Both humans started.

"Deor!" Bill shouted.

Her grandmother drew in a sharp breath, and her eyes brimmed with tears. "It's really you! How are you? Where are you?"

"How do these things work?" Bill shouted over her shoulder. Between the two of them, Deor could just make out that they were in her grandmother's dining room, seated at the table with the china hutch behind them.

"Merry Christmas!" Deor said. Her own eyes pricked suspiciously. "How are you all doing?" Both were still in their night clothes. That made her heart ache and ease at the same time. At least they were together, taking care of each other.

"Never mind us. Tell us about you!" her grandmother said. "It's been months with not a peep out of you. You look healthier. Are you?" Worry creased her forehead.

"I'm going to be fine. I found my father, and I found a good heal— doctor. She says I'm all healed up. All the color came back, and I'm not sick anymore."

"Where is your father?" her grandmother demanded. "I'd like a word or two with him."

"He's not home right now. I've been staying with him."

The other two gasped.

"Does that mean you're not coming back? Are you stuck there?" Bill said. "If you need help, blink fast."

Deor's nose stung and her eyes blinked extra fast, trying to stop the tears from falling. "I'm not signaling for help, Bill. I told you, I'm fine. I'm not stuck — I'm just taking my career in a new direction. Getting to know my faerie roots for a while. Besides," she swiped a hand over her eyes, "it's not like I have a job waiting for me back in the human world. But now we can talk whenever we want. The mirror should stand up to the human world for a good long time. Now that I know it works, I'll send you one too, Bill. I'll replace them when the magic starts to wear out."

Her grandmother frowned. "How did you pay for something like this? Magic can't come cheap."

No. It never did.

"My father is rich, and he owes me," she said, with a flippant shrug. "Don't worry about it. It's the least he… I can do. It was nothing, really. Everyone has a mirror around here. It's just a smartphone with magic."

"So tell me about your friends," her grandmother said. "Who are they?"

"What are they?" Bill said. "And how can you tell?"

"Bill!" Both she and her grandmother said at once.

"Most of my friends are faeries," Deor said, "though one is a changeling like me. I've met some dwarves, pixies, and goblins too. And a pooka. And," she confessed, "a vampire. They're all just people. You get used to it."

"I'm sure the population is fascinating. But let's not change the subject. I want to hear everything from the beginning." Her grandmother nodded.

Deor leaned back against the fireplace screen, the dimming embers warm at her back.

"Go on now."

Deor took a deep breath and launched into a carefully planned, one might even say creatively edited, version of events since she had left California. She included Penny, Robbie, the funnier doings of her students, but left out any mention of royalty and the changes it was making in her life and attempted murders. Some things didn't need to be discussed at Christmas.

Dressed for dinner, Deor made her way to the dining room. She was the last one there, but no one seemed to think she was late, so that was fine.

"And what have you been doing all day?" Finn asked. He smiled, but his smile was brittle—like it was on the edge of breaking.

"Resting," Deor said. "That's what the holidays are for, right? At least where I come from."

Finn crossed the room and hugged her. "Are you feeling tired? You look distressed."

Deor shrugged. "I talked to my human family today." She drew in a deep breath, barely keeping the tears brimming in her eyes from spilling over. "I miss them, that's all."

Finn nodded. "I understand. They're family, too." He hugged her again. "Do you want me to have them brought here?"

Images of a ninja-dressed band of faeries breaking down her grandmother's door at three in the morning shot through her mind. "Bring them here?"

"Yes," Finn said. "I could arrange passage. They could come in through London the way you did, if you like. They are family. If you want them near you, then so do I."

"Really?" Her grandmother could use some travel, and Bill—still looking ill—could use a break. They could stay in the Palace, too, and they would be safe. Behind Finn, Astarte had her arm around Robbie, who stared at Deor with wide, frightened eyes. When she caught Deor's gaze, she shook her head, just slightly, as if to say no.

"I will start making arrangements when I return after the new year!"

Deor stared at Finn for a moment. "No-o-o. I think they would have a hard time here. Traveling would be too much for my grandmother, and Bill hasn't been well. They might react badly to the Winter Court."

"If you say so," Finn said, a dubious frown on his face. "I would love to meet your family, though, so keep the option in mind." He turned from her and offered Astarte his arm to lead her into the dining room.

"Wise choice," Rafe said, offering her his arm.

She did not ask why. She didn't need to. There was no way she could escape the Winter Court—Finn would hunt her to the ends of the Earth. What control over her would he have if Bill and her grandmother were trapped in the Palace, too? No. Sometimes it was better to take the risk by yourself. Even if her grandmother and Bill would be furious that they had the opportunity to join her, and she wouldn't let them.

"I'm leaving tomorrow," Rafe said, pausing in the doorway of the dining room. "The Palace guard needs to get going again, before the king returns."

"Oh." Deor shuddered at the thought of being alone here. "Do you have to go?"

"No," Rafe said. "But I'm tired of performing happy family." He dropped her arm and turned to her. "Aren't you?"

"Yes." She hated him a little for being able to go, but she understood why. She'd bolt when she had the chance, too.

"Come with me, then." He rested his hand on the small of her back and guided her into the room, to her seat. He pulled out her chair. "You likely want to continue your study of the court so that you will be comfortable and ready for the coming year?"

"God, yes!" Deor wanted to hug him. Instead, she nodded her head in thanks as she took her seat. "I'll be ready at six a.m."

He laughed as he slid her chair in. "We'll leave after breakfast."

Chapter Twenty-Four

The next evening, lounging in a chair before the fire, Rafe flexed the fingers of his sword hand, rolling a ball of ice back and forth between his fingers—an old swordsman's drill to keep the fingers limber. Across the room, as close to the fire as she could get without actually sitting in it, Deor lay on a couch reading a book and making notes on her tablet.

He watched her chew on the end of her stylus, the changing moods of her face telling him how she felt about what she was reading. Mild annoyance. Concentration. A comprehending nod of the head. Full eye roll. A look of sudden interest and she made a note on her tablet. She turned the page and went back to chewing on her stylus.

He realized he had been staring at her for ten straight minutes. Enough of this nonsense. His paramour would be back from her Solstice trip with friends soon enough. Hurling himself out of the chair, he called across to Deor. "I'm bored. How about you?"

Deor tossed the book down. "I think I've had all the degrees of politeness I can take for the day."

"Good. Let's get outside and do something fun."

"Define fun," Deor said, with a laugh. "Because I am not going out there to let you pelt me with snowballs."

Rafe thought for a moment. Enough snow had fallen already that the roads were coated and slick, with city maintenance crews keeping the snow packed and glassy smooth.

"How about a sleigh ride?" he said. "I'll show you the Solstice decorations, and you can bundle up as much as you like." He crossed the room and offered her his hand.

"Sold!" she said. As her hand touched his, a jolt of magic shot between them. For a split second, it was the Adoption all over again, and darkness surrounded him. There was only the two of them, joined by the silver blades of light.

Heat glowed between their clasped palms. Deor's mouth formed a round "o" of surprise, her wide, dark eyes staring up into his, their silver light a deeper shock than any jolt of stray magic between them. They both held still, him staring down at her, her face upturned toward him.

"Well," Deor said. "That was a surprise." She pushed herself off the couch. "I'll go get my coat."

"Yes," Rafe said, rubbing his hand down the fabric of his pants. "You do that. I'll call for the sleigh."

By the time they made it downstairs, the stable-hands had hitched a pair of grey horses to a red and gold painted two-seater sleigh made from half of a large seed pod with a curling tip. A fragile looking footman's platform extended from the back.

"That's adorable," Deor said. "It looks like a giant's slipper. But won't we—and by we, I mean me—freeze to death in that thing?"

Rafe resisted laughing at her as she stood in the sunny, snow-covered yard, her head wrapped in a round fur hat and the sleeves of a sweater poking out from her long coat's cuffs.

"Never fear," he said. "I'll put up a shield spell, and it will keep off the wind. Lieutenant Bolton, would you light Her Majesty's footwarmer for her?" Jake and Sam made a formidable team, but if he was taking the princess out in such an open vehicle, it didn't pay to have no guards at all.

"Certainly, sir." Bolton reached into the hidden compartment under the seat and pulled out a box about the size of a loaf of bread. The box began to glow from within. "There you go, Your Majesty. This should keep you warm."

As Rafe handed Deor into the sleigh, Bolton tucked the glowing box behind her feet and spread the sleigh's fur-lined traveling cape over her lap to hold in the heat. Rafe hopped onto the footman's platform and sat down next to Deor. She was small beside him, smaller than Robbie. He could have easily tucked her into the crook of his arm.

"What about the dogs?" Deor said. Jake and Sam sat patiently beside the sleigh, tongues lolling.

"Don't worry. They'll keep up." Rafe snapped the reins.

Deor held onto her hat and laughed as they sped down the long drive in front of the Palace toward the main gate. The bells on the horses' harnesses chimed in time to their hoofbeats, and the dogs raced along beside.

"I learned to drive on this sleigh," Rafe said. "Finn used to let me take it out when I was just getting my learner's permit."

"And how many snow drifts did you crash into before you learned to take a corner?" she said.

"More than I care to admit. Want to give it a try?" He offered Deor the reins, but she shook her head.

"I'm fine, thanks," she said, snuggling further under the fur robe. Her smile shone like the ice that glittered on the tree branches. "You were right. This is quite cozy. Speaking of which..." She turned around. "How are you doing back there, Bolton? I hope you're not freezing to death."

"Not at all, Your Majesty," Bolton called back. "You don't know cold until you've had to hunt down a lambing ewe in the middle of the night in a January rain."

Deor shuddered. "I'll take your word for it." She turned back to Rafe. "So, where are we going?"

"I thought we'd take a few turns around the Ring in the park. We're in Georges Street now. There's the Goblin Embassy." He pointed across the piazza, slowing the horses to a respectable walk. Deor made a noise in the back of her throat like she might spit. "And there's the werewolf consulate."

The merry mood in the sleigh dropped. Unlike all the other buildings along the street, hung with woven greenery and pearly mistletoe, the consulate stood dark and cold. No Solstice bonfire stood ready for lighting in a brazier before the door. Unswept snow piled up on the steps and window ledges. Beside him, Deor sighed.

"How many people had to leave in total?" she said.

"I don't have an exact count, but we estimate about three thousand including at least four hundred faerie spouses and changeling children who left with their were-parent. Some of the spouses stayed behind to mind the family businesses."

Deor's mouth was a grim line. "It's like the Japanese internments during World War II," she said.

Rafe nodded. He didn't recognize the events, but he understood her tone. And he'd seen the empty streets—whole neighborhoods reduced to a quarter of their usual population. There had already been more than a few break-ins as opportunistic thieves scouted for valuables forgotten or too big to take away.

"I understand Lady Penelope's family has made their objections official—her father wrote a letter, published in the paper and to be read into the record at the opening of next year's Parliament, declaring that no one in his family will take their seat in Parliament again until the wolves are restored to their rights."

Beside him, Deor shifted, pulling the robe higher. "It's a nice gesture, but I don't see what it accomplishes. If he doesn't show up, he can't vote."

Rafe nodded. "Amazing how fast things can change. When Rufus dumped those heads out onto the floor and stood there looking like he'd caught a rabbit, I wanted to punch him right in smug face. By evening, I was more inclined to stand on his side."

"It was still murder," Deor said. "Don't get me wrong—Finn's behavior is awful—but extrajudicial killings are evil. There should have been a trial. Or something."

"The Alpha's never been known as a subtle politician."

Deor laughed, a short bark. "Why do I get the feeling that's the understatement of the century?" She shook herself. "Maybe we can lean on Finn more when he comes back from Roger's."

"Maybe." If what she wanted was to make him even more angry.

Chapter Twenty-Five

After the sleigh ride, Deor pled sleepiness and retreated to her room for a nap. She snuggled down in her bed and tried not to think about being alone for the next few days with only Rafe for company.

A couple hours later, wrapped in a comfy robe, she wandered back into the shared parlor, debating if it was worth it to send to the kitchens for food or if she should just raid the snack closet.

Rafe stood there half dressed in casual pants. He held a shirt and his hair was damp. "I was wondering if you wanted to do something with me tonight?" He shook the water out of his hair, and it was dry.

"Like what?" she asked, pretending his being half naked brought no activities to mind.

"Do you like the theater? Rodney and Clarissa are in town, and there is a Solstice musical on. They are always a little sentimental, but fun."

"Sure!" Deor said. "What should I wear?"

Rafe shrugged and ran his fingers through his hair. A faint white line ran across his torso, barely visible, from his left shoulder to the middle of his chest. Otherwise, his skin was flawless. She reminded herself not to stare.

"I'm wearing these." He gestured at his pants. "And a button-down shirt and a jacket. Not my uniform. Nothing fancy."

Deor nodded. "Okay."

She was staring again. This time at the mark below his right eye. He hadn't glamoured it yet. Like the line across his chest, it was faint. He seemed to think it was noticeable, but if she hadn't been looking for it, she wouldn't have seen it. It looked like a shadow, a slightly darker shade of blue. A slash that thinned to a line near his nose. Another thin white line nicked the nostril. She glanced at his eyes. He was watching her. He was waiting for her to talk. That's what people did in conversations.

"Can I wear pants?" she blurted out. Suddenly all her "severe" dresses seemed far too plain and shabby, even if they were immaculate.

He frowned slightly. "You're the princess. You can wear whatever you like."

She nodded. "Not my jeans or anything like that."

He shrugged. "You'll draw attention." He smiled. "But that's not a bad thing." He shook his head. "I'm not the one to be asking that sort of thing. You'd do better with someone like Gen. I say, wear whatever you like. It's just me and a couple of my friends. We're meeting at the restaurant, Junior Flaneur, at six. Is that enough time for you to dress?"

She laughed. "I'll be back in no time." She showered, thrilled at the magic that dried her hair without frizzing it. Sure, Rafe with his fancy water magic could do it himself, but she was happy with the Palace doing it for her. She did her makeup—real, human makeup—and then sat on the couch in her closet for twenty minutes staring at her clothes.

"No," she said to herself. "You will not sit here and stare at dozens of outfits and then say, 'I have nothing to wear.' Oh! Too late." She grabbed a pair of leather pants—they were a dark brown, more comfort and utility than fancy—and pulled them on. They were lined with silk to keep her warm. She had a lovely corset to go with it, but she had no idea how to get it on. Was it even possible to put one on oneself?

She put on the chemise that went with the corset and tucked it in. She put on plain boots with a small heel—nothing made here had no heel—and laced the corset up as much as she could and still be able to shimmy into it. With it settled around her, she tried to reach behind, but ended up doing the circle dance every woman trying to close a back-zipper on a dress knows. Then, just to emphasize the futility, she tried to grab the other tie behind her and spun around in the other direction.

She hiked the corset up in place once more and sighed. She didn't really have time to change again. She'd have to ask Rafe to help her. She ignored the voice in her head that wondered if he was better at taking them off than putting them on. She started toward the door and stopped. She wasn't wearing any jewelry. Would it be too casual not to?

Deor searched her jewelry box until she found a plain gold set. Small gold hoop earrings, a single strand necklace, and a few baubles for her hair. She left her hair alone, already up in a French twist and secured with a comb, but wore the earrings and necklace.

"Princess?" she heard Rafe from out in the parlor.

She glanced at the clock. Five-thirty-eight. "Shit," she whispered to herself. "Coming!" she called and headed through her parlor into the main room. "Hi," she said, still holding the corset up with one arm clutched around her middle.

"That's an interesting outfit," he said, face expressionless.

"Thank you." She rolled her eyes. "I thought I might be able to get it on myself, and I'm sure there is a way, but I've got no idea what it is. Do you think you could...?" She gave him a pleading look and turned her back to him.

"Sure!" He tugged at the ties and Deor jolted back. "Oops. Too much. Sorry!"

"No problem," Deor said. "Here, why don't I stand behind the couch and hold on to the back."

"Good plan." He followed her around the couch. He tugged and pulled for a moment. "Dammit," he said.

"What?"

"Oh, nothing that bad. I pulled one tie free of its eye. I'm better at getting these off than putting them on."

Deor clutched the couch. "Somehow, I'm not surprised."

After a few more minutes of yanking and pulling, several deep breaths, and the couch now a few inches farther from the fire, he finished.

"All done. And in a nice bow, too." He headed for the door and grabbed her long wool coat from the coat tree. He held it out to her.

"Thank you." She turned her back to him and slid her arms into the sleeves. He drew the coat up over her shoulders. She grabbed one of her scarves and wrapped it around her neck, tucking it into her coat as she buttoned it. She retrieved her gloves from the coat's pocket and slid them on. "All set." She turned.

Rafe draped a patterned scarf over his shoulders and down his lapel. "You're not going to button up?" she asked.

"I probably will on the way home. But it's still light outside; it won't be too bad. I'm sure it is still a bit above freezing." He held the door open for her.

"Practically tropical then!"

The carriage ride made Deor feel like she was in a snow globe. A light curtain of large, slow-falling flakes drifted through the air, surrounding the carriage in a flutter of white. Caer Eisteddfod did Solstice the way small towns in stories about New England do Christmas. There were decorations everywhere. Mistletoe hung in shop windows and wreaths on shop doors. Lights glittered along eaves. Up and down the streets, couples were arm and arm or held hands.

The carriage stopped in front of a large building with a short set of steps to a single door. Rafe hopped out of the carriage first and then held out a hand to help her. She tentatively put her feet, one after the other, down on the sheet of ice that was the sidewalk, making sure she had traction. She took Rafe's arm, and he led her to the door.

There was no sign, not even a street number, to give a clue what was on the other side. Rafe raised the brass knocker and knocked three times, paused, and then knocked another three more.

"Is there some sort of secret code to get in? I'd think it would be more elaborate than that. All sorts of knocks and taps to make sure the wrong sort of people can't get in."

He smiled. "It is, of a sort. Mostly, though, it's a silly joke. When I was your age," he chuckled, "this club was brand new—the first new one in centuries. Membership was open so long as the person was male. So, a bunch of us joined. It proved to be a brilliant idea—we had a place to go where we wouldn't run into parents or anyone else who might report any mischief we made. It grew up as we did, and now it's mostly a standard club—though the membership is pretty much all close friends. Young folks who want to get in usually spend some years working here before they apply."

The door swung open. A man in a uniform nodded at Rafe and stepped back from the door, bowing them into the foyer.

Behind them, the door closed. "May I take your coat, ma'am?" the young man said. Now, in the light of the room, she saw how very young he was. He didn't have many pips or bars on this uniform—which had been so starched that she was surprised he could bend his knees and elbows.

"Thank you," she said, handing it to him. She handed over her scarf and gloves as well. Another young man had come in and taken Rafe's as well.

"Thanks, lad," Rafe said and patted him on the shoulder. "I'm glad to see you've decided to join." He turned to the young man who had taken her coat. "Off you go now. I'll have Gordie here take us back to the bar."

The soldier nodded, but didn't say anything, and, after another quick glance at Deor, hurried away through a door behind a counter.

"Your Majesty," Rafe said, "May I present Squire Gordon Limeux."

The squire, already tall, straightened like he was a marionette jerked by a string. He stared at her for a few moments, opening and closing his mouth.

"Good evening, Gordon," Deor said and held her hand out to him. "It is nice to meet you. How do you know Rafe?"

Gordie glanced at her hand and the back up at Rafe.

"In her country, people shake hands as a greeting, Gordie. Go on." Rafe smiled at the boy, clearly amused at his nerves.

The squire grabbed her hand and gave it a short shake, like it might zap him if he held it too long. "The Sword is my knight," Gordie spit out. "I mean, I service him." His face went white for a moment. "I'm sorry. I mean Lord Farringdon is the knight for whom I am a squire, milady." He gave a small bow. The 'whom' phrase had put up quite a fight, but he had wrestled it successfully out of his mouth and into the world.

Deor nodded and smiled at him. He must have been about nineteen, she guessed. Or would have guessed at home. Whatever the number, he was a young man, emphasis on young. He had turned beet red, a state made no better by the fiery glow of his many freckles and shock of bright red hair.

"Gordie," Rafe said, "we can walk and talk at the same time. Perhaps you could show us back to the bar. Are Roger and Clarissa here yet?"

"Yes, sir. Yes, sir, they are here." He turned away from them toward a hallway leading farther into the building. He turned back. "This way, please." He bowed and then moved down the hallway.

"Are you going to join the military when you are old enough?" Deor asked as they walked.

He nearly tripped, catching himself on the wall. "Excuse me." His voice was a whisper now, and his face redder than anything should get without exploding into flames. "Yes, Your Majesty. I hope to join the same regiment the Sword served."

"That's lovely." She glanced at Rafe as they followed the boy. He gave her a smile.

Is he okay? she mouthed.

Rafe nodded. "Gordie is an excellent squire. He's a decent horseman and making excellent progress in both hand-to-hand combat and bladed weapons."

Gordie's eartips were so red she thought they might steam. "Thank you, sir."

"He's gotten quite proficient in Faerie, too. Even Old Faerie—all the formal titles and ranks. He leads his class, I think. Arthur wants to turn him into a spy because of the language skills. And because he knows how to be quiet."

The boy tripped again, catching the edge of a table and sending a lovely vase of orchids crashing to the ground. He scrambled to his feet and gaped at the mess. He knelt and grabbed at the broken glass, then jerked his hand back. Blood welled in his palm.

Deor knelt in front of him and took his hand. "It's okay," she said. "Don't hurt yourself. I'll help you." She delicately picked up the larger pieces of glass and set them on the table, which Rafe had righted. "Gather the flowers," she said to him.

Without looking up, he piled all the stems into his hands, then picked up every single petal and leaf. He stood and laid them gently on the table.

Rafe whispered something. Gordie's eyes widened. "Go on," Rafe said.

Trembling, Gordie held his hand out to her. "Your...Majesty..." He drew a deep breath. "MayIhelpyouup?"

Deor smiled and took his hand, letting him raise her up, though she did most of the raising herself. "Thank you."

He let go and flailed at the doorway. "The bar, sir."

"Thank you, Gordie." He patted the kid on the shoulder. He dropped his voice, and Deor pretended she couldn't hear him. "You did fine."

Summoning the knowledge the throne had implanted in her, she said in Faerie, *"Thank you, young squire to the Sword. I acknowledge your effort in leading me. May the rest of the night, and the Solstice season, bring you great joy."*

The boy almost fell over again. *"Thank you,"* he managed to squeak out in Faerie before darting through a side door that, from the noises that came out, led to the kitchens.

"Come on," Rafe said offering her his arm. "I see Rodney and Clarissa."

Deor took his arm.

"That was kind of you, you know. The boy certainly will not forget this evening—I imagine he wouldn't have anyway—that was quite the tumble—but you addressing him in Faerie? I am certain that he will regale all his friends, whether they like it or not, several times in the next hundred years."

Deor laughed. "There's nothing hard about being polite. It took all I had not to laugh—not because his mistakes were funny, but because…"

"You remember when you were like that?" Rafe finished.

"Something like that, yes. Were you that all elbows and knees?"

"I was." He nodded. "And with just as much skill talking to beautiful women." He waved to Rodney and Clarissa as they got to the table. "Evening all," he said and pulled out a chair for Deor.

Chapter Twenty-Six

The morning after her outing with Rafe, Deor slept in. Or rather she lay in bed longer than normal, wondering what exactly to do with herself all day that didn't involve staring at Rafe and reminding herself that he was happily engaged. Or, at least, engaged.

"Brother, my ass," she muttered to herself. Finn might imagine the two of them getting along in filial bliss, but the spark that leapt between their hands when they had touched the previous day had nothing to do with brotherhood. And Rafe wasn't even adopted.

"Okay, that's enough of that line of thought," she said aloud to herself. She threw back the covers and hauled herself out of bed. Breakfast should be waiting in the dining room now that most of the staff were back from their Solstice holiday.

Barefoot and still in her pajamas, Deor scraped her hair into a bun and stuck a hairpin through it. At the rate it was growing, her hair would be to her waist by summer. The Winter Court seemed determined to turn her into a proper faerie whether she liked it or not.

She stopped in front of the vanity mirror and put her wings out, wiggling them. The air still tickled every time she moved her wings, but at least the sensation was fainter now, or at least she was getting more used to it. Still, after a moment, she pulled the wings back in.

"Rafe hardly ever puts his wings out, at least around here," she muttered and then wondered who she thought she needed to defend herself against. Still, she left her wings in as she went in search of some fruit and a muffin.

She was just emerging from the dining room into the parlor, a plate of food balanced on a tea cup and saucer when Rafe came in off the balcony, bringing a rush of cold air with him. His wings were out, but he wore his great coat bundled around him with his arms holding something inside it.

"Did you fly up here?" Deor said, hastily setting down her tower of food on a side table.

"I did." He grinned at her. "It's a perfect day for flying if you'd like a lesson."

Deor shivered. "How about an indoor lesson for a first timer? And close those doors. I can feel my hair freezing off. Muffin?" She offered him one from the plate.

"No thanks, I already ate. But I have something for you. Or someone, I should say. Think of him as a late Solstice present."

Deor raised her eyebrows as Rafe opened his coat.

A second later, she squealed in delight and darted forward. "Brand!" The thick-furred puppy squirmed and barked in Rafe's arms. As soon as Deor took him from Rafe, Brand licked her face all over, barking his delight.

Deor had to sit down to contain the squirming ball of fur and enthusiasm that was the puppy.

"Are you sure?" she said, clutching him to her. "He's the best of the litter. You said so yourself."

"He's all yours." Rafe's grin was as wide as it had been on Solstice day. "I just had to wait until he was fully weaned."

"Oh, thank you." Deor buried her face in Brand's thick fur and was rewarded with another round of puppy kisses. Tears pricked in her eyes, and she was glad for Brand's hiding them.

They played with Brand until nearly lunch time, sitting on the floor of the parlor, laughing at the puppy's antics. Eventually, Deor sighed and said, "I should go get dressed."

"Why?" Rafe said. "It's Solstice. And you look lovely just the way you are."

Deor laughed. "I look like I rolled out of bed and stuck a pen in my hair. Which is pretty much exactly what I did."

"It suits you."

"I don't know if that's a compliment or not. Slovenly isn't exactly a style. At least not in Fae."

Rafe shrugged and stretched out his long legs, leaning on one arm to be closer to her. "You look natural. Relaxed. I like it."

Deor pulled Brand into her lap, holding the large puppy up like a shield. "If I didn't know better, I'd say you were flirting with me."

"Who says I'm not?"

"Your fiancée, I hope."

"Ah yes, my fiancée. Who currently isn't my fiancée." Rafe sat up and rubbed his face. "We're on a 'hiatus' you see. To think about what we really want."

"I see. And what do you really want?" Deor let the squirming Brand slip away from her. He bounded away toward Jake and Sam, leaving Rafe and Deor facing each other.

"A kiss," Rafe said. "From you."

"I suppose I do owe you a Solstice present," Deor said, a half smile on her face.

"Kissing games are traditional this time of year, you know. Just look at all the mistletoe hanging around."

"Mmm. You make a very persuasive point." She leaned toward him, and he reached for her, his arm sliding around her waist. Their lips met, and for a moment that had nothing to do with the lingering throne magic, there was nothing in the world, but the two of them, touching.

Rafe pulled her closer.

Deor put her hands up to Rafe's chest and pushed him away. "I was engaged once," she said. "It ended really badly."

"I'm sorry."

"He brought my replacement to a party and announced she was his muse. And I wasn't."

"I hope you threw him through a window."

"No." Deor bit her lip. "I cried. It wasn't my most dignified moment. But my point is..."

"You're not her, and you wouldn't do that to another woman," Rafe finished for her.

"Right. Even if the two of you are on a hiatus." She pulled herself away from him and stood, looking down at his lounging form. "But if the two of you ever do figure out that you want someone else, give me a call."

With that, she gathered Brand up in her arms and retreated to her rooms.

Chapter Twenty-Seven

At his desk in the Tower, Rafe frowned at the latest intelligence reports. They were disconcertingly empty of details, and it was details he needed—some hint of where the next strike against the royal family would come from.

Arthur entered and pulled up a chair, closely followed by other officers, including Bolton and Montjoie, who did the same. All their chairs faced toward the large mirror over the fireplace.

Rafe raised an eyebrow. "Something I can do for you, gentlemen?"

"It's time for the king's annual New Year's speech," Arthur said. "You've got the best mirror in the building. Or had you forgotten?"

Rafe harrumphed and turned his chair around so that he, too, was facing the mirror. He hadn't forgotten by accident. Somehow this year he wasn't in the mood for a warm and fatherly speech from the sovereign of the nation, but with the highest ranked officers on duty already sitting in his office with their boots propped up, as they did every year, he could hardly snarl at everyone to get out and find their own mirror.

A few seconds later, the mirror darkened and then cleared to reveal Finn. Everyone in the room, Rafe included, got to their feet and saluted smartly.

"As you were, gentlemen," Rafe said, resuming his own seat.

Finn sat in a gilded chair before a fireplace, a few shelves of books on either side. It looked both homey and royal, even though it was Northfalls and not the Palace, and that, according to the king's Master of Ceremonies, was what really mattered.

"It's all about the tone. Nothing matters so much as tone," was his constant mantra.

On the mirror, Finn cleared his throat gently. "My dear people," he began. "What a tumultuous and yet joyous ending last year had. I am sure you share in my joy, as I share in yours, at the safe return of our beloved heir, the Princess Deor."

Rafe rolled his eyes to himself.

"So let the joyous celebration continue!" Finn said. "I declare that this entire year will be one of jubilee. Let every soul within the Winter Court be glad with us. The land itself rejoices. Indeed, so certain am I of this that I have decided to remit half the annual Harvest Tax come fall."

Cheers from the men sitting in Rafe's office. All of them, except Lieutenant Bolton, held title to some plot of land, however small, somewhere. Rafe nodded to himself, even as a small, traitorous part of his brain wondered if the king's exchequer would be quite so delighted at the news.

Finn's speech continued with the usual list of New Year's boons—gifts to schools and charitable institutions, awarding of help to the needier regions of the country.

"And finally," Finn said, his benevolent smile widening, "I intend to re-institute the Royal Progress, visiting in turn the principal regions of this country and their people."

Both groans and cheers greeted this news. Rafe and Arthur exchanged glances. Keeping the king safe while he roamed around the countryside, stopping to talk to any random peasant who took his fancy and staying the night at one ducal household after another was going to require the same level of planning and care as a war. In fact, a nice little skirmish or two along the border might be less complex. Rafe leaned his head on one hand, already mapping out potential routes in his head. Why couldn't Finn, for once, warn him about this sort of harebrained scheme ahead of time?

"I shall begin my journey at Northfalls on the first of February." Murmurs broke out in the room. "There I will receive the renewed pledges of fealty of all the peerage, and they will be allowed to pay their homage to their new heir, my daughter Deor."

Rafe's jaw clicked open. February first was the opening of Parliament, and the king had not only moved it to Northfalls, but commandeered it for a display of loyalty.

Northfalls was no southern pleasure palace either. It was a heavily fortified castle built first and foremost for defense. And the land around it was none too heavily populated. The nearest city was thirty miles from Roger's home and nowhere near the size of Caer Eisteddfod. The countryside would be filled to the brim with camping nobles. In the middle of winter. Beside a Scottish loch. And all of them lining up to kneel before the king. Forcing the entire House of Lords to travel north? As ambushes went, it was a brilliant maneuver. Whether it would succeed in bringing the discontented to heel or blow up in the king's face was another question.

"Well, gentlemen. You heard him," Rafe said with a sigh. "Call back the troops and let's get started on planning this pageant."

Deor stormed down the hall to Rafe's office. When she rounded the corner, she almost slammed face first into a small group of soldiers. She jerked to a halt, and they stumbled dodging her.

"Sorry, Your Majesty!" Arthur, the leader of the group, bowed his head. The rest followed suit, with bows and apologies.

"No, my fault." Brand butted her calf with his head and whined. She glanced down. He was panting, having run to keep up with her. She scooped him up and cuddled him. The men gave her a rather bemused look.

"So much for them being savage dogs from birth," Montjoie muttered, but he was smiling.

"Brand's a sweetie." She tucked him under her arm. "Is Rafe in his office?"

"Yes, ma'am," Arthur said. "I'm guessing you want to speak to him about the Royal Progress?"

"Got it in one," she said.

The men moved aside as she passed them down the hall. A bit calmer now, she knocked on Rafe's door and even waited until he said, "Come in!"

"Hey," she said as she opened the door. She hadn't been in this office in months, and hadn't been one-hundred percent sure the portal in the Palace would get her to the Tower, but it seemed to work fine. His desk looked like it had been swept clean, and, by the rows of semi-neatly stacked piles on the floor next to the desk, perhaps it had. He had a hologram-like map on the table.

Rafe looked up. "Hello," he said and gave a weary smile. "So, you watched Finn's announcement."

"Yep." Deor closed the door behind her. "Can I set Brand on the floor? Or do you think he'll mess up your papers?"

"Set him down." Rafe leaned back in his chair and laced his fingers behind his head. "He can chew on those all he wants—he can pee on them if it makes him happy. Won't make them any more useless."

Deor lowered Brand to the floor, and he scurried a few feet away, sniffing everything he could get his nose on. Deor sat in a chair in front of Rafe's desk. "Been awhile since I've been here." She smiled.

"Yep. You're not going to yell at me again, right?" He grinned at her.

"No. Then we had a common enemy and didn't know it. Now, I think we're pretty much on the same page." She sighed. "There's no talking him out of this, is there?"

"Nope." Rafe gestured at the map on the desk. "You remember Northfalls." He pointed at the large castle, heavily fortified. It certainly hadn't looked like a vacation spot over Solstice, even with the lovely yacht ride. The map seemed accurate down to the time of day and weather, and the place was half buried in snow and ice. "The place is a fortress, though it's the height of luxury inside. Really, unless we let the traitors in by the front door, you'd be almost as safe there as you are here. Nothing happens in that palace that Roger doesn't know about."

"Isn't he quite the gossip?" Deor seemed to remember his commentary in many of the papers she read.

"Yes." Rafe nodded. "At his February party, he always has loads of press plants at his parties—reporters disguised as wait staff, bartenders, valets, maids, even stable boys."

"And that makes his home safe?" What a nightmare. Deor had enough trouble keeping her mouth shut when she was on guard. She'd be worried the whole time that she was saying something she shouldn't.

"More or less. Roger loves gossip, but only the social kind. Who's bedding whom, who's fighting, who isn't wearing the latest fashion. That I know of, there has never been an untoward piece of gossip about the king or his family from Roger or Northfalls."

"Good to know, I guess." She stared at the map. "So, we'll be safe there?"

Rafe waved his hand over the map and it shrunk, showing the length of the kingdom from Northfalls to Caer Eisteddfod. "Roger's castle is on Loch Ness. It's strategically important—the narrowest part of the canal between the Summer and Winter Courts meets at Loch Ness. If there's going to be an invasion of the North by sea, that would be where it is. Everything else for miles in either direction is either the lake, or walled cliffs that are too high and difficult to manage for an army. But if North-falls were to be taken," he pointed at the map and the flat land from the duchy to Caer, "an army would have an easy road straight down."

"So, that's good, then?" Deor studied the map.

"I suppose." Rafe leaned back. "At least for us." He waved the map in close again. "As you can see, there's no city for miles—the capital city of his duchy is not where he lives. He lives in what used to be the fort. It's more than a day's ride to Drumnadrochit. So no one will be able to stay there." He gestured at what looked like rather rough land around the palace. "People will have to put up tents and camp."

"Camp? Like, sleeping bags and open fires?"

"No." Rafe laughed. "With silk tents and hordes of servants. The nobility camp in style."

Geoff had said as much about his own hunting trips. The living quarters would be amazing, she was sure. Once again, like something out of a medieval romance. More and more the "fiction" she'd studied rang true. The authors hadn't seen anything like that in their world, but maybe more than one had been to Fae. After all, poets were supposed to be a bit "touched" anyway.

"Still," Rafe said. "This is going to cost a lot of people a lot of money. It's more than a celebration, like the Adoption. This is a loyalty test. He's demanding every noble show up. If he asks for much more, he might bankrupt some of them."

"That's horrible!" Medieval kings had certainly done the same thing. Tour the nation and require the castles he visited to put him up. Him and his dozens of servants and knights.

"For some, yes. I'm sure smaller families will band together."

"Are we camping?" the thought of sleeping on the cold ground in February did not please.

"Not us, thank the Creator" Rafe said. "We, and some of the other favored families, will stay in Roger's castle."

"Oh. Okay." She shook her head. "I don't know why Finn keeps doing things like this. Can't he see he's alienating his own people? People he's been alienating for years?" She scooped Brand up into her arms. "It's like he hears negative things people are saying and then doubles down."

"Yes," Rafe said. "He is trying to display power and coming off like a bully."

"I wish—" but Deor was cut off by the mirror flaring to life.

"Rafe?" Finn spoke as the picture came into view. "Oh! Deor, you're with him. Good. I'd tried you on your personal mirror, but clearly it isn't with you."

"I hope you didn't worry," Deor said, remaining polite despite the rising pressure in her chest. She hated that he had such an ability to spy on her.

"No," he said. "It's Solstice—I imagined you were doing something fun. But here I find you both in the Tower. Is everything well?"

Rafe smiled. "I was getting some work done and watched from here. Deor came to talk about the upcoming events."

"Oh!" Finn's eyes lit up. "It will be splendid! Balls and feasts like the Winter Court hasn't seen in decades! Roger, Astarte, and I have been planning all morning."

"So you and Astarte made up, then?" Deor asked.

A dark expression passed over Finn's face, but it cleared. "Yes," he said. "Some." He stared at them for a moment, and neither Rafe nor Deor spoke. He went on, "The event will be a week long, culminating in a grand ball for everyone the night before the formal presentation. I see you have the map out!" Finn turned his attention to Rafe. "That's my boy! Already planning."

Rafe visibly flinched at the word "boy," and a chill rolled off him like he was a block of ice. Brand snuggled further into her arms.

"Yes, I am. It will take a lot of planning, sire." Rafe kept his voice even, but Deor could hear the anger swirling under it too. Or maybe he hid it entirely and the cold he was blasting out clouded her hearing.

If Finn noticed Rafe's distress, he ignored it. "Excellent!" He glanced to the side as though someone were speaking to him. "Yes, darling, right away." He turned back to them. "Astarte says it is time for our walk. I must go." He leaned in. "I know it is the end of Solstice, but I expect that you two will have done some work on this before I return after Twelfth Night." The tone was light; the expression was not. "Good afternoon." He smiled once more, and the mirror went black and returned to silver.

"Ugh," Deor said. "That last bit was a threat, right? You heard the threat, too?"

"Oh yes." Rafe said bitterly. "He wants his prize possessions on display and happy about it." He wiped his hand through the map, and it disappeared. He set his elbows on the table and leaned his head in his hands. The chill was dissipating. "Forgive me," he said. "I'll fix it."

"Thanks, but it's fine. I get it." She sat forward. "Look, it's our last weekend before everyone comes back to the Palace. Why don't we stay in and enjoy the fire and the company and pretend that there's nothing else to do?"

"That sounds excellent. I have an errand to run before dinner, but then I shall join you." Rafe stood. "Shall we?"

Deor nodded. For now they'd put Finn out of their minds, not that peace would last. Everything was a demand or a threat from him. Her heart pounded as she thought about him, and wondered how real Astarte's reconciliation was and how much was for the sake of her child.

Finn was going to keep on her, demanding things as her father, and she was going to push back. No matter how much she thought about it, how many solutions she tried to work, she and her father were headed for a serious confrontation.

Rafe offered her his arm, and she took it, happy to follow him back to the portal. The Tower was still a bit of the maze, and, to be honest, she hadn't seen the best parts of it.

He seemed off in his own world, too, as they made their way back to their rooms.

Finn wanted perfect. Perfect wife. Perfect son. Perfect daughter. When someone failed to be perfect, as they inevitably would, what then? Deor thought about the small scars she had seen on Rafe's body. They could have been battle scars, but some looked so faded that they had to be decades old.

Her hand fluttered to her throat, though the scars from the attack in the alley had long faded, their memory had not. Whoever attacked her hadn't had nearly the power the king had, especially not in his own house.

Rafe walked her to the heart of the household, saw her and Brand safely into their rooms. He bowed over her hand. "I shall be back in time for supper."

"Where are you off to?"

"I have an appointment," he said. "At the Mound." He tapped his forehead and with a smile turned away and walked down the hall.

Chapter Twenty-Eight

S olstice was over, and Genevieve was back from the Alps, pink cheeked and full of delightful stories of skiing. The fire burned cheerfully in the parlor of her London house. Like many other members of Parliament from far-flung regions, her family kept a house in town.

"It really is too bad you missed it, Rafe," she said. "Delaney and George came after all, and we had a marvelous time. But I did miss you."

"I missed you, too," Rafe said automatically, though his mind went to the day in the kennels, sitting in a pile of straw while four Molossian puppies clambered over everything and everyone. "But I think you were right that we needed time to step apart and think."

"Absence does make the heart grow fonder, they say. Have you had time to realize what you truly want?" she said.

Rafe took a deep breath. "Genevieve, I'm not sure what I want because I'm not certain of who I am anymore."

Her face softened in sympathy, and she put her hand on his chest. "I know losing the crown must be a devastating blow, but you're still the same man you were before."

Rafe took her hand, holding it away from him. "But that's what you don't understand. I never wanted to be king. I only wanted to please Sweordmund, to be his boy the way he'd raised me to be. To want whatever he wanted. And because of that I almost died, I almost killed the true heir, and I was removed from the one thing I was sure I did want, to be Sword. Now I just don't know—about any of it. Including us."

"So you want to end our engagement? Is that what you're saying?"

"No, I'm not. I'm saying that I'm struggling. I wonder how much of our engagement is a true mutual attraction and how much is simply me doing the right thing in picking out a future Consort."

Genevieve's shoulders drooped. "There's nothing wrong with being savvy about the prospects of your future spouse, Rafe. I admit I thought about what it would mean to be Consort before I said yes to you. That doesn't mean we're not right for each other, simply that we're adults ready to take adult matters into consideration. Marriage is no small thing."

"And how do you feel about being the wife of the Sword instead?" Rafe said.

"It would be an honor."

"Yes, I suppose it would. Just as it would be an honor to be the husband of the Harvest Queen. But is that enough, do you think? Do we love one another? Or are we just a highly suitable match?"

Genevieve leaned forward and kissed him. "I don't think there's much of a difference, do you? And what does it matter so long as we're happy?"

He kissed her back, wondering if she were right. She was beautiful, charming, gracious, a skillful political advisor, and she cared for him. What man wouldn't be delighted to have her as his fiancée? Perhaps he was simply longing for something that only existed in storybooks.

"You know," Genevieve said as the kiss ended. "I've been thinking about the opening of Parliament and the fealty oath the king is requiring. Those Wham! and Thorsen styles the princess favors may not send the right message. She's going to need something extra special to wear for the event. Do you think she'd take offense if I offered to introduce her to my dressmaker?"

Rafe smiled in relief. Genevieve was kind too. How could he have forgotten that among her many good qualities?

"I think that's a sterling idea," he said. "I'll mention it to the princess tonight, if you like."

D eor wasn't nearly as thrilled at Genevieve's suggestion, but Finn immediately declared it a splendid idea. When Deor tried to point out that she and Genevieve had as much in common style-wise as a willow tree and a holly bush, Finn put his foot down and ordered Deor to accept Genevieve's offer.

So the day after Epiphany, Deor boarded the royal carriage for her appointment. It took her to a fashionable street only a block from Theophilus's shop. Like Theophilus's establishment, this shop had no need to advertise its presence. A discrete white door framed by an arch of glossy green rose bushes bore the simple word *LaRouche* and nothing more.

Whether tipped off by the Palace or by Genevieve or just good journalistic instincts, the press was ready and waiting for her the moment the carriage rolled up. They shouted questions and waved their mirrors as the carriage footmen forced a passageway for Deor. At the door, Deor turned and half-opened her mouth. Perhaps she ought to at least answer a few of their questions. But Arthur deftly stepped between her and the press as a footman swung open the door. Deor stepped through, and the noise faded to nothing.

Unlike the days when she had struggled to see Master Artisan Theophilus, this time Deor was greeted by a row of three servants standing at attention. The first one swept off Deor's coat, the second knelt to wipe the snow and salt from her shoes, and the third gestured her inward. Deor advanced through the white painted showroom. Decorated with accents of rose and gold, the room held only four dresses, each one magically suspended in air and slowly rotating. Ribbons and lace featured prominently in all of them.

Genevieve, beaming, emerged from a door on the far side of the showroom. She swept Deor a deep and graceful curtsey. "Your Majesty, thank you so much for coming."

Deor forced herself to smile. After all, this was as much a command performance for Genevieve as it was for her. "Thank you so much for offering to help me select a ballgown, Lady Genevieve. It's very kind of you."

Genevieve laughed. "Not at all, Your Majesty. Mentoring young girls in the Harvest Queen's court is one of my duties. I'm only too happy to extend that duty to my king and his heir."

Deor's smile froze as Genevieve tucked an arm through Deor's and led her out of the showroom into a parlor. It took all Deor's concentration not to prickle with spikes all along her skin where Genevieve's hand lay. As it was, a short spurt of fire-white sparkles pinged off her skin.

"Something the matter, Your Majesty?" Genevieve said dropping Deor's arm and stepping back from the sparkles.

"No, no. I'm fine, thank you. I'm sorry—it's something that just happens sometimes. When I'm startled."

Genevieve's pink skin paled a shade or two. "I beg your pardon."

"It's fine," Deor said. "Don't worry about it. Should we...?" She gestured toward the door through which Genevieve and the servant had been trying to lead her.

The door led to a parlor where the rose and gold theme was even more strongly present. Two faerie women waited for her, one middle aged and the other stooped with age.

"Welcome to LaRouche, Your Majesty," they both said in chorus, bending their knees deeply.

"Thank you." Deor tried to curtsey back and succeeded only in bending her knees awkwardly while trying not to stick her rear end into the air. The diagrams in the *Nobble Babees Booke* were harder to follow in real life than they had looked on the page.

As Madame LaRouche and her daughter maintained their deep knee bends, Genevieve cleared her throat as softly as a sheep coughing. "If Your Majesty would care to sit down?"

Deor took the hint and sat, releasing the other women from their bows.

"Yes, please. Everyone have a seat," Deor said.

Genevieve settled next to Deor.

Despite the winter cold outside, Genevieve wore layers of diaphanous silk in pale apple green. Deor shivered at the thought of the wind whipping straight through those thin layers and tucked her fingers deeper into the sleeves of the oversized knit sweater she had ordered from Wham! & Thorsen. As the younger Madame LaRouche passed around a plate of deep pink macarons, Deor wished she were back at the other showroom with the manic pixie and her equally energetic partner. There'd been a sense of humor to their earnestness that was missing here.

Along with the macarons came tea, steaming and aromatic. Deor clutched gratefully at the delicate porcelain.

"So," she said as brightly as she could. "Shall we talk about dresses?" Neither of the two Madames LaRouche had a sketchpad visible the way Wham! & Thorsen had, but she hoped perhaps she could nudge things along.

The elder Madame LaRouche chuckled. "The young are so impatient. All in due time, my pet, all in due time."

The younger Madame LaRouche leaned forward. "You must excuse my mother, Your Majesty. We can look at dresses this minute if you like. Lady Genevieve?"

Genevieve rose and exited the room. "I'll be right back, Your Majesty."

A curtain on the far wall pulled back to reveal a small stage that extended a few feet into the room.

"The theme this year," the younger Madame LaRouche said, "is petals in the snow."

As she spoke, glamoured snowflakes began to filter down from the air. Flute music played, and Genevieve stepped onto the stage. She wore a pink, flowing dress whose edges curled and fluttered with every step. Paler pink crystals decorated the waist and arms. As Genevieve took her turn on the catwalk, Deor tried to hide the horror in her face.

Deor swallowed hard and said, "I don't think that's quite what I'm looking for..."

"Oh, don't worry at all, Your Majesty," Genevieve said. "This isn't your ball gown."

Deor sighed in relief. Just a preview of the line then.

"This is your *arrival* gown."

Both Madames LaRouche nodded in unison. Genevieve exited the stage. After a pause, she returned dressed in pale grey. While this dress had a blessed lack of fluttering, it was embroidered from top to bottom in rosebuds, done graduating shades of pink from palest off white to a deep rose near the bottom hem.

"Now this dress," Genevieve was saying, "will be for the ball..."

"I thought I only needed one ball gown," Deor said, fingers tightening on her tea cup.

Genevieve laughed her delicate, silvery laugh once again. "I've taken the liberty of consulting Lord Roger at Northfalls as to the exact sequence of events, and I assure you, you will need each and every one of these gowns." She turned to Madame LaRouche. "Shall we see the next one?"

"Before we do that," Deor said, "I would really like to talk about my preferred style of clothes."

Genevieve turned gracefully and exited again.

While Genevieve changed, Deor turned to the older Madame LaRouche, saying, "I really need to wear something in the Aethelwing house color. It needs to be black. And subdued. I need something dignified."

The elderly lady patted Deor on the knee. "Don't you worry, Your Highness. We have that all thought out." She gestured toward the stage where Genevieve had re-emerged.

"And here we have Your Majesty's gown for the day of Parliament," Genevieve said. She glided forward, her dress completely filling the stage with the petals of an iris in full bloom. Its neckline plunged all the way to her navel, her pale pink skin glowing against the midnight purple velvet fabric.

"Unbelievable," Deor said.

"Isn't it?" Genevieve clasped her hands together. "Madame LaRouche and her daughter have done an amazing job in such short time. Now all we have to do is fit you."

Deor ran her hands over her face.

"You really shouldn't have done all this without me," Deor said, her voice strained.

Genevieve blushed. "You're so very welcome, Your Majesty. I understand that you're impatient with matters of fashion and I, we, wanted to make things as easy for you as possible."

Deor set down the tea cup. "I don't think you understand me. I mean you really shouldn't have done all this without consulting me first." She turned to the Madames LaRouche. "You've done some truly amazing work in a stunningly short period of time, and I appreciate that. I really do. But these aren't suitable." Beside her, Genevieve gasped, but Deor went on. "I'm sorry. We'll have to design something else."

Both the elder and the younger Madame LaRouche were looking stricken, but they nodded along as Deor spoke. What the princess wished, the princess would get. But Genevieve seethed.

"May I have a word with you in private?" She stalked off the stage toward Deor.

Before Deor could say yes or no, Genevieve threw out her hand and a silver curtain seemed to settle around them, blocking off the rest of the room.

"What on earth are you thinking?" Genevieve hissed. "These are the finest gown designers in all of Fae."

"I'm thinking that these clothes send the wrong message," Deor said.

"Those are perfectly lovely gowns."

"They are lovely. For you. For me, they are entirely unsuitable."

"With all due respect, Your Majesty, how could you possibly know? You've barely arrived in the country. You still wear pants. You need to trust us in this matter."

Deor bit her lip in thought for a moment before saying. "Lady Genevieve, these are beauty pageant gowns. And they look stunning on you. But that's the exact problem. They look stunning on *you*. On me they would look..." she gestured toward Genevieve's cleavage, "like costumes. I'm not a statuesque beauty like you. I'm short, I'm curvy, and frankly, I don't have the stage presence to pull off something like this. I cannot be presented in public as the heir and future ruler in one of these dresses. Think what that would do to the kingdom."

Genevieve fanned herself with her hands, her delicate nails flashing seashell pink in the silvery light of the privacy spell.

"I'm sorry," Deor said, her voice taking on the firm, but gentle tone she used to tell a student she would not be changing their grade. "I'm sure you worked very hard on this, and I do appreciate it."

"These dresses...I helped design them myself!"

Deor nodded and said nothing. A tear sparkled in Genevieve's eye.

"You don't appreciate the hours of work that went into them. I considered your coloration, your figure, your everything!"

"Nonetheless, I will not be wearing these dresses," Deor said. She stood up, shattering the privacy spell around them. She turned to the madames. "Thank you both so much for your hard work. I have to go now, since I have other work to do, but thank you again for your time."

As best she could while wearing pants, Deor swept out of the room, through the showroom, and out to the waiting carriage.

She settled in and flipped open her mirror. "Wham! and Thorsen," she commanded. Across from her, Arthur raised an eyebrow.

"Your Majesty!" The cotton-candy-haired Wham answered the call. "How delightful! What can we do for you? Did you want to order more clothes?" The look in the woman's eye was eager, but not greedy, and though she used all the proper titles, she spoke conversationally.

"I do. Would it be possible to fit me in this afternoon?"

"Yes, Your Majesty!" The pixie waved someone over toward her and exchanged a few hushed words, then shooed the shop girl off again. "Any time you like!"

"Thank you so very much. I shall be there directly." Deor nodded at Arthur, who rolled his eyes but slid open the panel and told the driver the new destination.

"Is there anything you would like us to work up before you arrive? We have some wonderful new leather in—it would make excellent pants. And our new line of boots is available, too."

"That would be great. I need something for hunting on horseback." Deor winced at the thought. "And, also, I'll be need a ball gown, and a gown for Parliament. Is that possible? Or is this too short notice?"

Deor knew that, like her "request" for an appointment moments before, her request for ball gowns would be greeting with a resounding "yes," even if Wham and Thorsen themselves stayed up from now until Roger's party making them.

Wham's jaw dropped. "Absolutely!" She jumped up from where she sat, the mirror's image jostling with her movements. "Thorey!" she called out. "Thorey, come here. Right now!" She glanced back at Deor. "I'm sorry," she said, suddenly realizing Deor was still on the line.

"What is it?" Thorsen appeared in the frame. "Oh! Your Majesty. How nice to see you." The faerie man smiled in a kind way.

"She's on her way here to look at some new clothes."

"Excellent."

"She wants two gowns—one for the Duke of Northfalls' Grand Ball, and one for the opening of Parliament."

The faerie's eyes widened in alarm. "Well, no question, we can do that. We look forward to seeing you…"

"In a few minutes," Wham finished for him. "We will see you soon," she added to Deor, and the mirror went dark.

Deor set her mirror aside and glanced at Arthur. He stared out the window at the passing scenery as though he were the only one in the carriage. His hands made loose fists on his knees.

"You think this is a bad idea," Deor said.

He turned his gaze to her. "No. I can't imagine that dismissing the opinions of the most fashionable woman in the Winter Court to work with non-traditional peasants for the most important day of your life has any chance of going badly." He went back to staring out the window.

"Gee, thanks," Deor whispered to herself. Genevieve's "advice" had done Deor some good. She knew exactly what she did and did not want. There was no way she could get away with pants for either the ball or Parliament, and she wasn't going to try. There were moments to push the envelope and moments to fall in line. Looking the part—at least some-what—was a necessity.

The carriage rumbled to a stop in front of the shop. Unlike earlier in the day, there were no reporters. When the footman opened the door, Deor stepped out and walked into the building, not bothering to wait for either her guards or Arthur.

Inside, Wham and Thorsen were standing in front of their pedestal, a glamoured model of Deor circling slowly. They had, in mere minutes, created a black dress that made Deor's breath catch. No, this was neither flouncy nor be-ribboned. A simple black ball gown with small sparkles like diamonds woven in the fabric.

"Wow," Deor said.

The two turned, startled at her presence.

"You like it?" Wham asked, a pleading in her voice that made Deor smile.

"This is our starting place." Thorsen hurried toward her. "It is a bit plain, but we'll fix that."

"It's beautiful." As the model rotated, Deor gasped. The dress had vents for her wings. Against the black of the dress, the blood-red wings, with their black and silver veining, stood out, drawing attention. No question, walking into a room in that dress, she wouldn't look costumed, or worse, like a little girl playing dress-up.

"That's a dress that makes the right kind of statement," Deor said.

Wham clapped her hands. "Will you let us turn the volume up a bit?"

She bit her lip and glanced at Arthur, like she was worried he would object.

"I can't wait." She couldn't. The dread that filled her at the sight of Genevieve's dresses vanished. For the first time in years, she was excited at the prospect of trying on clothes. If the clothes ended up a bit beyond her father's—or Parliament's—expectations, so what? She was here to stay, and she wasn't about to change who she was to suit them.

Chapter Twenty-Nine

At his desk in the Tower, Rafe buried his face in his hands and groaned. It had taken him an hour on the mirror to calm Genevieve. Arthur knocked at the door.

"What do you want?"

Taking this as an invitation, Arthur let himself in. "I see Lady Genevieve has told you what happened," he said.

"You could have warned me." Rafe looked up at him. "I've never seen her so distraught."

Arthur nodded appreciatively and took a seat in front of the desk, one leg crossed over the other. Rafe glared at him.

"Did you want something or are you just going to sit there looking smug?"

Arthur had never liked Genevieve that much. As a member of the lower nobility—his father was only a baronet—and Rafe's "personal secretary," Arthur had never rated more than kind, but uninterested, politeness from Genevieve. She always treated everyone exactly as she ought to, and that was the problem. The very thing that made her a paradigm of good manners and propriety blinded his otherwise very astute fiancée to the messier calculus of intimate friendship that comes from trusting a man with your very life and having that trust proved valid time and time again.

It was the same with the troops. She could easily understand his oblig-ation as Sword to be on good terms with his men. His willingness to sit in the barracks at Yule with his boots off, drinking winter brandy and telling stories with the enlisted officers baffled her. It was unseemly. And Lady Genevieve, Harvest Queen of the Winter Court, was *never* unseemly.

After a few moments of looking smug, Arthur spoke. "The carriages are all prepared for the journey to Northfalls. There will be five of them, the royal one in the middle. The soldiers accompanying them have all been assigned—Montjoie is leading."

"Sounds good. What other precautions?"

"We're letting it slip to the press that the king and heir are traveling together, so that should draw attention to your little parade. No one will be looking for the magic necessary to open the portals for such a crowd on both ends."

Rafe nodded. Opening the portal between the Palace and Northfalls wasn't difficult for a handful of people. But the king's retinue? All of the valets and maids, all of the clothes and jewelry and special cooks, and guards. Rafe was exhausted thinking about it.

"Some of the servants will be traveling with the group—that will maintain the illusion that the king and princess are there."

"Right." Rafe stood. "Tomorrow morning we leave."

Astride his horse Sampson, Rafe cast a look up and down the column of cavalry and coaches. The wind was bitter cold, but they had spent three days on the road beside full baggage carts and the empty royal coach, its windows darkened, and not an incident yet. Crowds had greeted them on their progress through the countryside, some cheering, some shouting for a glimpse of the heir, but nothing had impeded their progress. In the distance stood Northfalls, a great pile of rock on the shore of the shining loch. They'd be at their destination come mid-after-noon. He glanced at the position of the sun. Deor and Finn should be arriving at the castle by portal any minute now.

Between the baggage train and the castle, however, lay three miles of snow-covered rocky ground and a road that wound in and out of craggy defiles and steep drop offs. And everywhere there was a flat surface, a city of tents had sprung up as every noble family in the land came to honor the king's demands for a show of loyalty.

Rafe was just tugging at the reins to turn back toward the end of the column when a shout from the front brought him around. Beside him, the carriage driver slowed so as not to run into the backs of the horses ahead.

"Full alert, gentlefolk," Rafe said to the men and women riding guard on the carriage before he spurred Sampson forward.

Around the bend of the road where it passed through a low dip into a narrow passage between impossibly steep hillsides a barrier had been thrown across the road. Behind the barrier stood a cluster of about a hundred faeries, unarmored and unhorsed, but their faces grim. Who knew what glamours they had hiding weapons and other means of attack.

Beyond the cluster at the barrier stood other faeries, gawkers and uneasy onlookers, clearly aware that something was happening, but not willing to commit to being a part of it. Elaborate encampments spread out on either side of the road wherever a flat surface could be found. Somewhere nearby a baby squealed.

A red-haired woman standing front and center in the group held a scroll in her hand.

"What is all this?" Rafe shouted. Already the outriders of the caravan were pushing their horses toward the barrier, lances lowered.

"This is a peaceful demonstration," the woman shouted. "We want to speak to the king."

Rafe shouldered Sampson between two cavalry riders, bringing the giant horse as close to the barrier as he could without knocking against. Sampson jigged and stamped his feet, sparks snorting from his nostrils, but the people behind the barrier refused to flinch.

"Don't be absurd. The king will not speak to you like this."

The woman ducked under the barrier, bringing herself almost under Sampson's chin. "I offer myself as a hostage. Take me to the king." The same woman who had supported Victor in Parliament.

Rafe drew himself up. "Do I look like your errand boy, woman? Send your petition to the king by the usual means."

The crowd behind the barrier rumbled. The woman's orange and black wings flared in anger. "And will he read it? Will he even know that it was sent? Either bid the king come speak to us or bring me to him so I can present this to him personally."

"Woman, I'm telling you the king will not speak to you today. Not if you sit in the road and turn to stone."

A dark-haired faerie moved through the crowd toward the barrier. Victor. Rafe's stomach sank, and he moved his free hand to his sword hilt.

"Please, brother," Victor said. "Can't you just take the petition? What possible harm could it do?"

Rafe scowled hard at him. "What the devil are you doing here with these people? Aren't you content stirring up trouble in London?"

The woman with the scroll raised it over her head. "What good is a king who will not listen to his own people?" she shouted. "We are the Winter Court, and we demand to be heard."

Behind her, the crowd murmured and stirred in agreement.

Beside Rafe, one of the cavalry officers spoke low. "Do you want us to disperse them, general?"

"Not yet."

Rafe leaned down out of the saddle, all too aware that the last time he'd taken a chance like that he'd been knocked in the head. And been roundly berated by Finn for being a fool too. Still, the woman had offered herself as a hostage. He had to try.

"I cannot be seen to carry your petition to the king, not like this. If I do, every upstart in the kingdom will think he can coerce an audience with the king," he said, his voice soft. "But I can give you a minute to explain yourself. Speak quickly."

But the woman did not keep her voice low. "We have had enough of a failed king!" she shouted, her voice rippling over the crowd on waves of magic.

Rafe sighed in frustration. She had to be an air faerie.

The woman went on. "Let his heir rule in his place."

"Deor—the princess is thirty," Rafe snapped. "And you're insane if you think the king will cheerfully abdicate his throne just because a hundred malcontents asked for it."

He straightened in the saddle. "Get out of the way. Now."

"Rafe, please. There's more to it than that." Victor leaned across the barrier, reaching for Sampson's bridle. "You helped petitioners once before. Why won't you do it again?"

"This is not the time or the place, Victor!" Rafe turned to the soldiers beside him. "Clear the way for the king's carriage."

Shouts and boos broke out from the crowd at the barrier. Onlookers came to swell their ranks. The soldiers wrestled the barrier out of the way, but the protesters stood firm, linking their arms and refusing to budge.

"Shall we drive into them, sir?" a cavalry woman demanded.

It would be so easy to simply run them down with his horse, to scatter them like leaves before the caravan. And he had to behave as if the king really were in the carriage behind him, his highest priority to get the king safely through no matter what.

Rafe shook his head. "There are children in this crowd, whole families come to see the king. We won't start the violence, whatever we do. Call up the other outriders. Clear the way—haul them off the road by their wings if you have to—and hold an open space with your horses for the carriages to pass through."

The look on the soldier's face told him louder than words what she thought of that strategy, but she obeyed. Inch by inch, they moved the protesters back. Inch by inch, the carriages moved forward through a crowd of booing, shouting faeries. It wasn't just the commoners come to shout—this was a crowd of people used to getting their way. Counter protests broke out as they crept down the road, partisans of the king trading shouts and punches with partisans of the princess and other factions.

Every hundred yards gained was a victory. Rafe rode up and down the line, encouraging a soldier here, restraining a blow there. Everywhere he went, he felt the tension of his soldiers—they had trained for war, not crowd control. This felt like an ambush and now they were being told to be gentle with the ambushers.

"Steady on," Rafe said again and again. "Eyes on the road and remember these are your own people. They aren't the enemy."

Angry, shouting faces pushed in close against the skittish horses around the king's carriage. "Show yourself!"

"Come out and speak to us!"

"All hail King Sweordmund!"

"Down with the monarchy!"

But whatever was shouted, the empty carriage rolled on in silence. It was nightfall by the time they reached Northfalls' gates.

Arthur came out to greet them as the gates fell shut. "You're late," he said. "The king was beginning to worry."

Rafe slid to the ground and threw his reins to a waiting groom. "You have no idea," he said.

"You could have called to the castle for reinforcements."

"I could have started a civil war," Rafe said. "Or caused another tragedy like Castle Mirrovere."

"Well, come on then and tell me all about it." Arthur smiled. "You've arrived just in time to dress and make it to dinner."

"Wonderful," Rafe said. "I can hardly wait."

Chapter Thirty

In the Palace's main reception hall, Deor stood at Finn's side facing the doorway. Much more pomp and circumstance surrounded this portal than had her trip to Roger's at Solstice. This wasn't a visit to a friend—it was *an arrival*, and there was an eager reception waiting for them. Melanie twitched one last non-existent wrinkle out of Deor's floor-length skirt and stood to one side with the other servants ready to accompany the king and heir to Northfalls. She wore a conservative dress—one that bored Wham and Thorsen, but won her father's approval. Her more dynamic wardrobe, with pants and corsets and stunning ball gowns, had been sent ahead earlier in the day.

"Take my arm, my dear," Finn said. "You remember the protocol?"

"Yes, I do." She put one hand in the crook of his elbow, though she refused to actually lean on him. Behind them, Arthur stood.

Two servants put their hands on either side of the door. Lines of magic rippled up and down the frame until the doors disappeared, replaced by a view of a stone castle, its own front doors flung wide and servants lined up to receive the king. In the castle's doorway waited Roger and Pookie, much more formally attired. Roger wore his own lavender tartan, Pookie a heather grey suit.

The royal trumpeters stepped through first, blowing a fanfare as they did. Finn followed, leading Deor with him. She caught her breath as she crossed the threshold, feeling as if she had been flipped inside out starting with her navel and somehow catapulted a thousand miles in the process. Her fingers tightened on Finn's arm.

Gravel crunched underfoot, and she panted a bit. Traveling directly from Caer Eisteddfod to the faerie equivalent of Scotland by portal was a much bigger deal than the multi-stop portalling she and Rafe had done. She plastered the smile back on her face as the two men came down the castle steps. Two servants, a man and a woman, followed behind them.

"Your Majesties! How good it is to see you in good health. Welcome, all of you, to my home." Roger beamed. He took Finn's outstretched hand in both of his and bowed deeply. Behind him, the servants bowed as well.

"Well met, Roger, Lord of Northfalls, Lord of the Winter Court Admiralty and our trusted friend," Finn answered. He raised Roger from his bow and kissed him on both cheeks. "We are most pleased to share your hospitality."

Deor held out her hand to Roger for the next step in the ceremony. Roger bowed deeply over her hand and kissed it. "Welcome to Northfalls, Princess Deor. It is an honor and a privilege to have you in my home."

"You are most kind," Deor recited from memory. "I... we thank you for your hospitality."

"Please, come into the house and enjoy some refreshments after your long journey," Roger said.

Deor smiled at that. She had literally taken only three steps, even if those three steps had covered a thousand miles, but Finn was thanking Roger and agreeing that a refreshment would be most welcome after the arduousness of the journey.

Deor glanced over her shoulder. Arthur had come through with them, even if Roger hadn't acknowledged him. He stood no less than three feet behind Deor's back. The servants, however, were nowhere to be seen, and the portal home had disappeared.

"I thought those servants were coming with us," she whispered to Finn as he led her up the castle steps. "Where are they?"

"They are coming in by servants' entrance," he whispered back. "The porters will have moved the portal for them."

"I didn't realize they had to take a separate portal." She had simply pictured the servants arriving and then walking around the house to a side door. Moving the portal did make sense, especially with the freezing cold wind whipping through the courtyard. The very short ceremonial exchange outside had made her fingers and toes go numb and her ears sting. Her nose was going to start watering in a second, too. Good thing Wham had encouraged her to order three dozen handkerchiefs, one of which was tucked into an invisible pocket this very moment.

More trumpeting and announcing of titles followed as she and Finn crossed the threshold into Roger's Great Hall. A glittering crowd of who's who in the Winter Court turned to bow in her direction. Should she wave? Bow back? The book had described what a young noblewoman or man when making an entrance at her or his debut into polite society, generally a ball held on the person's thirtieth birthday party, but this didn't seem quite the same thing. Besides, she had a pretty keen feeling that if she upstaged Finn she would hear about it later, so she settled for following his lead and merely nodding her head.

The crowd parted, and Astarte walked forward until she was within arm's reach of Finn. She curtsied deeply to him but did not bow her head as she did so.

"My beloved Consort," Finn said. "How good it is to see you again."

"The pleasure is all mine, Your Majesty," Astarte said, her eyes locked with Finn's. Deor pulled her hand off Finn's elbow and leaned as far away from the two as she could get without being obvious.

Finn raised Astarte from her curtsey and kissed her on both cheeks as he had done with Roger. Astarte returned the kisses.

An audible sigh of relief spread through the room. Conversations restarted. Finn turned away from Deor to speak to Roger and Astarte.

Deor scanned the room and did not see Robbie. She recognized some from the Overton's card party, including a group of men and women clustered around Genevieve across the room—no cheerful welcome there. She stood in a bubble of isolation, half the room still watching her from the corner of their eyes, but no one yet bold enough to approach. She took the opportunity to look around.

The outside of Northfalls was rough-hewn rock, a fortress built for defense, not comfort, but the interior hall glowed with gold leaf and natural light. Garlands of winter greenery draped everywhere, twining around the bannisters of the twin staircase. Glittering snowflakes danced overhead, as if caught in a perpetual fall, always moving, but never landing.

"Whiskey, Your Majesty?" A servant offered her a tray full of tiny stemmed crystal glasses. Finn already had a glass in his hand, so she took one. If this was anything like the wine Geoff had ordered on their first date, she'd need to nurse it carefully or end up giggling and on the floor.

"Haggis foie gras on neeps, Your Majesty?" Another servant held out a different tray to Deor.

"Thank you." Deor took what looked like ground beef and oatmeal dolloped onto a tiny slice of root vegetable. Great. Now she had her hands full of two things she didn't want to put in her mouth.

She was about to join her father and Astarte, when Geoff's familiar shape pushed through the crowd. Two goblin companions, both broad shouldered and unsmiling, followed.

"How delightful to see you again, Princess," he said reaching for Deor's hand to kiss it as he bowed. Deor waved off the kiss with her hands full of neeps and alcohol. "Good afternoon, Prince Geoffrey," Deor said. "How are you enjoying the weather?" If there was one thing *the Noble Babies Noble Book* stressed, it was the importance of discussing the weather. *No other topic is so safe, so unlikely to carry hidden pitfalls, as a discussion of the weather. Young lords and ladies should make liberal use of this topic, especially in the presence of elder folk who may have intrigues in mind. The state of one's companion's health is also an acceptable topic, though even here one must be circumspect.*

Geoff blinked at her for a moment. "We're inside."

"Yes. It's much warmer in here than outside, isn't it?" Deor gave him a bright and vacant smile.

"Ah yes. Yes, it is. I understand you've given up teaching at Eisteddfod. Whatever for?"

"There was a riot. I don't want people to get hurt. What are you doing with yourself lately?"

"Many things." He waved his hand. "The demands of state are so complex that I've been forced to set aside my studies for the time being."

"What a pity," Deor said flatly. "Academia's loss, I'm sure." She took the tiniest possible sip of the whiskey. She wasn't going to take a bite of the haggis thing in her other hand, not while Geoff was watching. She'd be sure to get too big a mouthful or have the flat chip shatter, sending gobs of goose liver and oatmeal across her chest and down her cleavage. "And how is the weather in Barizan these days?"

"Barizan doesn't actually have weather. It's entirely underground."

"What a pity," she repeated. Using the *Noble Babies Book* was turning out to be rather more fun than she'd anticipated. The look of frustration on Geoff's face made her wish for a camera.

"Barizan is beautifully temperate year round," Geoff said, the green on his face deepening.

"What a pity," she said for the third time.

"Indeed," a voice behind her said. "I imagine the lack of variation would become rather dull if one lived there long. I always find myself longing for open water and fresh air when I'm forced to visit the place."

As Geoff sputtered, Deor turned to discover Victor Farringdon.

"Please excuse my attire." He bowed. "I only recently arrived, and I did not want to miss the chance to speak with you before the formal festivities begin tomorrow."

Deor waved away the comment—careful not to fling food or whisky. "I'm afraid my knowledge of faerie fashion is quite weak. I wouldn't have known the difference had you not told me."

He had his mother's eyes. At the thought, Deor's stomach lurched hard. The skin around her throat and across her chest stung as if she had touched freezing metal. She tightened her grip on her glass, focusing her attention on the feel of crystal pricking her fingers. Healers had told her to ground herself in the present—to find a physical sensation and hold on to it—whenever remnants of the alley attack overwhelmed her memory.

"Are you well, Princess?" Victor looked genuinely concerned.

"I'm fine, thank you," she managed. She focused on the distance behind Victor, trying to avoid his eyes without seeming intimidated. He had assured her he was on her side. She had no reason to disbelieve him.

When a waiter cruised by again, Deor dumped her uneaten *amuse bouche* on his tray, but kept the whisky. Despite being inside, she was chilly, and the drink warmed her. Though she took baby sips to make sure of its effects.

"Perhaps the Winter Court isn't suiting you," Geoff said. "What with your human side and all."

Deor shot him a glare but didn't rise to the bait. He'd sworn that she would lose her faerie side and be fully human at the Adoption, if she would simply let the ceremony kill the king and Rafe. "No," she said. "I'm unused to portalling such long distances."

"Ah yes," Victor nodded. "That can be difficult. I rode up from London myself."

"Was it a long journey? Cold?"

"I rode with friends, part of it on my horse, and part of it sharing a carriage, so when it was too cold, I could always retreat there. We took our time—a couple days—so it was a pleasant journey."

"I enjoy road trips," Deor said. "Seeing the countryside."

"You'll love the king's tour, then, won't you?" Geoff said. "You'll see so many houses."

"I imagine," she said. She wanted to shoo him away, demand he leave, punch him in the face. None would work. Small talk was her only recourse. Weather had been exhausted. People like Geoff liked to talk about themselves, so what could she suggest? "That's a lovely ring, Geoff. I don't think I ever saw you wear it before."

"Oh this?" He held out his hand. A blue stone was set in white metal—probably platinum—and surrounded with white pearls. "This is a family ring. It has been worn by heirs for centuries." He held his hand out to her.

Up close, she could see that the setting around the stones was engraved. She whispered the words to herself, but no translation popped into her head. It must have been Goblin, which struck her as similar to Faerie, but not enough to be recognizable.

"What does it say?" she asked.

"Good afternoon, all," Rafe interrupted before Geoff could explain. He gave a polite nod to both Geoff and Victor. "I've just arrived."

"Victor has, too," Deor said. "Trouble on the road?"

"No," Both Farringdons said together.

"It was fine, if a bit chilly," Rafe said. "And you all?"

"I was just asking Geoff about his fancy ring."

Rafe and Victor exchanged glances.

"Go on," Deor said to Geoff.

Geoff grinned and pointed at the top. "Above the gem, it reads *For the Future of My People* and below, *Purity of Mind, Purity of Heart, Purity of Body*."

Deor snorted. "That last one is cute," she said.

"What's cute about it?" Geoff's voice cut through the air.

"Really?" Deor asked. "Purity of body? Maybe I don't understand the meaning of the word purity in this context. You mean sexual purity?"

"Naturally." Geoff's body was stiff, his tone formal.

The crowd had thinned some, with various nobles returning to their tents outside. Those staying at the house had remained, and the conversation had drawn their attention. Even the king and Astarte had made their way within earshot.

Deor glanced at her father, who raised his eyebrows, leaving her response up to her. There was no way she was letting this go. "So, no sex? How's that working out for you?"

"Quite well," he snapped. "Just as I would never, ever do my country the dishonor of bringing a bastard into this world, I certainly would not defile my body, nor would I allow a woman to dishonor hers."

"Ah," Deor said.

Geoff had puffed up—straightened his back, squared his shoulders. Even his chin was jutted out. He withdrew his hand from hers. "I wouldn't expect *you* to understand such things, given what you are."

Deor blinked.

Rafe jerked like he was going to bolt, his expression murderous. Victor laid a hand on his brother's arm, and Rafe eased back. Victor whispered something to him, and Rafe nodded, but crossed his arms.

"No, no," she said. "I understand. We have some people with similar attitudes in my home country."

Geoff snorted. "I'm surprised."

"No, it's really pretty common," Deor said. "People who use all sorts of wild parameters to claim that they are virgins—it doesn't count because it was in a car; it doesn't count because I still had one foot on the floor; and my favorite, it doesn't count because it was in a foreign country." She patted his arm. "It's a crock of shit."

Gasps erupted from around the room. A few women had covered their mouths, but looked more like they were laughing than shocked. Finn shook his head, but more disbelief than disapproval. Astarte and Roger both had sly smiles on their faces. Pookie looked ready to clap his hands and cheer.

"Excuse me?" Geoff said.

"Did you not hear me?" she said politely. "Or did you not understand me?"

"I will give you one chance to clarify—what you said could be taken as an insult."

"An insult?" Deor said, skepticism on her face. "You are an insult. And, I must say, not worth the trouble."

"You didn't complain when I was showering you with…" he paused dramatically "…attention!" He might as well have made air quotes, too, though they couldn't have made his point more clear.

"That's true," Deor said. "I didn't complain. On the whole, your 'attention,'" Deor did include the air quotes, "was adequate."

Victor barked out a laugh, and a few others followed.

"Oh, Geoff," Victor said, "you should have that embroidered on a pillow so you can fall asleep and wake up to the reminder of your adequacy."

"Perhaps," Rafe added, "you might have it added to your official list of titles? Prince Geoffrey the Adequate, heir to the Goblin Kingdom?"

"I could have it put on a t-shirt," Deor said, with a smile. "Or we could send it out as a public service announcement to all of the Winter Court."

Geoff's slit pupils flared, and a small blush crept into the tips of his ears. "You were just another Winter Court slut I tossed when I was done."

Deor barked out a laugh. "Oh, Geoff. That's cute." She smiled indulgently—like he was a child. "But that's not how I remember it. I remember breaking it off with you in the side room where you tried to kill me."

Geoff's eyes widened.

"Oh, wait!" Deor pressed on. "You must not remember, because by the time I told you we were through, you were unconscious on the floor."

His whole face was flushed now, and his pupils trembled slightly. He opened his mouth to speak.

"I'm not finished!" Deor cut him off before he began. "I understand that things in the Winter Court have changed a bit recently—quite quickly. So, in case you didn't know, you're done. Do not come into my country and try to shame my people, you pathetic hypocrite."

"You'll pay for this insult!" Geoff snapped. "Your words mean nothing. You can't hurt me." He crossed his arms as if that finished it.

"Really?" she said. "Then tell me why, now that you're blushing, I can see two perfect, parallel white scars on your eyelids and cheeks? Or did some other faerie wing you in the face?" Deor crossed her arms and leaned slightly back.

Geoff sputtered for a moment.

"That's what I thought," she said.

"Finn!" Geoff snapped. "You need to get your daughter under control! Behavior like this could cost you!"

"Are you making a threat to His Majesty?" Rafe cut in. "As the Sword, I do take all threats against His Majesty and his heir very seriously."

"There are several of us here who would take up the princess's cause," Victor said with a grin.

Geoff gestured at Finn, who shrugged. He spun to look at Roger. "Are you going to let this go on? Are you going to let your guest be insulted like this?"

Roger laid a hand over his heart, his eyes sparkling like they would flood the room. "My dear boy, no." He looked to Deor. "I am sorry, Your Majesty, for my guest's bad behavior. I had no idea that inviting him would cause you such distress. If it pleases you, I could ask him to leave."

"What?" Geoff demanded. "Ask me to leave?"

"No, Roger," Deor said. "But thank you. He is your guest, and I would never impose on you like that." Deor glanced at Finn, who glared at her with grey eyes. He arched his eyebrows. "In fact," she said hurriedly, "I am sorry that I put you in this position as host."

Finn's shoulders eased a bit, and he smiled. She'd done another good pet trick, apparently.

"There you go, Geoffrey," Roger said. "Stay if you like—it seems the princess can tolerate you. Though I would suggest you keep your amorous adventures to a minimum."

Geoff looked around the room, and more than one noblewoman had a gleeful smirk. She imagined they'd had their own run-ins with the crown prince.

He bowed stiffly. "Thank you for the advice." Geoff nodded at his two bodyguards and strode from the room.

"Well, Princess," Roger said coming up to her. "That was the perfect way to start off this little soiree." He gave her a hug. "Is there anything you need?"

"No, thank you." She glanced past Roger at Finn, but he had turned to Astarte and seemed to pay her no mind. "I think that I will lay low the rest of the evening and prepare for our ride tomorrow."

"Excellent!"

Rafe stepped up and offered her his arm. "Shall I show you to your room?"

Deor took it. "Yes, please."

Deor frowned and looked around at the set of rooms assigned to her. On the one hand, she'd never been to a sleep-over that included a full bedroom, bathroom, and walk-in closet to herself. On the other hand, she'd never had an entourage to look after.

"Where exactly are you supposed to sleep?" she asked Melanie, who was busily hanging up clothes.

"I'm meant to sleep in here, ma'am."

"On the floor?" Literally medieval. No. She was not making someone sleep on her floor like a dog in front of the fire. She sighed. The guest bed would certainly fit the two of them, but it might be a bit snug, especially given that Brand had already made himself comfortable in the middle of the bed. He watched her with wagging tail and bright eyes.

"Not exactly on the floor," Melanie said. She pressed a portion of the wall, and a trundle bed slid out beneath the dresses to fill up the walk-in aisle. "It's a bit old fashioned, but I'll be quite comfortable. It's meant to keep your jewels safe, you see." She showed Deor how the bed had a hidden compartment beneath the mattress. "Not that anything would happen to your belongings here. Someone would have to be mad to try to steal from the princess with the Sword in the house and the king in the very next room."

"I suppose. It seems a bit rude, making you sleep in my closet..."

Melanie tucked the jewel box into its compartment and replaced the mattress, smoothing the sheets into place and sliding the bed back into its hiding place in the wall. "I wasn't going to ask, Your Majesty, but since you mention it, do you think I might have permission to sleep away a night or two?"

"Of course. You shouldn't have to be on duty twenty-four seven."

"Thank you. Lady Clarissa's maid and I are old friends, and we hardly ever see each other. It will be a great treat to spend time together at the Servant's Ball. I'd be back bright and early to help you with your toilette."

Deor laughed. "No rush. How long can it take to get ready to go hunting?"

Melanie shook her head but didn't reply.

"Deor?" Finn called from the parlor. "Come out here!"

"Excuse me." Deor nodded at Melanie, who curtsied. "Stay." She pointed at Brand before she slipped out her door and closed it behind her.

"We need to talk," Finn said. He stood by the fireplace, staring into the flames.

Deor came to him. "That was quite the reception," she said, her voice soft.

Finn looked up to her and frowned. "It was quite the scene," he corrected. "And you shouldn't be making any scenes."

"But Geoff—"

"No!" He cut her off. "You will not embarrass me!" He stepped toward her but stopped when she pulled back slightly. "If I have to lock you in here and keep you from everything until the presentation to the people, I will. I will have guards on you every day and night."

"The only one who embarrasses you is you," Deor said, forcing her voice to stay low and level. "There wasn't a woman in that room who didn't want to cheer when I told that asshole off. Would you rather him call me a whore and me smile than risk losing an ally who openly insults you? That's insane."

"That's politics!" His voice roared again. "He is a horrible creature. I will not deny that. But right now, the Summer Court is particularly powerful, thanks to my…illness, and they are no doubt aware of that and planning for something—likely war. I do not know that we could win. I do know what the world would look like if we were to lose. My alliance with Gregory keeps the Summer Court in check."

Deor opened her mouth, but closed it again.

"There." Finn pointed at her. "You're not so bullish now, are you? What little insult would Gregory need to pull his friendship."

"Not a very good friendship…" Deor muttered.

"No! It's not!" Finn snapped. "We were friends, when we were young, but after I married Astarte, and then no children…then she took a child bearer, and I became ill…" He shook his head. His shoulders slumped, and he dropped his gaze to the floor. He looked frail again, for a moment. "I have not been in a position of strength for some time." He looked back up at her. "You are changing that. You are young, healthy, vibrant, strong. You are everything this nation needs, but you know so little." He shook his head.

"Finn, I—"

"Come here." He sat on the couch and patted the cushion next to him. "Please."

She did.

He reached out and touched her cheek. "Everything rests on you, daughter. I am sorry it is so, but it is. Geoffrey deserved everything you said, and more. I know this. But your behavior—it puts not just you, but everyone, in danger. If people think you are bothered by him, that you can't control your temper, that you're just a child. Any of those could be deadly."

Deor nodded. "I understand." She wanted to argue, to tell him that no, what was important was standing up to Geoff, to bullies like him. But she was wrong, and she knew it. This was a world of delicate sneers and polite exiles. Sure, the audience might have loved her dressing Geoff down, but in the long run? She was a child acting out.

"Do you?" He cupped her chin and stared into her eyes. The grey was soft, drifting almost toward white, like high clouds on a bleak day.

"I do," she said. "From here on out, a picture of decorum."

He frowned.

"Okay," she admitted. "I'll only hit back?" She paused. "And I'll not egg anyone on, either."

He laughed and dropped his hand from her face. "Yes, daughter. Only hit back." He leaned in and kissed her forehead. "And we'll hope nobody starts anything."

She was off to such a great start, and tomorrow, a hunting party. No problem at all, since she'd never been hunting in her life, and never held bow and arrow in anything but PE, and, city girl that she was, never been on a horse.

Chapter Thirty-One

A sharp wind whipped across the stable yard, the sky above bright blue with only the barest wisps of cloud. Even in her hooded fur coat and double-lined riding pants, Deor felt the wind. The Californian in her expected blue sky to mean warmer weather, but here it seemed only to mean that the cold had deepened.

None of Roger's other guests seemed to care. Most of them were already mounted. They laughed and sang snatches of hunting songs, telling jokes and checking their horses' gear while foresters and a pack of shaggy dogs like hairy, overgrown greyhounds dashed around between the horses' hooves. Deor tucked her gloved hands under her arms and shivered. She wished Robbie were going. Then she'd at least have someone to talk to on this merry olde slaughter-fest and picnic. But Robbie was still too fragile to be riding pell-mell across the countryside. And, Deor suspected, too afraid of the king to make herself visible as one of the party.

Finn, his head bare, strode over to her, a riding crop in hand. "All set to ride?"

She glanced at the riders around her. "Not really—but I'll give it a go."

Finn laughed. "That's my daughter. I'm sure you'll be fine."

"Don't worry, Your Majesty. Old Bessie here will keep you safely on her back." Thea, a famed horse-breeder according to Roger, strode up leading two long-legged bay horses. The horses' saddles were both above Deor's head. Thea dropped the reins on one and pulled forward the horse with a white blaze across its forehead.

Even Finn looked a bit skeptical. "My daughter is not accustomed to riding, Lady Thea. Wouldn't a pony would be a more advisable mount?"

Thea snorted in a heartily unladylike way. "Don't you think it. Ponies are tricky little shits. And the ones Roger's got in his stable are all cart broken anyway. I doubt any of them would have the speed to keep up with the main party. No, what you want is a nice pasture pet like Bessie here. Got a good steady temper on her, and she'll follow the rest of the hunt whether her rider loses the reins or not. I brought her up from the south myself." As she spoke, Thea jerked on the stirrup, lengthening the strap until it dangled just below Bessie's belly. She turned the stirrup toward Deor. "Up you get, Princess."

Deor eyed the stirrup and then Thea. "How? Exactly." The stirrup was still a good four feet off the ground. She'd have to raise her foot almost to chin level just to get a toe into the molded leather loop.

Thea just laughed. "You are a green one, aren't you?" She patted the horse on the shoulder. "Stand still, there's a girl. Now, Princess, get a good grip on the saddle, and I'll give you a boost." She looped her fingers together and crouched, signaling for Deor to step into her cupped hands.

Feeling as if she were about become a reluctant participant in an ill thought out acrobatic act, Deor grabbed the side of the saddle with both hands and put her left foot into Thea's hands.

"Up you get!" And up she did go. Thea tossed Deor skyward as if she weighed nothing. She landed stomach down across the saddle, feet flailing.

"Get your leg over, girl!" Thea bellowed at her and pushed Deor's right leg over the saddle. Deor scrambled to sit up and still hold onto the front of the saddle while Thea shoved Deor's foot into the stirrup and tightened the strap. "Hold on. I'll get your other side." Thea ducked under the horse's chin and repeated the move with Deor's other foot. "There you go. Good show. Now stand up."

"What?"

"Let go of that saddle and stand up. I want to check your stirrup height."

Deor shook her head violently. "They're fine. Very comfortable. Thank you."

Thea shrugged good naturedly. "If you say so. Bessie looks like she's tolerating it nicely, so you should be alright." She picked up the reins from where they lay on Bessie's neck and handed them to over. Deor clutched them hard enough that Bessie's head came up and she snorted.

"Ease up there," Thea said. "Just a gentle tug is all she'll need. Sit deep in the saddle, and for heaven's sake, don't grip with your knees like that. Keep your eyes between her ears. She'll do the rest for you."

Deor nodded. Focusing on the horse's ears did seem better than thinking about just how far off the ground she was, held up only by a glass-smooth piece of leather and two stirrups. Finn nodded, apparently satisfied, and went off to find his own horse, while Thea mounted. She didn't even use the stirrup—a flick of her wings and she was in the saddle.

"You're not wearing a skirt," Deor said. Thea rode astride like her, billows of cloth Deor had mistaken for a riding skirt spreading out like a cloak over her horse's back and revealing Thea's slim cut breeches and boots underneath.

Thea smiled. "Sidesaddle hunting is stylish, I'll give it that, but I prefer the feel of a good horse between my legs. Besides, a split skirt keeps you and the horse warm."

Deor admitted to herself that Thea had a point. Astarte's insistence that her riding coat have a long slit from the bottom edge to halfway up her back meant that now the two sides of her coat hung over her legs instead of bunching up behind her.

All around them riders were turning their horses toward the open fields. Huntsmen in Roger's tartan were blowing horns. The pack of dogs tore out the gate and across the field. Behind them, riders began to move, horses picking up speed. With no input on Deor's part, Bessie picked up her feet and ambled along with the other horses. Deor clutched the reins harder and gripped with her knees.

Ahead of her, she spotted Genevieve riding beside Rafe. She carried a bow and her dagged sleeves fluttered in the wind. Rafe carried a spear in his hand, the end resting on his boot tip and three more tied to his saddle. A number of the other riders also carried spears and bows, including Victor, who threw Deor a jaunty salute before riding off to join the head of the pack. Thea jogged along beside Deor at the rear.

"You've been assigned to babysit me, haven't you?" Deor said. "I hope I'm not ruining your hunt." Bessie's pace had quickened into a bouncing trot that slammed Deor's pelvic bone down hard on every other step. She gritted her teeth and clenched her butt, but neither helped.

"Not at all," Thea said. "I like the ride, but I'm not much of a one for killing. Come up a bit though. You'll bang your horse to pieces if you keep coming down on her like that." She flicked her own horse with the riding crop and both animals stretched their legs, picking up speed. The banging motion stopped, but now the ground flew by underfoot in a blur. Mud splattered across Deor's lap. God help the servants who had to clean all this gear at the end of the day.

"Heads up," Thea called.

"Oh shit!" Deor shrieked just in time to see the hedge looming in front of them. Deor pulled back on the reins, but Bessie took this as a signal to jump, lifting them both up and over the low hedge. They landed with a muddy splash in a hidden ditch on the other side, and Deor clung to the saddle as her horse scrambled up and out of the water. Off to her left, Thea was laughing.

"Well done, Princess. You've got bottom to you after all."

Deor spat muddy water and tried to scrape it out of her eyes without losing her grip on either reins or horse. "What the hell was that?"

"Just a bit of a jump. Come on. Stay close."

And on they went, following the pack of hunters that was already spreading out far ahead of them and disappearing into the woods. Deor did her best, but her best consisted of hanging on for dear life and hoping Bessie had the sense not to get lost. The horses slowed, weaving between trees and through underbrush. Hidden dips and rises in the ground made Deor sway and weave from one side to the other. No matter what she did, Bessie kept placidly moving forward. When she looked back over her shoulder, Deor could see no trace of their path. The trees overhead were so thick that she could barely catch a glimpse of the sky or tell what direction the sun was shining from. The interlaced branches overhead had caught the falling snow so that the ground was only dusted with white.

At least she could still see Thea a few feet to her left. The rest of the hunt was gone, dispersed into the forest. Somewhere in the distance, dogs were yapping wildly. A flash of red or blue, the crash of a horse's hoof broke the unrelenting green and brown from time to time. Occasionally a horn blew. Deor shivered again, not with cold this time. This must have been what Longfellow meant about "the forest primeval." She just hoped the horses had some idea how to get back to their stable. If they did, they didn't give any hint of it. Instead, she and Thea kept pushing forward, getting deeper into the woods.

A flash of white off to her left caught her eye. Astarte, riding a pure white horse and holding a spear with a golden tip, rode up to them. The tip was stained with blood.

Her eyes shone, and her cheeks were flushed. "How are you enjoying the hunt?" she called.

"It's just peachy," Deor called back. "Very, um, rural. Did you catch something?"

"Just a red stag," Astarte said. "The foresters are flaying it for me."

The horns echoed through the woods, a three-note call repeated twice. Astarte stood up in her saddle. "A boar! Now there's real sport." With a whoop, she spurred her horse into the brush, the white animal and her sparkling wings disappearing between the trees.

The unsettling silence returned. The horses walked delicately, picking their way between moss covered boulders.

"Thea," Deor called. "We're not lost, are we?"

"Never fear. We'll be fine."

"That's not what I asked. Do you have any idea where we are?"

"Not as such," Thea said comfortably. "But I can hear the horns, and the horses aren't spooked, so we've nothing to worry about. I expect they'll be winding us in for a good luncheon once they've killed that boar."

Hooves crunched on leaves as they trotted farther into the woods. The trees around them merged from oaks and other deciduous trees to thick pine that blocked half the light. She began to lose sight of Thea from time to time as Bessie picked the easiest route through the trees.

"Princess!" Thea called. "Stay closer to me, please."

"I'm trying," she called back.

White flashed in the trees ahead. Deor breathed out in relief. Astarte must have killed the boar and come back for them. Deor tried to tug Bessie toward the white patch. The horse planted her feet, head weaving back and forth. It didn't take an expert horsewoman to realize the horse was shivering with fear. Deor patted Bessie's shoulder the way she'd seen Thea do. It didn't seem to help.

"Deor. Don't move," Thea said. She too was watching the white thing that flitted between the trees.

"What is it?" Deor whispered.

The branches ahead parted, snapping and cracking. A unicorn burst through the undergrowth, its eyes wide and rolling with fear. Bloody claw marks scored its haunches. A second unicorn came after it, sweating hard. Thea's horse screamed and reared. Thea kept her seat, but only just, clinging to her horse's mane.

The second unicorn squealed and reared, turning in mid-stride away from Thea's flailing mount. Bessie flinched away, but too late. The unicorn cannoned into Bessie, striking her shoulder. Bessie stumbled and screamed. The unicorn snarled, its teeth sharp and canine. Bessie jerked away, her own teeth snapping at the unicorn's haunch.

Deor threw herself flat across Bessie's neck as the unicorn's horn stabbed the air where she had been a second ago. Underneath her, Bessie's muscles bunched, and the placid horse leaped away, hitting the ground at a full gallop and bolting into the forest. Her fingers gripping Bessie's mane, Deor clung to her runaway mount.

In her scramble for a handhold, Deor lost the reins completely. They flapped uselessly across Bessie's neck as Deor clung with knees and claws to the saddle. The reckless gallop slammed her ribs up and down against the hard saddle, knocking the breath out of her so that she could only gasp for air. She put her head down, shielding her eyes from slapping branches, and banged her nose on Bessie's neck for her trouble.

Bessie broke from the forest into a clearing, but didn't slow. Deor risked sitting up—ahead the clearing gave way to a drop, and the horse plunged on, with no sign of stopping.

Chapter Thirty-Two

Bessie plunged over the drop and down a steep slope, hooves slipping and sliding through the damp moss until Deor was sure both she and the horse were about to go ass over teakettle. But she gritted her teeth and hung on.

At the bottom, Bessie slowed to a trot, then a walk, and finally came to a halt, breathing hard and shuddering. Foaming sweat covered her twitching body, and she hung her head, tongue protruding between her teeth.

Slowly, Deor forced her fingers to let go of the saddle. Her inch long, bladed nails left a row of perfectly spaced cuts in the hardened leather. She sat for a while on Bessie's back, panting, until she could pat the still twitching horse on the shoulder without risk of stabbing it.

"It's okay. We're going to be okay. You stupid, panicky animal you."

She thought about getting down off the horse. Right now, she'd like nothing better than to never ride a horse again, but she decided against it. The muscles in her thighs and calves twitched and jumped in a way that told her she wouldn't be doing any running away, or even much fast walking on her own. And the horse was still her best chance of finding her way out of the woods back to civilization.

Deor risked standing up in her saddle, but she couldn't see out of the low spot where Bessie had led them. She still couldn't reach the reins, but she made clicking noises and kicked her feet until Bessie started to walk again. On either side, the ground sloped up too steeply for any chance of going back the way they came. She'd never done Girl Scouts, and her one attempt at summer camp, at her grandmother's insistence, had not been a highlight of her childhood. Still, she hoped if they walked along this flat, narrow space, it might lead somewhere.

"Thea!" she shouted. "Somebody!" No one answered.

They rode along in the silence, but the farther they went, the more Deor felt as if the natural magicks all around her were broken, twisted and jagged like barbed wire. Bessie picked up her pace, seemingly enjoying the relatively open low spot of ground she'd found. Her hooves clattered rather than thumped, as they had on the soft dirt. Deor risked leaning out of the saddle to peer at the ground—yes, she was riding on the remnants of an old road.

The open ground in front of them widened. Jagged stones reared up out of the ground cover. Some had scorch marks on them. The ground cover grew sparser, more full of brambles and thorns. The few trees she saw were stunted and bulgy as if they had tumors. She was riding through the ruin of an old building. Bessie stopped in the corner of a wall with half a window, head low. Her shivering returned. If Deor looked closely, she could see the natural lines of magic flowing through and across the ground, except the magic was puddled and smeared. Bits of it tangled together or ended in black ends like burnt matches.

"Hello?" Deor called again. Clearly no one had lived there for years, but maybe by now the hunters were looking for her.

"Tally ho, Princess Deor," Victor's voice called back.

"I'm over here!"

"Stay where you are," he called back.

"No problem," she said under her breath. Bessie kept her head low, eyes white around the edges.

Victor rode up the road where she had just been, picking up his pace as he spotted her. "Are you alright?"

"I think so. Just bumped and bruised a bit." She tried to smile. "Bessie got spooked by a couple of unicorns."

Victor leaned out of his saddle, gathering her reins. His usually smiling face was grim. Bessie leaned her shoulder against his horse's, seeming to take comfort in the presence of another horse.

"We shouldn't be here," Victor said. "Forgive the impertinence, but..." He turned his own horse, pulling Bessie along. He had no spears, and though his bow was slung across the back of his saddle, the quiver had only two arrows.

"What a nice coincidence this is," she said. "How did you find me?"

"Thea called us. There are others out looking for you. I just happened to be the one who went this way."

"This place scares me," Deor said. "It's...wrong. There's something very wrong about this ruin."

Instead of laughing, Victor nodded. "Too many innocent lives lost. The destructive magic unleashed here has poisoned everything, even the ground. Without intervention, it will take hundreds of years before this place is cleansed."

"What happened?"

His voice was bitter. "Your father happened."

"Whoa. Wait up." She reached for his arm. "Tell me what happened."

"Later. When we're away from here." He tried to lead the horses around the corner where they stood, but Bessie planted her feet and leaned back against the reins, jaw locked around the bit. Victor's own horse skittered and danced sideways, eyes rolling white.

Muttering swear words in faerie, Victor tried to reel in Bessie while calming his own horse. Neither horse was having it.

Deor wondered if she should tell him she knew what each word meant.

Finally, he reached into his pocket, pulling out a round mirror bearing the Farringdon crest and tossed it to Deor. "Call the Sword and let him know where we are. Please. Your Majesty."

"I don't know where we are. What do I tell him?"

"Tell him we're at Mirrovere. He'll know."

Deor flipped open the mirror and tapped it. "Rafe, Lord Farringdon, please." No one else said please to their mirrors when they made calls, but she still felt as if she might be talking to an invisible operator on some magical version of an old-time telephone exchange.

Rafe's face appeared a second later. "Victor, have you found her? Oh, Deor. Are you safe? What happened to your face?"

"Just a bump." The swelling on the bridge of her nose was spreading to her eyes. "Victor says we're at Mirrovere. I think there's something really bad going on, Rafe. The magic here is all jagged, and the horses are freaking out at nothing."

"I'll be there as fast as we can."

She tucked Victor's mirror into her pocket. Victor was still wrestling with the horses who were trying the huddle together while keeping their eyes square on the corner of the ruined building. Deor grabbed a handful of saddle for balance as her knee banged painfully into Victor's.

"I don't want to sound like the dumb girl in a horror movie," she said, "but I think we're in trouble."

"Hopefully it's just another unicorn," Victor said between gritted teeth, wrestling his horse's head toward the road. He tied Bessie's reins to his saddle, looped his own reins around those, and unslung his bow. "I can handle a unicorn, though I'd rather have a spear and a couple of dogs for the job."

Deor squinted into the shadows of the building's corner. Too much shadow there. Like the shadows Donovan the vampire wrapped around himself. She leaned forward, concentrating on seeing through the magic.

Cold, heart-pounding terror poured through her, the kind of terror that wakes you up at two in the morning and keeps you awake until the sun comes up over the horizon. It squeezed her chest. Something like a rotting wolf and an octopus and a snake moved in the shadows. A snake with eyes like the woman in the alley.

"Are you seeing that?" she hissed at Victor.

"A thing like a goblin mated with a wyvern? Don't look it in the eye. Don't turn your back on it." Victor was pale. He panted with fear, too, but he held his bow steady. "It's called a Nightmare."

The shadow moved.

"Focus on the horses. That's right, tiny little minds, tiny little fears," Victor muttered under his breath. He drew back the bow. The thing in the shadows was more snakelike now. It crawled forward, and the shadows came with it. Flames leaped around its legs. Victor's horse screamed. Victor kicked it, urging it to back up, but the horse's legs were locked.

Deor flexed her fingers, willing her nails' blades to grow longer and sharper. Whatever it was, she was going to claw the hell out of it if it came within arm's reach. Inside her sleeves, her skin rippled and stung with gathering magic.

In the distance, a horn blew. Hope leaped up against the fear squeezing her heart. The shadow thing lunged. It sank its alligator teeth into Victor's horse.

Victor's bow twanged. The arrow snapped and bounced off invisible armor. Bessie reared and screamed, striking at the thing killing her companion. Deor scrambled for a hold, but her clawed fingers scraped down the saddle leather as she tumbled backward, head over heels.

Deor scrambled to her feet in time to see Victor leap clear of his dying horse. He groped underneath the animal for the last of his arrows, shooting into the shadow that surged over the horse's neck. Bloody, bone-snapping sounds came from it, but the arrow didn't seem to slow it down.

"Run!" Victor shouted. "Go!" He drew a knife. Deor looked around for a stone, a broken brick, something to throw at the shadow monster. It reared up from the horse, weaving away from Victor toward her.

Be a good girl. Hold still, there's a girl. Come with me. She could hear it calling her in the same voice that had enspelled her in the alley months ago. Tendrils of black and green magic wove through the air toward her.

"No! You have no power over me." She forced her voice into an echo of Finn's, the voice of assured power within the Palace walls.

For a second, the thing faltered. Then it surged forward, even more eager. *You are mine.* That woman's eyes. Finn's voice.

Deor screamed as the thing knocked her to the ground and rose above her. She caught it as it lunged at her, clawing and digging her silver nails into what she hoped was its face. Stinging ichor burned her skin, but her nails scraped bone. Hooves pounded up the road behind her, and a horn blew bright and clear.

Shadows rolled forward around her, engulfing her arms.

"Princess!" Victor swung at the shadow thing with his knife.

"Get back! Victor, get her away from there." Rafe, spear poised, thundered into her peripheral vision, riding so close that his sleeve whipped against her cheek as he passed.

Rafe's horse lifted up into the air, leaping straight over the creature, as Rafe thrust his spear down into its body. Horse and rider landed, whirling for another strike. But Rafe's hand was empty.

The creature spun from her toward Rafe, and Victor grabbed her arm and dragged her a few feet back before returning to the fight.

"Don't run," Rafe said. "You'll draw its attention again."

"I won't."

His eyes shone bluer than the California sky, bluer than sapphires. "You've enough courage in you for a dozen Nightmares." He whipped a hunting knife out of his belt and handed it to her. "Keep it for a last resort."

Deor got a firm grip on the knife, knees bent and ready.

Rafe whirled his horse loosening a spear as he rode back to the fight where Victor dodged and feinted at the Nightmare with his knife.

"This is spear work, Victor," Rafe shouted at him. "Go guard the princess."

Victor looked furious, as if Rafe had suddenly robbed him of the glory of the fight, but he began to retreat in Deor's direction, always keeping his face and knife turned toward the Nightmare. Rafe hurled a second spear into the mass of monster.

The more Deor stared at it, the less she could make out its form. It had six legs, no four, no a dozen. No legs at all. A neck like a lion. A cobra's hood. And stranger things still. A dead man, his guts spilling out as he screamed. A fire-breathing toad. Thousands of winged things that crawled and creeped and came apart to let the sword blade pass harmlessly through them.

Victor swore. "Someone in our trio is afraid of cockroaches."

"Is that what it's doing?" Deor said. "Taking the form of our fears?"

Victor nodded, his eyes focused on the fight.

"One of us should bait it," she said. Rafe circled and slashed, circled and slashed, but the thing changed form as fast as he could move. Deor started toward the Nightmare.

"What are you doing?" Victor dragged her back by her coat.

"If I give it a fear to concentrate on, maybe it will stay stable and he can kill it."

"No."

"Come on! We have to do something! I won't get close enough for it to grab me."

"Absolutely not. You don't know what it can do to your mind." Victor kept his grip on the back of her coat. "Watch."

Deor turned back toward the fight. Rafe had dismounted and regained his spear. His wings shone behind him, edges glinting like swords, as he advanced on the Nightmare. He shouted at it, a battle cry in Old Faerie, and the thing reared up on its hind legs, sinuous and weaving. Magic crackled along Rafe's spear as the Nightmare focused its form on him.

Rafe rushed toward it, and its squeal turned to a roar. It grew, doubling in size. Rafe shouted back, thrusting the spear with his whole weight behind it into straight into the Nightmare's embrace.

"Oh God!" Deor said. The spear snapped. The Nightmare's shadows rolled over Rafe, hid him from sight. Flashes of blue and silver wings sparked through the shadow. Sounds like snapping teeth and metal on meat came from the rolling mess.

Deor focused, forcing herself to see through the shadow. Rafe and the Nightmare rolled on the ground, grappling. It screamed and clawed, trying to wrap its tentacles around him, but the edges of his wings sliced through them, and the tentacles fell to pieces, burning the grass where they landed. Rafe had it by the throat with one hand. His other hand held the foot-long spear tip, broken off from its staff, stabbing into the Nightmare's underbelly again and again.

He rolled it over and plunged the spear tip into the Nightmare's throat. It shuddered and lay still.

Victor let go of Deor. She raced toward Rafe where he knelt over the Nightmare's body. His dark hair hung wet about his face, slime dripping from him. He panted, the broken weapon still tight in his hand. His chest and stomach were scored and shredded, his clothes in tatters. Between the blood and gore, she couldn't tell how deep the wounds went.

"Wait!" He held up a hand, warding Deor off as she reached him.

"You're hurt." She stripped off her coat, meaning to use it as a compress to stop the bleeding.

"Not yet, Your Highness. The Sword must still kill it." Victor caught her arm, barring her from reaching Rafe.

She glared at him. "He's bleeding out, and you're not even scratched. Why can't you kill it?"

Victor's expression was pained. "Believe me, I'd be happy to, but it would do him more harm than good."

He leaned close to Rafe, but careful not to touch him. "Are you going to make it?"

Rafe nodded, still panting. He held up a hand, as if to ask for a moment.

"Better hurry," Victor said. "It's past noon."

Rafe nodded again. He gripped the broken spearhead in both hands and raised it over his head. Magic focused at the tip of the spear, white and blue like frozen lightning. Rafe brought the weapon down, plunging it into the Nightmare's chest.

He yanked, ripping open the chest cavity, and dug his bare hands into the gore. Kneeling over the Nightmare's body, he held the Nightmare's heart in his hands. It still beat.

Victor whistled at the size of the thing.

"It's a wonder you were able to kill it. I could never have killed that on my own."

Rafe looked over at his brother. "No man could have, brother. Your courage saved the princess's life. You have nothing to be ashamed of today." He struggled to his feet. "Someone get me a yew branch."

Victor took a knife into the woods, returning in a few minutes with a long flexible branch covered in short needles, which he peeled down to slippery rope. Then he gathered the broken spears from around the site and piled them on the Nightmare's body. The longest spear he jammed upright in the ground, its splintered end pointing up. Last Victor pulled water bottles from his saddlebags and gathered the two living horses as close to the pyre as he could coax them. No one spoke a word until they were assembled in a circle around the Nightmare's body.

Through it all, Deor stood beside Rafe, her coat wrapped around her stinging hands, watching the Nightmare's heart beat.

"Are we ready?" Rafe said.

"Never a fire faerie around when you need one," Victor said. "But I have a spark with me and the water bottles. I won't call water out of this cursed ground."

Rafe lifted up the heart and impaled it with all his force on the broken spear. "Ash for healing. Ash for luck in battle."

He took the peeled yew strip from Victor and wound it around the heart, tying it to the spear. "Yew for poison, returned to its source."

Victor poured water over the heart. "Cleansing water, wipe away the evil that lodged here."

Rafe spoke, and a wind blew around them. "Wind, blow away the shadows and fogs of dreams." Deor breathed in, the wind smelling like spring returning.

Each of the men then stripped off their outer clothes. Anywhere the

Nightmare's slime had touched them, they carefully wiped it away. Victor offered a clean sleeve to gently wipe away as much of the blood and slime as he could from Rafe.

Deor helped, feeling both very awkward and honored as she dabbed at his chest. Under the crisscrossed lines of his new wounds, she caught glimpses of pale white lines here and there, scars from other battles. How many other ways was his body marked, a map of where he had shed his blood in service to his king and country?

"I'm trying not to make it worse," she said quietly. "I don't know much about first aid."

"It's alright," he said. "A friend's touch helps."

Deor tossed her sealskin coat into the pile around the spear with the rest of the tainted clothes. The corset underneath was clean, but the Nightmare's slime had soaked up the sleeves of her chemise. She wrestled that off as well, wriggling it out from under her corset. At least her pants didn't have to come off. She tried to wipe the black slime of the creature from her hands and arms with the chemise, but it stuck like tar. She shivered and dumped the chemise into the pile.

Victor stepped forward with a device in his hand that looked like flint in some sort of metal wrapping. He clicked it sharply, and a spark leaped from the flint, catching the yew branch immediately. Fire wound around the Nightmare's heart. A dying scream shot through the back of Deor's head. She clapped her hands over her ears, but it made no difference. The scream was inside her mind. By the strained looks on the men's faces, they heard it too.

The Nightmare's heart became a burning lump that hissed and spat as the blood dripped out of it. Deor swallowed hard and followed the men's example, holding out her hands to the warmth. The fire spread. Victor knelt with the spark, and soon the pile of wood, gear, and clothes around the Nightmare's body burst into full flames.

The bonfire burned as the sun crept down the westward sky. Slowly, agonizingly the scream inside her mind faded as the flames went down. The Nightmare's heart was nothing but a charred lump. Rafe reached out with a stick and knocked it into the remaining embers. It fell to pieces. Deor shivered as the winter wind blew over her bare skin. She hugged her arms around herself, but it didn't do much good.

"Well, that's done," Rafe said. "Let's get away from here before it gets full dark."

Victor coughed. "It appears I am at a disadvantage. As is Her Majesty." His horse lay to one side, its throat ripped out. Bessie huddled with Rafe's horse, clearly favoring her right leg where the Nightmare had clawed at it.

Rafe led his horse over to Deor and bowed. "Would you do me the favor of riding with me?" She almost laughed at the formal language, as if he were asking her to dance, but he put his hand on hers. The spark of throne magic leaped up between them again, his wounds to her wounds.

"Yes," she said. "Please let me ride with you." He boosted her up into the saddle and used his wings to lift himself up behind her.

Victor took Bessie's reins. "I think she's ridable, but not at any speed. You two go on ahead. Quickly."

It took only a click from Rafe's tongue to send his horse down the road and away from Mirrovere as fast as its feet would go. At first, Deor tried to sit stiffly upright, leaning away from the cuts all over his torso, but the motion of the horse and her own exhaustion made that impossible.

"It's okay," Rafe said. "Skin to skin is comforting after a Nightmare attack." He laughed. "Sorry, that came out wrong."

Deor laughed too, a little shakily as her stomach and watery muscles reminded her she hadn't had anything to eat since breakfast. She leaned back, and Rafe's free arm wrapped around her waist. The warmth between them eased her shivers. The lingering fear, like poison in her veins, subsided a bit more as Rafe tightened his grip.

"Why is Mirrovere cursed?" she asked. "Victor said it was Finn's fault."

"He's right." Rafe shuddered and dug his heels into his horse. "The Lord of Mirrovere was a minor lord. He owed his fealty to Roger, but he got it into his head to rebel. He holed up in his little castle and sent out his fighting men on raids against Roger's cattle and fleet. One night they managed to burn Roger's private yacht. Pookie was almost killed. That's when Roger demanded recompense from the king."

The buried road flew by underneath the horses' hooves. Rafe's muscles were rigid with strain as he told the next. "I was in my first deployed unit. Arthur and Delaney were there, too. We were new-made knights only the year before. Finn sent us up from the south to threaten the Lord of Mirrovere that if he did not surrender in three days and submit to his liege lord's justice, Finn would take it as treason against himself."

"What kind of justice was Roger going to hand out?" Deor said.

"He promised to let the castle's people go, but he wanted to execute the lord and his wife and dispossess their only child."

Deor whistled in surprise. "That's evil. And stupid—dispossessed heirs come back gunning for blood and their family's land."

Rafe chuckled, a bitter grunt in the back of his throat. "It was worse than that. They refused. On the third day, Finn came to the battle himself. I—we—all expected him to make an example of the lord. Lay siege to the castle, execute the lord, and put his head on a pike. We didn't expect him to kill every man, woman, and child there. He called up the power of the land, and he broke Mirrovere with it." Rafe's voice caught in his throat. "There wasn't enough left of them to bury."

Tears, hot and stinging, rose in Deor's eyes, even as the wind whipped them away. Broken bodies. Broken land. Broken promises—to his people, to her mother. What hadn't Finn broken?

"Is that why we found a Nightmare there?"

Behind her, Rafe nodded. She thought she felt a drop of water fall from his face to hers.

They rode the rest of the way in silence. When they reached the encampment around the castle, someone shouted their arrival, his voice carrying to the house. By the time the group arrived in the main courtyard, people had filled it.

In the center of the group stood Finn. Tall, pale, and very angry. The emotion radiated off of him, and Deor wondered if only she could feel it. Pookie looked worried—concern not anger. Roger and Astarte both stood behind the king, faces pale.

Rafe pulled his horse to a stop and jumped from the seat. He turned and held out his arms to Deor. Once again thankful for pants, she threw her leg over and hopped into his arms. He caught her and lowered her to the group. A collective sigh seemed to echo from the audience awaiting them.

From the crowd Thea burst through, charging forward, Deor assumed, to the horse. Deor yelped slightly when, instead, the tall woman threw her arms around Deor. "Thank Creator you're safe!" She let her go, and Deor saw the rivulets of tears—puffy, red rimmed eyes that said Thea had be crying for quite a while. "Please forgive me!"

Deor put her hands on Thea's shoulders. She scanned the crowd behind Thea and cleared her throat, making certain her voice would carry. "Don't be ridiculous! Nothing that happened—nothing at all—was in any way your fault. Clearly the unicorns were spooked by the Nightmare and were fleeing. Even the calmest of horses would freak out at that." She squeezed the woman's shoulders and smiled. "If I had a feistier mount, it might have thrown me, and I'd have broken my neck."

Finn's patience broke, and he strode toward them. Deor stepped past Thea, in between her and the king.

"You could have been killed!" Finn said, glaring at her. "I'm told that Victor Farringdon found you?"

"Yes," Deor said. "He—"

"Did he take you to Mirrovere?" he demanded. His face had set in that white-ice color he turned when he could barely contain his anger. His eyes were silver. He had crossed his arms and tucked his hands where they couldn't be seen.

"What? No. He found me there. I was calling for help, and he heard me. He had ridden that way while others had followed different paths to look for me. Right, Rafe?"

She turned back to him. He was standing stone still. The ichor and blood from both the Nightmare and his own wounds shone in streaks across his body. "Rafe?" she said and took a step toward him. She laid a hand on his chest, and he jolted, like he had been dreaming. He pressed his hand on top of hers and looked down at her.

"I'm sorry," he said. "What...what can I do for the princess?"

"That's it!" Arthur stepped forward. "Time for you to go inside."

"No one is leaving until I am satisfied as to who is responsible. Wounds can wait!"

Arthur looked for a moment as if he would tell the king exactly where to go and how to get satisfaction, but Deor spoke first.

"You want to know whose fault it is?" she snapped. "I'll tell you who is responsible. While riding in the company of Thea, my horse was spooked. It ran wildly and blindly to a devastated, horrible place."

She glanced back at the men. Rafe's eyes seemed to drift in and out of focus, and he shook his head as if to wake himself up.

"Mirrovere is an evil place." Deor locked eyes with Finn. "A horrible thing happened there. A horrible monster fed on the broken magic and grew full and fat. Evil begat evil."

"That's quite enough," Finn said, but his voice was softer. He looked past her. "Clearly we owe you a debt of gratitude, Rafe. Please," he stepped out of the way, "go and rest. We will celebrate your victory tonight."

Behind her, Arthur snorted too softly for the king to hear. "Come on, soldier," he said wrapping Rafe's arm around his shoulder. "Let's get you walking. One step at a time." He led Rafe forward, and Genevieve broke from the crowd. She slung Rafe's other arm over her shoulder. She whispered something in his ear as they walked. The crowd parted in front of them, opening a path to the door.

As Rafe took a step forward, the sound of a limping horse echoed across the gravel courtyard. Victor slid to the ground as a groom rushed up to take Bessie's reins.

Arthur moved off with Rafe, leaving Deor standing in the winter cold. She shivered. She ought to do something. She ought to go inside. But her feet refused to move. Dark shadows swirled around her mind.

"You too, Princess," Victor said. "You need to get cleaned up and rest, too. The longer the Nightmare is on your hands, the worse the night will be."

"Okay," Deor said. She didn't move.

Victor slipped his arm around her waist before she fell.

"Easy, there." He waited for her to get her balance. "Do you want me to carry you?"

Deor laughed out loud. "No. Thank you." The laughed cleared her head a bit. "But I will lean on you, if that is alright."

He led her through the path cleared by Arthur and Rafe. "You took a lot of the Nightmare, too. Second only to Rafe. You had your hands on it, just like he did." He spoke loudly, and Deor realized he wasn't speaking to her. He was telling her story to the crowd. "It came at you, and you fought back."

"Clawed it. My nails, its face. I thought I hit bone, but I don't know."

Around them, the crowd gasped. They were almost to the doorway, and she wanted nothing more than to be through it and away from all of these people—these staring faces. It was like the Adoption all over again. Violence and her bloody—again with someone else's blood—and a stunned audience. She leaned a little harder on Victor as he led her up the couple steps and into the house. Her eyes were focused on the ground, but she could feel the people moving around her.

"I've got her," a voice said.

She looked up in time to see Victor sway, and his valet grab him. "Easy," the man said. "You've had your share of excitement too." He led Victor away.

A hand on her shoulder. "Princess?"

She turned to see the kind face of Pookie—more worried and grey than usual—staring at her.

"We need to get you upstairs."

"Okay," Deor said and headed for the sweeping staircase.

"Oh, no." Pookie swept her up in his arms, and she squeaked. He laughed. "Yes, I am stronger than I look. I am a Pooka, after all. Strong as horse, whether I'm in that form or not." He carried her to a doorway arch on the wall. "Main suite," he said. The door swirled, and he carried Deor through directly into the parlor. He did not put her down, but brought her to the closet, where he set her on a bench.

Breathless, Melanie ran in, Brand hot on her heels.

Pookie waved at her to be quiet. She gave a quick curtsey.

"Help her out of her clothes. I will go draw a bath, and I'll be back to help her to it."

Melanie nodded.

In the outer area of the suite, there were voices. Her father. Astarte. His voice raised a bit and so did hers. She heard the door to her bedroom close and saw Pookie pass by the closet on the way to the bathroom.

Deor leaned back toward Melanie as the girl wrapped a robe around her shoulders. "Can you stand for me?"

Deor stood, swaying slightly. Melanie came around the couch and secured Deor's robe around her waist. Brand sniffed and snuffled around her feet and whined.

"It's okay, boy," she said, her voice barely a whisper. She leaned down to pet him but swayed and Melanie caught her.

"Easy," she said. "He's fine. He'll follow you. Do you think you can walk to the bathroom? Or do you want to wait for his lordship?"

"I can walk," she muttered. She put one foot in front of the other, leaning heavily on the doorway to the closet and breathing hard. Maybe she *would* wait for Pookie.

Finn's voice was louder now—she still didn't understand what he said, but he was angry—angry and afraid.

Chapter Thirty-Three

R afe sat back on the couch in his parlor and stared at the fire. He
was in a robe and slippers, skin still raw from the scrubbing it
took to free himself from the Nightmare's stain. He'd sent
Genevieve down to dinner to make his excuses, not that he needed them,
really.

"Jake?" he called. The dog bolted from its waiting position next to the
fire and knocked Rafe's hand with his head. Rafe scratched him. Sam
trotted over, too, laying his head in Rafe's lap. "Good boys," he muttered,
and kept staring into the fire.

Not much time left until full dark and the nightmares that would rock
him. He could try to stay awake all night, but it wouldn't make it better.
Putting it off, even if only to sleep in daylight, only made it worse.

"Okay, boys." He put his hands on his knees and eased himself up,
letting the aches wash over him. He stretched some of the soreness, the
tightness, away, but the tension was still there. He shuddered at the
memory—riding up to see Deor on the ground, the thing lunging at her.
But she hadn't had flailed or tried to block it, nor did she try to get away.
No. She had the thing by the face. He laughed to himself. In the end, she
probably would have lost, but it would have been close.

A knock came at his door.

"Come in?" he said and turned to it. He hoped it wasn't Gen, or worse, Finn come to lecture him about Deor and her safety.

"Good evening." Victor stepped in the room and closed the door behind him. "I wanted to see how you were doing." He held up two bottles. "Fresh water, from Roger's spring. It should help."

"Thank you." Rafe gestured at the bar at the side of the room. "I think I'd prefer whisky," he said, but smiled. "But I'll stick to water."

"Good." Victor popped open the top on one and poured two glasses. "Here." He strode across the room and handed it to Rafe. "Why are you up?"

"Were you hoping to catch me in bed?" Rafe smirked.

"No." Victor frowned at him. "But I figured Arthur would be here guarding you."

"He's making sure the horses are okay."

"Right." Victor laughed. "Making sure Thea is okay, too?"

Rafe smiled. "I imagine so." He took a long drink of water. "Thank you," he said. "That's good." He waved at the couch. "Sit?"

"No," Victor said. "I won't keep you. You need rest, and, frankly, so do I. Dinner without you or the princess? How dreadfully boring." He grinned. "I came to say, though hopefully I don't need to, that I did not lead the princess there. I did go there on purpose. I asked myself what the worst place she could end up was and went there hoping not to find her."

"That pretty much does it," Rafe said. "And I know. I know you didn't. That thing came after her, didn't it?"

"Like she was a beacon of light in a wall of fog."

"She is amazing, but damn if she isn't a walking, talking magnet for trouble."

Victor laughed. "Yes. It does seem to find her. Though the Geoff episode made her friends, no matter what the king thinks."

"He was furious with her for that one." Rafe shook his head and sipped the water again. "I can't protect her from him, not all the time. And she's not going to let me protect her much at all. And even if I do, and people see it, it makes her look weak, which isn't good. But Geoff," he sighed, "he could do so much damage." Rafe finished the water and placed the cup on the bar. "Can you help me keep her away from him?"

"Do you really think he'll try to hurt her here?"

"No," Rafe said. "I don't. He's not stupid. But he will needle her if he can. I want him away from her—"

"For his own protection?" Victor snorted. "I'll do my best."

"Thank you. Besides, you enjoy making Geoff uncomfortable."

"I do," he said. "He's a twit and a disgrace." Victor stared at his brother for a moment. "Tell her to be careful at the loyalty ceremony."

"That's not what it's called." Rafe frowned. Why did things always have to get political?

"Call it what you want. She needs to be careful."

"Are mother and father up to something?"

Victor rolled his eyes. "When are they not? But I am hoping that it remains nonviolent."

"You are involved?"

"No," he said, but frowned. "I expect mother to speak against the king. He dragged her all the way here. Do you expect her to bend a knee? But I hope that it will be a public statement, not an attempt on someone's life."

"And you'll be right there, helping?" Rafe didn't bother to hide his anger, and the cold seeped off of him, though his brother showed no sign of noticing.

He shrugged. "I am not a traitor. But I do not support the king. Look at his behavior today! He was looking for anyone to blame—even Thea—anyone but himself. So, if our parents vote no confidence in him, I'm not challenging them. That said..." He crossed his arms. "Michael is with them. They housed him since the Adoption—don't bother chastising me. You couldn't have gotten to him anyway."

"And now?"

"Michael is not well. He's haunted, furious. Damn near insane, I think. So, watch out for him. I will watch out for him, too."

"So," Rafe said. "You're saying that you'll publicly undermine the king and his heir, but you wanted me to know what? You're sorry? And there might be this other threat that you won't help with either? Thanks, Victor."

Victor rested his hands on his hips. "Fine," he said. "I will not support the king. But I will follow your lead with the princess. You bend a knee to her, and I'll be right there with you. And I'll mean it, too. Good enough?"

Rafe nodded. "Good enough. You keep her away from Geoff—or at least not alone with him—and I'll watch for Michael. If you see anything, let me know. After this whole thing is done, we'll talk about other ways you can help."

"Until then, we're still estranged?"

"Yes. Why confuse everyone now?" Rafe ran a hand through his hair. "I have to rest," he said.

Victor came forward despite Jake's growl. "Let me help you."

Rafe didn't argue. He leaned on Victor and let his brother help him to bed.

"Do you want me to find Arthur to check on you?"

"No." Rafe smiled. "Gen will be along in a little bit."

"Right," he said. "Remember, you need rest." He patted his brother on the shoulder. "I think I'm going to retire, too."

Rafe watched his brother leave and waited until he heard the door to the outside hall click. "Go see," he said to Jake. When the dog returned a moment later, he beckoned him and Sam up onto the bed. "Good boys," he said.

Genevieve would be annoyed that they were up in *her* bed. It was too bad that a Nightmare had ruined their first week together since she'd gotten back from her Solstice trip, but that's the way it was. The boys made him feel better. She could live with the dogs, or she could sleep somewhere else.

Despite the bath and the snuggles from Brand, nightmares haunted Deor all night and into the morning, jarring her out of sleep not long after dawn. She crept out of bed to stand next to the window, letting the sunlight hit her face. She clenched and unclenched her fist, her nails flicking from silver to normal. Most of the nightmares were lost in the morning light, but the feel of her nails on the flesh and bone of the Nightmare's face persisted.

"Your Majesty?" Melanie spoke from a few feet away.

Deor hadn't even heard her come in. "Hey," she said, unable to manage "good morning."

Melanie shook her head. "You need to go back to bed. Are you hungry? I can bring breakfast."

"No." Deor didn't move.

"Okay!" Melanie clapped her hands and Deor started. "Let's get you back into bed. She shooed Brand around the bed as she remade it, tugging back into place the sheets and blankets that Deor had pulled loose and bunched up in her sleep. Once she had the sheets smoothed and pulled back, she disappeared into Deor's closet, emerging a moment later with fresh pjs. "Do you want to put these on?"

Deor frowned at the slightly patronizing tone—she wasn't a child.

"Your Majesty?" Melanie tried again.

Deor realized that she had been standing still for several moments— what felt like seconds had been much more. "I'm sorry, Melanie," she said. "I can't seem to focus."

The maid shook her head. "It's the Nightmare. You need more sleep."

Deor shuddered. "No—"

"It's after dawn," she said. "There won't be any more nightmares—your dreams may not be happy, but they won't be as brutal as they clearly were last night."

Deor wrapped her arms around herself, a chill wracking her body. "How do you know?" Even to her own ears, Deor sounded like a frightened child.

Melanie sat on the bed and patted the spot next to her. Deor sat.

"When I was little, I was out in the forest with my father. Lord Farringdon had gone hunting, and we stayed behind in the camping tent. Lord Farringdon never minded if my father brought me along on things like that," she smiled. "My father has been his valet since the Sword arrived here as a child.

"Anyway, he was out hunting, and I was about, oh, fifteen. I had run off into the woods to take pictures of plants and flowers, my father following at his own pace. I remember finding wild roses, I remember a patch of shadow just beyond them, and the last thing I remember is the terror. I screamed so much and so loud that I tore my throat. My father came, and he chased off the Nightmare. It was small, smaller than Brand. As my father was cradling me, Lord Farringdon arrived—he'd heard the screams. Father told him what happened, and he ran into the brush after the Nightmare. He caught it and killed it, too, or my dreams would have been much, much worse. I didn't have nearly the contact you did, but I did have some." Melanie lifted the hem of her dress. A jagged line, like a tear, ran down her leg from mid-calf to ankle. "The healers couldn't keep it from scarring—and Lord Farringdon made sure I saw the Palace heal-ers. I had horrible dreams that night. When I woke in the morning, like you, I felt a bit lost. My father put me back to bed, with the curtains open so I slept in the sun, and I didn't have another nightmare."

Melanie gently maneuvered Deor into bed and pulled the covers up. "Come on, Brand." She patted the bed next to her, and Brand came up and snuggled close. "Try to sleep as much as you can," she said. "Ring for me, and I'll bring you food whenever you like." She pulled open the curtains, and white light spilled into the room. "The Grand Ball is tonight—if you believe you can come."

"Certainly," Deor mumbled, her eyes already drifting closed. The little girl in her couldn't wait to be a princess at a fairy ball, though she'd claw her own tongue out before she said that aloud.

"Very good. I will leave a fresh glass of water next to your bed."

"Thank you," Deor managed before rolling onto her side and curling around Brand.

Melanie must have left, but Deor didn't hear her go.

Chapter Thirty-Four

Later that afternoon, Deor sat in the parlor as Finn, angry again, paced back and forth in front of her. Astarte leaned in the doorway to their suite.

"Whatever," Deor muttered under her breath. Aloud she said, "I understand your concern, but no. She's not a threat, physically or politically. Spending time with her does not make you look bad, so I am not breaking my promise."

Behind Finn, Astarte gave Deor a smile. "Finn," she said. "Let her go. She's being gracious."

Finn turned on his wife, and Deor braced herself for some horrible string of words, but he drew up short, probably knowing too well what her expression said. Something like *go ahead, make my day.*

"Fine," Finn said without turning around. "Go. Have Melanie dress you there."

"See you at the party," Deor said and headed to her own room and closed the door.

From her room, she heard Finn's voice raise slightly, but Astarte's stay calm. His voice increased over the next few exchanges, and then plummeted. No doubt he'd gone a step too far and now was having to fake-apologize or smooth things over. There was so much to learn from the Winter Court's Consort.

Deor pressed her fingers to the mirror on her vanity. "Melanie?" she asked.

Immediately the mirror flashed to Melanie's quarters. She bobbed in front of the mirror. "Yes, Your Majesty? I was about to come up to help you dress."

"Wonderful!" Deor said. "But we're going to be dressing in Robbie's suite."

Melanie nodded. "I'll have your wardrobe moved there immediately. Will you be sleeping there as well?"

"Alas," Deor said. "No. She and I are going to get ready together. She's coming to the ball. Apparently that is irking some people."

Melanie dropped another small curtsey. "Yes, miss."

The mirror went black, and Deor's reflection returned.

Deor scanned her vanity trying to decide what to take with her to Robbie's. Melanie would bring makeup—she had a whole kit. Deor went to the trundle bed in her closet and dug out her jewelry box. Silly tradition, she thought, especially since her maid was not sleeping in her closet. She hauled out the heavy wooden box, twice as large as a shoebox, made of curly maple. A princessly crown had been etched on the top and inlaid with gold.

As she opened it, the top layer split in into two separate trays which swung out, each holding a crown. Thankfully, they were more circlets than massive emblems of state. The first was intertwined strands of platinum and yellow gold. Astarte had noted that it was a perfect for a young princess—not a child, she had emphasized—to wear to the Grand Ball.

The second crown was a circlet of brilliant black stones. The center was a netting made of fine velvet and dotted with flawless diamonds, like snow on black earth. Perfect for Parliament—conservative with a flash of winter in the colors of the Aethelwing house.

The next level held necklaces, and the drawers below contained the matching bracelets, rings, earrings, and hair jewels matching not only the crowns, but also the other outfits she had brought with her. She had no intention of wearing all the jewelry—too much weighed her down and she felt like a little girl playing dress up. Given her tendency to break spells on accident, hair jewelry was a risk of falling out and getting lost.

She snapped closed the case and stood, carrying it in her arms.

When she knocked on Robbie's door, Deor was a bit startled that the girl herself answered it. "Hello, Robbie. Can I come in?" Deor asked.

"Yes, Princess." The girl bowed and stepped aside.

"Please," Deor said. "It's Deor. You don't need to use my title any more than your mother or Rafe does."

The girl nodded, but Deor knew that the next time Robbie addressed her, it was going to have a royal honorific. She sighed inwardly. Maybe she was asking too much of Robbie. Such informality might get in her trouble—Finn wouldn't like it, and that might fall hard on the young woman. Robbie didn't need any more shit than she'd already got.

"You call me whatever makes you comfortable," Deor said as she came into the room.

Robbie smiled and nodded. She led Deor into the suite and to the right, to a small parlor and through into the dressing room. A vanity sat at one end of the room, and a small bench in the center. On one side, there was a small dais in front of a trifold mirror. On the other side, rows of clothes. Opposite the vanity, by the door, was a chest of drawers. On each side of the mirror was a mannequin. On one, Deor's chosen dress for the evening. The other one was naked.

Melanie was already there, and servants had laid out Deor's dress, shoes, and all the bits and pieces that went with them. Deor's massive makeup kit sat the floor next to the vanity. Melanie pushed an unseen button, and the contraption rose and unfolded itself into a table. There were dozens of small sections, and a small cabinet rose at the far side of the table, opening to reveal the shelves lining the doors, and inside, a series of drawers. Every possible space was occupied by some kind of makeup or tool.

"Wow," Robbie said, her quiet demeanor gone for the moment. She sped over to the box. "This is all human-world makeup, isn't it?" She looked at Deor. "This is awesome!" She picked up and put down different items, studying them. After a moment, she looked up. "This is all yours? Why?"

Deor sat down on the bench. "Magic sometimes slides off me."

"Slides off?"

"Glamours won't hold on her face. It's rather disturbing to watch one slide down like she's melting." Melanie smiled. "So!" she said pulling out the chair to the vanity. "Who's first?"

Robbie looked at Deor. "You want your maid to do my makeup?"

The girl seemed shocked. Maybe Deor had put her foot in it again. Maybe offering to do this was tantamount to saying that Robbie hadn't done a sufficient job herself, instead of a sisterly experience. "If you want to," Deor said. "If you have your own all set, that's great. I didn't mean to suggest that your makeup was wrong..." The words tumbled out, a kind of verbal flailing that, over many years of stepping on toes, Deor had perfected.

"No, no." Robbie cut her off. "That's not what I meant. I just..." She looked at the cosmetics and back at Deor. She turned her gaze to the box Deor had placed on the floor at her feet for the first time. "Is that your jewelry box?"

"What?" She followed Robbie's gaze. "Oh, yes. I thought maybe we might find you some to wear if you liked—I'm sure you have plenty of things here, though."

Tears welled in the girl's eyes.

"Oh God!" Deor stood up. "I'm sorry!"

Robbie shook her head as a few tears streaked down her face. "No!" Robbie crossed the few feet between them nearly at a run and flung her arms around Deor. "I didn't think...after you became the princess...I... My mother said that you would be polite, but she didn't say you'd..." The girl let go of Deor and stepped back. "Why?"

"Because I was hoping we would be close?" As soon as it left her mouth, Deor knew she sounded stupid. She sounded like she was trying to buy Robbie, and, she had to admit to herself, she kind of was. But wasn't this the kind of things that sisters did? Makeup and hair and talk about boys?

Robbie wiped her eyes. "I thought sure you would send me away. I wasn't going to come to the ball. Rafe said it would be okay—"

"He was right. Robbie, unless you don't want to go, I want you there."

The girl chewed her lip for a moment. Her eyes narrowed, sizing up Deor's sincerity. The look on her face said this might be some kind of horrible setup that would end in Robbie humiliated and covered in pig's blood.

"I want you there," Deor repeated. "I swear."

Robbie shook her head unconvinced. "The king doesn't—"

"Fuck him," Deor said flatly. "Fuck him sideways with a stick. He doesn't tell me who I see—he doesn't choose my friends or my family. Roger himself said that this ball was all about me. So fuck him."

Robbie's eyes widened. "Princess," she shook her said, "you can't say things like that!"

"Fuck him? Things like that?"

Robbie nodded, expression shifting from wonder to fear. "He's..." She trailed off.

"He's scary," Deor finished for her. He was. Deor should be scared of him, and she knew it. But she still wouldn't let Finn hurl Robbie into exile. "I know. Don't worry, it's my problem. I'll handle it."

Robbie pursed her lips, concerned. "But if he gets angry—"

"It will fall on me. I'll take the brunt of his wrath, and I'll be the focus." She reached out and laid a hand on the girl's shoulder. "I'll stand between him and you. I won't let him hurt you."

Robbie said nothing for a long moment. She stared at Deor and bit her lip again. Whatever she was thinking, there was some serious social math going on in her head. "O-o-okay," she managed.

"You'll come to the ball tonight? With me? With my makeup—if you want it?"

"Yes." She nodded her head. In a flash, the anxiety in her expression was gone. She spun and darted to the dress rack. "I was sure that I couldn't wear this," she said, pulling a garment bag free and hanging it on a stand. She undid the clasps and revealed a dress.

"This," she pointed at the first, "was for tonight—in case I wanted to go."

"Wow." Deor came up to the dress. Up close she could see that it was layers of airy ivory fabric on top of a sleeveless ivory shell. Overlaying that was a long-sleeved shell of an even finer cloth, almost transparent, shot through with gold embroidery to look like falling leaves. "That is amazing!"

Robbie snatched it from the hook and held it up in front of her. "It's beautiful, right? My mother had it made for me."

Once Deor saw the dress that close to Robbie, she had no doubt that Astarte had commissioned it. The ivory and gold brought out the golden flecks in Robbie's normally mundane brown eyes. Her skin, too, seemed to shift—the freckles that dotted her face flashed for a second like golden dust.

"Let's get that up on the mannequin," Deor said.

Melanie, smiling, took the dress from Robbie and draped it perfectly over the form.

Deor sat on the bench again, facing the dresses, and patted the seat next to her. "Sit down with me." When Robbie sat, Deor hauled the jewelry box up onto her lap and opened it.

"Ooh," Robbie said when she saw the crowns.

Deor split the tray with the crowns and ran her fingers over the jewelry sets in the second box. To go along with the crown, there was a choker made of multicolored golden leaves, with earrings and hair jewels to match.

"How about these for your dress?" She held up the necklace so the light flashed off the leaves. "I think it matches well." She turned to her maid. "Melanie?"

"Lovely!" she said.

"I can't wear those!" Robbie exclaimed. "That's the jewelry that goes with your crown. Aren't you going to wear them?"

"No," Deor said. "The neckline of my dress isn't really suited for a choker," she said, making it up as she was going along. She thought they would look beautiful on Robbie, and that was enough. "Plus," she said, "I think that the circlet and some simple earrings are enough." She handed Robbie the necklace.

The girl held it delicately, as if too tight a grip might break it. "You're sure?" She didn't take her eyes off it.

"Positive," Deor said. "Now, let's talk about makeup."

Chapter Thirty-Five

In a rare case of telling it like it is, the Grand Ball took place in the Grand Ballroom—a two-story open space in the center of North-falls. Guests entered at the second floor and traveled down a massive center staircase to the lavender and white marble checkerboard below. Each guest was announced by a herald with name, title, and whatever honors, if any, they had. The king and his Consort arrived nearly last —and most who arrived after were not announced.

Deor and Robbie, however, were running late.

Deor held Robbie's hand as they walked down the short hall to the ballroom. They had laughed and experimented with possible hair and makeup long enough that they were, perhaps, pushing the bounds of fashionably late. Deor's dress was a nod to the role of heir. Unlike tomorrow's dress, it wasn't black but a deep silver. As she moved, the dress caught different angles of light and seemed covered in falling snowflakes.

They were halfway to the ball when Arthur met them with a frown. "I was once again dispatched to fetch you."

"I'm sorry Arthur," Deor said. "It was my fault. We were having fun getting ready, and I ignored the time."

"Such is your prerogative." He bowed slightly and gestured at them to step past them. "This way."

Deor recognized the sarcasm of his reassurance. She stepped past him, still holding Robbie's hand as the girl trailed a bit behind.

The footmen at the door bowed as she arrived. He opened the door and announced, "Her Majesty Princess Deor, heir to the Winter Court."

When he stopped at that, Deor whispered in his ear.

His eyes widened slightly, but he added, "And Lady Roberta Ellington Gemalsdottir."

The room turned to look at the two women, who had so clearly stopped the show. The lovely string quartet had frozen mid-song and the room had turned, *en masse*, to see the princess. Robbie clutched Deor's hand tightly enough that she lost circulation for a moment.

"We'll be fine," Deor whispered to her.

Robbie barely nodded. The girl had no idea why the people were staring, but Deor did. Robbie was beautiful. When she was playing human, Robbie looked rather drab, like all humans did to the Fae. But tonight, with her hair swept back, makeup perfect, and the gown and jewels of royalty, she looked the part.

The spray of freckles sparkled against red-gold skin. The embroidery of the dress caught the light too, reflecting a soft glow around her. Her brown eyes were no longer flat. The flecks sparkled in them like sunlight dancing off water. Standing there, poised—though, Deor conceded, likely frozen—with her bloodline's magic shimmering around her, she could easily be called the most beautiful woman in the room.

No one could doubt she was a royal daughter of the Summer Court.

Deor scanned the crowd, not stopping on Finn to see the horrible glare he must be giving her, but sought out Astarte. She had been dancing with Roger and stood next to him, her hand still on his arm. Her dress was the mirror of her daughter's, the palest gold embroidered with flowers. Behind her, the one element Robbie lacked, her gold edged, translucent wings. In the light of the glittering chandelier above, her wings shimmered with color, like a rainbow through a prism.

Rafe and Genevieve were also on the dance floor. Him looking like a son of the king, though in blue, not black, and Genevieve looking every part a prince's Consort, her delicate iris-petal dress a perfect companion to his blue suit. It was also the dress that Deor had steadfastly refused to wear, and it looked even better out on the dance floor than it had in the shop. Because of course it did.

Deor squeezed Robbie's hand and tugged it gently. She moved down the steps into the room, Robbie at her side. The movement jolted the audience from their paralysis. They politely clapped, and the quartet began its music again. Most of the dancers swept back into their partners' arms and continued their rotation around the room.

Astarte and Roger slipped through the crowd to the edge of the floor, where they met Deor and Robbie.

Astarte's eyes glistened as she looked at her daughter. A tight smile formed on her lips, and she held her arms open to Robbie. The girl stepped into her mother's embrace, clinging a few more seconds than a simple greeting.

When they parted, Roger caught Robbie's hand and kissed it. "You are stunning," he said to her. "You both are," he added with a nod to Deor.

Astarte nodded but didn't speak. Finally, she flung her arms around Deor, hugging her tight. "Thank you," she whispered into her ear.

Deor opened her mouth, but nothing came out. What was there to say that wouldn't take a thousand words. "Any time," she managed before the Consort released her.

"Come," said Roger. "Join the party." Robbie and her mother huddled close, walking to the side of the room with the refreshments. Roger offered Deor his arm, and she took it. He guided her, too, toward the refreshments and, she couldn't help but notice, away from her father. "I was feeling put out by your delay," he said.

"I'm sor—"

"But the wait was certainly worth it!" He grinned.

"Thank you," she said. Roger had a penchant for drama and anything that would make a good spectacle. Judging by the looks she was getting and the whispers floating all over the room, her entrance had provided drama galore.

"Excuse me," he said and drifted away to check on one of the bartenders serving drinks.

At the refreshment table, Astarte put her arm around her daughter's waist and leaned in to kiss her cheek. Deor hoped that the rest of the guests didn't think her entrance was a stunt—a plea for attention—but given how much everyone was talking, she was sure some people thought it was. Well, let them. Robbie deserved the same respect as any noble here, and more. She was the daughter of the Summer Court's first heir—and though Astarte had given up her political connections when she left to marry Finn, she had not lost her considerable magical power. Robbie's appearance tonight proved that her daughter had inherited more from her mother than people previously thought.

"Quite the entrance," a voice at her elbow said. "Especially for someone who insists that they don't want the attention."

Deor turned to Victor. "Would you believe getting attention for me wasn't what I intended?"

He looked around the room. "Yes," he said. "Without question. You did this because you hate the way the king treats his step-daughter."

"Exactly." Deor gestured at the girl. "How could anyone resent her? How could Finn fear her?" Deor shook her head and stopped talking. She didn't need to be saying things like that in public, especially not to Victor. Her father was probably livid when she came in with Robbie. Now, if he heard her, he might have an aneurysm. The nasty part of her wondered, before she could shut it up, whether that would be a bad thing.

"Would you like to dance?" Victor asked and offered her his hand.

She watched the sweeping couples on the floor. Every few turns—though it never seemed to be the same number—the man would catch the woman's waist and lift her into the air, continuing the circle and setting her down on the opposite side of him. The two would come together again and continue their turns around the floor.

"No," she said.

"Oh." Victor's voice carried a hint of hurt. "I beg your pardon, Your Majesty."

"Deor," she automatically corrected him, not taking her eyes from the dancers. Of all the couples out there, Rafe and Genevieve were the most perfect, and in the center of the room. He was as tall or taller than all the others out there, so when he lifted her into the air, she soared above the rest of the crowd, her shimmering platinum wings flaring out behind her.

"You know," he said conversationally, "you are as lovely as she is."

"What?" Deor snapped her head around to look at him. "Why do you say that?"

"Forgive me." He bowed his head slightly, though his lips were curled in a small smile. "You seemed to be watching my brother and his fiancée. I may have been mistaken."

"Oh." She'd been that obvious. Dammit. "I don't know the dance. They seem to do it well."

"Indeed," he said. "Is that why you don't want to dance with me? Because you don't know the Farendelle?"

"Yes," she said. "I am sorry I was abrupt. It wasn't about you."

"Good to hear." He nodded at the dancers. "This will be over soon, but I would be happy to teach you. It is much easier than it looks. In this particular dance, the lifting partner leads. The other person has nothing to do but follow."

"Well," Deor said, matching his wry smile, "I seem to have a very hard time following."

Victor laughed loud enough that a few others nearby turned to look. "Indeed," he said. "I could teach you the first part, if you like, though I'm not sure you could lift me."

Deor snorted. "Certainly not like Rafe lifts his fiancée."

"Are you jealous?" he asked, a hint of teasing in his voice.

"What? No!" she insisted a touch too emphatically. "I'm not jealous of her. At least not, I think, in the way you mean."

"You dislike her?"

"What's with the twenty questions?" she snapped. "Is this an interview?"

"My apologies." He bowed his head slightly. He still smirked, though, and that didn't change. She was digging herself a hole.

She blew out a sigh. "I don't like her." She kept her voice low. "I've tried to, but everything about her pushes my buttons. She's lovely—in that socially pristine way. She doesn't make any mistakes. Ever. She never has a hair out of place, probably because her hairs are afraid of the lecture they'll get. Everything about her is perfect."

"I see."

She looked him in the eye. "And I'm well aware that everything about me is not."

He nodded. He smiled again, but with not a hint mockery. "Ahh, yes. I understand." He shot a glance at the dance floor. "I am familiar with feeling less-than."

"There is nothing wrong with her!" Deor couldn't stop herself. "And that's just...I don't know." She gave up.

"That's wrong?" he asked. "How much perfect can one person be?"

"Yes!" Deor gestured to the dance floor. "And she is polite, and kind and...helpful to the environment!" She spun, turning her back to the dance floor. "I have to stop."

He laughed. "It's not just the perfect, is it? What happened?"

Deor looked around them. They were alone in that there didn't seem to be anyone nearby listening in. "She took me shopping at the finest establishment. They'd made a whole line of dresses for this part on incredibly short notice—she modeled them. Perfectly. That was to be my ball gown. I—" She paused, searching for the right, inoffensive words, "I turned down the opportunity."

"I can't imagine," he said.

Deor shook her head, trying to clear it. "It looks far better on her than it ever would have on me."

"You two do have markedly different styles," Victor said. Why wasn't Finn using this man as a diplomat?

"Yep. It isn't that she's mean—though I bet she can be polite in a way that would sear a steak. It's that every word that comes out of her mouth is a pronouncement of *the way things are.*" Deor shook her head. "I have to stop talking about this." She looked out at the floor again.

The dance had ended, and Rafe was leading Genevieve their way.

Deor grabbed Victor's arm as the quartet started another song. "Oh look! A waltz! I can do that. Come on." She pulled him forward.

He soon caught up and led her to the floor with a nod to his brother as they passed. A slight chill buffeted them, and Deor didn't miss the satisfied smile that flashed across Victor's lips.

She didn't comment.

After two dances with Victor, he was replaced by Delaney Overton, Rodney of Northfalls, and finally, Lord Farringdon himself. Deor was startled when he hip-checked Delaney's younger brother George out of the way and bowed slightly before her. The quartet struck up a Farendelle.

"Oh, no." Deor shook her head. "I don't do this."

"Nonsense," he said and took her in his arms.

Before she could stop it, they were gliding around the room. He dropped her arms, and his hands caught her waist. She gasped as he spun her into the air and back down. Before she could stumble, he had her in his arms again and was moving around the floor.

"See?" he said. "Easy with the right partner!"

"Right." Deor was less interested in talking than she was in making certain that she didn't fall and take several other dancers with her.

"Did you have a nice chat with my brother?" Rafe asked.

"Yep," Deor said, eyeing an approaching couple. Deor froze and braced for the collision, but then she was in the air again and down, safely out of harm's way.

"That's nice," Rafe said. Well, those were the words.

Deor nodded.

They finished the dance in silence. Every time he lifted her in the air, she tensed. Her fingers curled into his jacket's shoulders. The lift should have gotten less difficult, but the more it happened, the more nervous she became. Each turn was one more turn in the dance—and odds were eventually she'd screw up and tumble them both down.

The music wound down, and Deor sighed in relief. She had actually made it—Nope! Rafe dropped his hands to her waist and swung her in one last arc. She panicked when her feet left the floor. She gave a small yelp and clutched his shoulders.

Rafe winced and drew a sharp breath in between clenched teeth. He didn't waver. He completed the arc and lowered her gently to the ground. They both applauded politely as the final notes sounded.

"Shall we step off the floor for a moment?" Rafe said, his voice slightly strained.

"Sure." Deor took his offered arm. "Are you okay?" He looked slightly pale, and his jaw was set.

He didn't reply but led her from the floor to the far side of the room, where very few people mingled. He dropped her arm and drew a deep breath. He blinked at her, as if waiting for her to say something.

"What?" she said.

"Why did you do that?" he asked.

"Do what?" she said. "I panicked a bit on that last lift because I thought we were done. Did I miss a step?"

"No," Rafe said and tugged at the sleeves of his jacket. From the sleeve, a small stream of blood trailed down his hand.

"What happened?" She grabbed his hand and pulled it toward her.

He drew in a sharp breath again, wincing and clenching his teeth. "Careful."

She turned his hand this way and that but couldn't find the wound. She pushed his sleeve up, but the trail disappeared up his arm. She scanned up to his shoulder and saw it.

The shoulder of his jacket—both shoulders—were frayed, like they had been ripped. She pressed two fingers to it and drew back blood. "I did that?"

He nodded. "I'm afraid so. But clearly you didn't mean to."

He was trying to soothe *her*! "I'm sorry," she said. "We need to get you to a healer."

"Nonsense. We don't need to do anything." He forced a weak smile. "I will be back shortly." He ducked out of the nearest side door.

"What was that?" Arthur said behind her.

Deor spun around. "Were you doing that sneaky thing again?" she demanded.

"No. Unless by 'sneaky' you mean walking up to you like any other normal person. What did you do?"

The breath caught in her chest, and her heart contracted. Tears prickled in her eyes. The drawback of human makeup—if she cried, it would run. How indecorous.

Arthur's irritation shifted to concern. "What happened?"

"I cut him," she said, her voice a whisper. Her hand trembled as she brought it up to cover her mouth. "We were dancing, and I cut him." She swallowed hard. Her breath came in shallow bursts, and the trembling had spread. Hysteria was rising.

Arthur took her arm. "Come with me." He pulled her out the side door that Rafe had used into a small hallway clearly designed for servants' ease of movement. "Tell me, calmly."

She explained the dance, and what had happened, that she hadn't meant to, she hadn't even realized she'd done it.

Arthur took her by the shoulders. "Pull yourself together." He turned her around to face the door from which they had come. "Go back to the ball before someone notices and comes looking. I will find Rafe. He is probably changing clothes." He gave her a little shove. "Go."

She wiped her fingers under her eyes, hopefully cleaning up any errant mascara and straightened her shoulders. She fixed her best "well, now, isn't everything grand" smile on her face and marched herself back into the swirling mass of people.

Chapter Thirty-Six

Thankfully, nothing was amiss. The ball was going on as merrily as it had been when she left it. Victor came up to her. "Are you alright?"

"Yes. I stabbed Rafe."

"What?"

Deor sighed. She didn't want to repeat the story, but she did. It got worse when Victor snickered. "It's not funny."

"No, no," he agreed and covered his mouth to hide his smirk.

"It is *not* funny," Deor repeated, but her tone had softened. "Is this thing about to wind down?" Deor asked.

"I'd give it another two hours before anyone starts to leave. It cannot end until the last stroke of midnight, right?" He offered her his arm. "Even if we do have to be up for Parliament in the morning."

Deor let him steer her to Rodney and Clarissa.

"Hello." Victor nodded at both of them. He kept a hand firmly on Deor's back. "How are you this evening?"

"Well, thank you, Victor," Clarissa said. "Roger does throw quite a party."

Rodney rolled his eyes. "He certainly does."

"I've had a lovely time," Deor spit out when Victor nudged her in the back. "Northfalls is beautiful. So..." Deor said searching her memory for something about these two other than, one, they were paramours—she didn't like that too-Harlequin-romance word—and two, Rodney was Roger's nephew and heir. Someone had said something about the wine.

"Oh!" she said, lighting up. "Clarissa Rangley." Deor put the names together. "Your family are vintners, right? The wine Roger has served is amazing." Even if she had only been able to drink one glass.

"We are!" Clarissa lit up. "Thank you." She seemed genuinely pleased. "Roger was serving some of our best from the harvests before..." She trailed off and looked at Rodney like she might have made a mistake.

"Before the king's illness," he finished for her.

"Oh," Deor nodded. "The crops weren't as good after that, right?"

Clarissa shook her head. "No. We made due, and the wine is acceptable from those years, but not much better than that."

"Hello all!" Genevieve swept up to the group, and Clarissa stepped aside to make room for her.

"Good evening, Genevieve," Rodney said. "We were just talking about the recent crops."

"Genevieve helped a lot," Clarissa said hurriedly. "Without her, I think we would have entirely lost some of the crops in the south. Up here, the winters simply were not cold enough to let the vines rest. They flowered far too soon for the grapes to be good."

"Don't be so modest, Clarissa," Rodney said and put his arm around her waist. "Without you, the situation would have been much worse."

"We all did what we could." Genevieve smiled at Clarissa and Rodney. "But now that you're here," she turned to Deor, "things should improve."

The tone was supposed to be hopeful, Deor knew. Why then did it sound like a threat? "I'll do my best."

Genevieve seemed to consider her response and then nodded. "That is a lovely gown," she said to Clarissa.

"Thank you." Clarissa held still, like some kind of prey animal waiting for the predator to strike.

"Its plain style suits you well." Genevieve smiled the sincere smile of someone who knows she is completely following the rules.

"Thank you." Clarissa's voice was even softer. A quick scan of Clarissa's face told Deor everything she needed know about the woman's relationship with Genevieve. Her face was a frozen smile, eyes staring at a spot somewhere near, but not directly at, Genevieve. Behind her, her wings fluttered—she was taking deep, calming breaths.

Perhaps Deor had discovered a kindred spirit. Everything anyone had told her about the Rangleys, and Clarissa specifically, had been lovely. Lovely followed by talented, smart, and excellent with plant magic. Deor couldn't see Genevieve rooting around in the dirt. Perhaps Genevieve saw Clarissa as competition?

"Hello, darling!" Rafe swept up behind Genevieve and kissed her on the cheek. "How are you?"

"Starting to wonder where you had slipped off to. Did you change your jacket?" she asked.

It looked like the exact same jacket. It was the exact same jacket—aside from the fact that the earlier jacket now had gaping holes in the shoulders. What kind of person noticed something like that?

"It is." Rafe said as he slipped an arm around her waist. "I'm afraid the other got a stain."

"Pity," she said.

"So, what are we talking about?" Rafe asked.

"The flowers in Lady Genevieve's hair," Victor answered.

Deor wanted to elbow him, but his expression was completely innocent—he was passing along accurate information. She wanted to elbow him and stomp on his foot.

"Genevieve, you hold a Parliament seat, don't you?" Deor asked.

Rafe's eyebrows shot up, and he cocked his head slightly, giving her a "don't you dare," expression.

Behind Rodney, far enough away to not be a part of the conversation, but close enough to hear, Finn and Astarte stood, along with Roger and Pookie, with Robbie on his arm. The music had stopped—intermission for the quartet, so everyone had gathered around to talk, and Deor happened to be in the cool kids' circle. Within moments, Delaney was involved, too.

"Yes," Genevieve said, her easy demeanor tightening. "My family has a seat, and I am the one who typically represents us."

Deor nodded. "Right. I remember seeing you at the last Parliament."

"You weren't there—?"

It had to be common knowledge that the king watched sessions, didn't it? It couldn't have been that people thought if he wasn't in attendance he wasn't paying attention? She didn't dare look toward Finn.

"I'm sure the princess means in the papers following the session," Victor cut in. "Every paper had something to say and pictures to match. And you always make a lovely picture, Lady Genevieve."

"Yes," Deor said. She should be grateful to Victor for the save, but she was more irritated than ever at Genevieve. "I was curious—you represent the Winter Court as the Harvest Queen, right?"

"Well, I like to think I do," Genevieve said with a faux-modest smile. "The Harvest Queen standards have often been seen to embody a Winter Court lady."

"You certainly fit the part!" Deor said with a glance at Rafe. Why had he gone back to her? Aside from the beauty, charm, poise, power, and social status, that is. Everything about her grated on Deor's last nerve. She talked down to people—including Deor herself. She had power, but never seemed to have considered whether or not she deserved any of it. "So," she said, "as the Harvest Queen, and a member of Parliament, how do you feel about this whole House of Commons business?"

Everyone in the circle, even Victor, gaped.

Genevieve opened her mouth to speak, and then closed it again.

Deor arched an eyebrow.

"I don't," Genevieve finally said.

"You don't?" Deor asked. Out of all the responses Deor had predicted, this one hadn't even made the list. "You don't think about all the people out there at all?"

"Why would I?" Genevieve straightened her shoulders. "People shouting and waving banners in Parliament aren't helping themselves. Why should I listen to a bunch of irrational peasants who destroy property and pick fights?"

Rafe closed his eyes and took a deep breath. "I think," he said opening his eyes, "that what Genevieve means—"

"I'm perfectly certain Genevieve can speak for herself, Rafe," Deor snapped.

Next to her, Rafe stiffened and another chill—not a blast, but an aura —radiated off him. "I simply mean that Genevieve's role in the Winter Court is quite complex."

"Thank you, Rafe." Genevieve wound her fingers through his and lifted his hand to her lips. "But I can answer for myself." She glared at Deor. "You seem to resent the nobility an awful lot for being at the top of it. Or is it only me you dislike so much?"

Deor flinched. Every word she had studied in the *Noble Booke* prepared her for such a moment. She could smile and back down, assuring Genevieve that she had not meant to insult. A glance at her father in the outer ring of spectators also told her that this was not the time to press further. Stirring up trouble was the one thing she should avoid. Why did it seem like the best idea of the evening?

"It's not personal," she lied. "It's politics. I dislike people in glass castles. People who refuse to listen to legitimate complaints—or refuse to listen at all, to see if complaints are legitimate—who dismiss them out of hand."

"Well, that would be most of the nobility," Genevieve said flatly. "Excepting your suitor there, though I wouldn't believe everything he's told you. Or anything, really."

Deor glanced at Victor. "He's not a suitor. And I'm perfectly capable of thinking for myself."

Genevieve rolled her eyes. "You've been here fifteen minutes and you believe that you know who you can and can't trust as friends? The whole of the nobility knows that he was a part of the plot to kill the king. You started with the Goblin Prince. Are you going to make your way through all the suspected traitors in the kingdom?" She gave a decorous snort of derision. "It seems a rather unsafe test of character."

"It's better than sleeping my way up the ladder to royalty, Miss would-be-Princess-Consort. Funny how things didn't start to go south between the two of you until he wasn't going to be heir anymore."

Genevieve gasped and pressed a hand to her heart. "How dare you imply that I'm using Rafe to climb the social ladder!"

"How dare I? Pretty easily, really. I'm sure I'm not the only one thinking it." She scanned the crowd. No matter how many people might agree, there was no stampede to join her.

"You don't know anything!" Genevieve snapped. "You might be an educated adult in the human world, but here you're nothing more than an ignorant child playing dress up. You don't know anything about me or the Winter Court, but you're perfectly happy to criticize." She stepped toward Deor. "People here have sacrificed and bled for their country. People like me and Clarissa Rangley, who poured our magic into the land at the expense of our own health."

"Genevieve," Clarissa said softly.

"No!" she snapped at the woman. "You almost died. Don't pretend it isn't true. You saved so many plants because you poured enough of yourself into it that it almost killed you. How long did it take you to recover?" she demanded.

"I'm fine—"

"She's not," Rodney said. He put an arm around Clarissa's waist and held her close. "You're not," he said quietly to her. "You're getting better, and you'll *be* fine, but you're not fine." He kissed her cheek.

"Lady Genevieve, I don't think this scene—" Victor tried to cut in.

"Stop!" She pointed at him. "There are so many reasons why you don't get to talk at all about this. You can't tell me Wellhall didn't suffer too, can you?"

"No, but the princess—"

"The princess what?"

"Had nothing to do with that," Victor finished.

Genevieve arched one eyebrow. "But she's here now, and she could bother to learn what's happening in the Winter Court before having opinions on how it should be run."

"You know," Deor said, stepping up, "I'm right here. You don't need to yell at Victor."

Genevieve turned on her. "You're right. There is not a person in this room who wasn't hurt by the king's illness, and there isn't a person who didn't do what he or she could to help. Except you. And that's not your fault. But you can do a hell of a lot more than making snide comments at me because you don't like my dress."

"It has nothing to do with the dress..."

"No? Nothing at all to do with the dress, then?"

"It wasn't suitable for me. This," Deor waved at her own body, "looks nothing like that!" She waved at Genevieve. "You're tall, I'm short. You've got broad shoulders and have a body like a cross between an Amazon warrior and a runway model. Me? I'm six inches shorter than you are and weigh more. That dress, while lovely, would look horrible on me. Horrible! I don't know who told you it would be a good idea for you to design me a dress, but it wasn't me, and whoever it was, they were a complete idiot!"

Genevieve turned her head to look directly at Rafe. "On that count, Princess, I agree with you."

"It was your idea?" Deor asked Rafe.

"I'm afraid so," he said. Chill buffeted off him and raised goosebumps on her skin.

Deor shook her head. "It doesn't matter now. It's fine."

"Fine?" Genevieve crossed her arms. "No. Not fine. Out of everyone in the court, Rafe gave up the most—he almost gave his life for you, and he didn't know you existed!"

"I know," Deor said. "I am sorry—"

"No, you're not." Genevieve shook her head. "If you were sorry, you'd behave better. You flaunt disobedience like it is a fashion trend." Her eyes narrowed. "I simply cannot believe that no one has told you how to behave. You live with a model for decorum." She glanced at Astarte. "So, picking a fight with me?"

"I wasn't picking a fight," Deor insisted.

"Do you know when His Majesty became king?"

"What?" Deor stammered, confused by the change in subject. "When he was about one hundred years old."

"Do you know when that was?" she asked. "Or when his father became king? Or what his mother did in court? Do you know when the current ducal and county boundaries were established? Or, an easier question, do you know all the ducal families?"

"There's Rafe's and Roger's..."

"Yes. Do you know how many ducal families there are?"

"Not off the top of my head."

"How about how many members of Parliament?"

Deor shook her head.

"I see. Do you know how Parliament works? How laws are passed? How kings make changes to law? How the courts work? Inheritance—"

"I know that one!" Deor cut in. "Inheritance is based on family choice except rare circumstances."

"Well," Genevieve said, "I suppose it is unsurprising that you know how your own fortune works."

"Come on," Deor said. "I haven't been here that long."

"No," Genevieve said with a small smile. "But you've been here long enough to challenge me on my political position, without having any idea what that would mean."

"That's too far, Genevieve," Rafe said, taking her arm. He looked at Deor. "I'm sorry, Your Majesty."

Genevieve yanked her arm away from Rafe. "You're apologizing to her?" She backed a few steps away. "Why?"

"Why do you think?" His voice was low. "Now, let's go." He reached a hand toward her.

"No." She took another step back. "Look at her!" She pointed at Deor. "She could destroy the kingdom!"

"She could save it," Rafe said.

Genevieve rolled her eyes. "Sure. She *could*. But does it seem like she will?" Around the room, murmurs of agreement with Genevieve started to rise.

"I didn't ask to be the heir!" Deor snapped.

Genevieve turned her gaze back on Deor. "Well," she said, "that puts you with the rest of the people in this room. We didn't ask for you, either. Most of us were thrilled with Rafe."

"I do not want to be king!" Rafe yelled.

Genevieve jerked back like she had been hit. "No," she said softly. "And you don't have the sense to realize that made you an even better choice." She looked at Deor and shook her head. "Rafe, you're everything a great knight could be. Right down to the unquestioning loyalty."

"That's my job." The cold was coming off him in waves now. Deor shuddered slightly at the chill. Genevieve was close enough that Deor could see the goosebumps on her skin, but the woman didn't flinch. She didn't move a muscle.

"Is it?" she asked. "I thought your job was to be Sword."

"No!" Deor took her turn to shout. "Don't you dare, Genevieve. Don't you dare disparage him. Call me out all you like, but leave him alone."

"You're right, Princess," Genevieve said, not taking her eyes off Rafe. "I think I will leave him be." She grabbed the ring on her left hand and twisted it back and forth until she slid it free. "Here." She threw it at his face, and he barely caught it before it hit him. "It never fit right anyway."

"You can't be serious," Rafe said. He took another step toward her. "Genevieve, please. Let's go somewhere and talk about this."

She smiled sadly. "You were never good at political negotiations, Rafe. So, no." She turned to go, the crowd parting for her, but stopped and glanced back. "Tomorrow morning, we're to bend a knee to you, Princess. Do you think you'll be worthy of it by then?" With a swish of her skirts, she walked away.

The crowd closed behind her and turned their attention to Deor.

"I—" she started. Her eyes were filled with tears, blurring the room. "I —" She choked back a sob. She looked to Rafe, moved to put her hand on his arm. "Are you okay?"

He jerked his arm away from her. He bowed stiffly. "Excuse me, Your Majesty." As he moved toward the crowd of people, they fell open in front of him. The only sound was the click of his boots on the floor and the *thunk* of the door closing behind him.

When the door closed, the spell broke. Around the room, conversations exploded. People glanced sideways, from the corners of their eyes, at Deor, as she stood in a widening circle of people. Her father glared at her, but said nothing, taking Astarte by the arm, with Robbie following, and leaving.

As the crowd broke, a voice spoke from slightly behind her. "Princess?" Victor asked.

"Deor," she corrected, her voice a hoarse whisper.

"Shall I escort you to your rooms?" He offered her his arm.

She took it with a grateful smile. "Thank you." Across the room, she saw the doors open to the balcony. "Could we perhaps step outside for a few moments?"

"Certainly." He led her through the doors.

The balcony was dusted with snow, and small flakes tumbled through the air. The cold air stung her skin—she wouldn't be able to stay out very long, not without a coat. Then again, the room was clearing quickly.

"I'm an idiot," she said to no one.

"You're young," Victor said.

"I'm an ignorant idiot," Deor corrected. "I poked Genevieve because I was bothered by her, and everything she said was right."

"Not everything," he said, but did not sound convinced.

She chuckled bitterly. "Close enough. Do you think this is going to screw up tomorrow?"

He turned her to face him. "Yes," he said. "I'm certain of it. Or at least it is going to make the loyalty display that much harder. People were already annoyed and suspicious. This is going to make it worse. Tomorrow is a session of Parliament," he reminded her. "Your father is not the only person who can make statements and motions."

"So, what? Is someone going to suggest I be barred from being heir?"

"I hope not," Victor said. "But a vote of no-confidence is not impossible. And that would be bad."

"A coup?"

"Not quite, but it might set the stage for one. And I don't think your father will react well to a challenge. He's not known for taking criticism well."

Deor laughed out loud at that. "No. He's not. And, apparently, like father, like daughter."

"It's something everyone could work on," Victor said.

"You're very good at diplomacy."

"I try." He offered her his arm. "Come along," he said. "The crowds are gone now, and I don't doubt that if you delay, your father will be even more angry than he already is."

Deor shuddered. She hadn't broken her promise—she hadn't said anything against him. Then again, she hadn't needed to. Genevieve did all that for her. With the full approval of the nobility. Even worse, the nobility at the Grand Ball were supposed to be those most loyal to the king. If they were losing faith, tomorrow would indeed be a mess.

"Go on," she said shooing him along. "Thank you for the offer, but I'm afraid if he sees me with you, it will make it worse for you."

"I think I can handle it," Victor said.

"Well, I can't." Deor stepped back from him. "I can't handle one more bad thing being my fault tonight. He doesn't trust you. This will make that worse."

"If you say so," Victor said. He bowed slightly to her. "Goodnight, Deor."

"Goodnight, Victor."

Deor stood alone on the balcony for a few more moments. In the distance, through the falling snow, she could see the encampments of those stuck out in the fields. Lights twinkled in makeshift castles and cottages. She'd never seen tents like that before—not even at the most fancy of Renaissance Faires. By now, word of her fight—if it could be called that, really, it was more like a beating—with Genevieve must be reaching them. Tomorrow morning, everyone would know that she was an ignorant fool and that she broke up the most beautiful couple ever to have graced the Winter Court.

"Your Majesty." A soft voice caught her attention.

She turned to see Arthur, at parade rest, hands behind his back.

"My father wants me," she said.

"Yes." He turned to lead her inside. "Quickly," he said. "He was in quite the state."

"I'll bet," she said, and followed him.

Chapter Thirty-Seven

Deor followed Arthur to the suite, going over in her head what she would say to Finn to try and make this better. Not much came to mind.

Arthur stopped in front of the door. "Here we are." He knocked once and opened the door. "Your Majesty." He bowed slightly.

Deor stepped past him into the room. She squinted as her eyes adjusted to the darkness. Finn sat in one of the chairs by the fire, the light flickering off his eyes and the silver nails of his hands as they rested on the arm of the chair. She glanced over her shoulder. "You can go, Arthur," she said.

He did not move. "Your Majesty?" He spoke past her to the king.

"Go on, Arthur. You might check on Rafe."

"Yes, sir." Arthur nodded to her and left, closing the door softly behind him.

Deor walked to the fireplace and took a seat in the chair across from Finn. Her heart pounded in her chest, and her blood rushed in her ears. The tips of her fingers burned silver, and she closed her fists to hide them.

"Someday you'll learn to control that," Finn said. "It's not particularly wise to do that in political conversations. Unless you want to be seen as hostile or afraid."

So, his nails were silver by choice. Deor didn't know whether that should make her feel better or worse. Was he trying to frighten her? To make a point?

"Should I be afraid?" she asked.

"Of me?" He sat up and rested his hands on his knees. His fingernails remained sharp. "I don't think so," he said slowly. His gaze wandered around the room, and he seemed to come to a decision. "I was very angry."

"I figured." She shifted in her seat, kicking off her shoes and tucking her feet under her. She smoothed her dress so that the skirt fell across her legs and down, keeping her warm.

"What possessed you to ask Genevieve about Parliament?" He leaned forward, as if getting closer would mean that he could understand her better. "Do you have something against her?"

"No," Deor said too quickly. She frowned. "I shouldn't, I know. She tried with the dresses, but come on, could you see me wearing what she was tonight?"

Finn seemed to consider it. "I suppose that your choice is better. Is that what that was? A dispute over fashion?" His eyes flashed silver.

"No." Deor shook her head hurriedly. "It wasn't about that. There's something about her that rubs me the wrong way. She's perfect—and I should love her—everyone loves her—she's all grace and poise, and she's heroic—"

"I wouldn't go that far." Finn sighed. "I suspect that you caught her at a fraught moment, too. Especially given that after she put you in your place, she gave Rafe his walking papers, too."

Deor dropped her head into her hands. "Don't remind me." She looked up. "I didn't mean to cause that—I have to apologize to Rafe."

"No." Finn shook his head. "Or at least not tonight. By tomorrow they may have mended it. But likely, even if they have, it won't last. Spending the Solstice Season apart from your fiancée when you don't have to? That's not a good sign."

"Apparently they were on a 'hiatus.'" Deor mimed quotes in the air. Another wave of guilt washed over her. He had kissed her, but she should have seen it coming and certainly could have headed it off. She hadn't. She hadn't wanted to.

Finn laughed. "Well, there you go." He grew serious, folding his hands in his lap. "So, what shall we do about this?"

"Tomorrow you mean? I don't know. Should I not go to Parliament? You go without me. I'd be a distraction."

"No," he said. He stood and paced in front of the fire. "That would be seen as weak. Either you'd be running away, or I'd be keeping you away because I didn't trust you to handle the day."

"Do you trust me?"

He rested a hand on the mantle and leaned toward the fire. "No." He did not look at her. "But I cannot show that in public." He turned his head to look at her. "It is fine for you to dislike Genevieve. Many women do. It is even perfectly acceptable for you to shun her in public, though I wouldn't recommend it—not for a few decades at least, until you have established your own circle."

"Tonight was too far?"

"No. Or rather the first step was already too far. You challenged her loyalty to the nation. Asking a complicated political question? There was no answer to that, not in that moment, with Parliament tomorrow, with you being her superior—"

"I'm not her superior," Deor insisted.

Finn sighed and pushed himself away from the mantle. "You are. Like it or not. There is only one person in that room tonight who is higher ranked than yourself."

"You."

"Yes. Perhaps I should have stepped in, sent you to your room, but I'm not certain that wouldn't have made it all worse."

Deor shrugged. "I don't know." She dropped her feet to the ground and stood. "I am pretty good at this point at finding 'the worst.' There were worse things, I'm sure, but those would have likely involved violence or out and out treason. I went after the heroine of the Winter Court. And she made me look like a fool."

"She did." Finn rested his hands on her shoulders. "Tomorrow, you say nothing except when I speak to you—and you always answer in the affirmative. Be a perfect display of humility. Thank the people for their loyalty, praise Roger if you like for his hosting, compliment the Winter Court. Do *not* speak to or about Lady Genevieve or tonight's events. The ceremony should be short."

"Is it a group thing? Like will everyone stand at once and pledge?"

"What?" Finn let go of her and stepped back. "No. The family holding every seat in Parliament, or at least someone from the family, will come up, kneel, and pledge their fealty the Aethelwings. I will be seated; you will stand at my right."

"How many people is that?" Deor asked.

Finn shrugged. "A few hundred I would imagine."

Deor gaped. "So, no, this is not a quick ceremony, Finn. That will take all day! Is everyone required to stay as it happens?"

"It will not take all day. The fealty oath is short. Normally the Shield would lead the oath: 'do you swear to…' and so on. But Michael is not here. Rafe will volunteer his loyalty, he will say the oath for Roger, and then Roger will do so for the rest of the people."

Deor hoped that her shoes were comfortable. "Wouldn't it be easier on everyone to do some group pledge?"

"Ah, but then how would we know everyone participated?" Finn smiled. "Establishing power is challenging, daughter. Sometimes it is a wise choice to remind the people of your authority. Standing for an hour or two won't kill anyone. No one will forget their public promise."

Bullying. That's what Finn was doing. Demanding loyalty from people who had never seemed anything but loyal. Deor didn't have to know everything about the Winter Court to know this was a draconian display of power dressed up in party finery. "And choosing the opening of Parliament? That reminds everyone that you can refuse to allow Parliament, right?"

"Exactly." Finn leaned in and kissed her on the cheek.

Deor froze, forcing herself not to recoil from his touch.

"Pay attention to everyone there tomorrow, Deor. It will be obvious, no matter the smiles, who our real friends are."

"Right."

"Good." He shooed her away. "Now, off with you. To bed. Parliament opens at noon tomorrow, but that doesn't give us too much time in the morning. We will breakfast at nine, and Melanie will help you dress. I will enter before you. Once I am seated, Astarte will bring you to me. Roger will make some speech," he rolled his eyes, "and it will be quite flowery. And then we begin. And you…?"

"Don't talk at all," Deor answered dutifully. "Got it."

He nodded. "Good." He turned from her and disappeared into his and Astarte's rooms. Deor headed for her own.

When she opened the door, Brand leapt from the bed, barking, and ran to her.

"Hush, hush!" she said, but smiled. She swept him up into her arms. He squirmed and writhed, licking her face and making small yips. She dumped him on the bed. "Hush!" she said again, and he stopped barking, but his tail wagged furiously.

She glanced at the clock; it was well past one in the morning. She sighed and headed for her closet. She took off her jewelry and placed it back in the box. Her dress buttoned up the back. She reached behind her head and unfastened a few, but she couldn't reach enough to get her dress off over her head. She dropped onto the chair at the vanity.

"Melanie?" she called to the vanity mirror. "I'm sorry, but I need your help getting undressed."

The girl appeared. "Right away, Princess." She dropped a quick bow, and the mirror went black.

Deor pulled the pins from her hair one by one, tendrils of hair dropping free with each.

"Good evening, Your Majesty," Melanie said from the doorway.

"I'm sorry it is so late," Deor said.

Melanie giggled, "Oh, miss. No. Several people have not yet called their valets and maids. Many people are still enjoying each other's company."

"What about Rafe?" Deor watched in the mirror as Melanie swiftly removed all the pins—almost like magic.

She brushed Deor's hair and tied it back, not saying word for so long that Deor began to think the girl hadn't heard her.

"My father left some time ago," she said. "His lordship needed help moving to another room."

"Ugh." Deor wanted to drop her head to the vanity and bang it a few times, but she didn't move, as Melanie was sweeping her makeup away with a warm, damp cloth. "I'm sorry about that."

"I wouldn't be, miss," Melanie said matter-of-factly. She gestured for Deor to stand up, and she complied. She gently turned Deor away from her and unbuttoned the first of the twenty-some buttons on her dress. "My father thinks that this is for the best. He didn't particularly like Lady Genevieve."

Deor looked to the mirror to catch Melanie's eye, but the girl was studiously focused on her task. She didn't even glance up. "I see."

Melanie dropped to a crouch to finish the last of the buttons. "All done." She stood and slipped the dress from Deor's shoulders and brought it down to the floor.

Deor stepped out, trying not to stomp on the delicate material. Melanie gathered the dress and put it in one of her trunks. "I'll see to it when we get back to the Palace, if that is alright with you."

Deor grabbed the sides of the vanity as Melanie undid her corset. Once free from that, she helped Deor into her pajamas. Though she didn't need the help, there was something comfortable in the systematic movements. She smiled as she remembered her mother doing something similar when she was a little girl—helping her get ready for bed. Several times she had shooed away her mother's hands claiming she could do it herself. Tonight, it was nice to have someone else do it for her. "Thank you, Melanie."

Melanie curtsied. "I shall be in at about eight to wake you for your bath. I will get your dress and jewelry ready while you breakfast with the king, and then we will get you dressed and made up. Is that acceptable?"

"Yes, thank you. You know how all this is done. Whatever you say, we do."

Melanie smiled. "Thank you. Goodnight, miss." She slipped out the servants' entrance, and Deor followed her into her bedroom.

Deor shooed Brand from the center of the bed and climbed in, snuggling under the warm blankets. Brand turned circles as Deor settled herself on her side, and he flopped down close to her, resting his head on her hip.

Chapter Thirty-Eight

On the morning of the loyalty ceremony, silver flickered on Deor's fingertips as she reminded herself not to wipe her palms on her dress. Pearls, fastened not with magic, but with real hair pins imported from the human world, cascaded through her hair. The tiara of diamonds and platinum that she had brought from the Palace weighed on her head.

"You look amazing," Robbie said.

"Very regal," Astarte said as Melanie fastened the black silk sash across Deor's silver and black brocade dress and pinned on the diamond-studded eight-pointed star of the Aethelwing house.

"Thank you," Deor croaked. She swallowed hard against the dryness in her throat. She didn't need to be nervous, she told herself. It wasn't complicated. She didn't have any lines to flub up. Only speak when spoken to, and briefly, too. All she needed to do for the next two hours was stand still and smile. Stand still and smile while dozens of pissed off nobles knelt at her feet one by one to swear their fealty to her and her father.

With a deferential knock, Gordie let himself into the room. "Is Your Majesty ready?

"As ready as I'll ever be." Deor glanced once at Melanie before saying,

"Lead on, MacDuff." A pang of homesickness struck through her as she said it. Bill, her grandmother, any of her doctoral study group from home would have laughed and corrected her intentional Shakespearean gaffe. "It's 'lay on' not 'lead on'!" someone would have shouted.

Instead, Gordie simply turned a deeper shade of red and bowed again as Astarte whispered, "Gordie is from Cornwall, not Scotland, dear."

"Thank you," she said and followed Gordie out of the room, down the corridor toward the Great Hall where the ceremony was to be held. Ahead of her, trumpets blared and heralds sang out the name of King Sweordmund VIII.

At the entrance to the Great Hall, as planned, Astarte took Deor by the hand to lead her up the center of the room to Finn. Deor had objected to this detail when the Master of Ceremonies had explained the plan. Too like a wedding or a christening. Too much like Astarte was her mother. But now she was grateful for the friendly support. Her own fingers felt icy cold in Astarte's warm ones.

On either side the room was hung with black velvet bunting, each loop holding a shield that bore the eight-pointed star of the Aethelwings. As she and Astarte passed up the central aisle, the crowd swayed like grass in the wind, bowing low.

It was a long walk through the massed nobility. *Stand still and smile*, she told herself, as she took her place next to Finn. *Anyone can do it*. On the walk to the front, she had been too focused on not falling to observe much else, but now she looked around the room, staring back at all the faces staring at her. There was a subtle gradation to the room she realized.

No matter what rank, each member of Parliament was wearing his or her chain of office. One of them was Genevieve. If Deor were very lucky, she wouldn't melt into the floor in humiliated embarrassment when Genevieve made her pledge.

Everyone present was dressed in their glittering finest. The whole room sparkled. Still, the farther back she looked, the less glorious the crowd became. Colors were a touch more muted, jewels a touch smaller and fewer. And she saw fewer familiar faces. Towards the front of the room stood the highest in the land—the Farringdons, Rangleys, and Overtons among others. Penny's family was harder to pick out of the crowd, lost as they were in the middle of the pack. Farthest back stood the gentry—landless knights and wealthy farmers, merchants who stood high in society but lacked lands and titles—invited as a courtesy to watch the show and fill the hall. None had a chain of office.

Victor Farringdon stood near the front with his parents, but many of his friends stood toward the back. Deor recognized them from the disastrous Parliament session. In particular, a woman with an arrow through her auburn hair stood out from the crowd, a sardonic smile on her face. Deor wanted to simultaneously hand her some sort of gold medal for the sheer chutzpah of bringing a weapon in disguised as a hair ornament and have Arthur search her for a hidden bow.

Smile and hold still, Deor told herself, stifling a sigh. If this were grad school, she and the red-haired woman might have had a chance to become friends, but from their current places, they might as well dwell in separate countries.

As Deor let her thoughts and eyes wander over the crowd, Ama Nefasta, wearing her Bardic robes and waving a mistletoe branch like the one she had used during the Adoption, intoned a blessing and well-wishes from the Bards.

If she hits me with that thing, Deor thought, *I'm going to take it and snap it in half.*

Next to her, Finn raised his hand. The already quiet room fell deeper into stillness. No one moved.

"My people," he said, voice echoing enough to make a few people flinch, "we thank you for your generous presence here today. While it is not often that the monarch chooses to attend the opening of Parliament, today is a special occasion. Today, my people, I present my daughter—a child of my body—Deor, Heir to the Aethelwing House and Princess of the Winter Court."

Deor held her breath, as all eyes settled on her.

"I declare Parliament open," Finn flung his arms out wide, "and invite everyone to come forward and pledge their loyalty to your monarchs."

Roger stepped forward and spoke. She tried to pay attention, really, but her mind wandered once he got to the third praise for the king and family, and she went back to scanning the crowd. No one seemed happy to be there.

Deor wondered how she might get to know those people, the ones who stood in the back, who lacked a voice in Parliament.

And now Roger was inviting anyone who wished to come forward and affirm their fealty to their sovereign and his heir. Deor writhed internally. Finn wanted all of this to look entirely voluntary. As if he hadn't ordered every one of these people to pack up their households in the dead of winter and come north for this exact purpose.

No one moved. Deor felt a horrible urge to laugh.

There was movement among the Farringdon contingent. Deor spotted Victor and his father Edgar flanking Madeline in a cluster of retainers and hangers on. Deor squinted. One of them seemed fuzzy, dimmer than he should have been at that distance. Madeline smirked and stepped forward, her mouth opening.

"Allow me to be first." Rafe's voice echoed through the room. Before Madeline could fully emerge from the crowd, Rafe had crossed the open space and taken a knee at Deor's feet. He drew his sword and held it out to her on open palms.

"As I swore fealty to my king upon my knighthood, so I swear it now to his heir, Deor Smithfield. Princess and lady, my sword is ever at your service."

We thank you. That was her line. That was all she was supposed to say. Finn had drilled her on it endlessly. But now it seemed pathetically curt. Rafe still knelt before her, sword extended.

Without glancing at Finn, Deor stepped forward and laid a hand on the sword's blade. A good blade, perfectly tempered and not a drop of iron in it, her senses told her as soon as her fingers touched the metal.

She cleared her throat, remembering her Malory. "I thank you, Rafael, Lord Farringdon, Sword of Peace and Justice. And I shall strive always to be worthy of your loyalty, a good and gracious lady to you," her voice rose, "and to all my people."

Rafe nodded curtly at her and rose, sheathing his sword and returning to his position next to the king. The icy stare he gave her made her wince —he was doing his job, being loyal, but he was not happy about it, or her.

"Members of Parliament," Madeline Farringdon called out as she stepped forward. "I have a motion." She raised a scroll above her head.

"Traitor!" Finn shouted.

"Not at all, Your Majesty." She curtsied deeply before the king, dropping her eyes to the ground. "I have no quarrel with your reign, no question about your rule." Deor rolled her eyes. "But this creature—what is she? Who is her mother? What proof do we have that she's even a faerie? Not the child of a proper child bearer at all, but some bastard conjured up from the human world. I say she's a trick, a hoax to cover the failure of the Adoption magic." She spun to face the crowd. "And thus, I call for a vote by the Lords and Ladies of Parliament. Have you any confidence in this creature?"

Voices rose in chaos, some agreeing with her, some not.

"Silence!" Finn stood. The room went silent. He scanned the crowd, challenging anyone to speak, before focusing on Madeline. "How dare you speak such treason in my presence? You have no right to say such things."

"On the contrary," she said. "This is Parliament, as you have said. And I, as a high-ranking member of Parliament, have the right to put forth a motion. Will you deny me my rights?"

Finn quivered with anger, his irises silver, and leaking to swallow his pupil and whole eye. He held her gaze for several moments. "No," he finally relented. "Make your pathetic motion, and let's get on with it." He flung himself back in his seat, like a bored teenager.

She inclined her head at him. "Thank you, Your Majesty."

Deor glanced at her father. He wasn't even looking at Madeline. She had the rapt attention of everyone else in the room. No wonder the king feared her—she was a politician and a showman to the core.

"I call for a vote of no-confidence in this woman, this would-be heir."

Deor winced. She could feel Finn's stare at her back but did not look to him. Instead, she held Madeline's gaze. No magic hovered around her, and Deor detected nothing in her voice that reminded her of the whips of will magic that had lashed her body, leaving spiraling black marks across her that had taken a month to dissipate. No. Today that woman was relying on good old-fashioned rhetoric.

"I second," a man called from close to the back of the room. Deor did not recognize him—he hadn't been at any of Roger's events, that she could remember. Next to him, the woman with the arrow through her hair smiled.

"Order!" A woman—the Speaker of Parliament—clapped her hands for lack of a gavel. "We have a motion and a second. Is there any debate on the motion before we call the question?"

Silence again fell. Madeline turned a circle, scanning the crowd and returning to face the king, but her eyes were on Deor. Deor glanced to her right. Finn drummed his nails on the side of the chair, inch long silver blades chipping the wood with each strike. Beyond the king, Rafe stood at parade rest, his eyes forward, staring at some vacant spot half way through the crowd.

Finn had told her not to speak. She should bow her head and say nothing. She should be a *good girl*.

Madeline grinned. "I move to call—"

"I have something to say!" Deor stepped forward, and all eyes snapped to her. She looked to the chair. "May I speak?"

The woman started, shock crossing her features. "Yes, Your Majesty."

"Thank you." Deor nodded. "I don't want to speak out of turn."

Someone in the crowd actually snickered.

She let it go.

"First," Deor said. "To Lady Genevieve and all those present at the Grand Ball last night, I apologize."

Gasps from the crowd.

"I behaved horribly," she went on. "It is no surprise that Duchess Farringdon would make such a motion today and less surprising that so many would support it. You do not know me. I am a changeling, whisked away as a child and brought back. Why would you trust me? Especially over Lord Farringdon, a man of impeccable character, skill, and love for the Winter Court, and to whom I also apologize."

Murmurs rose in the crowd. She knew better than to look to Finn. If looks could kill, his probably would—or at least maim.

"So, I ask a favor of you," she said, spreading her arms out. "Please, give me another chance. I've no right to ask for it, but I am. I am young. I am inexperienced, and I was wrong." She smiled. "I hate admitting I am wrong—it is something that, if I am to be a good ruler, I must work on."

A few people chuckled or smiled back.

"So please. I am thirty. Do not decide today that I never will be more, or better, than I am today. Give me time. My father is healthy. The land is recovering. Surely there is a little space for me to grow up. A vote of no-confidence cannot be undone. I don't ask that you give me your support

—not yet. I ask that you table the duchess's motion. Give me one year. Next February first, open parliament with this vote. I will do everything in my power to be worthy of your confidence then. Including meeting, as much as I am able, with you, talking to you, and, if need be, personally assuring each and every one of you. Thank you."

The lady in charge scanned the room. "Lady Farringdon, do you want to call the question?"

"Yes," she said.

"All those in favor of voting on no-confidence?" she said.

A few people—far more than Deor hoped—called "aye."

"All those against?"

"Nay!" The voices rose above the others, and echoed, loud enough to be definitive.

"No vote today," the woman said, and clapped her hands again.

"Thank you." Deor put her hand over her heart and bowed.

Madeline was far from finished. She moved forward, nearer to Deor and Finn. The Farringdon party as a whole moved toward her, including the fuzzy retainer who stayed fuzzy even as he got closer. Deor squinted and the focused her magic. Her nails lengthened and grew sharp.

Madeline went on. "I say it is our duty to the realm to compel the king to take a child bearer—a proper one of faerie blood, approved by the Parliament—to bear a proper heir."

"Are you offering yourself?" Rafe snapped. "At your age and after two children, I doubt that's wise, Mother." He unsheathed his sword as he stood between Finn and his mother.

For a moment, Madeline looked as if she wanted to slap him, but she composed herself, holding her hands out in a gesture of appeal to the crowd. Faint traces of shimmer filled the air around her hands, as if heat radiated from her. The shimmering disturbance in the air spread and thinned, drifting into the crowd.

"Finn, she's doing something," Deor hissed.

"She's inciting treason."

"No, not that." Deor yanked up her skirts and stepped off the dais toward Madeline. "I can see you!" Deor said. "Whatever magic you're doing right now, stop it. Stop it this minute." Angry sparkles spit off her as she stalked toward the woman.

Mouth open in shock, Madeline turned to look at Deor.

"Deor, be careful." Rafe stepped away from Finn, moving to intervene between the two women.

Everything happened at once. The magic in Madeline's hands disappeared into her. Something—someone—fuzzy, just glimpsed in the corner of Deor's eye, rushed forward. A knife gleamed.

"The king!"

Rafe whirled, sword raised. Too late. Michael, his shock of red hair gone grey, but fire burning in his hands, slashed wildly at Finn. Finn's arm came up to block the attack, armor suddenly glistening along his forearm. A whistling in the air and sickening *thunk* of knife hitting meat. Michael gasped, stiffened, and fell forward, a knife made of ice embedded in his back.

"Are you alright, Your Majesty?" Victor Farringdon stepped forward, a second knife in his hand.

Rafe moved to put Deor behind him, but she side-stepped him and went up to Finn. "Are you hurt?"

"Guards, disarm that man!" the king shouted, waving at Victor.

"Finn, he just saved your life," Rafe shouted. "I saw it with my own eyes."

A roar of approval, the first sign of unanimity, went up from the crowd. Victor laid his remaining knife on the ground and stepped away from it, his hands visibly empty. The crowd's approval grew.

On the dais, Finn seethed. Rafe laid a hand on Michael's neck and nodded. "He's dead. We'd better get you to a healer, Your Majesty."

"I'm fine. My clothes are singed is all," Finn snapped. He strode forward, nails silver and seized Deor's wrist.

"Ow. What are you doing?"

Finn held Deor's hand high over her head. "Do you see?" he shouted at the nobles. "Do you see her hands?" He held up his own bladed fingers beside hers. "There's your vote."

Still holding Deor by the wrist, he turned and strode from the room, with Rafe trailing behind. Locked in Finn's fierce grip, she had little choice but to run along next to him, trying not to look like a toddler being hauled from the room by an angry parent.

"Rafe, fetch Astarte," the king said as he hauled Deor toward the foyer.

"Shouldn't I make sure you two get safely to your rooms?"

"No!" Finn shouted. "You should make sure you do as I say!"

Rafe glanced at Deor and gave the king a short nod. "Yes, sire." He turned from them and headed back toward the ballroom.

"Finn!" Deor said as he hauled her toward the foyer. "Wait!"

He did not stop. He did not acknowledge her at all.

Deor planted her feet and hauled her weight backward, tugging against Finn's grip. "Stop!" She stumbled forward again as he refused to hear her and kept on. "Dammit, Finn!" He winced at her cursing, throwing a silver-eyed glance over his shoulder. She persisted anyway. "Madeline is still in there. She's going to pick up where she left off. We have to go back!"

Finn halted so abruptly she nearly ran into him.

He jerked her toward him, and she yelped.

"We are not going back," he snapped. "You promised not to speak."

"I was going to be—"

"No!" Finn shouted, and it reverberated off the walls of the foyer. "If I had wanted you to speak, I would have granted you permission." He clenched her arm tighter, squeezing her bones. "I could call your choice today treason."

Deor winced. "That would go over well," Deor said before she could stop herself.

"It will go over how I say it goes over!" he snapped. "That is what you need to learn. I say what is and what is not. I say who speaks and who remains silent. That makes a king!"

Deor opened her mouth to argue, then shut it. There was no arguing with a madman, and anyone who thought he made reality was crazy.

"Wise choice." He turned toward the stairs curving up to the household rooms from the foyer. Only steps away she had entered with Finn a few days before.

She planted her feet and held her ground. "I'm not going with you."

He turned to face her. "Do not defy me, daughter."

As her father, as her king, it didn't matter. He was wrong. "If you do not go back, you lose," she said. "I know it. Madeline is in there now, whispering to people. That's what she does. She's controlling the narrative!"

"What that traitor does is no concern of mine. We will deal with the *narrative*, as you say, later. I will decide what it is—"

"It doesn't work that way," Deor snapped, voice rising. She jerked on her hand, but his grip was sure.

His eyes went silver. Deor gasped as stabs of pain hit her wrist. His nails were silver, and drops of blood were pooling at their points.

"Stop it," Deor said. She didn't cry out, or yell, but kept her voice level. "Let go of me. Right now."

"Or?" A wicked grin crept across his face. His silver eyes glittered. An open challenge to defy him.

"Or this." Deor's vision flashed with a silver aura as she forced magic into her wrist.

"Gah!" Finn cried out and dropped her wrist. Small silver peaks wringed her wrist, rising above the blood smeared there. A line of fine red dots crossed Finn's palm.

Before he could do anything, Deor turned on her heel, gathered her skirts, and ran back to the ballroom. She slammed open the door, expecting buzz and discussion. A wall of silence hit her.

She stumbled but stayed standing. Power swirled around her—it was like walking through thick water. She drew a deep breath to make sure she still could. The magic slipped into her, coating her mouth and throat, trailing down into her lungs. With a puff, she forced the air out, but the magic lingered.

Deor had entered the same way she'd left—behind the dais. Madeline stood center stage, facing away from her. Everyone in the room had stayed, it seemed, when she and Finn had bolted. Now they all stared at Madeline who gestured and waved as though she were making some grand speech, but Deor heard nothing. Instead, glimmers of blue magic sparked through the air.

No one had noticed her entrance. She slipped out of her heels and gathered her dress and crept behind Madeline, hoping to get a better view of the room without drawing anyone's attention. She needn't have worried. No one's gaze left Madeline. Deor could have stripped naked and done a dance, and no one would have moved.

A sound behind her jolted Deor around. In the back of the room, crouched by the throne, were Astarte and Rafe. A golden glow encompassed both of them, and from the fierce look in Astarte's eyes, it was all her magic. Rafe looked dazed, a slow blink the only change in his blank expression, focused on nothing. Astarte had him sitting beside her, her arm around his shoulder. Astarte glanced at Deor and started, surprised. With her free hand, she waved at Deor to come to her.

"Hurry," the woman mouthed. She pointed at Madeline.

Deor turned back to look. The glimmers of blue magic hung closer in the air to her, and instinct made her dodge as one flicked toward her. She glanced back at Astarte. Worry lines creased her face, and she flailed again at her.

"I'm fine," Deor mouthed and shook her head. She returned her gaze to Madeline and focused her attention on the magic. In seconds, the coils of magic revealed themselves. As Deor stepped closer, she saw that Madeline's gestures weren't rhetorical—she was weaving the magic into the air itself.

Deor crept closer, until she was parallel with Madeline. Thick cables of magic spread out from a single coil, the centerpiece of a cat's cradle she constantly manipulated. Her lips were moving, and if Deor concentrated, she could make out the faintest whisper—no doubt amplified into Madeline's victims' ears as she wrapped them in her magic. Madeline's eyes flicked in Deor's direction, and a coil of magic shot toward her. Madeline hadn't moved a muscle.

Deor threw her arm up to block the blow, and the magic coiled around it. In a flash of blue light, Deor was in the alley again, heavy twines of magic lashing around her shoulders, trying to haul her back. Panic flooded her as it had that afternoon, and she felt herself, even as she watched, struggle against it. Now, though, she could see clearly the face of her attacker. Madeline, armed with the same expression she now wore, wove binding after binding of will magic and sent it after her. The memory rolled on, and Deor flashed her wings out, shredding the magic with their sharp edges. Madeline stumbled backward, and Deor fled the alley before she could regain her feet for another attack.

Deor blinked, and the world swirled back into view. The coil of magic had worked its way up from her wrist to her elbow. The whispered words were loud and clear in her mind. Madeline smiled grimly at her.

Deor grinned back.

The words were gibberish—snippets about what a bad man the king was, what a good family the Farringdons were, and how she, Madeline, was the rightful heir to the throne. Deor rolled her eyes, but in the crowd of people before her, several nodded, many teary eyed.

Deor rolled her wrist so that she could grasp the coil in her hand. "Madeline," Deor called, breaking the silence. "Let these people go."

Madeline scowled, fury lining her features. "I will deal with you later."

A shock of pain shot through her hand and arm where the magic touched her.

Deor gasped, sucking air in through her teeth at the pain, but rolled her wrist again, gathering more of the coil around her hand and tightening her grip. She wrapped the fingers of her free hand around the thick rope of magic and hauled it toward her as hard as she could, wrenching Madeline away from the crowd.

For a moment, people in the crowd seemed to stir, a few blinking.

Madeline focused on Deor. The coil binding her vanished, leaving burns in its wake. Before Deor could respond, Madeline seemed to fling the cat's cradle toward her. Rather than a single coil, a net flew. Deor shrieked and held up her hands to block, but the net slammed into her, thick and heavy, knocking her to the ground.

Everywhere it touched her flesh, it burned. The weight of Madeline's will woven into the netting itself blocked out the rest of the world, and her words blared like a siren. Deor clutched her hands over her ears, but words echoed in her head. The point wasn't persuasion, but pain. Deor screamed as she clutched the netting and hauled it off her body. Her nails, instinctively silver, did nothing against the magic, and her sparks gave her only the barest of shields.

She scrambled away from the netting, kicking it away from her and scooting back. Blood dripped down her forearms and oozed out of her palms where she had gripped the net.

Madeline had already refocused, and any of those waking had succumbed again.

Deor stood. She tucked back a few strands of hair and smoothed her dress. She glanced back. Astarte and Rafe were still safe under Astarte's golden shield, but Madeline's magic crashed against it like the tide, and it was only a matter of time before it gave way.

The path to the door was clear. She could get help. Finn was out there, and with his voice, his power, he could shut this down. That made the most sense. She turned, and something tugged her foot. A small thread of blue magic wound loosely around her ankle.

Get help flashed again and again in her mind, keeping time with the pulsing magic. She kicked her foot free and stomped on the thread, grinding it beneath her heel like Eve encountering her first post-Eden snake.

Deor had fled Madeline's magic once. Never again.

She willed magic into her fingers, and her nails lengthened. Sharp and shiny, but no match for the tight cords Madeline made. Certainly not the cat's cradle—the source of the spell. It would take more than claws to tear through this web.

Deor studied her palm, opening and closing it like she was gripping the hilt of some unseen dagger. She closed her eyes. She pooled magic in her hand and imagined it coalescing into a narrow hilt, a perfect fit. A crossbar pommel nestled against her closed fist. A straight blade, edged on both sides, tapering to a sharp point. All of it white-silver gleaming in the light.

A single piece of metal.

"No," she corrected herself, her voice soft but clear. "A single piece of magic—of me."

Tightening her fist around her creation, she swung it a couple times, its weight cutting through the air. She opened her eyes. Not a dagger.

A sword.

Deor strode toward Madeline, her sword slicing through the blue aura like a boat through rough water. She slammed a hand onto the woman's shoulder and spun her around, sending her flailing.

Madeline's mouth formed into a small "o."

Deor lifted the blade and brought it down through the cat's cradle, shredding it to pieces.

Madeline stumbled backward, jagged threads of magic blackening and crumbling to dust in her hands.

"These are *my people*," Deor snapped, advancing on Madeline. "*Mine.*" She spun to face the crowd. "It's okay," Deor called. "The spell is broken."

Several of them shook themselves and rubbed their hands over their arms and bodies, as if brushing away some invisible debris.

Madeline shook her hands free of the broken magic and drew her arm back as though she might strike again.

"Go ahead and try it," Deor said and leveled the sword at her.

Madeline glanced around the room.

Several people had started to advance on them—none of them looked happy. Toward the back, the woman with the arrow in her hair pulled it free and, glaring at Madeline, shoved people aside as she headed for the dais.

Madeline spun from Deor, and a flash of magic exploded from her hands. Deor blocked with her sword and free hand, sending sparkles flying. A wall of ice crystals had slammed into her and the audience, knocking dozens to the floor. Several were bleeding from the glass-like shards of ice. Sparks swirled in the air around Deor—any ice that had gotten through to her had melted on the way, peppering her skin with drops of cool water.

A side door slammed, and Deor turned to see Madeline and her followers ducking out. Victor lay in a crumpled heap against the wall, nose bleeding, crisscrosses of angry red welts, like netting, marring his face. A jagged icicle had been jammed into his shoulder.

"Victor!" Deor called.

"I'm fine." He hauled himself to his feet. He gripped the icicle, and it dissolved, magic melting into a puff of steam. "It wasn't deep."

Deor spun to face the crowd. "Is everyone okay?"

Most people had regained their feet. "We're fine, I think." Roger spoke. He came toward her a few feet and then stopped.

"What?" Deor said.

"I think," Rafe said, stepping beside her, "he's a bit intimidated by the sword."

"Oh." Deor looked down at her hand. The silver-white blade was still as she'd imagined it, sparkling in the light of the chandeliers. "Right. Sorry." She wasn't sure what to do with it. She didn't have a scabbard.

"What is going on?" Finn demanded, slamming into the hall. His eyes widened when he saw the sword in her hand.

"Madeline tried to enchant Parliament," Astarte said, holding her hand out to him.

"Deor stopped it," Rafe finished. "Madeline ran."

The king eyed Deor but took Astarte's hand. "You made that?" He nodded at the sword.

"Yes," Deor said. She immediately but gently lowered it to the ground. As soon as her fingers loosened from it, it vanished into a flurry of sparkles. The crowd around her gasped, as if they only now believed in magic. Deor stood and tried to curtsey. The world around her spun, and she staggered.

"Deor." She heard a voice, felt someone grab her, and the world went black.

Chapter Thirty-Nine

When Deor came to, she was in her room, on her bed. A quilt had been spread over her. Her shoes were off, but she was still in her dress. The curtains were pulled back, and the sunlight shone through.

"So I haven't been out long," she said to the ceiling.

"About twenty minutes." A voice spoke from a few feet away.

Deor jerked up and saw Rafe sitting at her vanity, chair turned toward the bed. He smiled at her. "How do you feel?"

Deor flung the blanket off and sat up. She swung her legs off the bed. "I'm okay," she said. "A little weary."

"You fainted after you let go of the sword. Too much magic loss."

Deor nodded. "Right." She looked at him. "Is everyone okay?" Brand whined and forced himself under her arm. She snuggled him close.

"Yes. Thanks to you."

She leaned forward. "Did you arrest the Farringdons, or at least Madeline? I saw her with magic in her hands."

"She and my father fled. They had a portal ready-made and waiting for them." Rafe shook his head. "People remember hearing her speak, but they can't explain her magic."

Deor threw up her hands and rolled her eyes. "So she gets away again. Great."

Rafe stood and gestured at the bed. "May I?"

"What?" Deor shrugged. "Sure."

He sat next to her. "You're taking this all really well. It's okay if you need to cry or shout or something. I'm the only one here—feel free to rave a bit if it makes you feel better."

Deor let out a short laugh and swiped at her eyes. "It all happened so fast I didn't have time to be scared."

Rafe nodded sympathetically.

"I'm getting a bit sick of people almost killing me. Though to be fair, I think Michael was going after Finn."

Rafe nodded again.

Deor shifted on the bed to face him. "I wish I could run away from it all for a little while—get outside the Palace world and be somewhere safe and quiet. Do you ever feel that way?"

"I do. It's why I run every morning."

Deor laughed. "Don't let's go crazy here. I said I wanted to get away, not get up at dawn to do it." She pulled Brand up onto her lap, her fingers buried in his fur. "I also want to apologize to you. I am sorry about last night. If I can do anything to fix things with Genevieve, I will. I'll go apologize again, I'll make a statement in the paper, I'll go to her personally— whatever you need."

"Stop." Rafe frowned. "I was angry last night—I was angry today. But the truth is, we were headed for that. You might have sped it up a bit, but she was right, I'm not good at politics. I'm not the right man for her."

"She's an idiot," Deor said out loud, wincing as the words escaped. Some things were meant to be kept in one's head. "Sorry…"

"She's not an idiot," he said, but he smiled. "She's amazing."

Deor's shoulders dropped. He was pining for her already. "She is."

"She got an Aethelwing to apologize. That's unheard of." His expression was serious, but his eyes sparkled..

Deor laughed. "I'm still sorry—and I'm sorry I don't like her."

He shrugged. "Some people are like that—they just rub you the wrong way. Hopefully you'll both come around. She would be a great ally to you."

"I know."

"And, if we're being honest here, I never should have tried again." He shifted to face her and leaned forward until he could have easily reached out and touched her. "If everything had been right, if we'd just needed a break, I never would have kissed someone else."

"There is that, I suppose." Her voice came out breathy and quiet. She leaned toward him. He'd broken up with his fiancée the night before. She couldn't, well, *shouldn't* kiss him. Not now, and probably not ever. But his eyes were crystal blue, and the scar under his eye only made him more handsome.

He slipped his fingers into her hair and brought her face toward his. This time, when their lips met, she did not stop him. She savored the feel of his lips against hers. She leaned forward and wrapped her arms around his neck. He dropped his hand to her back and pulled her toward him, slipping his other arm under her legs and settling her on his lap.

She wrapped her arms around his neck. Her heart raced and the sparks that leapt between them when they first touched months ago returned, arcing energy between them, wrapping them in their own world.

A knock came at the door.

"Princess? Lord Farringdon?"

Deor shoved herself away from Rafe and leapt to her feet. "Yes?" she called to the door as ran her fingers through her hair, smoothing it, and wiped a hand across her lips.

The door opened slightly. "You and Lord Farringdon are needed." Lieutenant Bolton nodded at both of them. "The king would like to see you."

Rafe stood and headed for the door.

Deor followed. "Come on, Brand!" she called, and the puppy caught up to her, and followed her and Rafe out of the room.

Finn's shouting lasted well into the evening. He shouted at Rafe, at Astarte, at Roger and Pookie, at Deor, at any passing servant. He shouted throughout the ensuing scramble of leaving guests, through Roger's repeated, increasingly abject apologies. He went up in volume when it was reported that Madeline and Edgar Farringdon had left for their own encampment and were roundly denying having ever set eyes on Michael, let alone encouraging his crazed attempt on the king's life. And now he was shouting in the next room as servants scrambled to pack everyone's belongings and Astarte murmured soothing things at him. She'd convinced her husband to spend the night, but nothing would persuade him to stay beyond the next morning.

Breakfast the next morning was a tense affair, but at least the shouting was over. At the table, Finn lurked behind the newspaper, which was both a relief and a stressor—Deor wasn't sure if he'd simply run out of anger or was now giving them all the silent treatment. He hadn't mentioned her magic-made sword once.

Everyone else at the table, Astarte and Robbie especially, seemed content to let him sit behind the paper undisturbed.

Finally, Deor cleared her throat. "Finn," she said. "Instead of taking the carriage with you, I think I'd prefer to ride." After the incident with the Nightmare, she couldn't believe she was volunteering to get back on a horse, but the prospect of cold fingers and a sore backside seemed preferable to a three-day journey sitting opposite Finn.

The newspaper snapped down, and Finn glared at her over it. "Ride? How? With whom?"

"With me in the vanguard," Rafe said. "It'll be perfectly safe, sire."

"Plus, it might be a goodwill gesture. It will let me see more of the countryside, maybe even stop and talk to people a little bit on the way."

Finn grunted. "You do have a point there."

"No time like the present to get started on making people like me," Deor said.

"It's the peerage that's going to be voting their confidence in you, not the commoners you're so fond of."

"But many of the lords listen to their people," she persisted. "And more importantly, I can listen to them—find out what their needs and concerns are and how life looks from their level. That will help me know how to address the House of Lords better. After all, won't they be happier with me if they know I understand the needs of the country?"

Finn snorted this time and frowned. "Very well, go ahead and ride in the open. Perhaps it will do people good to see you in the flesh after all. Then the idea that they have an heir will seem more real and substantial to them."

"Thank you."

"But remember your promise."

"That I won't speak against you?" Deor nearly rolled her eyes but remembering his rage the night before managed not to. "Finn, you have to stop being afraid that I'll undermine your authority."

As she said it, the truth of it struck her. All his raging the night before, his attempts to control her—he was afraid. It seemed absurd, but the more she thought about it, the more she was sure she was right. What had Arthur called her? Chaos incarnate. She might be the heir Finn had longed for all his life, but she was also the stark reminder that someday his reign would come to an end.

"Thank you," she said again. "I appreciate your letting me do this. If you'll excuse me, I'll go ask them to saddle Bessie." She rose from her chair and quietly walked toward the door.

As she passed his chair, Finn's hand shot out and caught hers in a tight squeeze. "Be careful, daughter," he said.

"I will," she said. "I promise."

I n the stable yard, Rafe adjusted Sampson's girth strap and patted the horse on the shoulder. Beautiful day for a ride across country—hardly any wind and the sunlight sparkled on the drifted snow. Arthur walked across toward him, cloak wrapped tight.

"Where's your mount?" Rafe called out to him. "We're almost ready to leave."

"The king has another errand for me today," Arthur said. "I'll be going back to London the short way."

"Ugh, bad luck."

Arthur shrugged. "Duty."

"Speaking of duty, can you believe how the princess handled the Farringdons yesterday? It was masterful."

Again, Arthur shrugged. "It certainly put off the crisis. How often in history has an Aethelwing said 'I'm sorry'?"

"Exactly. She may be new at this, but she's learning fast."

"Is she learning the right things though, do you think?" Arthur said. "I hear she's riding with you instead of in the carriage."

"And what's wrong with that?"

"Every time she goes out in public, she makes statements. I would have thought the king had had enough of that sort of thing for the time being."

Before Rafe could respond, Arthur shrugged again and saluted. "I'll see you back at Caer Eisteddfod in a few days."

Rafe returned the salute and watched as Arthur went off whistling to himself. Whatever errand the king had for him, it must be a pleasant one, at least by Arthur's measure of such things.

Bundled in a coat over sweaters layered over shirts and wrapped in a long muffler, Deor managed to scramble her way up onto her horse with the aid of a stable boy and a mounting block. Rafe nudged his horse over next to hers, laughing.

"Are you sure you'll be warm enough?" he said.

"No, no I am not," she shot back as Brand, snuggled in her coat, wriggled around to poke his head out so he could see. "But this will have to do for now. If I get too cold, I suppose I'll have to retreat to the carriage with Finn and Astarte." She pushed back the hood of her coat so she could see him better. "You don't even have a hat on. Won't your ears freeze?"

"I'll risk it," he said with a smile. "Come on." He turned his horse with an easy, one-handed movement of the reins, and Deor did her best to follow suit. Bessie turned and gave Deor a look, then shuffled off to follow Rafe's horse.

"Close enough," she said.

Slowly the king's caravan formed up and departed through the gates, Roger and Pookie waving a last good-bye from the castle steps. A vanguard of armed soldiers rode first with Deor and Rafe following them, closely followed by the king's own carriage. Trumpets sounded, and they rode off to a merry fanfare.

"Nice touch," Deor said. "Makes it seem less like we're slinking home with our tails between our legs."

Rafe chuckled, and Deor waved to the people lining the roadside to see them go. She wondered how much of this was Roger's orchestration and how much was simple sightseeing. After all, it wasn't every day that you got to see a king, or at least the outside of his carriage. She waved cheerfully, and Rafe waved with her.

As they did so, a cheer went up from the crowd. Deor sat a little straighter on Bessie and kept waving. The nobles might not think much of her, but at least the commoners seemed to like her a bit. They might not hold the vote, but she promised herself she wouldn't forget to care what they thought, no matter how Parliament voted in a year.

Epilogue

Victor waited until Deor and her retinue rounded a corner and he could no longer see them before turning back to the courtyard to find his own mount. His friends had gone ahead of him, in a large, slow-moving group. He'd catch them before lunch if he pushed his horse, but even an easy ride would have him arrive before nightfall.

A stable hand held the reins of his horse—Roger's horse, actually, since Victor's had been killed. Once he rejoined his group, a servant would return the horse to Roger, and he could ride in a carriage the rest of the way. He took the reins from the man, who nodded and disappeared.

A strange quiet filled the courtyard. Roger's home was always so vibrant, so full of life and people when Victor normally visited, but now the cold grey walls were more like a prison than anything else. He lifted his foot to the stirrup.

"Victor?" A voice behind him.

He turned. Arthur bowed slightly. "I was hoping to catch you before you left."

"Captain." He nodded. "I'm rather glad you did. I expect Rafe suggested you speak to me? He and I talked some at Solstice and after the Nightmare, but we haven't had a chance to talk since last night."

"No." The captain shook his head. "Rafe didn't send me to speak with you. I don't believe he knows I am here at all."

"Ah." The courtyard wasn't as empty, a few stable hands, large burly men, hovered around. At least they were dressed like stable hands. "I see."

"The king, however, did ask me to find you. He requests your presence."

"About?" Victor said. There was only one way out of the courtyard, through the gate, and Victor heard it shut—quietly, but firmly—behind them. There were at least three men, including one of the best—and most devious—fighters in the kingdom.

"It is not my place to ask," Arthur said.

A slight tremor rolled through the ground under Victor's feet—Arthur also wielded earth magic—the kind that could split the ground beneath him or shake it until it rolled like the sea in a hurricane.

One of the men had taken hold of his horse's bridle. The other waited, hands clasped in front of him, a few feet away.

"Is he in the parlor?" Victor asked.

"His Majesty requests your presence in Caer Eisteddfod." Arthur gestured toward a path leading to the carriage house.

"Am I under arrest?" Victor said, not moving. "Do you have a warrant?"

"No," Arthur said. Then he smiled. He flipped his lapel back to reveal a badge—a shield bearing the king's eight-pointed star. "I don't need one. I'm the Shield. You are simply being detained at the king's pleasure."

THE END

About the Authors

Sarah Joy Adams is co-author with Emily Lavin Leverett of the Eisteddfod Chronicles. She is also the author of the Kinslayer Winter series, about modern day berserkers in Buffalo, NY, forthcoming from Falstaff Books. When she is not writing about faeries, vampires, and Norse warriors, Sarah teaches medieval literature and creative writing at Azusa Pacific University. She lives in the LA area with her husband Thom, where they are raising their child to be fluent in all dialects of Geek. She can be found on Facebook or http://sarahjoyadams.blogspot.com/.

Emily Lavin Leverett is a writer, editor, and English professor. She is the co-editor of *Lawless Lands: Tales from the Weird Frontier* and *The Weird Wild West* with Misty Massey and Margaret McGraw. Her first novel *Changeling's Fall*, co-written with Sarah Joy Adams will be followed in 2018 with *Winter's Heir*, the second novel in their contemporary fantasy faerie tale series *The Eisteddfod Chronicles*. She is currently working on another urban fantasy novel set in Raleigh, NC. Her scholarship focuses on the connection between Medieval English Romance and the *Discworld*

novels of Terry Pratchett. She lives in North Carolina with her spouse and their three cats, where they remain stalwart Carolina Hurricanes fans.

More by these Authors

Sarah Joy Adams & Emily Lavin Leverett

Changeling's Fall

Emily Lavin Leverett (editor)

The Big Bad

The Big Bad II

The Weird Wild West

Lawless Lands

Falstaff Books

**Want to know what's new
And coming soon from
Falstaff Books?**

Try This Free Ebook Sampler

https://www.instafreebie.com/free/bsZnl

**Follow the link.
Download the file.
Transfer to your e-reader, phone, tablet, watch, computer, whatever.
Enjoy.**

Made in the USA
Middletown, DE
26 November 2021

53504373R00184